This book is published by
Grosvenor House Publishing Ltd
Link House
140 The Broadway, Tolworth, Surrey, KT6 7HT.
www.grosvenorhousepublishing.co.uk

A CIP record for this book
is available from the British Library

ISBN 978-1-78623-859-7

**FT
Pbk**

Introduction

It was whilst I was living in the house behind the crumbling remains of Old Slains Castle that I began to wonder what the lives of its occupants must have been like; and the question of, why the wife of Francis, 9th Earl of Erroll stayed behind in a local farm when he abjured the realm just had to be answered.

Sitting on the edge of a cliff overlooking the North Sea and frequently windswept, it cannot have been the easiest place to live in. But, none the less, Gilbert Hay had done very well for himself. Some might see the reward of Slains Castle for his services to Robert Bruce and to Scotland as a poisoned chalice but the power, honour and riches which accompanied it were exceptional.

Bruce's plan was have the north east of Scotland in a safe pair of hands and, considering Gilbert Hay to be a great friend as well as supporter, there could be none better.

The castle was to remain in his family's hands for almost three hundred years before it was destroyed and during that time there must have been many adventures and tragedies.

We do not have birth records until Francis Hay – the last owner of Old Slains Castle; indeed, there were probably numerous children of whom, for one reason or another, we know nothing. We do have many other records though and it had been an adventure searching through them. The inscriptions for the Abbey of Coupar Angus tell us where and when the early Chiefs of Clan hay died and many other fascinating records survive. Although we know the dates of their deaths, other than those who died in battle, we do not know the cause of their deaths. These I have made up.

As most surviving documents are of a formal nature they give no clues as to character and, although I must apologise to those whom I have misrepresented, I feel sure there were bad as well as good amongst them.

Marriage amongst the aristocracy was for gain and support rather than affection or love but I feel that many must have grown close to their spouses and perhaps even to love them – and others to hate each other!

I make no apology for the repetitious names – these were the actual names of the characters. Family names were usually passed down, often being repeated should a child die. Indeed, King James III had two legitimate sons called James who were both living. That must have been confusing!

Delgatie Castle is now the Clan Hay Centre and Clan members gather there on the first Sunday of every August for lunch.

I have tried, wherever possible, to be factually correct, but where details are not known, I have let my imagination fill in the gaps. I hope you will enjoy the results.

I am indebted to Alan Hay and Angus Hay for their help with historical research, to Lord Erroll for his help and support, to Lady Jane MacRae for her advice and encouragement and to my husband, Ralph, for a never ending supply of coffee.

Glossary.

Alaunts – Hunting dogs.

Besom – difficult woman

Braies – trousers

Breeks - trousers

Galoot – idiot

Gang- go

Hoor – whore

Keech - excrement

Keek – look

Loon – young man

Lymer – dog; valued for its scenting skills

Mon – man

Stookie – immobile person

Toon – town

Wean – child

Wha – who

Wheesht! – quiet

Wifie – old woman

Wrang – wrong

CHAPTER 1

August 1314

The thunder of hooves announced the approach of soldiers. Armed and threatening they pounded across the open ground scattering all before them. The inhabitants of Slains Castle had heard the news that Robert Bruce had given the Barony of Slains, taken from Hugh Comyn in 1306, to Gilbert Hay. Fleeing for their lives the inhabitants of the castle pushed the tiny fishing boats out into the bay, not waiting to collect their meager belongings, but frantically struggling to preserve their lives and those of their loved ones. The sea was calm for once and they took to the oars, racing to pass Blind Man's Rock and escape along the coast to the town of Peterugie. Most of their men folk had left and the majority of those who remained at Slains were women and children.

Still euphoric from their success at Bannockburn where he had fought as Bruce's right-hand man, Gilbert Hay, the 5th Lord Erroll and Constable of Scotland was eager to survey the castles and lands which Bruce had bestowed upon him some time ago. He had been given Slains and Delgatie Castles and the tower of Bowness by Bruce as reward for his support. Battles and commitment to Bruce had denied him the opportunity to install himself in his new property and he was

1

anxious to do so now. His mighty figure sat tall in the saddle, a confident, powerful noble. His long fair hair tied back and his short pointed beard giving length to his face. Beside him sat his brother Sir Hugh; a mountain of a man, rippling with power.

As he and his men drew nearer to Slains, those who had been unable or unwilling to make their escape, stood fearfully within the castle walls keeping their distance as Gilbert's banner bearer preceded him through the gates. The rumbling of hooves and clatter of weapons thrust fear into the hearts of those waiting but slaughter was not at the forefront of Gilbert's mind. Calling to a loon to take his horse, Gilbert dismounted and strode across the courtyard. Timorous maidservants whispered together as he passed, admiring the strikingly rugged, handsome knight who bore the features which had earned his clansmen the title 'The Handsome Hays'.

In three strides he reached the top of the steps and turned to face the people. Standing over two yards high he made an imposing figure. 'I bear nae enmity tae ye,' he declared. 'Those of ye who wish tae stay and serve me will be well treated and respected. Those who wish tae leave will be free tae go but must be gone afore sundown.' Murmuring could be heard from groups of women until an ancient figure stepped forward and challenged, 'Wha' aboot our menfolk? Will they be allowed tae return tae us?'

'Ye have ma word,' Gilbert replied, 'Those who wish tae return will be received with good will. I ken ye fear the Bruce. I am Bruce's man but I'm nae Bruce.'

Gilbert understood the value of local knowledge and would truly value the advice and services that these people could provide. Many of the people had fled to the protection of Slains Castle when Robert Bruce and his brother Edward had raped the lands of Buchan. Gilbert had with him but a handful of men and needed the villagers to provide for the needs of his men and castle.

There was silence which seemed to stretch out for an age until a bonny young woman strode boldly towards him with the words, 'I'll show ye around the castle if you will, Sir. The steward left when Comyn was gone. I am Morag. I served Comyn but would offer those services to a new master.' Nods of agreement could be seen from others.

He gave a brief nod of acknowledgment and as he followed Morag into the castle his standard, bearing three red shields, rose above the tower fluttering proudly and announcing that the new laird had arrived.

Although those with the most severe wounds had been left behind to be treated at Coupar Angus Abbey, some of Gilbert's men who had arrived with him bore injuries from the battle. Women brought salves and herbs to the hall and began to treat the injured whilst Gilbert and his Brother Sir Hugh made their way through the castle.

Gilbert's men took the horses into the stables and called for food to be prepared. Figures ran about, eager to maintain their homes within the protection of the castle.

Seated on a promontory on the coast of Buchan, Slains Castle was surrounded by the North Sea on three sides and stood five stories high in a commanding position. A curtain wall enclosed not only the tower but also a stone built gathering hall adjoining which was a kitchen. A small chapel served the religious needs of the community; a barn and numerous other workshops and homes provided for their more earthly needs. Steep cliffs, an often turbulent sea and a narrow lane as the only land access, protected the castle from attack. Boats made use of the relative safety of the bays to north and south to deliver provisions and made transport to many areas along the coast preferable to using the unmade roads on land.

Morag led Gilbert into the first floor of the castle. A long table sat in the middle of the room with a bench on one side and two ornate armchairs on the other. Within a stone arch, there was a window which looked north over the sea and either side of the window were seats built into the stonework. A cupboard stood against the wall with a pewter jug and some wooden goblets on a tray. The walls were skimmed and finished with paintings which brightened the room. To the right of the table, they passed through an archway to a staircase which rose majestically to the next floor.

She opened a large studded door and stood aside as Gilbert passed through it. He stepped forward ducking through the low doorway and looked about him. A magnificent table lay bare, an ornately carved chair placed behind it. The pair dominated the room. In the wall was a huge stone fireplace with figures of griffins at either side. Against a wall stood a sideboard with finely carved doors. In the centre of the beautifully molded ceiling was a shield bearing the Comyn arms. Surprisingly large windows looked out to the east and north over the sea giving light into the finely furnished room. A colourful tapestry depicting a stag hunt brightened the wall opposite the fire. As he turned he saw a gallery above their heads. The curtains were swept aside but could be closed to give privacy and shelter from draughts.

Through another studded door a spiral stairway rose through the thickness of the wall to take them up to the private chamber. A bed draped with fine linen reflected the importance of the laird. More tapestries brightened the room and gave it a cosy feel. 'Ye'll want tae refresh, m' lord,' suggested Morag. 'I've instructed the maids tae bring water.'

As she spoke a tap on the door indicated that her instructions had been obeyed. A number of girls passed silently into the room carrying buckets of steaming water. Each dipped a brief curtsey as she entered and proceeded to tip the contents into the tub before the fireplace. An elderly woman stooped to light the fire and within moments it was blazing and giving off a glorious heat.

As discreetly as they had arrived, the servants left, leaving Gilbert and Morag alone in his chamber. Her abundant, red-gold hair fell in curls about her shoulders and no man could deny her beauty. Without a word, Morag began to remove Gilbert's hauberk. He raised his arms to assist and stretched enjoying the freedom of movement. She moved on to his chausses which dropped to the floor. Morag continued to undress him until he stood naked and slid gratefully into the steaming water. He sat with eyes closed luxuriating in the warmth; an experience he had not enjoyed for many a month. His eyes sprang open as Morag's hand explored beneath the water. 'Is this a service ye offered tae yer last master?' he asked with a quizzical smirk. 'Aye, this and others,' she replied grinning.

※ ※ ※

Gilbert sat at the laird's table; his brother Hugh at his right hand as they discussed their day's findings. Meat and pies were laid before them and they ate hungrily after their day's exertions. The maids curtsied as they brought each platter and set them before him. The food was simple but tasty and was served on fine silver. The meal finished Gilbert called for the cook. A small round figure appeared before him trembling and almost stumbled as she dropped a deep curtsey. 'Laird, I did ma best wi' the food available. With nae men tae hunt fer deer there was little but mutton and fish tae be had.'

Gilbert held up his hand for silence. 'Ye did well woman. I sent fer yea tae to express ma pleasure. Ye use herbs well and cook a fine meal. How is it that it comes tae me on silver platters? I had thought to find all valuables stripped from the castle.'

'Laird, I am too old tae be traipsing about the countryside looking fer a new home. When Hugh Comyn was killed I ken that we would be exposed tae looters and hid what I could in the dungeon. I ken nobody would leuk there.'

'Canny woman' laughed Gilbert. 'Ye serve the castle well and serve food well too! If others follow yer example they will find me a good master. Show me the dungeon. I would see where ye hid ma wealth.' Bowing as she turned, the rotund figure led him to a stairway near the entrance. Stone steps led down to a lower level where bottles of wine, barrels and sacks of provisions were stored. In the centre of the floor lay an iron grid covering the entrance to the prison pit which lay deep in the rock. A ladder propped against the wall provided the means of entering the dungeon, only to be removed when the prisoner, or his remains, was to be taken out. Gilbert thrust the ladder into the hole and descended into the darkness below. He stood whilst his eyes grew used to the darkness. The space was damp and cold. There was no need for irons as escape was impossible and a bundle of rags on the floor showed that prisoners had been held here from time to time. As Gilbert peered around him he heard a scuffle and a scream followed by a thud.

The ladder was lifted out of the prison pit. He made a grab for it but missed and fell forward striking his head on the bare rock. Stunned, he thought he heard a moan and gurgle. Something hit his leg and through his clearing vision, he saw a body lying beside him. A dirk between his ribs left no doubt that the figure was dead. The light dimmed as a head leaned through the opening blocking out the light. 'Gilbert!' called a familiar voice. 'Ye owe me a favour.'

Hugh turned to look at the crumpled figure of the cook. Her head had made contact with the wall as she was thrust aside by the assailant and a pool of blood surrounded her head. Hugh examined the figure and saw that she was still breathing. He leaned through the doorway and yelled up the stairs for someone to help her. As he cradled her head and shoulders on his lap, a disembodied voice called up from the dungeon. 'Hey, ye mind me? How about getting me oot? If it's no too much trouble...'

'Well now, if I were tae leave yea there, I could be laird,' quipped Hugh.

'Ha! Ye dinna save my life just tae leave me here,' returned Gilbert laughing.

The ladder appeared before him and Gilbert clambered up. 'A group of menfolk returned and this bastard was amongst them,' explained Hugh, indicating the body which had fallen into the dungeon. 'I saw him break from the group as they ate and followed him.'

'I'm right glad ye did. Round up the others and hold them in the hall. I'll be with yea in a few minutes.' He turned to the figure surrounded by people who bathed her head and lifted her from the ground. 'Take her tae ma room and care for her,' ordered Gilbert.

He strode from the chamber and made his way to the hall. The men who had returned were surrounded by Gilbert's men who had drawn their swords and stood guard. Gilbert demanded silence.

'I have declared that any that wish tae return and serve me are free tae do so. I tak no revenge on those who were servants of Comyn. However, I will suffer nae treachery. Any who seek tae betray me will be put tae death. Those who dinna wish tae support me, gang now and tak yer families wi yea. From those who stay, I expect total support. You will swear fealty tae me. You will train hard and work hard. I suffer no idlers. In return ye will be cared for, defended and fed.' He gave them a moment before ordering his men to put down their swords and allow any who wishes to, to leave. One scowling individual moved away looking over his shoulder expecting others to follow. When none did, he bit his thumb towards them and left.

Gilbert gestured with his head to two of the guards who followed the man out.

'I give yea one hour tae wash yerselves and make yerselves presentable. Each man will then attend me here tae gie ma his name, skills, and tae swear fealty.'

Gilbert spun away. He made his way to his chamber and knocked gently on the door. A serving girl opened it abruptly intending to dismiss the intruder with a torrent of words that would make their ears bleed. She opened her mouth to speak and stopped, gabbling and curtseying as she saw who stood before her. Gilbert edged her aside and strode quietly towards the bed where the cook now lay sleeping peacefully. 'How fares she?' he asked.

'I put five stitches in her head. She sleeps now from an infusion I made from herbs.'

'Leave her here the night. I will sleep above in the guest quarters. See that she is cared fer.' After a moment's thought, he asked, 'Can ye cook?'

'Aye, Sir.'

'Then ye shall run the kitchen this evening.'

Gilbert left the chamber and sent for his brother, Sir Hugh, to join him in his upper room.

It was some time later that Hugh arrived. He had been checking the stores and watching the returning men reuniting with their families. Grinning, he explained to Gilbert that word of his care for the cook had spread like wildfire and clearly the villagers were relieved to discover that they had so fair a laird.

'We'll have enough to do here in Buchan without our ain folk agin us,' Gilbert explained. 'We need the support o' these people as much as they need us. The handful of men who came with us from Coupar Angus are not enough alone tae hold castle and land. And anyway......she's a good cook' he smirked.

The meal that evening was roasted mutton but lacked the good flavour that the cook had achieved. Gilbert chewed a slice which he had cut from a leg and pulled a face. 'Tak good care o' cook,' he demanded, 'I miss her fine food already.'

He filled his goblet with wine and gulped it down. 'That's me away fer ma bed,' he declared and strode from the hall.

He was awoken by a blood curling scream from below. Leaping from the bed and groping in the dark for his braies he raced down the stairs. He was met by Sir Hugh coming up. The screams continued and it was clear that they came from Gilbert's room. He threw open the door and was startled to see cook sitting up in bed screaming mercilessly. 'Hold fast,' Gilbert comforted her, ''tis just a dream. You hit your head and....'

'Nae she bawled. Twas nae a dream. A hand at ma throat....threw back the covers tae ravish me!'

A stifled giggle brought their attention to a figure behind them. Gilbert spun round. 'You!' he declared seeing Morag.

'I thought 'twas you in the bed she laughed. I was about tae show you some o' the other comforts I offered. I dinna expect yea tae scream.' She let her eyes roam over his naked chest hungrily and fell into peals of laughter. Gilbert looked to Hugh who lifted a quizzical eyebrow. 'Comforts?' he enquired.

'Yese'll get the thrashing ye deserve the morrow ma girl!' declared cook, gradually recovering her senses.

'Hold yer hand woman,' said Gilbert. 'She meant nae harm. I'll deal wi' her.'

Morag stepped towards him and ran her hand down his body. 'Oh Laird, don't be too harsh with me,' she grinned. He took hold of her wrist to stop her progress.

'I'm much recovered thank ye, laird. I'm away to my kitchen,' said cook in a huff as she swung her legs out of the great bed and made for the door. Sir Hugh followed her out leaving Gilbert and Morag alone. As Gilbert turned, Morag's kirtle puddled at her feet and her long red hair fell loose about her shoulders. She slipped between the sheets and turned them back to welcome him.

꙰

'Sleep well?' asked Sir Hugh with a knowing look.

'Well enough,' replied Gilbert. 'We have much tae do today. You checked supplies?'

'Aye. We've plenty o' grain, straw and herbs; mutton and rabbit are in good supply and there's bloody choukies everywhere! The well has never been known tae run dry and gives clear, fresh water.'

'Where is it?'

'Within the walled area beyond the tower. The brew house is next tae it.'

'How are supplies o' weapons and wood?'

'Few weapons remain. The men took most o' them tae the fighting and those remaining, were taken in the boats as we arrived.'

As they spoke a number of small boats appeared in the bay. A man jumped from each and pulled them further up the beach. A couple of the men scrambled up the rocks to the castle and approached Gilbert and Sir Hugh.

Explaining that they had heard that Gilbert would show mercy and welcome them back, the men offered to pledge allegiance and their services if they could return. Gilbert took them into the castle and took their pledges recording the names and skills of each. It was becoming clear that they would be able to find men to provide for all of their needs from those who had returned.

'Hugh,' called Gilbert. 'You said we were short o' wood.'

'Aye. As ye see, there is none growing hereabouts since the Bruce harried the whole o' Buchan. We need tae tak carts and collect some.'

'Tak those who arrived yesterday. I've work tae do here and will set these tae work tae prove their worth.'

Hugh called to the men to ready the carts. He took some of their own men with him so that they could experience the area and get to know the castle men.

The journey took almost an hour. The road from the castle was steep and uneven and, although the weather had been dry for some weeks, some roads still bore ruts created by horses and carts which had passed in wetter times. Finally, they arrived in a thickly wooded area and set about cutting trees and collecting timber. The stoutest trees were loaded onto the largest cart and would be kept for making and repairing buildings and such. The smaller were loaded on smaller carts to be used for firewood.

The men worked with a will and Hugh worked alongside them. Suddenly he was thrown to the ground. He saw a glitter of sunlight on a blade and he was tossed over again. Reaching for his own knife he felt the blade across his throat. Yells and curses rang in his ear as he put his hand to his neck. Blood covered his hand. He wasn't going without a fight. A Hay, a Hay, a Hay he yelled, surprised that he could still make so much noise. He felt a pulling and the weight on his back rolled away. A pair of arms lifted him to his feet and a grinning face looked into his. 'Yer no' sae bad Sir Hugh,' the face said. 'Ye will need that neck looked at but it is only a flesh wound.' He indicated a badly mauled body on the ground. 'Ye ken the loon who decided not to stay with the new laird? He musta thought he could tak us all on. Bloody keech! Well, he'll nae bother us nae more. Awa now, we need tae get that wound looked at.' The man tore a strip from his tunic and wrapped it around the still bleeding wound.

'I'd ken yer name,' said Hugh.

'I'm Rabbie. I'm the smith' he said flexing his muscles. 'He chose the wrong one tae wrestle!' The men nodded in agreement.

Sir Hugh and Rabbie took the large cart and made their way back to Slains. Tough as he was, Hugh was shaken, but glad to be able to report to his brother that the men had proved their allegiance.

Their return to Slains was greeted with a flurry of activity. Rabbie called for the women to treat Hugh and went himself to tell Gilbert of events.

'So die all who stand against me!' declared Gilbert. He went to find Sir Hugh and discover the extent of his injury. Hugh dismissed his concerns and belittled the cut, which the women had finished dressing, as, 'just a scratch'. 'That's a lot o' blood fer a scratch,' observed Gilbert indicating the bloody cloth on the floor.

'Haud yer wheesht! I'll live'

As they spoke a disturbance in the yard drew their attention. Hugh had expected it to be the other cart arriving and wondered what the excitement was about. They were both surprised to see that it was a party of people on horseback. The group was led by a figure they both recognised. It was their brother John who was parson of Erroll. In the midst of the guards sat Gilbert's wife, Elizabeth and his young children Nicholas aged 9, Thomas 7 and 5-year-old Margaret.

Three loons ran forward to hold the bridles of the horses and Gilbert strode across to Elizabeth's side, sweeping her from the saddle and planting a resounding kiss on her lips.

'Ma bonnie Betsie! I had nae looked tae see ye arrive sae soon,' Gilbert declared. He lifted her from her horse and set her on her feet and ruffled his sons' hair. 'I've barely arrived myself.'

'Sir, I carry a message from Robert Bruce and thought it wise tae bring yer family too,' explained John.

Elizabeth had spotted Hugh emerging from the steps of the castle. She saw the dressing at his throat and turned to her husband. 'I thought you came through the battle with but minor wounds.'

'Aye and so we did. Come inside and I'll tell ye aboot it. And ye can gie me the news frae Erroll.' He put one arm around her waist and the other on Thomas' shoulder. Nicholas followed them inside holding little Margaret by the hand and looked around the hall. 'May we explore?' Thomas asked.

'Aye, son, but I want yea both back here by sundown.'

Elizabeth had taken the message from John and held it out to Gilbert. Breaking the seal he opened the folded paper and read in silence. His face gave nothing away. 'Is all well?' she asked.

'Bruce wants me tae go tae England tae negotiate a truce.'

1 3

'No!' she cried. 'Sweet Jesus! He wants you to travel the length of England, to journey to London with the English still smarting from their defeat!'

'Dinna tak on so. King Edward has granted me safe conduct. I'm Constable of Scotland and its ma duty.'

Knowing that his words were true was little comfort to Elizabeth. 'But now that I'm here, and your sons, who will protect us?'

'I've three months afore I've ta gang. I'll leave Hugh here and tak John with me as far as Erroll. Then I'll collect men tae accompany me tae London. It will gie the boys some time here afore they gang tae Sir John Gordon. They must learn their duties and train in weaponry. Aye and learn to speak correctly if they are tae go tae court. John Gordon is a good man and will bring them up as we would wish.'

'I hoped we could wait a little longer before you sent them away,' Elizabeth moped, 'we have all missed you so much whilst you have been with Robert Bruce. It seems that since your father's death I've hardly seen you.'

'We hae two fine sons and a daughter who give the lie tae that and I'll no have them grow up Jessies.' He smiled and held her to him. 'Now I must speak tae ma brother and apprise him o' the message and ma plans. Morag will show ye tae ma chamber and help ye tae refresh.'

Letting his hand slide down her arm lingering at her hand and looked back over his shoulder, he left her to find his brother.

They discussed who would leave with Gilbert and it was decided to leave Rabbie, the smith, at Slains to support Hugh. What weapons remained at the castle they would take with them leaving his brother to organise the production of more to defend the castle should it be necessary.

Elizabeth bathed and Morag combed out her hair for her whilst Margaret slept peacefully in a crib. The boys burst into the chamber chasing around the furniture and squealing with excitement. Elizabeth reached out and grabbed at Nicholas' tunic as he passed. 'Hold fast young man. Your father will wish to speak to you before he leaves. Tidy yourself up and go down to the hall below.'

Nicholas ran his fingers through his hair and set off down the narrow stairway to find his father.

'Away in, Nicholas,' instructed Gilbert his tone indicating that this was to be a serious conversation. 'I needs must hae words wi' ye.' He stood and moved thoughtfully about the room as he spoke.

'Yea ken that I fought beside Robert Bruce at Bannockburn and that Robert is King o' Scotland.' Nicholas acknowledged with a nod. 'Bruce has rewarded me fer ma services, not only with this castle and all that lies aroun' it, the Barony of Buchan, but also he has made me Constable of Scotland. This is a great reward but also a great responsibility.

Bruce has asked me tae gang tae England tae talk tae King Edward about a peace. This is best for oor country because the people have suffered long with battles and lost kin. Now that Robert Bruce rules Scotland we need peace so that oor people can recover and live their lives again.'

'I understand faither.'

'One day this great title will be yours. You must grow up tae be wise and strong. Your training will start while I am away. You are tae look after yer mother and brother and tae begin learning tae use a sword.'

Excitement gleamed in Nicholas' eyes. He had been longing to move on from the wooden weapons that he had played with at Erroll.

'When I return you and Thomas will gang tae Sir John Gordon tae train as squires. I will expect yea tae work hard and learn well.'

'Aye, faither,' replied Nicholas trying to control his excitement and longing to be dismissed so that he could tell Thomas and his mother.

'Whilst I am awa', your Uncle Hugh will stand in ma stead but ye will look out fer yer mother, brother, and sister as a young squire should. We are living amongst people we do nae ken. I believe we can trust them but we canna yet be sure. Keep a watchful eye. Treat the people well and they will repay ye.' Gilbert indicated that his son was dismissed and Nicholas walked steadily from the room before breaking into a breakneck run to find Thomas.

John had been making preparations for Gilbert and John's departure. Horses were saddled and caparisoned and stamping their feet, eager to get on their way. The men who were to accompany them were mounted and waiting. Elizabeth emerged from the castle steps and he took her in his arms and kissed her. 'I'll return as soon as I can,' he promised. 'Dinna fret, I'll be safe.'

'You must return,' she said, then whispered something for his ears only. He held her at arm's length then hugged her again and swung up into the saddle grinning.

To his left stood cook and Morag. Cook stepped forward and pressed a package into his hand. 'Something tae refresh ye on the way' she explained. He gave a wink in their direction as he rode away leading the party through the castle gates.

They were undoubtedly a small party to accompany such an important lord but Gilbert was confident that the menfolk were still busy getting back to their farms and trying to bring them back from the ravages of Bruce's work. They would not rise again against Bruce or his man.

His belief was correct and they travelled to Erroll without hindrance. Gilbert was given a hero's welcome. His men, led by his brother, Nicholas, came out to greet the party. Gilbert swung out of the saddle, landing with a thud of boots and jangle of spurs. He stretched to ease his muscles before slapping Nicholas on the back and hugging him. The horses were led into the stables to be rubbed down, fed and watered whilst Gilbert and his party were faced with a barrage of questions.

'What was it like fighting with Bruce?'

'What was the battle like?'

'Were ye wounded?'

Then Nicholas expressed concern. 'The Lady Elizabeth and your sons, did they arrive safely at Slains!'

'Aye and I was verra glad tae see them.'

'Well if they arrived, why have ye come here and left them there?'

'Bruce has asked me tae gang tae England and work fer a truce. He's right; the people need peace. There's no a village or town nae lost men these last years. The land has suffered and needs tae be tended. We sent Edward's army home with its tail atween its legs but we dinna want them tae return with new forces. A truce will serve us well.'

'Will ye stay a while afore ye go on tae England?'

'Aye, a night or twa tae see how things fare here and select men tae come wi me. Then I must awa.'

There was a flurry of activity as preparations were made to celebrate Gilbert's return and his success. His people were clearly delighted to see the laird return. Musicians were sent for to entertain that evening and as they dined Gilbert discussed the holdings in Erroll and preparations for his journey, with his brother, Nicholas. As the evening progressed, tales were told of bravery and betrayal on the battlefield and of more mundane events at Erroll. Anecdotes of minor mishaps and his son's antics amused Gilbert and he found it relaxing to be home and amongst his own people for a while.

The following day saw much activity. Weapons were prepared and sharpened, armour repaired and parts replaced. Men were chosen and carts prepared to carry supplies for the journey.

Amidst all of the noise and clatter, Gilbert's attention was drawn to shouts and movement near the gate. The arrival of a nobleman had drawn men and boys from their tasks to deal with the party.

'Guid Sir James!' Gilbert greeted him shaking him warmly by the hand.

'I heard of your arrival and wanted tae greet ye. I've nae seen ye since Bannockburn.'

'I went with Bruce to Coupar and then on to Slains. I needed to establish myself there.'

'Aye, ye did well. And well deserved.'

'As did ye, Black Douglas,' returned Gilbert. 'Join me in toasting oor success.'

James Douglas followed him in and they spent some time reliving the battles they had shared.

'There was something I wanted tae say tae ye, Gilbert.' He recognised the pause as permission to proceed. 'Ye will have heard that ma wife gave birth tae a girl child last Easter. I would ask ye tae stand witness fer her baptism.

'I'd be honoured tae James.'

'I'm grateful tae ye.' He paused thoughtfully.

'There was something else?'

'Aye….would ye consider promising yer son Nicholas tae her?'

Gilbert whistled. 'I've just arranged fer him tae gang as a squire with John Gordon. I had nae thought tae arrange his marriage yet.'

'It would be a fine alliance, Gilbert. We're nae talking o' them being wed this year….nor fer many a year yet, but promised tae each other!'

'I'll think o' it James. I've work tae do fer Bruce yet. I'll give ye ma answer on ma return.'

For now, James had to be satisfied with that. Gilbert was not a man to be pushed and James knew him to be both fair and wise. He could do no better than to link his family with the Hays and the Constable of Scotland at that. As chief of his clan, he was duty bound to forge bonds with powerful clans but he wanted the match for reasons of friendship too.

They passed the evening in good sport with music, singing and dancing. Wine flowed freely and good food was placed before them. James strummed a lute and sang whilst Gilbert relaxed.

Gilbert enjoyed spending an evening with James and Nicholas. He felt at home and it was good after so long away with Robert Bruce, often living rough and enduring many deprivations whilst harrying the English. He knew he must now spend much of his time in Buchan, establishing his rule there and restoring his possessions to make them profitable and powerful. But tonight he would enjoy for tomorrow he must ride for England to negotiate the peace.

CHAPTER 2

1315

The screams cast fear into the hearts of all who heard them. Even the menfolk, used to the cries of the dying on battle-fields and of prisoners put to the torture, shrank from the sound. Not just because of the pain and anguish which drew them forth but because they came from their good lady, Elizabeth. The child she carried was desperately trying to make its way into the world but its struggle was in vain and the Lady Elizabeth was failing.

Morag, her sleeves rolled up and her apron bloodstained mopped Elizabeth's brow and encouraged her to push but by now she feared for the life of the child and her lady too. She sent for a maid to bring fresh cool water. The maid opened the door slowly and stood fearfully in the doorway. 'Away in stupit quyne!' called Morag, now frantic to get the baby out and save at least one of them. By the light of a single branch of candles they worked, fearing that too much light would be dangerous for the mother and child.

Elizabeth weakened and her cries became mere groans. She looked pleadingly at Morag. 'Help me,' she pleaded.

As the first light of dawn grew on the horizon, a baby girl was delivered. Her feeble wailing reflected the struggle which had brought her forth and her frail condition. Morag wrapped her quickly against the cold and laid her in her mother's arms. Elizabeth's lips trembled into a smile as she gave up her last breath.

Morag knelt at the side of the bed. She laid her head on her Lady's hand and wept from exhaustion and grief. She wept for Elizabeth and for the tiny bairn whose mewling was so pitiful. She wept for Gilbert who would return to find his beloved had passed. She pulled herself to her feet and lifted the child, tenderly moving Elizabeth's arm from around her.

Cradling the bairn in her arms she moved slowly to the wooden crib which had been placed by the fire. She sat in a low chair and rocked gently as tears trickled down her cheeks. She had grown to love Elizabeth for her gentle ways, wisdom, and humour. They had latterly spent many hours together as Elizabeth had grown great with child, stitching and laughing together. Morag would miss her badly.

A scratching at the door drew her attention as a wide-eyed serving maid peered into the room. She called her forth and spoke in a whisper. 'Go tae the kitchen and ask cook fer a little ewe's milk fer the bairn.' The maid stared over towards the bed. 'Is she…?.' Morag nodded and the girl rushed away to do her bidding.

Cook came herself bringing the warmed ewe's milk and a cloth. She dipped one end of the cloth into the milk and gently twitched the other end on the bairn's lips. It made a feeble movement towards the cloth and drew it into its mouth but its suckling was so weak that it could not draw the milk through the cloth and into its mouth. 'Leave it be the night,' suggested cook. 'Tomorrow we'll try for a wet nurse.' *'If she makes it through the night'* she continued in her thoughts.

Morag spent the night next to the crib. Her efforts to help Elizabeth had tired her out and before the hour was spent she slept.

Waking with a start as the previous day's events returned to her thoughts, Morag leapt to her feet and peered into the cradle. She was amazed to find that the child still lived and she breathed a sigh of relief.

In spite of her relief, she knew full well that the bairn had little chance of survival. She was puny and weak and her breathing was shallow. Even if cook managed to find a wet nurse there was scant hope.

A knock on the door was followed by the appearance of Sir Hugh. 'Dinna blame yerself, Morag,' he advised. 'Ye did all yea could I'm sure. But now we must get a minister tae baptise the child. I've sent Ewan tae fetch him. May I hold ma niece?'

Morag gently placed the child in his arms. He walked over to the bed and looked down at Elizabeth. 'We'll name her fer her mammie,' he decided. 'She's the very picture of her.' He returned the bairn to its crib and strode from the room before Morag could see his weakness.

During the hours before the minister was brought to Slains Castle, Morag prepared Elizabeth's body. On his arrival, no time was wasted in getting to Gilbert's chamber where Elizabeth's body still lay and the child, so like her, was silent in her crib.

Sir John lifted her up and the minister recited the words he knew so well, adding his own thoughts of the sorrow brought to Gilbert by such a tragedy. As he spoke the last word the child drew a shuddering breath in and gently exhaled her last breath.

A howl of grief from Morag expressed the thoughts of them all. The minister, though used to the duty of burying many an infant, could never come to terms with such loss.

Sir Hugh took the tiny body and laid her in her mother's arms.

The only comfort to the small circle of grieving figures was that her mother had seen her if only for a moment.

'I will stay and carry out the funerals,' offered the minister.

'Nae. Tis kind of ye to offer,' said Sir Hugh, 'but Gilbert would want them tae be laid at Coupar Angus where he will, one day, join his ancestors.'

And so it was arranged that Hugh would take the bodies to the abbey to be interred.

⁓

Gilbert had met with little success in England and decided that to stay longer was futile. He made his return with all haste wishing to manage his lands and, most importantly, to see his family again. The many separations during his years spent fighting with Bruce had been a trial. Only for brief visits had he been able to return to his lands and see his family. When he arrived at Slains he had hoped to settle for a while. For his beloved wife and children to arrive and be seen so briefly was torture to him.

He stopped at Erroll to break his journey and oversee his estates there. He was surprised at the looks given to him by his people. Nicholas came out to meet him. His expression was grim and Gilbert knew that something was amiss.

'What is this, brother?' he enquired.

'Awa' inside, Gilbert. We needs mun talk.'

In silence, they made their way in. Nicholas called for whisky to be brought to the Laird's chamber and led Gilbert there to a seat before the fire.

'Spit it out, man! What ails?'

'Tis Elizabeth, yer good wife.'

'Nae, she was in fine health when I left six months ago and confided in ma that she was tae bear ma another son.'

'She bore ye a daughter but her confinement was lang and difficult. The child was the wrong way 'bout and weak. I'm afeard Elizabeth succumbed to the suffering.'

Gilbert put his head into his hands and groaned aloud. 'What of the bairn?' he asked.

'She lived a day.'

'Did Elizabeth see her' Gilbert whispered.

'Aye.'

'Leave ma,' ordered Gilbert. Nicholas hesitated at the door, about to say something then changed his mind and left. Gilbert gave way to his grief, silently at first and then sobbing. He had had so little time with his beloved Elizabeth. Why was God so cruel? He raged and wept until he was exhausted and fell asleep where he sat.

Some hours later Nicholas returned.

'Gilbert...' he said touching his arm. 'I dinna want tae leave ye too long. Sir Hugh is bringing Elizabeth and the bairn to Coupar Angus tae be buried with your ancestors. If ye hurry, ye'll be in time tae say farewell.'

Nicholas went with Gilbert to the Abbey where they were both greeted warmly and with sympathy. The Abbey was built of sandstone and was one of the largest of its kind, the buildings covering over an acre of land and the lands spreading for miles in every direction. Most of the land had been given by Gilbert and his ancestors, and the Hay arms were to be seen on many tombs and plaques around the abbey church. Nicholas, as Dean of Dunkeld, was given permission to carry out the service. His words were heartfelt and Gilbert stood in silence as he reflected on her short life. At that moment he vowed that he would not marry again. He had two sons and could not share his love with another after Elizabeth. She was his first and last wife.

Sir Hugh had brought young Nicholas and Thomas to say their goodbyes to their mother. Margaret, being thought too young, had been left in Morag's care at Slains. Gilbert put a hand on the shoulder of each and gently squeezed. 'Ne'er fear to greet fer yer bonnie ma. We'll all miss her sorely.'

As he spoke the sound of the pipes could be heard playing a lament. Gilbert led his sons away, through the cloister where their footsteps resounded in the covered walkway and into the Abbot's chamber, followed by his brothers.

Wine was brought and the Abbott left them indicating to his prior to follow him.

'We shall return tae Slains tomorrow,' decided Gilbert. 'I must return tae my lands and see what progress has been made. There will be a year of mourning for Elizabeth. My sons, yea will not gang tae Sir John Gordon as planned.' Nicholas was sorely disappointed but he and Thomas bowed their heads in submission to their father's decision.

The boys were dismissed and ordered to return to the abbey's guesthouse for the night.

Gilbert and his brothers spent the evening in quiet conversation drinking the fine wine provided by the Abbot and planning the future. The next day Hugh would return to Slains with him whilst John and Nicholas returned to Erroll.

The following morning horses were made ready and food prepared by the abbey kitchener. The day was dark and cold and clouds overhead threatened snow before long. Gilbert set the pace and moved them along rapidly, wanting to reach Slains before the snow started if possible. It was not to be so and before they had passed Meigle, large flakes began to fall.

By midday, they were all in need of a rest and some food. None of them had eaten much before they left the abbey; they had no appetite. Now the cold and exercise had changed that and, finding a shepherd's hut, they stopped to refresh themselves.

They didn't bother to make a fire as Gilbert wanted them to get started again as soon as possible. A crackling sound was unexpected and they were taken quite by surprise by the thug who hurled himself round the doorway wielding a dirk and demanding their food.

As Gilbert drew his sword and took a stance to defend himself, Hugh edged the boys out of the door. Nicholas and Thomas backed out of the doorway and, keeping their backs to the wall, edged round to make their way back to the horses.

Nicholas thrust his hand over Thomas' mouth. 'Shh...' he whispered, 'There's another of them by the horses. 'I'm going tae get over there. When ye see ma signal I want ye tae throw a stone tae the other side of the horses. Got it?' Thomas nodded and Nicholas slowly removed his hand. He slid like a shadow into the nearest trees and slowly made his way through the cover of woodland, to the horses. Thomas watched his every move and when Nicholas nodded, Thomas picked up a stone and threw it as hard as he could.

The man who was untying the horses turned to look and as he did, Nicholas snatched his little sword from his saddle. Without a second thought, Nicholas surged forwards towards the back of the thief. As he did so the man turned raising his hand to grab at whoever was approaching. He did not expect his attacker to be a child and reached too high. At that moment Nicholas lunged towards him thrusting his sword into the man's belly. The thief's forward movement pushed him further onto the sword. His eyes opened wide in surprise as he realised what had happened and that his assailant was so small. His arms came down to grab at Nicholas' head but he was too weak and Nicholas stepped back out of his reach and withdrawing his sword as he did so. The man crumpled to the ground.

Thomas jumped and clapped his hands at his big brother's success. He turned suddenly as a figure emerged from the shepherd's hut. His father, nursing a cut on his arm, stepped out to see to his sons' safety.

'Nic killed the robber!' squealed Thomas.

'No Thomas, your father did' explained Hugh stepping out from behind Gilbert.

'No! Look!' shouted Thomas pointing. 'Nic killed the man who was stealing our horses!'

They looked where he was indicating and saw Nicholas standing staring at the body. It was the first time he had killed a man.

'I was going tae tell ye how well he was doing in his training when we got home,' began Sir Hugh, 'but it seems he decided tae demonstrate his skills the day.'

'Come here son, I'm well proud o' ye,' said Gilbert.

Nicholas continued to stare at the body. Gilbert went to him and put his arm around him. 'I ken it's the first time ye've killed a man but it'll nae be the last. You did well to defend us, and agin a man twice yer size,' he pointed out. 'Without yer quick thinking and canny swordsmanship we could have lost the horses and without them, we probably would hae frozen tae death on the road. Ye did the right thing. Always defend the right. He deserved what he got and Scotland is better without him. Come now, we must awa.' And with that, he began to mount his horse. Nicholas was brought out of his shock and clambered up on his pony as Hugh helped Thomas.

'When we get home I'm going to tell mot....' Thomas realised that his mother was gone and fell silent.

'Aye,' helped Sir Hugh, 'Morag will be proud of her charge.'

The boys were both accomplished riders in spite of their lack of years and their ponies accustomed to long journeys but by the time they finally reached Slains, both boys and ponies were exhausted and frozen. The horses were taken quickly to the stables to be cared for and Morag raced to gather up the boys in her arms and lead them in to find food and warmth.

Supper was filled with Thomas' excited chatter telling of the great fight in which Nicholas and his father both beat their opponents and killed the thieves. He pranced about waving his arms and demonstrating how it was done. Nicholas had overcome his initial shock at what he had done and was enjoying his brother's hero worship and the astonishment of the gathering. Margaret wash thrilled with the story of her brothers' adventures and squealed delightedly as Nicholas demonstrated how he had fought the thief. Gilbert was immensely proud of his eldest son and enjoyed being told by Hugh of the great progress Nicholas had made in his training.

That night Gilbert lay in bed looking at the beams of the ceiling. They were painted with biblical scenes and texts. His eyes were held by an image of Mary holding the baby Jesus. She looked so like his beloved Bess that a tear rolled down his face and he gave vent to his grief.

CHAPTER 3

The following morning Nicholas was keen to take up his sword and begin his practice. He thrust and cut sending young Fulk, his sparring partner, holding up his hands in submission. Gilbert had been watching from the stables.

'Ha! Indeed ye have learned well,' he said with pride, 'but remember; you are still young and hae much to learn. Don't think ye can tak on grown men. Ye did well, but a wise man kens his weaknesses as well as his strength.'

'Aye, faither. I ken well I canna' beat a grown man in a battle yet but one day I'll fight by yer side.'

Although Gilbert knew this full well, it disturbed him to think of his son on a battlefield amongst the sights, sounds and smells of dying men and horses and the danger he must one day face.

'Now put up yer sword. Enough fer the day.'

'Aye, faither. I'll clean it first, though.'

Gilbert turned away so that Nicholas could not see his smile. 'Ye've trained him well Hugh,' he said.

'Aye, but he works hard and listens. He'll do well.'

Having finished cleaning his small sword, Nicholas headed for the stables. He loved horses and loved to spend time with his pony. In the next stall, Fulk was grooming a pony. He put down his brushes and crouched behind the partition. As Nicholas entered, Fulk sprang out and hurled Nicholas to the ground. 'Best me would you?' Fulk growled in his ear, 'I'll serve ye fer that!' Fulk was five years older than

Nicholas and bulky if not heavily muscled. The two boys rolled in the hay and pummelled each other as they struggled. Fulk gained the uppermost and knelt astride Nicholas who suddenly yanked on the back of his belt sending Fulk sprawling on the ground.

Across the courtyard, Gilbert heard the noise and turned to intervene. Hugh put a hand on his arm. 'Wait'.

The bigger boy leapt to his feet and grabbed the beam above his head; swinging his legs he aimed a kick. Nicholas ducked and sidestepped grabbing a passing foot and keeping hold of it, he turned the owner over onto his knees. Sitting himself on Fulk's back whilst holding his legs so that he could not move he cried, 'Submit!'

Fulk had no choice but to admit defeat.

Nicholas stood up and gave Fulk his hand to help him to his feet. Both boys were laughing and slapped each other on the back.

'The lads enjoy a wrestle much as we did as boys,' Hugh explained.

'His skills are a credit tae ye and him. I think now it's time fer him tae learn tae hunt,' decided Gilbert. 'I hear there are some deer tae be had tae the north.'

'Aye but roe deer, not red,' explained Hugh. 'We need tae go a day's ride tae find red deer.'

'Roe will do tae start. If he handles himself well we can keek fer red deer later.'

As they sat at supper, Gilbert explained his plans to Nicholas. Thomas begged to go with them but was firmly told that hunting was men's work and he'd to stay with Morag. Seeing Thomas' crestfallen look, Gilbert softened and told him that he needed someone to hold the castle whilst he was away. Thomas brightened at this and was happy to listen to the discussion about the coming day. At the end of the meal, Morag took Thomas' hand to lead him away to bed. Nicholas clasped his hands behind his back so that she did not take his as he strode along beside her, feeling every bit the young noble.

❧☙

Preparations made and corsers saddled, the hunting party set off early. Three of the castle alaunts and one lymer accompanied them as they cantered off, harnesses jingling and a merry atmosphere surrounding them.

They made their way north towards Ward of Cruden and onwards towards Peterugie. As they rode, Gilbert explained to Nicholas about the hunting method they would use. Although hunting *par force* was considered to be the noblest form, today they would use *bow and stable*. The hunters would gather in a pre-determined place and lie in wait. Beaters and dogs would drive the deer towards them and they would use swords and spears to kill them as they raced past.

When they reached the forest which offered shelter enough for deer they split into two groups. Sir Hugh led five of the men silently through the woods. As they went they searched the ground looking for signs of deer. While they did this, Gilbert took Nicholas and a couple of other men to a clearing over to the north.

The beaters moved stealthily keeping low and communicating by hand signals. They had sighted a small herd and were keeping downwind of them. When there was a man behind and one either side they closed in before setting them off in the direction of the hunters.

A loud cry alerted Gilbert to the fact that Sir Hugh's party had spotted the herd and were chasing them towards the hunters. Nicholas was startled as three deer broke from the cover of trees and charged towards them. In a flash, two had passed only to be shot by the huntsmen who stood behind him. The third, large for a roe deer, was wounded by Gilbert's spear. Gilbert leapt from his saddle and with a single stroke of his knife he dispatched the beast.

Nicholas was laughing, watching his father dispatch the buck and did not notice the approach of another large buck which was running wildly through the woods, terrified by the uproar behind it. It raced past within inches of Nicholas. His horse was taken by surprise and reared up. Nicholas had no time to bring it under control and was hurled from the saddle, landing with a sickening crack on the ground. Winded by the fall he lay still for a moment before letting out a moan. Gilbert was by his side in an instant. 'What is it son?' he asked, more shaken than he cared to admit. He tried to roll Nicholas over but his screams stopped him instantly. 'Leave me alone! Dinna touch me! Go awa!' Nicholas was shaking with pain and shock. His left arm was badly broken with a displaced fracture. When Gilbert managed to gently turn him he was shocked to see the shape of his son's arm. Trying to conceal his fears from Nicholas he spoke through gritted teeth. 'You'll be fine lad. We'll get ye home and strap it up. Morag will give yea something fer the pain.'

Nicholas braced himself as he was lifted up to Gilbert to sit in front of him and share his horse for the ride home. Gilbert held him closely but in fear of worsening the injury. He was relieved when Nicholas lost consciousness. He was not in pain, at least for the present. The men used Nicholas' horse to carry the kill home and the party travelled in concerned silence. Even the dogs, running alongside were subdued.

Villagers from the castle saw the hunting party returning and many ran to meet them. There was shock when they saw

Gilbert cradling the terribly still body of his son in his arms. Hugh galloped ahead to order preparations to be made. Gilbert handed Nicholas down to Hugh's waiting arms before dismounting himself and looking around for Morag. Spotting her amid the group he called her forward.

'We need a bone setter. The lad's arm is badly broken.'

'The best in these parts is Old Nell at Whinnyfold. I'll send men to fetch her.'

Within moments two men were on the beach hauling a small boat into the water. They grabbed the oars and pulled strongly towards the north and were soon out of sight around the rocks.

Nicholas was laid on Gilbert's bed. He briefly regained consciousness and moaned, trying his best to be brave and not scream with the pain as he would dearly loved to have done. Morag wiped the beads of sweat from his brow and trickled some poppy juice between his clenched lips. 'Try to swallow' she coaxed, ''twill ease yer pain.' Some moments later he slept yet still soft moans escaped him from time to time.

'How long will it take them tae get tae Whinnyfold?' Gilbert asked.

''Tis only a couple o' miles up the coast. They should be back within the hour.'

'The break looks bad. I've seen such on the battlefield.'

'Old Nell is a canny woman. She's skilled in such things. I'm sure she will be able tae help.'

Almost an hour passed. Gilbert paced around the room stopping each time he passed the window, peering out for sight of the boat returning. Becoming impatient he roared at Morag, 'Where are the galoots? Yea said they would be here by now!'

Just then the bow of the boat appeared from behind the coastline. Gilbert raced down the stairs and grabbing Old

Nell's sleeve he hauled her out of the boat, ignoring her protests, and pulled her up the stairs towards his room.

'Hold yer hurry man. Are yer breeks afire?'

'Well, dinna stand aroun like a stookie wifie. Ma son's in a bad way.'

He pulled her through the doorway then stood back as she hobbled over to where his son lay.

Old Nell gently took hold of Nicholas' arm and examined it. She felt along the length of it carefully probing to find how the bones lay.

She stepped away from the bed and drew Gilbert and Morag to the far side of the room. Speaking quietly so as not to alarm Nicholas, she explained that it was indeed a bad break. The fracture was displaced and must be pulled to correct it.

'I'll nae deceive yea,' she said, 'to right it will cause the bairn grievous pain. Twill be best if yea can fetch ma bag frae the boot. We will need tae gie him something tae help kill the pain.'

'I'll fetch it.' Morag offered and slipped away.

'Yea'll need tae hold him still.' Old Nell directed. 'I need tae pull the arm until it comes straight.'

'I'll get Hugh. He's stronger than you,' said Gilbert.

'Tis no sae much strength that is needed as skill. Tis best I do it.'

'Verra well.'

Morag returned, breathless from running and worry.

Old Nell took the bag from her and fumbled inside it. She drew out a small jar with a wooden stopper. The centre of the stopper was hollowed out and she poured a measure of the contents into it. Bending over Nicholas she spoke gently to him. 'Word is that yea are a brave hunter and fighter,' she told him. 'I have tae mend yer arm and I won't lie tae yea, it will hurt. This will make it more bearable for yea.'

She held the stopper to his lips and Nicholas swallowed making a face at the bitter taste.

'Guid lad.'

She stepped away from the bed and spoke softly to Gilbert. 'Gui him a moment fer that tae work.'

They stood watching the child as he became sleepy. Finally, Old Nell went across and touched his arm. He didn't flinch and she nodded her head to Gilbert and Morag indicating that they should come and help.

'Hold the lad's shoulder and the top o' his arm,' she told Gilbert. Morag was instructed to take the pieces of bone from the bag. She took them out and looked questioningly at them. 'Tae hold the arm straight when I've pulled it,' explained Old Nell. 'I allas use a bone tae set a bone. It draws strength from it.'

As Gilbert took hold of Nicholas' shoulder, Old Nell held the wrist in her right hand. Gently at first she felt with her left hand for the break and where it needed to go to correct it. Gilbert felt her slowly pull the arm, the pressure building as she pulled harder. He heard a grinding as bone moved against bone then a muffled click as the bone went into place.

Old Nell felt along the arm and shook her head.

'What's wrong?' Gilbert asked.

'It's nae right. One bone has fixed but the other is badly broken and will nae meet up.'

'Will it mend?'

'With time it will heal but it will ner be right. Let him sleep fer now. The herbs I gave tae him were powerful so he'll sleep fer some time.' She wrapped the arm in strips of cloth then told Morag to hold the sheep bones either side of the arm and put further strips of cloth around to keep them in place. Satisfied that she had done the best that she could, Old Nell made to leave, explaining that the cloth and sheep bones could be removed in a month. As she went out through the door, Gilbert told Morag to go to the kitchen with Old Nell and see that she had a meal before she left and a parcel of good things to take with her. He handed the old woman a purse of coins and, hefting it in her hand, she nodded her acknowledgment.

He sat by the bedside as Nicholas slept wondering how badly damaged the arm would be and grieving for his son who was just learning to be a warrior and may never be able to fight again.

After an hour or so Morag returned. 'Go and eat she suggested. I'll sit with the wean. Sir Hugh is below and worried. He feels responsible.'

'Never, he could nae hae stopped the beast nor held Nicholas' pony.'

Gilbert went down to find Hugh and put his mind at rest. He found him in the chamber below pacing the floor. As Gilbert entered the room, Hugh strode over to ask how the boy was and apologise for not preventing the accident. Gilbert would hear none of it and told him to stop blaming himself.

Gilbert threw himself into a chair exhausted and rested his head back with his eyes closed. The day's events had taken their toll and within moments gentle snores indicated that he was sleeping.

Sometime later a noise from within the courtyard woke him. Still reclined in the chair he rubbed his eyes and opened them. Staring at the ceiling he rubbed his eyes once again and peered up. He looked over towards Hugh. 'Wha?' he exclaimed.

Hugh looked up then smiled. 'While you were in England I took the liberty of having John Comyn's arms removed and yours put in their place,' he explained. Above their heads was a silver shield bearing three red shields upon it.

'Ha!' roared Gilbert, 'a bonnie sight if ever there was! And made with great skill. Which man did this?'

'Donald, the castle mason,' replied Hugh.

'Then he shall do more work within the castle,' declared Gilbert.

Feeling the need to take some fresh air, Gilbert went in search in Donald and found him chiselling stone to replace a damaged window. He explained to him that he was pleased with the work in his chamber and asked him to design some new door frames for within the castle. 'Fetch them tae me when ye have done them,' he instructed.

Returning to the bed chamber, Gilbert was pleased to see that Nicholas was awake but drowsy. Gilbert ruffled his hair and sat beside him. 'Och, how are you feeling?' he asked.

'Nae sae bad. Is it all fixed?'

'Nae quite, son. The woman could nae fix it properly. Yea'll be alright but she could nae tell how well it will mend. Still....tis yer left arm nae yer right. We've tae be glad fer that.'

Nicholas was still feeling drowsy from the potion Old Nell had given him and soon drifted back to sleep. Gilbert decided not to disturb him and climbed in beside him to spend the night.

It was still dark when Gilbert became aware of a voice close to his ear. In his half sleeping state he thought it was Elizabeth and his arm reached out to draw her close. He woke with a start as his hand felt a hot, sweating body. He sat up and remembered the previous day's events. Nicholas lay beside him writhing and murmuring in a state of great agitation.

Gilbert leapt from the bed and raced to fetch Morag. 'The wean has a fever,' he told her. 'He's burning up.'

Morag followed him to the bedroom and looked down at the boy holding her hand to his head. 'Aye, he suffers from the injury. We must get Old Nell back.'

Gilbert left the room and sought out the men who had brought Old Nell earlier but as he stepped outside he found that the haar had come down and it was impossible to see more than a couple of feet through the dense mist. No boat could find its way safely through the puffin covered rocks even with a lantern. He returned to Morag raging, 'What in God's name will we do?'

'We need tae cool him.' She fetched a bowl of water and a cloth and began to bath the child's head, cooling him and talking gently to him.

It was all too common for fever to set in after an injury even without an open wound and both knew that there was no guarantee of recovery. Neither Gilbert nor Morag would give way and leave the child to the other's care and the morning found them both still sitting beside the bed.

At first light, they were disturbed by Thomas arriving to see how his brother was. He was horrified to see the still figure in the bed, his face glistening with sweat and glowing rosy with fever. His father took his hand and pulled him onto his lap holding him closely and burying his face in the boy's hair.

'Yer brother ails from his injury, son. Will yea fetch Uncle Hugh tae me?'

Aye faither,' said the child and ran to find Hugh, eager to do something to help.

Hugh insisted that Gilbert and Morag take some rest and sat himself beside the bed. Within the next hour, Nicholas' fever raged and he rambled on incoherently. Hugh mopped his brow and soothed him as best he could, knowing that soon they would know if he would recover or not.

After what seemed like days, Nicholas began to calm and fell into a healing sleep. Hugh took the opportunity to slip away and report the progress and brought Gilbert and Morag who crept into the room and took up their earlier places beside the bed.

It was some time later that Nicholas opened his eyes and looked from one to the other.

'Is it supper time yet? I'm starving.'

The words brought howls of laughter from his carers. Gilbert pulled Morag into his arms and hugged her with relief. Nicholas whistled which brought renewed laughter. The sound brought Sir Hugh and Thomas into the room and Thomas was sent to ask cook for something tasty for Nicholas whilst the others congratulated each other on his recovery. Cook arrived in the room bearing a bowl of broth which Nicholas ate hungrily much to the amusement of those watching.

That evening Nicholas was able to join in the family's meal and even exchanged an occasional joke with Thomas. Clearly, he was recovered from the fever but Gilbert watched him discreetly, very aware of the bandaged arm and the damage it had suffered. Would the wean ever regain the full use of it? It seemed unlikely.

When Gilbert retired Morag slipped quietly into his room. She drew back the blanket and slid in beside him. He reached out and drew her to him, feeling the need of comfort. Elizabeth was no more and his son and heir was badly injured. 'I can nae marry ye, ye ken,' he whispered into her ear enjoying the scent of lavender which delicately fragranced her hair.

'Aye, I ken' she replied tracing her thumb across his cheek. 'But I'm nay a hoor. I'll be mistress tae none but ye.'

Chapter 4

February 1320

Shouts and cries greeted the King as he arrived at Slains Castle. The ride had been long and hard but the message he had for Gilbert Hay could not be entrusted to a messenger and besides, it was far too long since he had spent time with his good friend and supporter.

Gilbert raced out to meet him and dropped to one knee. Robert Bruce threw his leg over the horse to leap to the ground and, taking Gilbert's elbow, lifted him to his feet to embrace him. Both men slapped each other on the back and hugged with power that would have broken the ribs of most men.

An absolute hulk of a man, Robert Bruce, although not as tall as Gilbert Hay, was bull-necked and broad of shoulder but for all of his bulk he was surprisingly agile. His legs rippled with muscles. His features were solid and rugged and he often quipped that he inherited his looks from his mother. Certainly, he gained his character from her, stubborn, determined and powerful.

A squire took the horses to the stables whilst food and lodging were organised for Bruce's men. There was much activity and Thomas Hay was delighted to have responsibility for supervising the arrangements. He was growing into a fine young man, bright of mind and strong of arm. Gilbert had often glanced his way wistfully, regretting that it was his first son who now carried an almost useless left arm and an increasingly bitter nature.

Nicholas had accompanied the king and his father into the castle where Sir Hugh was waiting to greet them. Wine was brought and they partook of it whilst reminiscing and catching up with events.

'You've certainly made this castle you own,' observed the king looking at the ceiling boss bearing Gilbert's arms. 'The stonework is that of a master mason,' he continued looking at the door cornices which were now decorated with ivy stems forming a heart in the centre and snaking out to a flower at each end. 'I would meet the maker. I may find work for him.'

'You would rob me of my mason?' joked Gilbert.

'Aye, Gilbert. I cannae have my constable with a finer castle than mine now can I?'

'I'm sure I can spare him for my king,' said Gilbert bowing.

'Well young Nicholas,' said Robert, 'when are you going to get yourself a wife?'

Nicholas scowled. 'I'm not the finest catch, now, am I?' he asked indicating his arm. Although the bone had set where Old Nell had pulled it, one bone was displaced and broken in more than one place making it impossible to align the ends to enable them to knit together as they should. It gave Nicholas pain sometimes but more importantly, it was weak and he could not use it properly.

The king raised an eyebrow at the lad's tone but continued, 'One day you will be Constable of Scotland and a fine catch for any maid.'

Nicholas shrugged and put his head down.

'Faint heart never won fair maid,' pursued the king, 'nor man,' he laughed. 'My mother held my father prisoner until he promised to marry her!'

Nicholas looked up unbelievingly. 'Tis true!' declared the king, 'he told me the story often.' This was greeted by laughter and chatter amongst the men and one or two coarse remarks. They were finally brought to silence by the king. 'I would speak now in private with you Gilbert,' he declared. 'My visit is nae purely fer pleasure.'

Sir Hugh and Nicholas rose and went to see how the preparations for Robert's stay were progressing, leaving the king and Gilbert alone.

'I'm sorry tae see that Nicholas' arm has fared sae badly. I had heard of his accident but hoped fer a better result.'

'Aye, and he bears it badly too. He is bitter that it hinders him so. He has nae hunted since the accident which is a failing I fear will hinder his fighting skills when he is called upon to do so.'

'He can still bear a sword?'

'Aye, for as you see, tis his left arm which suffered.'

'Yet another reason we need tae avoid further fighting. The English king still harries us. He seeks the Pope's support and gets it because the Pope wants Edward tae send men tae fight in the crusades.'

Bruce's knew that their excommunication distressed his people and to maintain their support he needed to get it lifted.

'Since we were excommunicated the Pope turns a deaf ear tae our case. This is why I come tae you the day.'

'What can I do? I was excommunicated too along wi' all the Scottish people. He'll nae listen tae me.'

'He'll nae listen to any one of us but I hae a plan. Three letters will be sent tae him. The first I will send. The second will come frae the clergy. There is hope that he will read that with an open mind. The third will come frae the nobles of Scotland, including ye, of course. I've arranged fer ye all tae meet at Arbroath Abbey. The Abbot is making ready tae receive ye. I'll leave the wording tae yourselves but I want the document tae look as though the nobles hae power tae get rid of me if I don't do what they want and protect Scotland's independence.'

'Strong words indeed; and ye wish us tae say this?'

'Aye and more. It must be powerfully worded and show that the nobility o' Scotland tae stand together tae support Scotland's independence. It must show that we will no' be subject tae English rule.'

'I have sworn allegiance tae ye and ye ken I'm faithful. As you ask, I shall do. I shall set off tomorrow for Arbroath and return only when the letter is on its way tae the Pope.'

'I knew that I could rely on ye Gilbert. You need not set oot sae soon, though. Many o' the nobles have far greater distances tae travel and will not arrive fer many a day yet. If you leave on Monday you will reach Arbroath in plenty o' time.'

'In that case, we can spend the next couple o' days catching up with what's been going on since Bannockburn. I've missed yer company and I've heard many a tale o' what you've been up tae.'

With that, they rose and made their way to join the others.

The evening was spent enjoying good food and good wine. Musicians had been brought to the castle to entertain and told tales and sang songs to cheer the company. When they had finished eating, Gilbert took Nicholas to one side and told him his plans to find a wife for him. Nicholas was furious but he dare not argue in front of the king and spinning away he stomped from the room.

Gilbert sent Thomas to fetch him back. No son of his would turn his back and leave the room in the presence of his father and especially in the presence of the King.

Thomas found Nicolas skulking near the stables. Before he could speak Nicholas yelled at him, 'I will nae marry just tae make a good match. I'll marry whom I like. I'm not going tae tac some ugly bitch o' a girl I've never even met, and she won't want tae marry me when she sees ma arm. I'm nae good tae anyone like this and I'm nae going tae suffer the humiliation o' being rejected by some bitch because o' this,' he said indicating his arm.

'She'll do as she's told,' remarked Thomas. 'If her father says she is tae marry yea she'll have no say in the matter.' That's what daughters are for; tae make good marriages and bring wealth and power tae their families. I expect father will find a husband for Margaret soon and she will have no choice in the matter.'

'I know that but I will no have a wife who pities me and regrets a marriage that she is forced intae.'

'Well, dinna bother yerself too soon. Her father may not agree and then the marriage willna happen.'

'And which man would not see his daughter married tae the next Constable of Scotland? '

'Faither is waiting; we best get back'

'Aye.'

'Aye, Gilbert. I was truly sorry to hear of Elizabeth's passing. She was a bonny lass and sweet natured. You'll miss her sorely' said the king.

'That I do. We were well matched and I worshiped the ground she walked on.'

'We all must lose loved ones but it never gets any easier.' After a moment he continued. 'That boy o' yours grows tall and strong. Tis a pity about his arm. He grows churlish and mun see that what is done is done and cannae be changed. But I'm sure you are the man tae set him straight. If he grows up tae be as wise as his faither he'll nay be bad.'

'You were right tae mention that he mun find a wife.

Malcolm, Earl of Lenox has a daughter I hear. I presume he will be at Arbroath. With your permission, I will speak with him there and see if he is agreeable.'

'Aye, that would be a grand match. Malcolm is true tae oor cause and I would be glad tae see his daughter as your son's bride.'

The two returned to the hall. Gilbert frowned at his eldest son but said nothing for the moment. He turned back to the king and carried on the conversation.

'Yea keep a good table, Gilbert,' observed King Robert.

'Aye, I ken. I've a good cook and she serves me well.'

The evening was passed in convivial conversation and reminiscing over battles and adventures that they had had together. Such good friends were they that Gilbert was quite relaxed in Robert's company and there was much laughter between them. As the evening drew on they became increasingly merry as glasses were emptied and refilled time and time again.

Finally, Bruce decided that it was time to turn in for the night. Gilbert led him to his own chamber whilst he himself would make do with the guest chamber.

Morag fussed around making sure that everything was ready and comfortable for the king's stay. Robert's eyes followed her if she moved around the room. 'Stay woman and bear me company the night,' he said to her.

'Sire, I am faithful tae ma master as he is tae you. Dinna ask this o' me as I would nae wish tae disobey a command o' ma King.'

'It is good tae see that my constable commands such faith and steadfastness. I would nae ask you tae betray him. My apologies, Gilbert, I shall find some other wench.'

'I shall find a willing girl tae warm your bed my liege.'

Gilbert and Morag left the room and true to his word Gilbert found a girl amongst the servants who was more than willing to do service for her King.

The King and his company stayed at Slains for the remainder of the week before moving on.

The day after his departure Gilberts made ready to set out for Arbroath Abbey. He travelled with just a small number of retainers. Enough to protect him should the need arise but few enough not to draw unwanted attention to the group.

The journey passed quickly and their arrival at Arbroath Abbey found the monks to be in a state of anxiety due to the large number of noblemen and their followers who were arriving each day. Although the abbey had ample guest rooms for most occasions this unusual number of significant and powerful visitors was uncommon and they were hard pressed to find suitable accommodation for them all.

Lay brothers ran around caring for horses and finding places for the retainers to bed down for the night. Nobody knew how long the guests would be staying for. It might be just a day or two or possibly months if the discussions dragged on. Bruce had told him what the contents of the document should be but the tone and the wording was to be decided by the nobles. Painfully aware how difficult it was likely to be to get so many people, each with their own best interests in mind, to agree, Gilbert was resigned to the fact that his stay was likely to be an extended one.

The lay brothers were tasked to take chairs and tables into the Abbot's chambers so that the nobles could all be seated and discussions held in private. This would also be the dining room for the nobles, whereas the retainers would join the monks in the refectory. Gilbert was impressed by the opulence of the Abbot's apartments, as fine as any king's palace and sparing no expense. Beautifully upholstered chairs and finely carved tables and cupboards were of the finest quality and beautiful tapestries depicting biblical scenes covered the walls. A huge fire roared in the enormous fireplace giving the whole room a cosy feel.

The Abbey Gardens were filled with the fragrance of herbs and the warm spring sunshine made it a pleasure to take some relaxation here before the work began.

The table that night was laden with food befitting the status of the diners. The monks provided fine wine which disappeared in vast quantities very rapidly as the eight earls and thirty-eight barons refreshed themselves after their journeys. Some had travelled great distances at the command of the King to be present at the drafting of the document.

The next day discussions began and it became apparent very quickly that it was going to be difficult for all to agree the wording. Abbot Bernard decided that he should take responsibility for recording the letter for security. He began time and again to record the thoughts of the group only to have to scratch them out and begin again when people failed to agree. Tempers became heated and words were exchanged between individuals. In this unsettled time, many nobles wanted to establish their precedence and many were unwilling to go unheard. Arguments broke out and there was a danger of violence, so divided was opinion.

Sir Adam Gordon stepped between the combatants and held up his hands for silence.

'It is for the good of Scotland and of us all that we are gathered here. Put aside your differences and self-seeking. We have to write words that will turn Pope John to support us.'

After many weeks of discussions and debates, it was agreed that the document should begin with a greeting to the Pope and naming all of those whom the document represented. This to show solidarity and the support of so many Scottish nobles for the cause. It would continue by documenting the history of the Scottish Nation and its independence. This was to be followed by a statement of the religious calling of the Scottish people in an attempt to convince the Pope of their support for him. They would then relate the barbaric behaviour of King Edward until their freedom had once again been restored through the success of Robert Bruce.

There was shock amongst many when Gilbert suggested, as Bruce had directed him, that they should declare that the Bruce ruled only with their agreement, and, should he betray their rights to independence, the nobles would remove him from power.

'...we have been set free... by our most tireless prince, King and lord, the lord Robert... Yet if he should give up what he has begun, seeking to make us or our kingdom subject to the King of England or the English, we should exert ourselves at once to drive him out as our enemy... and make some other man who was well able to defend us our King.'

He explained that this was a strategy to display their solidarity. They confirmed their commitment to independence with the words,

'For so long as there shall but one hundred of us remain alive we will never give consent to subject ourselves to the dominion of the English. For it is not glory, it is not riches, neither is it honours, but it is liberty alone that we fight and contend for, which no honest man will lose but with his life.'

Finally, the letter was agreed and Abbot Bernard wrote out a fresh copy. He read it back to the gathered nobles. There were nods of approval and a few grumblings which were quelled by the majority.

It was agreed that a copy should be made in case the original should be intercepted and that Sir Adam Gordon should deliver the letter to the Pope in Avignon. It was addressed; *'Letter of Barons of Scotland to Pope John XXII.'* and each present attached their seals.

For many the gathering was a chance to catch up with events and Gilbert was pleased to spend time with Sir Robert Keith. They discussed their new acquisitions in Aberdeen and exchanged news of family and friends. Sir Robert had a grandson, his namesake and was in agreement with Gilbert that it was time they started to seek wives for their offspring. Sir Robert was keen for his grandson to marry well and put it to Gilbert that uniting their lands, which were in such close proximity to each other, would be advantageous to both families. After some negotiation, Gilbert was in agreement and before they parted an agreement had been struck.

Eager to return to their estates, the signatories set off early the next day. There was much bustling and shouting in the abbey forecourt as nobles and their retainers gathered and mounted their horses. A few held back to speak privately with the abbot, before their departure, to make donations to the abbey and request prayers to be said for them or their loved ones. Each party received a blessing as they set out and soon the peace of the abbey was restored.

Gilbert was the last to leave. He mounted his horse which bore a saddle of the finest leather, tooled with Celtic scrolls and oiled so that it gleamed. His squire and retainers mounted up and fell into a rank behind him ready to return to Slains.

Jenni, the serving wench who had offered her services to Robert Bruce during her stay at Slains Castle, was now sure. She was with child and she was positive it was the king's bastard. She bragged amongst her friends that she carried the king's child and daydreamed about how she would be rewarded by Robert Bruce. He had only one living son and if he should die her son might be acknowledged. She even dreamed he might marry her and legitimise her son and she was sure it was a son by the way it kicked. When there was work to be done she shirked it saying that she mustn't risk the king's child and so it was not long before everyone within the castle precincts knew of her condition.

It had been a glorious summer and as autumn approached the evenings were balmy. The full moon shone on the sea casting its light onto the rippling water in a widening, shimmering path towards the castle. She stood on the edge of the cliffs looking out and dreaming of glories to come. Thomas had seen her from the window and decided to join her to enjoy the peaceful evening. He made his way down the stairs and out through the doorway. His footsteps were silent on the wooden steps leading down to the courtyard. As he made his way towards the edge of the cliff he became aware of the presence of another person. A shadowy figure stepped out towards Jenny and tried to kiss her. She pushed away and said something to her would-be lover. Before Thomas knew what was happening the figure had reached out and pushed Jenny forward. He heard a scream as she lunged forwards and hurled over the edge of the cliff. There was a sickening thud as she hit the rocks below. As Thomas raced forward he became aware that the figure who had pushed her was his brother, Nicolas. Without thinking he hurtled forward to challenge Nicholas, shouting as he went. Nicholas grabbed him and thrust his hand across Thomas' mouth. Nicholas did not think twice but, knowing that he could not restrain Thomas with his weakened arm, he pulled his hand around holding Thomas' face and pushed him backwards with all his might, hurling Thomas onto the rocks below, his body landing beside that of Jenny. He stood back, suddenly shocked by his own actions. He had murdered not only the serving wench but also his own brother. He stepped a little closer to the edge of the cliff and looked down at the two bodies lying crumpled on the rocks; two victims of his bitterness and jealousy. He strode away without any regrets, thinking only of how he would defend himself should any accuse him of this horrendous deed. The castle gates were locked for the night and it would be impossible to leave without being noticed. He decided that his best course of action would be to return to his room and claim to have been there all evening.

It was early the next day when the bodies were found. Fishermen from Whinnyfold were arriving with their catch to sell to the castle. As they rounded the head of the cliff one of the men spotted something on the rocks. They could not get closer with the boat for fear of it being damaged but as soon as they had pulled the boat up onto the pebbly beach they scrambled up the rocks to raise the alarm. Men raced down with them to investigate the find whilst women and children peered over the edge of the cliff and gasped as they saw the two bodies. Jenny was lying face down and was not readily identifiable but the body of Thomas could not be mistaken. The men lifted the bodies from the rocks and carried them round to the beach. Ropes were lowered to lift the bodies up the steep cliff. A woman screamed as she realised who the girl was. There was shock as Thomas' identity was confirmed and a loon was sent to fetch Gilbert.

As he arrived at the scene people stepped back to allow him to see the dreadful site. For a moment he was speechless. The body of his beloved son lay before him broken and bloodied. 'What happened?' he whispered fearing to speak out loud as his voice was quaking. When there was no response from the frightened people he asked again this time in a roar, 'I said what's happened, why is my son lying here dead?'

One of the men who had recovered the body was trying to explain how they had been discovered. There were whispered conversations amongst the people behind but all agreed; the night being calm there was no reason why anybody should have fallen. A woman stepped forward declaring that she had heard a scream the night before but she had taken it to be that of a wench fooling around with one of the stable lads. 'But there are two bodies,' declared Gilbert. 'Thomas had his favourites amongst the girls but Jenny was not one of them and I don't believe he would force himself on an unwilling lass.' There were murmurs of agreement as Thomas was known to be a caring young man, and being strikingly good-looking he could have his pick of any number of girls without forcing himself on any.

Gilbert declared himself determined to root out his son's murderer and offered a substantial reward to anyone who could bring him evidence of who the murderer was. His anger knew no bounds and Nicholas feared discovery if he did not cover his tracks well. He approached his father and added his own challenge to people to find the murderer. 'My beloved brother lies dead,' he bellowed 'I shall not rest until his murderer is brought to justice.'

The bodies were taken away and laid in the chapel where the women came to prepare them for burial. As they did so one of them noticed that although Jenny had fallen face first onto the rocks damaging her features almost beyond recognition, Thomas' injuries were to the back of his head and his neck was broken. She went quietly to Gilbert and took this information to him. 'What does this mean?' He asked of himself. 'If his head bore the injuries that killed him and his face is unmarked, he must've fallen backwards.' It did not take Gilbert long to realise that this confirmed that Thomas had been pushed from the rocks rather than falling. Gilbert dismissed the woman telling her not to share this information with anyone. He paced the room thinking and wondering who could possibly wish to harm his younger son. He raged at fate and at God for taking his wife, maiming his eldest son, and now taking his younger son from him. He wondered what else could possibly happen to him and was inconsolable in his grief.

CRUS

A messenger had been sent to Coupar Angus Abbey for preparations to be made and within the week the party of mourners set off. A likely target for outlaws who knew they would carry gifts for the abbey, the party included not only Gilbert, Sir Hugh and Nicholas but also armed men surrounding the cart which carried the coffins. It had been decided to take Jenni's body with them for burial in the grounds of the abbey.

They were surprised to be greeted by Robert Bruce with the abbot when they arrived. He stepped forward and spoke to Gilbert. 'My condolences, friend. Ye have suffered much these last years.'

'Aye, life has not been kind tae me. But I still have my eldest son.'

They turned to look at Nicholas and Bruce was shocked to see the smirk which crossed the face of Gilbert's heir.

Frowning Bruce continued, 'I am told the lass carried my child.'

'Aye, so she said.'

'I shall see her family right in this. Take this purse to them, Gilbert, and should they want for anything, I would have word of it.'

'I shall see it done,' promised Gilbert.

The service was a sombre one and even though Scotland was excommunicated, the service was a full mass. The chanting of the brothers melodic and sweet brought a tear to the eye of even the menfolk, yet Nicholas stood dry-eyed and thoughtful.

The following day Robert Bruce spoke to Gilbert as they broke their fast.

'Have ye given any thought tae your son's marriage yet?' asked Bruce.

'Aye, Malcolm Lenox is agreeable and will bring his daughter to Slains to discuss the match.'

'Tell him the match has ma blessing,' offered Bruce, turning to ensure that Nicholas had heard his words and understood their meaning.

❧

Before Gilbert entertained Lenox to discuss Nicholas' prospective bride, he felt obliged to proceed with the agreement made with Sir Robert Keith and rode with his daughter to Dunnattor Castle. Margaret was pleasantly surprised when she was introduced to Robert. A tall and muscular figure he was fair of face and many a maid had cast a longing eye in his direction. He took her hand in his and planted a kiss upon it. Leading her by the hand he showed her around the castle and explained the recent alterations and additions which had been made to it. Robert's quiet attentiveness and chivalric behaviour re-assured her and she was not displeased when it was agreed that the marriage should take place as soon as possible.

As Gilbert was anxious to return to Slains to prepare for his son's marriage, he was delighted that Margaret's marriage was acceptable to all. Sir Robert provided Margaret with a maid to prepare her for the wedding and it was the next day that both families went into the castle chapel for the ceremony.

Chapter 5

1321

Slains Castle had rarely seen such preparations. Only Robert Bruce's visit had caused more of a stir. Chambers were made ready and food prepared to greet The Earl of Lenox and his daughter in order to show them the finest welcome and display the wealth and status of Gilbert Hay, Constable of Scotland.

The arrival of the party was greeted by Gilbert himself with Nicholas beside him. Nicholas was surprised to find that Malcolm's daughter, Beatrix, was very beautiful and petite. Her long yellow hair was braided and tied with ribbons. She was only 13 years old and an obedient but fearful daughter. Her parents had told her that she was to meet her prospective husband and that if he found here pleasing, she would wed a man who was set to become the most important man in Scotland after the king. Overcome by this honour she was determined to make herself agreeable to Nicholas. She dreaded letting her father down and would be mortified if she were rejected.

Nicholas helped her down from her pony appearing every bit the young gentleman whilst his eyes roamed over her appraisingly.

Leading her by the hand, Nicholas took her into the castle hall. Her eyes glimpsed his arm but she looked away quickly.

She knew that many men were injured in battle and she was lucky to be offered to a man who at least still had four limbs and bore no ugly scars. Nicholas was relieved by her acceptance of his appearance having expected her to flinch at his touch.

Gilbert and Malcolm followed them into the hall and suggested that Nicholas showed her around whilst they discussed the match. Her father was aware of the honour being shown to him and was keen for the match to go ahead but was reluctant to offer a huge dowry as he had other daughters to wed yet.

As fortune had smiled upon Gilbert, at least financially, in the last years, he was prepared to accept a somewhat smaller figure than he otherwise would have looked for. He was also keen to find a match for Nicholas as his only remaining son so that heirs could be secured.

୶୶

An agreement was reached and it was decided that the ceremony would take place that week.

Malcolm, Earl of Lenox sent for his daughter and told her that he expected her to be a good and obedient wife. He was sure that Nicholas would be a good husband and it was a fine match.

If Nicholas had to be wed to a girl who was not of his choice, he decided that this one would do. She was young and weak. He would do with her as he wished.

After supper, Beatrix excused herself blaming a headache. She left the table and started on her way to her room. Her maid prepared her for bed and left her to sleep. She lay awake thinking of what was to come. She would rarely if ever see her family again and would live in this castle on the edge of a cliff where the wind blew so strongly that doors could not be opened and two people had recently been murdered, including the laird's son!

Silently the room of her chamber opened. Nicholas stepped in and barring the door he strode over to the bed. As he took hold of the coverlet she was startled and clutched it to her. He put his hand over her mouth to prevent her from screaming and whispered into her ear. 'Don't make a sound. It is me. If you are to be my wife I want to see how good you will be to me.'

Beatrice trembled and clutched the blanket tighter. 'Sir, we are not yet wed!'

'You are promised to me. I need to see that you will be a good and obedient wife' he said his hand roaming under the blanket.

'I am an obedient daughter, sir,' she told him pushing his hand away. 'My father would not wish this.'

'Sod your father!' he exclaimed, heaving on the bed covers. 'He would want you to obey me.'

With a final pull, he removed her covering and she curled up trying to protect herself from him. Nicholas showed no mercy as he forced himself upon her, muffling her screams with his hand as he used her.

She sobbed as he rolled away, spent. He lay for a while, smiling and caring nothing for her distress.

'You'll do I suppose,' he said finally. 'But you've a lot to learn if you are to satisfy me.'

He left her and returned to his own room, well pleased with his success.

For the following days, Beatrix kept to her room. She knew there was no point in revealing what had happened as no other man would want her now and Nicholas was bound to deny it calling her a liar, saying she must have lain with some other man. She replied to requests for her company with messages that she was preparing for her wedding day. In reality, she was terrified of this brute of a man whose wife she must become.

⁂

The day dawned when the wedding was to take place. Nicholas stood waiting with Gilbert as Malcolm led her down to meet them. Beatrix kept her head down to hide her tears but this was seen only as a sign of her humble agreement to the marriage.

The wedding took place with all of the pomp and ceremony to be expected of the son of the Constable of Scotland. Nicholas played the attentive husband but his whispers to his bride were not endearments but threats of what would become her if she resisted him.

Wine flowed freely and there was not a sober person to be found. When Nicholas began to lead his new wife away to their chamber, there were calls for the bedding ceremony. Nicholas laughed as they were followed up the stairs but as he and Beatrix entered the bed chamber he quickly turned and bolted the door. He was not averse to showing off his prowess in bed but he would not have them witness him fumbling with his damaged arm. He threw off his own clothes then turned to his cowering bride. Ripping her dress from her shoulders he threw her onto the bed. Pausing he turned back to his clothes. Taking his dirk from his belt he pressed the blade into his hand and smeared the blood onto the bed. He was not concerned that the servants would believe that this gentle maid was not as innocent as she looked but he would not have them doubt his ability to serve her.

Beatrix had suffered every humiliation that Nicholas could inflict upon her in the privacy of their room, yet in public, he showed no sign of his contempt and ill treatment of her.

As the months passed she grew big with child and Gilbert looked forward to the arrival of his grandchild. Nicholas secretly hoped for a son yet outwardly showed little interest in the forthcoming event. In due course, Beatrix was confined. Her maid, familiar with the bruises which she so often witnessed on her mistress' body was, none the less, shocked to see fresh marks even now.

Her labour was long but straightforward and she was delivered of a fine healthy boy. Holding the child against her she smiled at him and placed a gentle kiss on his head, hoping as she did so that he would not grow up to be such as his father.

Nicholas marched into the room. 'Give me my son,' he ordered snatching the child from her. Meekly she said, 'I should like to call him Malcolm after my father.'

Nicholas did not care what the child was called but to spite her he would deny her even this.

'He will be called David,' he declared choosing the first name that came to him. He left the room taking the child with him to show off his success whilst Beatrix was left to gently weep out her sorrow.

Gilbert tapped on the door and entered quietly in case she was sleeping. He was surprised to see tears and strode across the room to the bed. 'There now lassie, Nicholas will bring the child back to you shortly. He just wants to show him off,' he said mistaking the reason for her tears. She brushed them away and in doing so Gilbert caught sight of her bruised arm. She swiftly covered it so he made no comment but suspected that it was no accident.

Chapter 6

1327

News that King Edward II of England had given up his throne in favour of his son was greeted with excitement and celebration. The actions of Edward's wife, Isabella, and Roger Mortimer and the favour shown by Edward to Hugh Despenser the younger had destroyed his standing with the nobility of England. His son, Edward III, was crowned on 1st February. The messenger who brought the news to Slains Castle was rewarded with a purse of gold pieces. Gilbert gave orders for preparations to be made for celebrations to take place at the end of the week. Musicians were sent for and food supplies were brought to the castle. This, he hoped, could mean a halt to the hostilities between England and Scotland; something for which all could be grateful.

1328

The news came to the castle by messenger. Robert Bruce had signed a treaty in Edinburgh which meant peace between England and Scotland. This was the news they had been waiting and longing for. War was an expensive business both in monetary costs and in lives. Scotland could not bear it much longer and needed peace.

The terms of the treaty were costly but acceptable in the long term. Scotland would pay England £100,000 sterling and in exchange, the English crown would recognise Scotland as fully independent and Robert Bruce, his heirs and successors as the rightful rulers. The border between the countries would be as that recognised under the reign of Alexander III.

There was great cheer in Slains Castle as Gilbert ordered preparations for celebrations.

Sir Hugh was away in Perthshire so it was left to Nicholas to oversee preparations. Boats were sent out to fetch extra help from Whinnyfold and Collieston and wine was sent for to supplement the castle's already extensive cellar which was kept full thanks to the local people who had an agreement with French sailors.

October of that year saw further celebrations as the Pope lifted the Interdict from Scotland.

Robert Bruce was once more celebrated as the hero of Scotland and took the opportunity to see his son, David, who was just four years old, married to Joan of the Tower, daughter of Edward II. The marriage took place at Berwick on Tweed significantly near the border between England and Scotland and Gilbert Hay, his son, Nicholas and many other nobles were invited. As the prince and his new wife were so young, the children of other nobles were also invited and after the ceremony they enjoyed a party whilst their elders celebrated this consolidation of the agreement between Scotland and England as much as the actual wedding.

But Robert Bruce, whom rumour had it was suffering from leprosy, was failing fast. He was fated to have little time to enjoy his glory for, little over a year later, on 7th June 1329 he died at Cardross.

There was great mourning in Scotland as the hero of their time was taken from them. His ravaged and battle-weary body was buried at Dunfermline Abbey before the high altar and next to his queen. The abbey was the traditional resting place for Scottish kings and his nobles took care to make this final gesture to him. Bruce, on his deathbed, had regretted his failure to fulfil a vow to undertake a crusade to fight the Saracens in the Holy Land and asked his knights to go on a crusade on his behalf. He requested that his heart be carried with them. They could not deny him this favour and Sir James Douglas had agreed to carry this relic of Scotland's hero.

'Robert's death is a great blow to us and to Scotland,' remarked Hugh to Gilbert. 'His son is a mere child and we cannae trust the English to honour the agreement signed in Edinburgh.'

'We are none of us getting any younger' observed Gilbert to a group of knights at Bruce's graveside. 'Edward Balliol is a threat to us all and with Robert Bruce's son yet an infant we must depend upon Sir Thomas Randolph who rules as Guardian of Scotland.' Many of those gathered expressed their concerns. They trusted Randolph but Edward Baliol was bound to have the support of King Edward and the Scottish numbers were still low as a result of the many battles and skirmishes which had ravaged their land and people for so many years. Their suspicions were justified and it was not long before Edward Balliol came forward to claim the crown of Scotland. Edward III and numerous lords who had lost their lands as a result of Bruce's victory were all too ready to support him.

Chapter 7

1332

A loud hammering on the gates of Slains Castle was answered gruffly by a guard.

'Who's there? The gates are locked for the night. What are you doing travelling after dark, it's asking for trouble?'

An urgent voice responded, 'I bring a message for The Constable. I demand entry in the name of Sir Thomas Randolph.'

'Sir Thomas who?'

'Just open the fucking gate you moron!'

'I'll have to ask....'

'Your master will have your head if you don't open these gates right now!'

Grumbling and cursing the guard stepped back and called up to his fellow on the look-out, 'Is he alone?'

A nod re-assured him and he drew back the plank which locked the gates.

'Idiot!' barked the messenger as he rode past him making sure that his foot caught the guard a hefty blow as he passed. 'Fetch you master and be quick about it!'

'He's not going to like this,' muttered the guard as he set off to raise Gilbert. 'Watch him,' he called to the other guard as he went as much by way of a slight as through any perceived threat.

It was some time before Gilbert appeared in the courtyard. At fifty-seven years of age, he was suffering from old battle scars and the ravages of age. He could not move with the agility he had displayed as a young man and was preparing to hand over the reins to Nicholas.

The messenger held out a rolled document which bore an impressive seal. A single glance told Gilbert that the caller was genuine and he commanded him to accompany him into his hall. Taking a taper he took a light from a torch and lit a cluster of wax candles which stood on his desk. In silence he read the document, his face forming a frown as he read.

Edward Balliol was proving their suspicions to be well founded. He had gathered forces and was sailing for Scotland. He had English troops and mercenaries with him.

Gilbert lowered the paper. 'How long have yea taken tae get here?'

'Three days. The roads were bad but I wasted no time.'

Gilbert called for his servant whom he knew would be outside the door having heard his master rise. 'See that this man is well fed and rouse Nicholas.'

The man immediately went to do his bidding and within moments Nicholas appeared.

'What cause have yea tae bid me rise?' he questioned churlishly.

'A cause which could cost Scotland its freedom,' responded Gilbert. 'Edward Balliol comes and would attack Scotland tae claim the crown. Randolph summons us tae Perth. We are bound tae provide men tae fight in the king's cause. Sir Hugh is already at Erroll and will reach Perth afore us. We will meet him there and prepare tae do battle. Go and say farewell tae your wife and son.'

'No need. I'll let them sleep and see them when I return.'

'There is never any certainty of return when we go tae battle. See them while yea may.'

'I said nae! Dinna tell me wha' tae do old man!'

'Yea forget yer sel laddie! I'm nae deed yet!' but Gilbert was too busy to continue the argument and set about preparing to leave.

Men were roused and kitted out. Those without decent weapons carried whatever they may to fight and defend themselves. There were horses enough for most of the men but a few were without and must march. Nicholas had a shield which was modified to help his damaged arm. The baldric strap which went across his shoulder was doubled to take the weight and a grip on the reverse enabled him to hold it in place with ease. The design was useful but compromised on mobility.

As soon as men and supplies were ready they set off at as fast a pace as the marching men could manage.

The bustle and noise had woken Beatrix and a few questions had brought her the news of events. Not wishing to take leave of Nicholas she made her way to the chapel where she knelt in prayer offering a request for safe deliverance for Gilbert and for herself.'

Her prayers were to be answered.

On arriving at Perth, Gilbert sought out Thomas Randolph only to discover that he was dead. He had died at Musselburgh on his way to repel the invasion and rumours suggested that he had been poisoned by the English. A great and honest leader had been lost at this crucial time. He was replaced as the King's guardian and Guardian of Scotland by Donald, Earl of Mar who would fight beside them this day.

On 12th August 1332, the Scottish troops faced an army of English soldiers and mercenaries at Dupplin Moor.

The Scots heavily outnumbered the English and were confident of success. They knelt as Gilbert's brother, Nicholas, Dean of Dunkeld, prayed for the deliverance of the Scottish army and blessed them before they went into battle.

The English drums were beating and the drones of bagpipes could be heard as the pipers struck in their pipes. The sounds of battle had commenced and the conflict began. The order to attack was given and horses and soldiers charged forwards towards each other. Battle cries of each clan could be heard as they fell upon the English. Screams of men and horses mingled with the sounds of metal on metal as men, boys and horses were struck down with horrific injuries. The smell of blood assailed their nostrils as death found them on the battlefield.

The Scots had the advantage and English troops were suffering dreadful casualties but the heat of battle had hidden the fact that many English men had remained motionless throughout. It was only when a cloud of arrows rained down on the heads of the Scottish fighters that they realised what was happening.

Gilbert's horse reared up throwing him to the ground. As he fell his wounded horse, in its panic, stepped back onto his leg. A sickening crack declared it broken and the pain took consciousness mercifully from him.

སྐུ་

Nicholas Hay rode forward into battle. He had never taken part in anything much more than a skirmish and was unused to such large numbers. His horse lunged fiercely towards the English and he held his sword aloft ready to strike. Swinging the weapon to left and right he struck out at men around him. As he looked to his left a sword was descending towards his head. He lifted his targe on his damaged arm to intercept the blow but in doing so the strap which supported it from his shoulder hindered the movement. The descending sword caught the targe and dragged it behind him with the momentum of the attacker's horse. The strap pulled across his throat and yanked Nicholas' head backwards. His head hung loosely from his shoulders as his horse continued forwards carrying his limp body.

In the fading light figures moved amongst the dead and dying relieving them of armour, valuables and weapons. Parched lips called for water and some begged for the mercy of death. A number of women passed amongst the bodies left on the battlefield slitting the throats of the dying and helping themselves to rings and chains as they did so.

A few searched amongst the bodies for those they knew. Gilbert dreamt he heard his name called from a long way off. He tried to respond and heard a cry of pain close by. As he re-gained consciousness he realised it was he who had made the sound. His leg was a throbbing mass of pain and blood.

A figure stood over him. He recognised his brother, Hugh. He felt himself lifted through the fog of pain and vaguely realised that Hugh was carrying him. The jogging movement and searing pain seemed to last for hours before he felt himself being lowered gently to the ground.

As if the pain was not bad enough he suddenly felt a burning liquid poured over it. Hugh held a flask of whisky which he was using to wash the wound.

'Give me that!' ordered Gilbert snatching it and holding it to his lips. The burning liquid poured down his throat gradually easing the pain.

'My son?' asked Gilbert. 'Bring him to me.'

'I cannot, Gilbert,' said Hugh sadly. 'He was victim to an English horseman. He died instantly.'

'Where is Mar?'

'He is dead also. Just ten days as Guardian of Scotland and he lies amongst the dead. We must appoint a new Guardian for the king as soon as is possible.'

The Scottish forces had been decimated. Sir Robert Bruce the illegitimate son of King Robert also lay amongst the dead.

Gilbert was carried to Erroll where his brothers cared for him. Servants tended his wounds with herbs from the monks at Coupar Angus. The whisky which Sir Hugh had poured over his leg had helped to keep infection at bay but the break was bad and would not heal.

Sir Hugh rode to Slains Castle to deliver the news and tell Beatrix in person of her husband's death.

Beatrix could scarcely hide her relief at the news. Taking David's arm she entered the chapel and knelt before the altar. Those close to her were sure that her prayers were of thanks for being freed from her bitter and abusive husband. To others, it seemed she was praying for her husband's soul. Her precious son was now doubly so as he was Nicholas' only son and would one day become Constable of Scotland.

Beatrix decided that, with Hugh's help, she would ensure that David grew up to be a well-balanced young man. He would learn to fight as he must but he would also learn to be honourable and fair.

Gilbert's recovery was slow. The news that Edward Balliol had been crowned King of Scotland by the English had distressed him badly and although Balliol had been forced to flee back to England by December, he remained a threat to Scotland. The pain in Gilbert's leg was often unbearable without the herbal infusions which Brother Wilfred from the Abbey of Coupar Angus provided. Although it was a clean break and the flesh healed, the bone refused to knit and he could only walk with the aid of crutches made from birch wood. After several months he found the pain increasing and his need for the relief given by the herbs was growing. Ulcers appeared over the broken bone and in spite of Brother Wilfred's efforts they would not heal. Maggots were brought to put on the festering tissue but the sores grew worse, as did the pain. The smell which came from the open would was sickly and the good brother feared for Gilbert's life. 'I have seen this before in battle wounds,' he told Gilbert. The only hope is to remove the leg.'

'Will this ensure my recovery?'

'I cannot promise. Some die from the surgery but some make a good recovery. The leg is beyond repair. I must ask you what I should do.'

'I do not fear the knife,' declared Gilbert in little more than a whisper. 'If there is a chance of its success I must ask you to go ahead.'

Brother Wilfred left Gilbert to gather the help and equipment he would need.

An hour later he returned with four strong men and an assortment of instruments. As he opened the door he was immediately aware of the stillness. Holding out his hand to still the others he approached the bed. He held his ear close to Gilbert's mouth to listen then standing up, he placed his hand on Gilbert's chest.

'The Lord has taken him,' he announced and closed Gilbert's eyes with his fingers.

⁂

William, Gilbert's cousin from Erroll rode to Slains carrying the news of Gilbert's death. Beatrix' shock brought her to her knees where she held her hands up to the Lord to pray for Gilbert's soul and for her young son who was now the Constable of Scotland. Scotland now had a King of only seven years old and High Constable of twelve years of age. Many other senior nobles had also fallen at Duplin Moor leaving Scotland with few experience leaders. The stability of Scotland was at risk and the threat from England was increasing.

But for now more imminent matters must be dealt with and Beatrix must make preparations for their journey to Coupar Angus for Gilbert's funeral.

Boatmen set off from the bay to make their way to Peterugie to secure the services of tailors to prepare mourning clothes for Beatrix and young David. They must be readied at all speed as they must set off in three days.

The boatmen returned with the tailors who brought with them the materials they would need and began work immediately. David must have clothing befitting his new role as High Constable and no expense was spared in producing a black velvet tunic and breeks, finished with pearls and silver buttons for David and a dress of black satin with velvet cloak for Beatrix.

The party set out for Coupar Angus Abbey at first light, accompanied by a guard of fifty armed men. Armour and weapons had been polished to perfection and, at the head of the procession a guard carried the banner which bore the Hay arms of three red shields.

As they arrived at the abbey the great bell was already tolling. They were greeted by Abbot John Orwell holding his crosier.

'Greetings my lord,' he addressed David, 'my condolences on the death of your grandfather. It must come hard so soon after your father's death.'

'He was indeed dear to me Father Abbot and will be sadly missed. He was a good and honest man.'

Gilbert had provided a tutor for his grandson and Beatrix was proud of how he confidently answered the Abbot. Abbot John turned to Beatrix. 'My lady,' he said bowing, 'my sympathies to you also. I know that you held your husband's father in high esteem.'

'Thank you, Father Abbot. He will be much missed. He leaves my son with huge responsibilities but he provided well for his education but as yet he has no Latin and little knowledge of the scriptures. If you can spare a brother to return with us as his tutor I will see that you are well recompensed.'

'Madam, we are well provided for in Gilbert's will and he has made just such a request of us. Brother Lambert will accompany you on your return journey and stay for three years to educate the young master. Lord Erroll also requested masses to be said for his soul which we will gladly perform.'

Abbot John led David and Beatrix to the guest house and showed them to their rooms. Water and towels were brought and after a short rest, they were invited to dine.

The Abbot's table reflected his status and fine food was accompanied by good French wine. David and Beatrix were hungry after their journey in spite of their grief.

'I am sorry that we were unable to bring your father's body here for burial,' Abbot John told David, 'following the battle it was simply impossible to make arrangements for so many nobles to be brought back to their families. I said prayers for their souls at the battle site and we will, of course, say masses for him at the abbey.'

'I do understand,' said David simply. He did not wish to discuss his father and knew that it distressed his mother to do so.

The meal complete, preparations were made for the service. Mass was said by Abbot John and Gilbert's body lowered into the tomb which had been prepared for it within the abbey church. Light poured through the stained glass windows and picked out facets of the gold chalice and plate upon the altar. Gilbert and his ancestors had bestowed money and land upon the abbey and signs of its wealth were all around them.

Following the service, Beatrix walked with Abbot John in his garden.

'The boy is young to carry such responsibility on his shoulders.'

'Yes but he is not only the double of his grandfather in appearance, he has his courage and strength.'

'You must take great care of him. He must produce heirs and carry on the noble line of Hay.'

'I will see to his care and with the help of his uncles and the good Brother Lambert, he will grow to deserve the great title which he bears.'

'But his uncles are not young men. Should you need my help do not fear to ask. The abbey owes much to the Hays and will do all we can to support them.'

'I thank you, Father.'

'Now, will you join us for compline?'

'It would be a privilege.'

As they spoke the abbey bell began to ring once again and the gentle slap of sandals could be heard as the monks made their way in silence towards the abbey church.

The voices of the monks raised in song were soothing and gave David an opportunity to consider his future. He himself would have liked to follow a monastic life but his future was determined by his duties.

The following day David and Beatrix rose early and attended Lauds before preparing for their departure. The horses were saddled and ready and they took their leave of Abbot John. They passed through the gatehouse, bridles and spurs jingling and the creak of leather as they broke into a trot.

Chapter 8

1340

David's progress with brother Lambert was rapid. He was a studious young man and absorbed all he was told. His training in sword skills and warfare out-passed even his academic progress and he was rapidly becoming a force to be reckoned with and a downy shadow on his upper lip proclaimed the approach of manhood. He grew as tall as his grandfather and was recognised as an honest young man. In good weather and bad he hunted, visited his tenants and oversaw the running of his estates. He grew in wisdom as well as stature.

His mother was proud of him and of Slains. She cared for the people of the castle and the procurement of supplies. A devout woman, she provided for a priest to serve the castle's little chapel and attended every service herself. It was she who greeted the messenger who arrived at the gatehouse in a cloud of dust. The weather had been dry for weeks and the sun had baked the road to Slains into a cracked and dusty way.

The messenger was clearly from the king as could be seen from his livery. Following the victory of the English at the Battle of Halidon Hill in July 1333, the young King David and his wife had been sent, for safety, to France, reaching Boulogne on 14 May 1334. King Philip had received them graciously and given King David Château Gaillard as a residence.

The messenger leapt from his horse and knelt before Beatrix. 'My lady, I bring you greetings from King David.'

'Please, come inside and refresh yourself. I shall send for my son.'

On David's arrival, the messenger explained that the Scottish forces had gained enough power and influence in Scotland for it to be safe for the King to return. Even now plans were being put in place for his journey back to Scotland. David Hay, Constable of Scotland, was commanded to provide a guard for the king on his return. Details would be provided as the plans progressed.

The messenger did not stay long as he had more nobles to alert to the king's plans for returning to Scotland and after taking refreshment he went on his way.

David sent men out to the furthest reaches of his barony at Slains to ensure that they had weapons and horses ready to form a guard when the instruction came. He sent also to Erroll to his estates there and to his uncles and cousins so that they too could make ready.

The date and place of the king's arrival would only be made known to them shortly before the event and it was imperative that they were ready to act as soon as the alert came.

David was delighted when he heard that Sir Robert Keith and his wife, Margaret, David's aunt, would be arriving at Slains Castle shortly. It was some time since he had seen them, the last time being when he had visited them at Dunnattor Castle to celebrate Christmas. It had been quite a family occasion and he had enjoyed hunting with his cousins William and Edward. Hugh Arbuthnot had joined them and David found him to be a skilled hunter both with falcon and sword.

Hugh had offered for his cousin Margaret's hand and there were great celebrations when Sir Robert Keith agreed to the match. David was quite envious of him as both Keith girls were very beautiful and accomplished.

The party arrived by boat and were ferried ashore at Slains in smaller vessels. David was delighted to find that their daughter Barbara had also made the journey and he took her hand to assist her ashore.

He welcomed the party to Slains Castle and gave orders for their trunks to be taken to the guest chambers.

During their meal that evening, musician entertained the group with lively tunes and songs. The fiddler struck up a merry tune and, the meal ended, David leapt into the middle of the room and placing his sword on the floor and with another across it, he entertained the gathering with his skills, dancing over and across the swords without touching them. There was laughter and applause as he bowed deeply to his appreciative audience. Barbara rose to her feet clapping and laughing at his antics. 'You must be over warm, sir,' she said. 'Perhaps you should take the air to cool a little.' She took his hand and with a little skip in her step, led him out of the door and down the stairs. They tumbled into the courtyard laughing together and turned towards the sea. The moon was casting its silver light on the water. 'It looks as though you could walk along its silver pathway right up to the moon,' Barbara mused. David slipped his arm around her waist as they looked into the sky. 'Yea're a very forward young lady,' David observed.

'I know what I want and I intend to get it. Besides, you are my cousin and I can speak freely to you, can't I?'

'These are exciting times,' David told her. 'King David will soon return tae Scotland.'

'My father is to join you in receiving him on his return.'

'We could make it even more exciting.'

'How so?'

He turned her in his arm and looked into her eyes. Slowly he lowered his head until his lips brushed her brow. He placed a trail of gentle kisses down her nose until his lips found hers. His kiss deepened as she responded returning his embrace and pulling his body close against hers.

'Would you care tae stay at Slains forever?'

'Cousin?'

'As my wife' he smiled.

She reached up and pulled his head down so that her lips could reach his.

'I'll take that as a yes then,' he told her. 'I'd better speak tae your father. I hope I can get him tae give you a good dowry. How much do you think he would pay me tae take you off his hands?'

She gasped in feigned shock then pulled him back to her and kissed him again.

Sir Robert Keith was thrilled with the match. 'It will take a powerful husband to take Barbara in hand,' he warned, 'but if any man can do it, you can David!'

'I must be mad,' David quipped, 'I have tae fight enough battles without courting trouble!' for which he received a most un-lady like punch. There was much laughter as David picked up a stool and pretended to use it as a shield to defend himself from his future wife.

It was decided that St Machar's Cathedral in Aberdon would be a suitable venue for the wedding and Robert returned home with his family in order to make preparations. The cathedral was still undergoing repairs from the damage done by King Edward but the dean assured Robert and David that it would be fit to hold the ceremony.

Family members had arrived at Slains Castle from Perth for David's wedding. He took the opportunity to catch up with matters in his Perthshire estates and spent much time in his chamber listening to accounts of minor disputes and events.

Two prisoners were held awaiting his judgement, one accused of murder and the other of theft. These would have to wait until David had time to travel to Perth and deal with them which he promised to do as soon after his wedding as could be practical.

⋙⋘

The arrival of Sir Robert Keith and his family at St. Machar's was greeted with fanfares and cheers. The bride looked radiant in her new green velvet dress and with flowers woven into her hair.

David had arrived some time earlier and grew nervous as the time for his wedding approached. His cousins teased him about Barbara's forceful character and jibes about their wedding night.

As a piper led her and her father to the cathedral porch the priest came out to meet them. He greeted the assembled families with a blessing before proceeding with the cere-mony. As he concluded, David took Barbara in his arms and gripped his around the waist. 'Now you must obey me,' he crowed to the laughter of their guests.

Celebrations went on well into the night with music, stories and dancing. The atmosphere was one of celebration and mer-riment. Robert had bestowed David with two carucates of land, a pair of fine hawks and a considerable about of gold and silver as Barbara's dowry. It was a wonderful match for her and if he were honest, Robert was relieved to have found a husband for his strong-willed and forthright daughter.

David laughed off the jibes made about their bedding and grabbed Barbara's hand racing her off to his bedchamber. As he arrived at the door he turned to the people who had chased after them laughing and making ribald comments.

'Enough!' he shouted over them. 'Leave us now. I will nae have my wife subjected tae your gaping. You've had your fun…and now I shall have mine!' and with that, he dashed through the door and bolted it.

For some time there was hammering on the door as drunken people demanded to watch the bedding and made colourful comments about what they were doing. Eventually, they got fed up and left the couple in peace.

'Now we'll see who's master here,' laughed David as he threw Barbara onto the bed laughing.

⟡

In due course, Barbara was brought to bed of a fine healthy son and David was determined that his son would not be named Nicholas after his father, and decided to honour his uncle, Thomas, in preference. His mother was relieved and thrilled that the succession was secure with the arrival of a sturdy boy.

It was only now that David found time to travel to his estates in Perth and was delighted to carry the news of his son's birth. He invited two of his cousins to witness young Thomas' baptism along with the child's maternal grandfather.

The arrival of a messenger at Dunnattor Castle was no surprise, however, there was much consternation and excitement when it was discovered that he came from the king bearing orders for Sir Robert Keith to attend him at Inverbervie in Kincardineshire on 2 June. This was where he proposed to land on his arrival back in Scotland.

The same message was received by David Hay and both made ready for immediate departure. Armour and weapons were kept at the ready and highly polished but none the less, armourers and squires rushed about making final adjustments. From both castles, almost simultaneously, parties set out to receive the king.

They arrived to find that a number of nobles had already gathered and there was much noise and bustle as excitement grew.

A fleet of ships came into sight and Robert Stewart, who had led the Scottish nobles in re-taking Edinburgh Castle and Scotland for King David, gave orders for people to assemble. A big bluff man, Robert was a likeable sort, able to rally men and charm the ladies. Men craned their necks to see what was happening as distant figures disembarked from the ships into smaller vessels. All wanted to catch a glimpse of the returning king.

After some time a murmur could be heard, 'There he is.....the boat nearest shore. The king!' The horses, sensing the excitement, stamped their feet and jostled restlessly. As the boat reached shore a cheer went up. 'The king! Hooray!' Robert Stewart dismounted and approached the king who shook his hand and placed his hand on his shoulder. 'It's good to be back,' he said simply.

King David was given a black horse of immense stature and the finest quality. It tossed its head with a spirit to equal that of the king. He mounted and turned to address the men.

'Greetings. It makes my heart glad to be back in Scotland; the land of our fathers and a land from which we will drive out our enemies and defend our freedom!' This was met with a tremendous roar.

'Many of you have lost kin and born injuries for the freedom of our land. This will not be forgotten and those who support me will reap the benefits. But the fight is not yet over! Edward still threatens our land and we must repel his assaults whenever and where ever they occur.

You have proved yourselves to be good men and true and your Scotland applauds you.'

The nobles were delighted with King David's speech. Still a very young man, he had returned to rule in his own right and they had every confidence that he would prevail over the English. The king called several of his nobles including David before him and knighted them. A number of the nobles and their men, including the now Sir David, accompanied the king to Perth where he was to set up his court whilst plans were compiled for the continuing repulsion of English attacks.

Chapter 9

1342

During his stay at Perth, Sir David sat in judgement of two felons who had been languishing in prison awaiting trial. The man accused of theft was dragged before him. He was a stooped and bedraggled figure. A hacking cough racked his body as he tried to catch his breath. The fellow had been caught taking goods from a draper's stall in the market place. Witnesses were brought who swore that they had seen him take the goods. Nobody spoke up for him and there was no doubt that he was guilty. David sentenced him to be flogged and the woeful figure was dragged away. He would be stripped naked, tied to the back of a cart and flogged through the town. In his present condition, he probably would not survive the beating.

The second man who stood accused of murder was an even more hopeless figure. Suppurating sores at his wrists and ankles were the result of being chained in the cell since his capture. His ribs showed through his torn clothes and the smell which he gave off caused people to cover their noses with anything to hand and to turn their heads away. The man was very short of stature and balding.

David sat at a table with a scribe beside him to record the case. 'Give me the details,' he demanded. The sheriff, Sir John Inchmartin, a belligerent-looking man, stepped forward.

'John Baxter was found dead in the church-yard. This bastard, Peter Taylor, was seen sneaking away from the churchyard after dark having killed him.'

'Who saw him there?' asked David.

''Twas William Key, sir.'

'I would hear it from his own lips. Is he here?'

William Key stood up so forcefully that his chair fell behind him causing laughter from the gathering. A court official called for silence.

'I am William Key,' he declared.

'Did you see Peter Taylor near the body?'

'Didn't know there was a body until next day, sir.'

'So you didn't see him commit the murder?'

'Not actually kill him.....but he was there and John is dead. Nobody hangs around the graveyard after dark. Spirits lurk there. You wouldn't see me dead in the graveyard after dark.'

This brought peals of laughter from the people gathered to witness the trial.

'Very well, I take your point,' said David concealing his mirth behind his hand. 'But how was he behaving?'

'Behaving?'

'Yes, was he hurrying?'

'Nae, sir. He walked slowly and peered around him guilt-ily,' he explained miming a furtive gaze.

This brought shouts of, 'Hang him,' from the crowd.

David turned to the coroner. 'Did you examine the body?'

'Yes, sir. He had been dead for some time because he was cold.'

'What would you say was the cause of death?'

'He had been stabbed. The knife was still in his back.'

'Has the knife been identified?'

'It has!' declared the sheriff gloating. 'It belongs tae Peter Taylor!'

More roars from the crowd greeted this and the official had to call for silence four times before order was restored. Turning to Peter Taylor he asked, 'This is your knife yet you say you didn't murder him.'

'Ma knife was lost,' shouts of derision and disbelief greeted this. 'I had been tae ma wife's grave tae tend it and used my knife tae plant a shrub on her grave. I must have missed it in the dark and left it near the graveside.'

'Why were you at her grave after dark?'

'My wife died the week afore this happened. I had a lot of work tae catch up with because I had tae take time off tae make arrangements and bury her. By the time I had finished work that day it was already growing dark. I went tae plant the shrub. It took longer than I expected because the ground was hard. By the time I had finished I could hardly see my way.'

'Show me the knife,' ordered David. He looked at the knife turning it over in his hand and running his finger along the blade. The tip was bent and there was damage to the edge. It certainly looked as though it had been used for digging.

David looked at the man accused and thought for some time. Mutterings in the crowd indicated that they were looking forward to a hanging and were impatient to get on with it. They had waited a long time for David's visit and were excited at the prospect of a day's entertainment. Finally, David called the coroner forward. 'Describe the victim tae me.'

'Well he was tall, o'er two yards high I'd say. He was heavy built and powerful.'

'How did the knife enter the victim?'

'Between his shoulder and neck.'

'Were there any other marks on his body?'

'His knees were scuffed,' came the hesitant reply.

After a few moments contemplation, David declared, 'I find Peter Taylor not guilty.'

There was uproar in the crowd. Shouting and shoving the townspeople were shocked.

Raising his voice to be heard, he continued, 'He could not have reached to drive a knife into a man so much taller than he is. The marks on John Baxter's knees suggest he fell to his knees after being stabbed; therefore he must have been standing when it happened. The knife is damaged at its tip and blade as could be expected if used as a digging tool. I believe Peter Taylor is telling the truth. Set him free.'

One or two people in the crowd cheered, others were astonished at the wisdom of the judge and some were just disappointed that they were not to have a hanging to entertain them.

As there were no further cases which needed his judgement, David stood up and turned to leave, his fine cloak swirling as he went.

❧

David's return to Slains Castle met with some delay as there were many documents awaiting his signature and land transactions to be agreed. He had decided to give a parcel of land to his kinsman, William Hay of Leys, and needed to have the paperwork signed and witnessed. This was to be done by Patrick Dunbar but his horse had thrown a shoe making him three hours late.

By the time David reached Slains it was growing dark and Barbara had already retired for the night. She was sleeping soundly when he slipped into the bed beside her and, with a sigh, he slipped his arm around her luxuriating in the comfort of her body against his. She murmured and snuggled into him without waking.

The following morning she was awoken by the clash of steel. Fearing that the castle was under attack Barbara leapt from her bed and flew to the open window only to see that David was below and was practicing his arming sword skills with one of the guards. David clearly had the upper hand and as she watched he brought his opponent to his knees. Barbara applauded his success. He smiled up at her and giving his sword to the armourer he saluted her and strode away to meet her.

'I didn't realise you were home,' she greeted him. 'I fancied you were in my bed last night but I thought it was just a dream.'

'I trust it was a pleasant one,' he countered with a smile and planted a kiss on her lips. 'It is good to be home. How fares young Thomas?'

'Come, I'll show you.'

Barbara took David by the hand and led him inside the castle. Thomas lay in his crib with his nurse sitting next to him. He was bound tightly in strips of cloth to make his limbs grow straight. As David entered the child opened his eyes and smiled. 'You see,' boasted David, 'he's glad to see me home too.' He lifted the baby from the crib and held him up high. 'One day all of this will be yours,' he predicted. Little did he realise how soon his words would come true.

Chapter 10

1346

Philip VI of France saw an opportunity to distract the English forces by setting up an attack near the border with Scotland. Under the terms of the Auld Alliance, he called upon David Bruce to support him by attacking England, thereby reducing the numbers which Edward could deploy in France. King David, having no choice but to comply, called together his nobles to plan their attack.

Sir David Hay was dismayed when he heard that the king was to launch an attack. There had been so many skirmishes with the English over decades and he had hoped that Scotland would soon have a period of peace to rebuild its resources. Riding to meet the king with a small party of retainers he soon came upon other nobles who had also been called upon.

As usual, there were some who relished a battle but the more experienced realised that the cost would be high in every sense.

There were those who rightly felt that Scotland was being used as a decoy by France to distract the English and allow the French to defeat their diminished forces. Whatever their opinions, the king was bound by the alliance and they, in turn, were bound to the king.

They met in the castle of Stirling and the great hall echoed with voices as they rose in competition with each other.

As the king entered, silence fell on the hall. David II looked every inch the glorious monarch. Made in the image of his father, his red-brown hair hung almost to his shoulders and his beard was full. A prominent nose gave a mature look to him in spite of his less than thirty years. His robes woven with gold thread and trimmed with ermine hung finely on his proud figure. He wore his crown with confidence and dignity.

Striding to his throne he sat and indicated to the gathered noblemen to be seated. He greeted them respectfully and explained that it was not his will to attack England at this time but he was duty bound by the alliance to support France. The French were at war with the English at Normandy and a Scottish attack in the north would draw English troops away to defend their border. There was unrest and muttering from those listening but he brought them to silence with a gesture. He continued to explain his plans and where they were to meet. They would gather south of Edinburgh and from there travel on to Carlisle. Those who were travelling from further north would join them later along the route and those from further south were to add their forces along the way.

Sir David Hay, as Constable of Scotland, would be one of the leading commanders along with John Randolph, Earl of Moray, Niall Bruce of Carrick, Robert and Edward Keith, Thomas Charteris, Robert Stewart and Robert Peebles. The nobles were dispersed to make preparations and gather their men as pledged to the king.

David returned to Slains with mixed emotions; the thrill of going into battle again beside the King wrestling with concerns for the Kingdom of Scotland and his own family. He was greeted by an anxious Barbara who bombarded him with questions. Who would he take with him? Who would he leave to protect her and their son Thomas? How long would he be away? Did he have to go? The last question she knew was pointless. Her husband owed fealty to the king and must do his bidding. He must not only go himself but must provide men and weapons to fight for the king.

Although he had so many arrangements to make David took time to sit with her and comfort her as best he could. He would arrange for her sister, Margaret, wife of Hugh Arbuthnot, to stay with her. It would be company and, as their father was also called upon to fight and provide soldiers, she and Margaret could support each other. Barbara knew he must go and was determined to try not to make his leaving any more difficult than it must be.

On the morning of his departure, she kept to her chamber as long as she could bear. Finally, she made her way down to the courtyard. David sat astride his horse. Both he and the animal wore armour and looked quite forbidding. His visor was up and what little of his face she could see smiled when he saw her approach. Horses and men milled around and there was shouting and swearing as men secured their weapons and made final checks before leaving. The creak of leather and clank of armour was fearsome.

Barbara approached stealthily knowing that war horses could be dangerous, unlike the mild-mannered mare she herself rode. David leant down and spoke into her ear. 'Fear not. I'll be home before you know I've gone. Look after young Thomas and yerself. Yours is the first face I want to see when I return to Slains.'

With that, he held up his hand to indicate to the soldiers to form up and they left at a steady trot with Sir David's standard carried aloft before them. Barbara covered her face with her hands and sobbed. A comforting arm wrapped around her as her sister led her inside and put a glass of wine in her hand.

The silence of the castle was unbearable. Most of the men had left with David. The smithy was silent and the usual bustle of the castle courtyard was still. A murmur from the crib reminded her that she must stay strong to care for their son until his father returned. The precious child needed her.

⚮

Sir David stopped at Erroll on his way south in order to see his cousins and give directions to them in his absence. Before he left he cut a sprig of mistletoe from a bough of the oak tree in the grounds. Almost a hundred years ago, Thomas the Rhymer had said that so long as it grew on the oak on their lands at Erroll the House of Hay would thrive and it was believed that a sprig of it cut on All Hallowmas Eve with a new dirk would keep them safe. We are in October so close enough perhaps, he thought. As the troops travelled towards Edinburgh groups of soldiers met up and joined together.

By the time they reached their destination there were thousands of men, horses and supply carts. Camp followers were there to cook and look after the men's needs. Pipers and drummers played for entertainment and to pit their skills against each other. The noise went in waves as David passed through between the tents. At one point he passed a group sitting and listening quietly to a harpist; a much more soothing sound.

The commanders had been summoned to meet with the king. Scouts had been sent out to assess the route and the king wished to consult with his men. It was decided that they would go on the next day to Jedburgh before going on the following day towards Durham. The original plan had been to go on to Carlisle first but a messenger had been received from the town carrying protection money which was accepted. It would be of use in purchasing supplies and paying soldiers. Little was to be gained in attacking the town in any case and time would be wasted. The king was expecting little resistance from the English believing most of their forces to be in Normandy. It was a mistake which was to prove costly.

As they travelled southwards, men from the borders joined King David's forces swelling their numbers and instilling confidence in the troops. Barbara's father had joined them and asked after her and their son. 'War is always hard on the women,' he observed.

The march to Hexham was long and arduous over hills and through woodland. From time to time the pipes would strike up to keep up their spirits or the drummers would rattle out a beat for them to march to.

They stopped short of the town and King David selected the commanders he wanted to go forward keeping some of his troops back.

They met with little resistance and greatly outnumbered the English forces based there. They sacked the monastery so that it could not offer succour to English troops and took with them valuables which could be sold. Sir David was glad that he was not amongst those chosen for this task as he was deeply religious and was disturbed to see the ruin of so fine a religious house and the ill-treatment inflicted upon the brothers.

Encouraged by this success, King David led his forces on towards Durham burning land to either side of their march to deprive the English of resources.

They arrived at Durham on 16th October and were met with an offer of £1,000 protection money. King David believed their offer meant they were unprotected and was unaware that the English had put troops in the area in preparation for his invasion. They did not have a large force and the Scots outnumbered them by two to one but the element of surprise was to be their weapon.

The following day, troops under the command of William Douglas, stumbled upon the English. The English were ready for them and inflicted heavy casualties upon Douglas' soldiers.

Douglas, dirty and bloodied, reported back to King David who was shocked at the presence of English soldiers having expected only a token resistance from old men and farm hands. He decided to remove his forces to higher ground and took them to Neville's Cross where he arranged his men into three battalions and prepared for battle.

Still reeling from the surprise attack he decided to put up a defensive stance. The English having fewer numbers also felt attack was too risky and chose defence. The sun glanced off their helmets as the Scottish soldiers prepared for battle.

Finally, the English decided to push the Scots into making a move by bringing forward their archers. It was the skills of these men who had won the day at Dupplin Moor and the Scots were not about to stand as targets for the arrows again. They began to move forward, Sir David Hay leading his men on the west and Robert Stewart to the east. As they advanced the ranks began to fall apart. Men fell and their fellows rushed forward to attack before they fell victim to the rain of arrows. Men and horses were stumbling over each other and English arrows were claiming victims by the second. A man fell against David's horse throwing it off its stride and as he lurched forward the sprig of mistletoe fell from his helmet. On the downward slope, it missed its footing and fell, trapping him beneath its weight. The horse's throat was exposed and an arrow found its mark killing the horse instantly. David was trapped. One of his men tried in vain to pull the horse off him.

The rain of arrows had stopped and English soldiers were upon them. His would-be rescuer was struck down by a sword blow. Sir David himself felt a sharp pressure at his neck then succumbed to darkness as his life blood spurted away. Robert Stewart had called his men away and he with others escaped.

Over a thousand Scots lay dead or dying and many were taken prisoner but King David had managed to escape.

The king parted with most of his men as it would be difficult to conceal a large number of soldiers from the English. He thanked them sincerely for their support and wished them success in their safe return to Scotland. To travel by night would be safest so, having put a few miles between himself and the battle, the king concealed himself under a bridge to wait for nightfall. The sound of hooves and voices told him that the English were in the area searching in trees and undergrowth. He froze as he heard somebody on the bridge, his heart thumping as he squatted down to make his shape as small as possible.

Suddenly a cry went up. An English soldier had seen the king's reflection in the water and he had been discovered. There was no hope of fleeing and it would have been dishonourable to do so. King David stood up and stepped out from his hiding place. The English soldier grabbed his arm roughly only to be rebuked by his leader, John de Coupland. 'Unhand him!' he bellowed. 'He is a king and will be treated as such.'

King David bowed briefly in acknowledgement and strode towards his captor. He turned his sword and presented the hilt to John who took it with a bow of his head in acknowledgement. John called for a horse for King David to ride with the soldiers to Odiham Castle in England as a prisoner. Coupland knew that he would be well rewarded by King Edward for such an important prisoner.

❧

On his return to England, King Edward was delighted to find King David a prisoner and ordered John de Coupland to deliver him from the Tower of London, where he was now held, to Windsor Castle.

David found himself in a comfortable suite of rooms within the castle, guarded by men who showed him respect and who were willing to make his time there bearable. He was permitted to walk within the Castle precincts and converse with visitors. He played chess and was provided with quill and paper so that he might write letters to his family.

From time to time he received messages from King Edward pressing him to acknowledge him as his feudal superior. These he declined and returned messages asserting his rights as King of Scotland.

As time went by and there was little sign of his release, King David grew weary of lingering in the English Castle and longed to return to Scotland. He became more circumspect in his responses to Edward's demands leading the English king to interpret this as David acknowledging him as his feudal superior. If this meant freedom, David was happy for Edward to think it so.

Sir David's family at Slains Castle received the news of his death with great sorrow. His wife hugged young Thomas to her as she and her sister mourned not only David's death but also that of their father. At only four years old Thomas was now the Constable of Scotland and Scotland's king was a prisoner in England. Although a powerful woman, she now felt vulnerable and isolated at Slains she decided to take the child to Erroll where his uncles could defend him and support her as the boy's guardian. As the sole heir to the title, he was a very important child. It was vital that he learned the skills of a knight and courtly manners, to speak correctly in Scots, English, French and Latin and to interact with courtiers and diplomats.

◈

Edmund Hay of Leys greeted their arrival at Erroll.

'My sympathy,' he offered 'You have suffered much with the loss of your husband and father.'

'It is the lot of women to suffer so when men must do battle to defend our country,' she said gallantly and yet a tear denied her strength.

'We live in difficult times,' he replied. 'I would have been with them on the battlefield were it not for my infirmity' he pointed out indicating his leg which had been damaged in an earlier battle requiring him now to use a stick to support him when he walked. The injury meant he could not stay in the saddle safely enough to ride into battle. 'I am deeply sorry that it is such sad circumstances that bring you here and yet I am glad to see you.' He took them inside and called for refreshments to be brought. 'It will be good for Thomas to spend some time here. He can become familiar with his lands,' said Edmund.

CHAPTER 11

1348

King Edward's beloved daughter, Joan prepared for the journey to France. Her servants moved silently about packing clothing and jewels which she would take with her. No expense was spared and when Joan left Portsmouth a fleet of four ships set out for Bordeaux to meet her betrothed.

People talked of a terrible illness which was raging in Europe but everybody was too busy to listen to gossip. There was always illness and disease, especially in the summer months.

It was soon after their arrival in Bordeaux that members of her entourage began to fall ill. This was like no illness they had seen before. The victims suffered firstly from cold like symptoms but the large black swellings which appeared in their neck and armpits set it apart from anything which had been known before.

Joan was rushed out of town to a small village where it was hoped she would be safe, only for her to be the first in the village to die. Her death was swift and painful and left her entourage shocked and stunned.

It was not long before the dreadful sickness reached the shores of England. It soon took hold and people were dying in their hundreds every day.

The people of Durham, afflicted by the plague and in fear of a further attack from the Scots began to riot. Their fears were well founded. 'By the foul death of England!' declared Robert Stewart, 'I will use this chance which God has given us to take vengeance on the English. They hold our king and God is punishing them!' He called upon other Scottish nobles to meet with him in the forest of Selkirk. There they plotted their attack. 'God has seen fit to inflict this pestilence on Edward's kingdom. The English are so busy burying their dead that they cannot give fight. Now is our hour come!'

The crowd cheered and set out to gather men and supplies to invade England.

Within a very short time, the attack had begun. The length and breadth of the border Scots poured into England but it was not long before they themselves were struck down by the dreaded illness.

Douglas' men came in panic to him. 'Laird, the foul death of England is upon us! Two men lie sick with the black swellings we have heard tell of.' Within hours the men developed a fever and within a couple of days, they were dead. This set panic amongst the men.

Word spread as rapidly as did the disease and, before long, dozens of men were dying each day. Dead and dying lay all around them and it was becoming impossible to bury the dead fast enough. Within a few days, five thousand Scottish men were dead. Douglas asked Robert Stewart for an audience and a number of other nobles gathered with them. Terror was in their hearts and Robert could see that it was pointless to pursue his attack. 'Men are deserting and others are afraid and like to leave before long. No army can succeed with fearful men,' Douglas said, expressing the thoughts of them all.

It was agreed that they would discontinue the invasion and they would return to their homes in Scotland. They packed up their camps and baggage and each returned to their estates relieved to be leaving the threat of disease behind but it soon became clear that the pestilence had travelled with them and it was not long before death claimed many thousands of lives in Scotland.

⁓

Believing it would be safer further from England, Thomas and his mother were escorted back to Slains Castle. The gates were barred and nobody gained admittance without waiting outside for three days to ensure that they were not carrying the plague. Boats from Whinnyfold and Collieston were not permitted to moor near the castle and men from within the castle precincts went out fishing and putting down creels to supply the inhabitants with fresh food. It was as if the castle were under siege. They were well supplied with water from the spring and they were hopeful that their precautions would protect them.

Winter came and reports of new cases were very few. It seemed that the Scottish winter had stopped the plague in its tracks.

The respite was short lived and as spring arrived so did a fresh outbreak. It was not long before it was clear that it was back with a vengeance. Huts were built outside the castle walls and any person showing the least sign of a chill or cold was compelled to live there until they recovered or died. Word came that somebody at Clochtow, a farm within the barony and frighteningly close to Slains Castle had succumbed to illness and fear gripped the hearts of the inhabitants.

The next week saw the worst storm they had seen for many years and as Barbra sat in her chamber working on a tapestry with her sister the waves crashed on the rocks below and the wind howled around the castle. The ladies sat either side of their work passing the needle through to each other. 'I fear that this storm will do much damage tonight,' Barbara said. Margaret agreed that the signs were that it was strong enough to bring even further misery to the people in the area.

Suddenly, a disturbance outside made her go to the window and look out. People were running about and a billow of smoke was rising from the bake-house. As she opened the window a cry of, 'fire!' was heard. Panic gripped them. Fire was one of the greatest threats to the castle and Barbara's first though was to get Thomas to safety. Rushing up the winding steps to the nursery she met the nurse-maid coming down with the child in her arms. She reached out and took him, turning and lifting her skirts to ease her descent. The door was open and castle servants were rushing out to form a chain with buckets of water to put out the fire. The smoke caught in their throats and Barbara pulled Thomas's blanket over his face to protect him.

'Get men down on the beach!' the steward ordered. 'Pass sea water up, the well is too slow!'

Barbara and Margaret were huddled together watching the progress and trying to stay on their feet against the wind.

'Gang intae the mews,' shouted the falconer, his voice being snatched away by the wind. 'It's far enough away to be safe and is built entirely of stone. It'll nae burn even if this wind blows sparks tae it.' Burning debris was being tossed about by the storm and to find shelter and safety was paramount so Barbara allowed the man to lead her through the smoke to the mews. His wife brought wooden cups of water to ease their throats from the smoke and stools for them to sit on whilst the falconer returned to help to carry water.

It was an hour before the fire was under control and folks could begin to go back to their homes. One or two cottars had damage to their roofs from stray sparks but as the bake-house had a slate roof there was no burning thatch to spread to other buildings. Given the strength of the wind, it could have been much worse. The baker was fretting about how he could bake bread for the next day but Barbara was resource-ful and suggested they use the facilities in the tower as had been done in the past before the bakehouse was built.

When this was settled she turned to Thomas, who was awake now and fascinated by the activity, and told him that he must go back to bed now before handing him back to his nurse-maid and retiring to her chamber with Margaret. 'Well! Just when we thought things were bad enough...'

'Everybody is safe and that's what matters,' Margaret reminded her. 'We can see what needs to be done tomorrow when, hopefully, the storm will have died down.'

At first light, Barbara rose and having dressed with the help of her maid, she went immediately to assess the damage. Many of the menfolk were already investigating and clearing out the burnt materials. It was mostly benches and flour which had suffered and they had plenty of flour stored in the barns. She gave directions to the men and set off to find the baker. The smell of freshly baked bread told her that he had coped with his new environment and they would not go hungry. For now, all was well.

It seemed that their precautions in locking themselves into the castle had been successful in keeping the inhabitants safe from the plague and they were now hearing less and less of new outbreaks.

Barbara had been strict in enforcing the rule about people entering the castle precincts and the inhabitants were more than ready to do her bidding but when Robert Stewart, regent of Scotland, desired entry it was difficult to refuse. The Lady of Slains went to the gates herself and spoke to him. 'Sir, you will no doubt have heard that I do all that I can to preserve the life and well-being of the Constable of Scotland.'

'Aye, Lady, and rightly so.'

'Then you will, I pray, forgive me if I delay your entry briefly.'

'How so?'

'I fear I must ask you if you and your party feel quite well. You have no aches or pains?'

'We are quite well.'

'No chills or fever?'

'No.'

'Have you been near any person who has been ill of this pestilence which strikes our kingdom?'

'We have not,' he replied.

'Then I am pleased to bid you enter.'

'You do well, Lady to protect young Thomas so fiercely.'

'It is my duty, Sir.'

'Would that all the king's subjects were so dutiful.'

Barbara took him inside but did not send for Thomas until she had had the opportunity to see for herself that Robert suffered no signs of the illness.

On his arrival, Thomas greeted Sir Robert formally. 'Sir, it is good to see you. We have had few visitors during the last year and more. I trust you are well.'

'Aye, Thomas,' Sir Robert replied, impressed by the child's courtly manners and maturity. 'This pestilence is a grave sorrow to our country. Many souls have perished. The fields lay un-harvested for lack of men and people fear to travel abroad. Your mother has done well to protect you.'

'How fares your new wife?' enquired Thomas.

'Well indeed!' laughed Sir Robert, amused at the lad's forthrightness. 'My wife is recently brought to bed of a fine daughter. You will no doubt have heard that Pope Clement VI gave us a dispensation that our older children are legitimised.'

'That is indeed good news,' acknowledged Thomas.

'Young Thomas does you credit, madam,' said Robert addressing Barbara.

'Thank you, Sir; I am anxious that he becomes his role.'

'I might yet find a bride for him in the future from amongst my daughters. Would you care for that, young man?'

'You honour me, Sir,' replied Thomas with a bow of his head.

Sir Robert Stewart spent some days with Barbra, discussing the situation that Scotland was in. The king was still being held hostage by King Edward of England and the English were inflicting punishing raids on Scotland all too frequently. Sir Robert hoped to unite the nobles of Scotland, to somehow secure King David's release and to protect their borders.

⚜

1351

King David, finding it difficult to enforce his rule from London, campaigned to secure his release. He reached an agreement with the English that, in exchange for a monetary settlement, the return of Scottish estates to English barons and an agreement that one of Edward's sons would be recognised as the next heir to the Scottish throne, he would be freed.

On hearing this Robert Stewart was furious at this undermining of his expectation, as a grandson of King Robert Bruce, to become the next King of Scotland. When the proposal was put before the Scottish Parliament, Robert rallied his family and supporters to use their influence to have it rejected.

King Edward was disappointed that his plan to bring Scotland under English rule and permitted King David to travel to Scotland in order that he might support a revised treaty. He presented it to the nobles, clergy and town delegates but again it was declined. King David was furious and began to believe that Robert Stewart was manipulating the nobles in order to keep him in England so that he could continue to rule as Guardian of Scotland.

❦

1353

Sir Robert Stewart returned to Slains Castle with a following which included a number of noblemen in addition to the knights and retainers who normally travelled with him.

Thomas Hay welcomed them and bade them follow him into his hall. Wine was brought and food for the travellers and while they ate Sir Robert explained the purpose of their visit.

'We can suffer our king's captivity no longer. The English weaken our country by holding him and if we do not secure his release soon and ensure that all know and acknowledge that King David rules Scotland, the power struggles which plague us and the attacks of the English will reduce our proud nation to subjects of the English throne.

My plan is to send a party of the highest in our land to treat with the English for his release. Thomas, as Constable of Scotland, I wish you to be a member of this Regency Council.' Thomas was taken aback. It was the first significant role which he had been asked to carry out.

'Of course I will be happy to go,' he said, 'I am the king's man.'

Arrangements were made and the knights who were to accompany him chosen.

The party which left Slains was a spectacular sight. Despite his lack of years, Thomas was every bit the noble and carried himself proudly, demanding the respect of all who saw him. His men wore his badge of three red shields and carried his standard with pride. They travelled to Edinburgh where they joined forces with the other commissioners who had been appointed to treat with the English.

Their journey was long and arduous. Although they slept in comfort most nights in the castles and homes of English nobles and were treated with the honour and respect due to them, they needs must spend some nights at inns where they were forced to endure flea ridden beds and inferior food. A squire was sent ahead each day to secure lodgings for the night and find the best possible rooms for them but all too frequently there was little choice.

Where ever they stopped each noble's squire would sleep across the doorway to prevent assassins gaining entry whilst they slept and conversations needs must be guarded but whilst they rode they felt safe to discuss their options.

Opinions varied on the course that discussions should follow and how much they should be prepared to offer in exchange for their king's release. The struggle for independence had already cost Scotland dearly and the shortage of workers, resulting from the thousands who succumbed to the pestilence, meant that they had little to trade with.

Their arrival at King Edward's court was well received. Edward's country had suffered the same ravages as Scotland and the Scottish king was a valuable bargaining tool. Most important to Edward was the Scottish crown. England had failed to take it by force but perhaps the Scots could be subjugated by negotiation.

The last thing on the minds of the Regency Council was to give away their country's crown to the English but they were prepared to offer hostages for the king's release and Thomas along with twenty others were accepted in this role.

He found himself in a sumptuous English court where life was very acceptable. The hostages were treated with respect and had a degree of freedom reflecting the trust which was expected of men of their standing.

It was to take until 1357 before King David would return to Scotland.

CHAPTER 12

═══ «◆» ═══

1355

Thomas had been back at Slains Castle only a few months when a liveried messenger arrived at the castle. He bore a letter from Robert Stewart inviting Thomas to attend his wedding to Euphemia of Moray. Robert's first wife had died some little time ago in childbirth and Euphemia, a beautiful and charming young lady had been a widow for nine years since her first husband, John Randolph, had died at the Battle of Neville's Cross when she was yet a teenager. She had born no children during her first marriage but this was not of concern to Robert who had ten children already.

As Thomas read the letter he knew that he would have to make many preparations before he departed for the wedding. As Constable, he was expected to attend but he was happy to do so and considered Robert Stewart to be a good friend. A gift must be found to give to the couple and new clothes prepared for Thomas and his mother who was to accompany him.

'A pair of silver goblets would be a fine gift,' suggested Barbara, 'they would adorn Robert's table well.'

'A perfect suggestion,' Thomas acknowledged, 'Robert is fond of his wine and will have good use from them,' he laughed.

Thomas' robes were of finest bright blue brocade stitched with silver thread. He made a handsome figure and would catch many a maid's eye.

The wedding was to be in May so heavy cloaks were not required but Thomas had a short cloak of a contrasting darker blue.

Thomas mounted his horse to depart. His mother rode a small grey palfrey and a cart carrying their fine clothes was pulled by two horses that were restless and eager to be on their way.

The wedding day was fine and Robert greeted each of his guests as they arrived. Thomas was pleased to see him and wished him well of his marriage. He gave Robert the goblets which he had had inscribed with Robert's arms, the couple's names and the date of their wedding.

Much merriment followed the ceremony and Thomas enjoyed the music and storytelling of the musicians. As the evening went on people began to dance to the traditional tunes and Thomas found himself dancing with a beautiful young lady who told him her name was Elizabeth.

'Ah! I see you have found my daughter,' said Robert as he passed. 'Take care, she will lead you a merry dance!' he quipped laughing.

'You are little Elizabeth Stewart? I did not recognise you!' exclaimed Thomas. 'The last time I saw you....' he indicated with his hand how small she had been. Her merry laughter tinkled as she smiled at him. 'Little no more, Sir,' she said, 'I am quite grown up now,' she continued looking at him from under her demurely lowered brow and dipping a fine curtsey. Thomas was quite taken with her beauty and her gentle manner and made sure he danced with her many more times that evening.

'You seem to enjoy my daughter's company,' observed Sir Robert.

'She is a beauty indeed,' agreed Thomas. 'Does she have any suitors?'

'Aye, many, but none I would entertain. Would you be one of their number?'

'I would be honoured,' he replied.

Their conversation was interrupted by horseplay amongst some of the young people and Sir Robert and David left off to discover what was happening and joined in the laughter at a squire's antics.

The next day Thomas took his leave but on his return journey, Elizabeth was much on his mind. His intentions to court her were interrupted when he was recalled to the negotiations in England. This time was to be more successful than previous attempts and on 3rd October 1357, a treaty was signed at Berwick on Tweed, under which Scotland's nobility agreed to pay 100,000 marks, to be paid at the rate of 10,000 marks per year, as a ransom for their king. In November the Scottish Parliament met and ratified the agreement and King David was finally free to return to Scotland.

Thomas and many others of the nobles were concerned at the burden which had been laid upon Scotland but knew that the strength and confidence of the kingdom depended upon King David being free.

On his return, King David summoned those who had been involved in the negotiations over the years to offer his thanks. Thomas was glad to see his king home and willingly answered the call but was concerned to hear the king say that Scotland could not afford the instalments of his ransom and that he fully intended to discuss with King Edward the possibility of bequeathing Scotland to one of Edward's sons as an alternative to payment. 'I know that our parliament will never agree,' he told them, 'but it will buy us some time whilst our forces recover enough to face the English army.'

After all that had gone before and all the efforts they had made, being absent from their families and lands for so long whilst negotiating for his freedom, they were disappointed to hear such talk.

The nobles returned to their lands with grave concerns. They knew that the population would be heavily taxed in order to raise the ransom money but the thought of their country being given to the English after all their hardships and loss of life created unrest and bitterness amongst them. Thomas was and always would be the king's man but he hoped that fighting between Scotland and England would not be renewed. Enough Scottish blood had been shed defending their kingdom.

⚜

1364

A royal wedding was usually justification for celebrations throughout the land but when it became known that King David was to re-marry in February, there were grumblings to be heard in every household. Thomas received visits from Archibald Douglas and William Fenton of Fenton, both of whom expressed concerns about the cost of a royal wedding when Scotland was struggling to pay the ransom and taxes were crippling. Their concerns were echoed throughout the land but there was nothing to be done to prevent it and the king would not be convinced to limit the expenditure.

On 20th February, his marriage to the widowed Margaret Drummond took place in Inchmurdach Manor in Fife and on the eve of the wedding, it being the custom for the king to endow knighthoods on the eve of his wedding, Thomas was one of those chosen for this honour for having served with distinction in battle and in the negotiations for his release. There were revels in celebration of the marriage throughout the land but when the festivities died down and Scotland was left to count the cost, there were grave concerns about the wisdom of such expense.

King David was angered by the response of his subjects to his marriage. He had heard talk of revolt. He knew that many of his nobles were becoming unruly and he feared for his crown if this continued. Ruling a country so diverse and far flung with many nobles residing in remote areas made control difficult but he was determined to hold on to his crown by using those barons who were loyal to him to wield his power in their localities.

Margaret was behind him in this. 'Have I married a king, only to find that he is subservient to his barons?' she would jibe. Small of stature she possessed a fiery personality and would constantly mock him about calling the barons to task. Having found little resistance to this she went on to goad him personally about having been a prisoner of the English for eleven years. Although this prompted him to take a strong stance with the nobles it wore his patience thin and it was not long before he began to bite back.

'We must talk about the northern barons,' she demanded.

'Not before I speak my piece,' David responded angrily, 'I will take no more of your constant rebukes and censures. I am king and you will remember it!'

'Then act like a king. You....'

'Quiet you old scold!' he ordered, 'Enough I say! You give me no children yet think you can rule the roost!'

'Well if I've not produced children, the fault is not mine! It took your father twenty-two years to sire you and **you** might never manage it. If you spent more time in my bed and less in that of your whore,'

'You were my whore until I married you and what a mistake that was! How would a man get sons with a woman

1 1 0

so meddlesome and officious? There's no warmth in my bed with you.' He turned on his heel and strode away. King David ordered his horse to be made ready and he, with his guards, left the castle. He immediately sent for his writer to set about getting a divorce. Their marriage had lasted just six years.

Although Margaret had gone, the effects of her provoking continued and David worked to bring the barons under his control. Thomas Hay and other like him were ordered to seek out dissidents who were ignoring the king's rule or provoking anarchy and report them to the king's forces. Continued negotiations with England kept border attacks at bay and gave the king an opportunity to focus on his problems at home.

CHAPTER 13

1371

News of the king's death reached Slains Castle on a stormy February night. The wind howled like a woman sobbing her sorrows into the darkness. His death had been sudden and unexpected while he was visiting Edinburgh Castle and some whispered that it was not a natural death. Thomas was sorry to hear the news as he was fond of the king but he was glad that it would be Robert Stewart would follow him and not an English man.

Thomas put Slains Castle into mourning for the dead king until Robert was crowned. All within the castle fasted as Thomas made ready to attend the king's funeral. His choices were to travel by sea sailing into the teeth of the biting wind and facing the risk of being shipwrecked before reaching Edinburgh or travel by road facing snow drifts and the possibility of losing the road altogether. It would take much longer by road and the risk of freezing to death, even wearing his cloak which was lined with fur, was a risk too far. Sea travel was the safer and faster option.

The funeral service took place at Holyrood Abbey and the great and the good from many parts of Scotland were in attendance but many had failed to arrive either through delays en-route or not even attempting to travel in such conditions.

Thomas Hay arrived safely if rather nauseated by the journey. What should have been a straightforward voyage in better conditions became a battle for survival against the turbulent sea and wind. The ship was tossed about and it was impossible to keep your feet. Water swept across the deck, pouring off the side as the ship rolled.

By the time they docked everybody was covered with a rime of salt from the spray and struggled to regain their legs.

Thomas' men removed his kists from the hold and found a carter to take them onwards. He was received at Holyrood Abbey and shown to the abbot's house where he changed into his fine robes before taking refreshment. He was surprised to find Sir William Hay of Locherworth, Sheriff of Peebles, at the abbey but was told that roads from the south were much clearer than those in the north and he and his retinue had been able to travel by road.

King David's body was still lying in state at the castle but would be brought in procession to the abbey for burial the next day. Thomas asked for a horse to be made ready for him and made his way through the foul streets towards the castle to pay his respects. The abbot had insisted on providing armed guards to accompany him protesting that it was not safe to travel alone even for the single mile. The streets of Edinburgh were home to many thieves and vagabonds who could steal and disappear down a passageway before their victim even knew they had been robbed. The streets were steep with many steps and infested with rats and stray dogs. Filth was thrown into the streets every day and rotting rubbish filled the gullies. The traveller who was lucky enough to avoid these ran the risk of disease; an ever-present threat.

Arriving at the Castle, Thomas decided it would be safer to remain in Edinburgh until the weather improved and the snow had cleared and spend some time with a number of like-minded guests at the castle. He came across Sir Robert Stewart on the rampart and strolled over to him. Thomas bowed his head to the man who was destined to be crowned king now that David was dead but Robert grabbed his hand and pulled him into an embrace slapping him on the back.

'Well met, Thomas. I'm glad to see you safely here.'

'It was a journey I would not care to repeat,' grimaced Thomas rubbing his middle.

'I was fortunate enough to be in Edinburgh when I received the news of David's death. I know he did not like me and would rather even an English man took the Scottish throne than I, but…well, here we are!' Robert threw his arm around Thomas' shoulder and guided him indoors to see where the king's body lay. A black candle stood at each corner of the open coffin and monks prayed before it. Armed guards stood as still as statues and could have been mistaken for such in the low light.

Sir Thomas, with Robert beside him, knelt by the coffin and prayed for the soul of their departed king.

The next day the sun shone on the lying snow as the nobility of Scotland formed a guard of honour, led by Robert Stewart, along the road between Edinburgh Castle and Holyrood Abbey. Standards were lowered and King David's standard was draped over his coffin. The sound of the abbey bell tolling grew louder as they approached, bringing a heavy feeling of solemnity to the procession.

When they reached the abbey they filed into the nave to the sound of the monks chanting.

The service culminated in King David's coffin being placed in a specially prepared tomb and a plaque being placed over it. A figure of the deceased king would be added later. The congregation drifted out into the icy air and many of the noblemen were invited to join the Abbot in his house.

Congratulations were offered to Robert on his rise to kingship and he took the opportunity to speak to Thomas about his role as Constable in his coronation the following month at Scone. Thomas was glad of the opportunity to discuss what he must do and, having his robes with him, decided not to return to Slains but to go to Erroll for the intervening weeks. He took his leave of Sir William Hay, sending his regards to William's wife and wishing him a safe journey. There were many desperate people on the roads south where crops had been repeatedly destroyed and livestock stolen in raids by the English. Anybody travelling was at risk; much more so a person of substance.

By the end of the week the snow had cleared and travel, although uncomfortable, was possible. Robert bade Thomas farewell and asked him to be at Scone a few days prior to the coronation for rehearsals and a chance to catch up with their news. Thomas shook him warmly by the hand and promised to arrive in good time. He set off for Erroll with a lighter heart, looking forward to spending some time with Robert and sharing their memories and family news.

He was met at Erroll with news of damage to barns caused by the weight of snow causing the roof to collapse. There had also been some trouble between a number of estate tenants and those of Sir John Drummond who held adjoining land at Strobhall. The disputes had been dealt with but the barn damage had resulted in the deaths of three men who had been working there at the time of the collapse. Their families needed support and this was being arranged. Thomas approved this and ordered that a close eye be kept on the boundaries to ascertain what was transpiring between the tenants. He was pleased with the work of his stewards and took trouble to praise them and reward their diligent work.

Thomas was keen to get to Scone, not only to spend some time with Robert again, but also to become re-acquainted with his daughter, Elizabeth whom he had been very attracted to on their last meeting. Robert had hinted that he would look kindly on Thomas as a suitor for her and he was anxious to court her.

With this in mind, he kept his stay at Erroll short and set out as soon as possible for Scone. Twenty men at arms accompanied him and his robes were carefully cleaned and packed for the journey. He travelled in his mail as full armour was too uncomfortable for a long journey but mail provided some protection in case of attack. His standard was held high to announce the approach of an important figure. He wanted to make an impression on his arrival as it would, no doubt, be witnessed by Elizabeth. The party made sure to keep to the centre of the road when passing through woods as it was a common place for outlaws to carry out an attack and Thomas' retinue would be a prime target as he was clearly a wealthy man.

Their fears were to prove justified as a whoosh was heard as an arrow flew between the branches of the trees and forced its way between the rings of Thomas' mail. He felt only a thud of impact at first and it was some moments before the searing pain followed. The mail had slowed the progress of the arrow reducing its penetration but it had still entered his leg about three inches. Experience on the battlefield had taught him not to pull the arrow out until he had something to stem the bleeding so, gritting his teeth, he snapped the shaft groaning with pain as he did so. His men had formed a circle around him and some had set off in pursuit of the attacker. A howl of pain told that they had discovered the culprit and were handling him none too gently. A struggling and bloodied figure was dragged from the forest and thrown to his knees before Thomas.

'You tried to kill me,' he accused the rogue.

'Bastard!' spat the figure.

'String him up,' ordered Thomas. As Constable, he had the right to judge all cases of rioting, disorder, bloodshed and murder if such crimes occurred within four miles of the King, the King's Council, or the Parliament of Scotland and clearly, this was one such occasion, he himself being the victim. The men took a rope from a saddlebag and carried out Thomas' orders leaving the body swinging from the rope as a warning to others.

Progress thereafter was slowed by Thomas' injury as every step his horse took was agony for him and using his injured leg was impossible. His horse obediently followed the leading mounts and eventually they arrived at the Abbot's Palace at Scone and were greeted by Robert Stewart and an anxious Elizabeth. Their approach had been seen from some distance and the alarm was raised that the party was travelling very slowly. It was clear that something was amiss.

Elizabeth covered her face with her hands when she saw Thomas' injury then, brought to her senses by her father's instruction to prepare what was necessary to treat the wound, she rushed to find Brother James, the infirmarian, and request cleansing materials and herbs to sooth and heal the wound.

Brother James gathered his equipment and waddled after her to the abbot's chambers. Thomas had been seated on an armed chair and was breathing raggedly with the pain. Although skilled in healing, Brother James, an ageing member of the community, was shaken at being asked to treat a man of such importance and fumbled with the arrow extractor that he proposed to use to remove the remaining portion of the arrow. Elizabeth had now regained her composure and, resisting the attempts of her father to remove her from the room, took the tool herself and took charge of the situation.

'Sir, I will help you first to remove your chausses so that I can more easily remove the arrow head.' Brother James drew in a sharp breath, 'Madam you cannot stay....,'

'He will need help not to pull on the shaft of the arrow as he removes them. I will see him without them when I treat the wound.' she began.

'I must insist, madam. It is not proper.'

'Oh, really!' she protested, 'well hold the mail up from his leg as you remove them and be sure not to drag on the arrow shaft.'

Brother James held the door and indicated that she should leave whilst the disrobing took place. As soon as it was done and a blanket draped across Thomas' lap she was permitted to return. Taking a block of wood which Brother James had provided she offered it to Thomas to put between his teeth and bite on whilst the task was done.

Shaking his head, Thomas declined the offer. Elizabeth sighed at the vanity of men and proceeded to open the area around where the arrow had entered in order to remove it without ripping the flesh.

Thomas regretted his pride and struggled not to cry out as the knife cut into his leg. Fresh blood flowed and the pain seemed to last for hours but in fact, Elizabeth moved swiftly and confidently pushing the extractor into the wound to surround the head of the arrow and prevent it tearing the flesh as it was withdrawn. She removed the arrow cleanly and pressed a cloth onto the open wound to stem the bleeding. Brother James passed her a goblet of wine and indicated that she should pour some over the wound. 'It washes away the excess blood which can rot and stop the wound from healing,' he explained.

Elizabeth did as he suggested before taking a needle and thread and stitching the flesh. In comparison to removing the arrow, the pain was insignificant but unpleasant none the less.

When she had finished, Thomas realised he had been holding his breath and exhaled a long breath. 'Thank you,' he said.

'You did well, Thomas,' she said, 'It must have hurt badly.'

He grimaced and she laughed. 'Well now I suppose I shall have to care for my patient whilst he is here. We must have you on your feet for the coronation.'

Thomas made to stand up protesting that he was fine but finding that this was not the case he slumped back into the chair.

'Rest,' advised Brother James, 'it will heal faster if you do not walk about for a few days.'

'I'll see that he rests,' Elizabeth assured him, smiling at Thomas. She was determined to do so as it would mean spending more time with this handsome young man whom she found most amusing and, according to her father, was a potential husband for her. Being a strong willed woman she was determined to have a say in her father's choice for her and having seven sisters she knew he would be delighted if she were to agree to a suitable match quickly.

For the couple of weeks leading up to her father's coronation, Elizabeth took great care of Thomas, bathing his wound and bringing him delicacies to eat. They spent a great deal of time together and she found herself enjoying his company more and more. As for Thomas, he found her company most agreeable. She was proving to be bright as well as beautiful and he was confident that she was more than capable of running a castle.

The day of the coronation arrived and Thomas had made a good recovery. There was no sign of Elizabeth today as she was being dressed and groomed for the day's proceedings. A squire was sent to assist Thomas into his robes and to show him down to breakfast. Finally, he buckled on his sword and carrying his robe he made his way downstairs. He sat on Robert's right side and they chatted together over a light breakfast of cold meat and cheese.

Robert offered Thomas a nip of whisky before they made their way to join the procession out to the Moot Hill, which he accepted gladly. Their path was flanked by monks and lay brothers who mingled with the minor barons. As Constable, Thomas walked immediately behind the king in the procession, standing aside only for the coronation.

The ceremony was greeted by cheers, some genuine but others merely polite. There were those who, like the old king, felt that Robert Stewart was not the best person to wear the crown and yet, along with Thomas Hay, many nobles took the oath of homage to the new king the day after his coronation.

The banquet after the ceremony was lavish in spite of Scotland's continuing poverty and wine was consumed in vast quantities as the celebrations continued. Thomas was seated beside the king with Elizabeth next to him, which gave him the perfect opportunity to speak to Robert about his wish to marry her. The wine gave him courage and he waited until the musicians were playing a quiet song to ask Robert for permission to wed his daughter.

'If she'll have you, Thomas, I would be delighted,' he laughed.

At that moment the musicians struck up a dance tune. Thomas stood and bowed to Elizabeth offering an arm to lead her out to dance. She gracefully placed her hand on his and the couple took to the floor. The following dance was a lively jig and they finished breathless and laughing. Thomas took her into his arms and whispered his proposal to her. Throwing back her head and laughing she replied, 'Why, Thomas, I would be thrilled to be your wife but do we have to live in that castle of yours on the edge of a cliff where the wind blows like the devil himself is howling?'

'I'm afraid so my dear. But I'll make it worthwhile,' he promised with a wink. 'Besides, I needs must spend a great deal of time in Edinburgh as I hold the keys to the Parliament House and must accompany the king when he attends parliament.'

As they returned to the table, Robert Stewart smiled and asked, 'you have accepted Thomas then?'

'Aye Sire, I think I can make a good husband of him.'

Gasps of astonishment greeted her audacity followed by lively chatter as people placed wagers on Thomas' chances of bringing his wife to heel.

'I'm afraid I cannot allow this,' the king told her.

'I don't understand father, surely Thomas asked your permission and..'

'I cannot permit you to marry a man who is not knighted,' he replied firmly, 'So that is final.'

'But father!'

'Enough! Bring me my sword.'

A squire appeared as if on a pre-determined signal and handed the king his sword.

'Kneel, Thomas Hay, Constable of Scotland.'

Somewhat taken aback, Thomas knelt on one knee before King Robert who promptly dubbed him a knight. 'Now, brave knight, you may tame the dragon!' This was greeted by cheers and raised goblets. The partying went on until well into the following morning and there was many a sore head the next day.

Before he left, Thomas was taken aside by the king. 'I shall require you to swear to the Act of Settlement of the Crown in April. You need to be in Edinburgh Castle for the beginning of the month.'

'I shall be there,' Thomas said simply.

CHAPTER 14

1372

In spite of numerous calls upon his time to repel attacks from the English, and his trip to Edinburgh for the king, Sir Thomas found time to make preparations for his wedding. The king gave him a charter of an annual rent of eighteen marks sterling out of the lands of Inchtultryll as a wedding gift.

He was to be married at the newly completed Dundonald Castle, which the king had had built on his accession to the throne. Although Sir Thomas was a man of substance and of high status, to marry a daughter of the king was to be a daunting experience as there would be great ceremony and the highest in the land would be invited. Of course, the king himself would be there but Thomas was not concerned about that as they had been close friends since he was a child but the ceremony and proceedings would be very formal and he must be sure to get things right.

As the time grew near he made his final preparations and set off. His stewards, retainers, knights and men at arms formed a magnificent procession as they left Slains Castle. They made good progress and at every town and village they passed through, people came out of their houses to cheer.

Dundonald Castle was dark and foreboding, clearly built for defence in these uncertain times when, not only the

English, but potentially the barons, might pose a threat to the king's life. It stood three stories high; the ground floor was used for storage of provisions, wine and fuel, the first floor housed the Laigh Hall where the Baron Court was held and feasting took place but the top floor, the upper hall, was reserved for the king and his family. Sir Thomas' arrival was celebrated with fanfares and cheers of delight. Thomas' bride to be stood beside her father and his wife, blushing in spite of her usual precociousness. She was about to marry one of the most powerful men in Scotland and one of the most handsome and considered herself fortunate indeed to have been able to choose her husband rather than having to submit to her father's choice.

Sir Thomas was shown to a guest chamber and provided with a bath of hot water to refresh himself and a man servant to assist him. His own steward remained with him and prepared his fine clothes for the evening and for his marriage the following day.

The meal that evening was sumptuous with courses of fish, dove, pheasant and game with spices used to enhance the flavour. This was followed by perys en composte, pears in wine and spices and sambocade, elderflower cheesecake. The wine was mulled with honey and spices which was Thomas' particular favourite.

Although there were musicians who had arrived in good time for the ceremony the entertainment was of storytelling and quiet songs punctuated by formal dances in order not to over excite the bride.

Thomas slept little that night but fell into a deep sleep just before dawn. He was awakened by his steward who had his robes ready and hot water waiting.

After washing and dressing Thomas made his way down to St Inan's chapel within the castle, where the wedding ceremony was to take place. Guests had already begun to arrive and were seated on benches whilst waiting. Thomas took his place, nodding to familiar faces and passing a word or two with close friends. There was a shuffling as the king arrived and the guests rose to their feet. Beside King Robert, stood the abbot of Kilwinning Abbey who was to preside over the ceremony.

A hush fell as Elizabeth entered the chapel. She was quite striking in a gown of gold, her raven hair styled in rings of plaits and a headdress of lace held in place by a ring of yellow roses. Sir Thomas turned as she approached and she smiled boldly at him. 'You are beautiful,' he said simply but his eyes said much more.

The wedding breakfast surpassed anything which even Thomas had seen before. A cock-o-trice formed the centrepiece and ducks, capons and chickens were served first. This was followed by fresh salmon poached in beer, vinegar and herbs, and pike in wine sauce. The main remove was roasted suckling pigs, venison and beef stew. Pies and delicacies abounded as did cheeses and eggs.

The meal lasted for hours and was followed by dancing and entertainment before, finally, Sir Thomas and his bride were escorted with much merriment and ribald comments to their chamber. Many of the guests would have stayed to witness the bedding but the king ordered them to leave the couple in peace and none dare disobey him.

They stayed at Dundonald Castle barely a week as Thomas found it a sombre building and wished to return to his Castle at Slains to introduce his new wife to his people.

The people of Buchan, eager to see the beautiful princess that their laird had married, lined the road to Slains. They cheered as the couple rode past at the head of a procession of knights, squires and men-at-arms, all of whom wore

Sir Thomas' arms and looked splendid as they approached. Thomas helped his new wife to dismount and led her into the castle, acknowledging with a gesture of his head the greetings and congratulations of his people. He showed Elizabeth around the castle and left her with her maid to unpack and refresh after the journey and to take a nap before supper.

Gradually Elizabeth began to learn the names of the staff and took over the running of the castle. She learnt new skills from some of the older servants and was happy to share her own knowledge with them. The environment was new to her as she had never lived on the coast before and was fascinated to see the boats arriving with the day's catch and seeing how the local people dealt with the ferocious winds which scoured the cliffs from time to time. Most of all she was stunned by the views out to sea and along the cliffs. She longed to visit the local villages of Collieston and Whinnyfold and Thomas promised to take her to see them soon.

Elizabeth insisted on meeting the people in even the furthest most parts of Thomas' lands and often rode out with an escort to visit and take food to people in need. She was much loved by people of all ranks, especially those within the castle precincts where she was to be seen each day checking on supplies and people's needs.

Her lady's maid, Shona, was also her confidante and they often shared secrets and scandals as they sat stitching. Elizabeth had decided to make a new shirt for Thomas for Christmas and was carefully working on the fine details when Shona asked, 'When do you plan to tell Thomas the news?'

'What news would that be?'

'Of the child you carry.'

'You know!'

'Of course I do.'

'Well, I want to be sure. I don't want him to be let down.'

'Well, I think it's safe to tell him now. It will be showing soon then you won't be able to hide it from him. And you wouldn't want somebody else to notice it before you have told him.'

'No, but he'll stop me riding out if he knows.'

'And quite right too. You don't want to risk his child do you?'

'Of course not. I'll tell him tonight.'

That evening after supper she could not wait to tell Thomas the news and suggested they retire early. With a twinkle in his eye, he readily agreed.

When they were alone he took her into his arms and kissed her, gently at first then deepening. She drew her head away and leaning back in his arms she told him of the child.

'You're sure?' he asked.

'Your son will be born in July,' she said confidently.

'It's a boy?'

'Of course it will be.'

Thomas guided her to the bed. 'You must be careful. No more riding and you must take it easy.'

'I'm not ill! I knew you would be like this.'

'No, of course you are not, but bearing children is dangerous. You must take care of yourself and the child.'

July arrived and with it the longed for child. Elizabeth lay sobbing as Thomas entered the room. Shona tried to console her with little success.

'What troubles you?' he asked. 'The child is well, is it not?'

Through her sobs, she whispered, 'I promised you a son but it's a girl.'

'Oh, my darling, don't fret. She's beautiful just like her mother. We will have sons in the future but now we have a daughter and I love her as I love you.'

Shona handed him the bundle which contained his daughter and he sat on the edge of the bed sharing her with Elizabeth. He kissed his wife's forehead and lay beside her with the child between them.

The first visitor to Slains Castle to see the new arrival was the king. Robert strode in proudly. He loved children having at least twenty-two of his own that he knew of. To be a father was wonderful but to be a grandfather was something special. Elizabeth was still in her chamber when her father arrived and he knocked gently before entering.

Hugging his daughter has asked firstly of her health and finding her well and recovering from the birth he looked around for the child. The crib lay beside the bed and he scooped the sleeping child into his arms.

'What have you named her?' he asked.

'Elizabeth, Thomas wanted her to have my name,' she told him.

'Well said,' he declared. 'You have a fine husband.'

'Will you stand as witness at her baptism?' Elizabeth asked.

'I will be proud to. Now where is that husband of yours? We must wet the baby's head! '

He disappeared in search of Thomas and loud greeting indicated his success.

Elizabeth smiled to herself. She had indeed a fine husband who loved and cared for her and her tiny daughter and she promised herself that the next child would be a son.

It was scarcely a year later that their next child was born; another girl whom they named Alicia. Elizabeth was disappointed as was Thomas though he would never let her know and made much fuss of her and the newborn. He was convinced that he hid his disappointment well until, out hawking one day; his gillie broached the subject quite directly. 'Ma wifie says ye should na worry sae, tis not uncommon tae start wi lassies and gang on tae ha lots o' laddies. Yer both young yet sae nae worries, ye'll hae plenty more. Just look at her father's bairns, there's plenty of both!'

Thomas thought for a moment before answering, 'Aye, I know you're right. I just hoped this one would be a son but she's a bonnie lassie and I love her well.'

'Aye, ye've twa bonnie lassies and there will be handsome sons to follow, mark my words.

The old gillie was right and Alicia was followed by three brothers, William, Gilbert and David. All were fine strong children with their father's good nature and mother's strong will. Close in age they played and studied together and were often a worry to their mother as they played close to the edge of the cliff. It was almost a relief to her when Thomas declared that he would look for a noble household to take them and train them in the skills of young noblemen.

John Leslie of Rothes was his choice and he had decided to visit him with his request. John had a son, George, of a similar age and proved more than willing to agree to an arrangement between the two families. It was decided that Thomas' sons would join John Leslie and study with his son George for half of each year and for the other six months the boys would reside with Thomas Hay. It was an unusual arrangement but worked well for both families and both Margaret and John's wife were delighted that they would be able to spend some part of each year with their sons.

The boys' tutor would stay with them at both locations but their weapons training and stewardship would be provided at each castle.

The boys had not met previously but soon became firm friends. There was rivalry in all of their activities and in the classroom but it was a healthy rivalry and contributed to their progress. Margaret and Alicia spent their days with their mother and her ladies learning to sew and the use of herbs. They skipped about the castle enjoying each other's company and becoming great favourites with the castle servants.

Occasionally their paths would cross with those of the boys who held themselves to be grander in spite of their lack of years. Never the less, they treated the girls with the respect expected from young squires and George, in particular, was careful to pay his respects to Elizabeth. Elizabeth for her part enjoyed the respect and flattery which George showered upon her. When he took her hand and kissed it she was at first tempted to giggle but with time she began to look forward to their paths crossing, knowing that she would enjoy the experience.

When John Leslie arrived at Slains Castle to collect the boys and take them back to his castle for the next six months he noticed his son's behaviour towards Elizabeth and found an opportunity to take him to one side.

'You show good behaviour towards the ladies,' he observed.

'Aye, father, I do my best to behave as you would have me. I shall not let you down.'

'Yea answer well, boy, but I think there is one lady whom you show particular favour too.'

The boy flushed but held his head high and looking his father in the eye he replied, 'The lady Elizabeth is most beautiful and cultured. I enjoy her company and find her most agreeable.'

'Yea speak as though you would not be averse to being betrothed to her.'

George was rather surprised. This was a step further than he had thought so far. He took a moment to mull over the suggestion before answering, 'Aye, father, I should like that very much.'

His father slapped him on the back. As a man who had an eye for a beautiful lady, he admired this in his son. 'I shall speak to Sir Thomas tonight and ask if he would be agreeable.'

John was as good as his word and when he and Sir Thomas retired from the table after their meal he broached the subject. The Hays and the Leslies had been close allies for many years and Thomas was not averse to the idea of his daughter marrying John's son. Their conversation progressed to talk of dowries and dates. George was several years older than Elizabeth, who was still only a child of ten years old but it was agreed that the marriage should take place the following year and the bedding could be postponed.

Later that evening as Thomas and Elizabeth retired, he told her of the arrangement.

'But she's so young!' protested Elizabeth. 'Must she marry so soon and leave us?'

'She will not leave us,' Thomas reassured her. 'John will continue his training as a squire and so he will be with us for six months of every year and Elizabeth will go with him when he goes to his father's estates but we can visit them there.

Elizabeth realised that this was a good arrangement and better than she could have hoped for. She knew that her daughters would be quickly betrothed as many a lord would wish his family to be associated with the Hays. She asked permission to break the news to their daughter herself and Thomas was happy for her to do so feeling it was better for the child to be reassured by her mother about the wedding.

Young Elizabeth was mature for her years and took the news philosophically. She had hoped for a prince as her father had married a princess but she liked George well enough and he treated her kindly. He was only a few years older than she and she knew that her duty was to marry well.

The young couple were brought together and both gave their agreement to the arrangement. John promised to begin the arrangements as soon as he returned home and a date for the wedding was settled. The wedding arrangements were swiftly put in place with invitations being sent to the king and many of the Scottish nobles who were associated with both families. St Machar's Cathedral was the chosen venue for the ceremony with guests retiring to Slains Castle for the wedding breakfast.

There were many young people at the celebrations including cousins from far and wide. Each family had a number of branches and a wedding was always a good reason to get together. As George and Elizabeth stood up to dance, George's uncle, Sir Andrew Leslie of that ilk, took the opportunity to approach Elizabeth's father. 'It's good to see you,' Thomas greeted him. I trust you enjoyed the ceremony.'

'Aye, indeed. It is good to see a match between our families. It is that I would speak of.'

'Our families have been close for many years. I am pleased to maintain our links.'

'In these difficult times, it is well to maintain our strengths. The more our families are bound together the better for us all. I would like to see this continue and, on behalf of my young heir I should like to offer for your other daughter.'

'While she is still an infant, I would, none the less, agree that it would be a favourable match. We must talk over the details in the coming days.'

As they grew up, Thomas's sons, William and Gilbert became very close, enjoying each other's company and taking every opportunity to train and hunt together. Their father spent a great deal of time away from Slains Castle in the service of the king. The boys were tutored in the king's household and so saw their father from time to time but were kept busy with studies, sports and knightly training. Gilbert enjoyed being at court but William resented the time which his father spent on business believing that he chose not to spend time with his sons.

The king was often pre-occupied and left many of his duties unfulfilled much to Sir Thomas' frustration with the English were an ever-present menace. King Robert had not only lost the respect of many of the barons but he was frequently at odds with his son, John who was frustrated at his father's failure to take control of the situation. The arguments between the king and his eldest son could often be heard bellowing around the castle and Sir Thomas knew that it would not be long before the king lost control of his kingdom. A truce had been arranged between England and Scotland but King Robert was unable to get his nobles to recognise it and so the costly war resumed and, as Constable, Sir Thomas must continue his duties. The king, however, more concerned with squabbles between his many children, took no active part.

The King of France was well aware of the situation in Scotland and was deeply concerned about the Scottish king's failure to take control. He needed Scotland's support against the English and fearing the nobility being caught up in an internal power struggle, he sent forty thousand francs to be divided amongst his friends and allies in Scotland. When Thomas received four hundred francs as his share with a letter from the French king reminding him of the Auld

Alliance, he was more than happy to accept. Although Elizabeth would rather the French king had sent a roll of brocade or fine silk, she was content with Thomas' promise to take her to Perth to have a fine new dress made.

King Robert's son, John was becoming angry at his father's ineptitude and lack of interest in his country.

The king refused to make any attempt to pay the ransom owed for the old king's release reasoning that David was dead now, as was King Edward, so they owed nothing. The English did not see it as so and the border battles re-commenced. John had been created Earl of Carrick before his father's ascent to the throne and, as such, was influential in the government of the kingdom but he longed to take over as king.

By 1384 the king was in his sixty-seventh year and John was frustrated to see his father failing to make decisions and being unable to stand by his decisions. He approached the government with his concerns and convinced them to depose his father and give him control of the country. Although King Robert made a show of his anger, he was relieved at his advanced age to give up the kingship.

Sir Thomas had had his own concerns about the king's ability, and even desire, to rule but doubted that John would do much better. He knew that John's brother, Robert, Earl of Fife, was constantly snapping at his heels and would not stand by and watch John eclipse him.

When Fife announced that he was to host a joust, knights from many parts of Scotland prepared to take part. Sir Thomas thought it would be an excellent opportunity for his sons to witness the excitement of the joust and he himself intended to take part.

He returned to Slains taking the boys with him. Elizabeth was delighted to see them all home but horrified when she learnt that Thomas was going to take part in the joust. She knew that many knights saw it as an opportunity to gain fame and fortune and no participant would hesitate to attack his opponent with all his skills and might.

Although Thomas did not need to prove himself and was already rich in wealth and status he knew he must take part in order to remind his rivals of his continuing strength and skills and as Constable of Scotland he must preside at all tournaments.

William, Gilbert and David were fascinated by the preparations and watched the castle armourer preparing their father's best hauberk and polishing it until it gleamed. Even his spurs sparkled. His destrier was exercised and groomed and a new shafron and trapper bearing his arms were prepared for his mount. Thomas' herald ensured that his weapons were in perfect order and was excited to be going with his laird on this auspicious occasion.

When they arrived the boys were mesmerised by the hustle and bustle of knights and their stewards preparing for the events and freelancers offering their services to take part in jousts on behalf of knights. There was to be a melee in which many knights would take part simultaneously whilst individuals would fight out their challenge at the tilt.

Tents had been erected for knights to change and rest in between matches and their squires took care of their weapons there. Pie-men and bakers hawked their wares and ladies tied their favours onto lances to show which knight they supported. David, who was always hungry, begged his father to let him buy a pie from a seller and was delighted to be given a coin to purchase one each for himself and his brothers.

For the most part, the atmosphere was of a fair but those taking part in the jousting took it very seriously. Fortunes could be won or lost and there was a real danger in taking part.

A trumpet sounded to indicate the first joust was about to take place. At each end of the tilt, a man was mounted on an enormous horse. One wore armour and was introduced as Sir Alex but the other, Sir Walter, had only boiled leather to protect him. Each horse's coat bore the colours of the knight creating a brilliant spectacle. The bridles were held by the knight's squires restraining the excited animals from charging too soon and so disqualifying the entrant.

There was an expectant hush until the trumpet sounded again and the horses charged towards each other. The arena erupted with cheers and shouts. Within seconds the horses met. Weapons crashed against shields and both men wavered in their saddles as they continued to the end of the tilt. Turning their horses they were handed fresh weapons by their squires.

They charged a second time. This time Sir Alex was hit by his opponent's lance and unseated; the lance shattering against his armour. Falling to the ground with a thud he struggled to his feet. Chivalry dictated that his opponent must also dismount to meet him. The fallen knight's squire rushed out to him with his sword scrambling out of range before the combatants met.

The clash of swords resounded around the arena as the men struck at each other swinging their swords with great skill and determination. In spite of his disadvantage against the lance, Sir Walter's leather protection now gave him the upper hand as he could move more freely and dodge his opponent's blows. The weight of his mail was telling on Sir Alex and it was clear that he was tiring. He fell to his knees and Sir Walter stood over him, his sword raised for a final blow.

Robert, Earl of Fife, sat in the terraces with his wife and daughters. As Sir Walter looked towards him, Robert indicated that Sir Walter was the winner, sparing Sir Alex from further hurt and humiliation.

Sir Walter held his hands in the air, accepting the cheers of the crowd. He had won a handsome purse of gold coins and his opponent's horse and armour and would go on to fight again later in the day. If his luck held he would go home a rich man this day.

Thomas' sons were thrilled by the spectacle, jumping up and down and cheering. He took them over to the terraces where places were found for them to sit to watch the remaining jousts.

There was a stir in the crowd drawing their attention from the men who were preparing the list for the next challenge. A mounted figure bearing the arms of the Earl of Carrick appeared between the spectators. The earl himself was to take part and had challenged James, Earl of Douglas.

The two knights took their places at each end of the tilt. Their restless horses were eager to begin. The signal was given and hooves thundered towards each other kicking up dust as they went. A crash indicated their impact and a gasp went up from the crowd as the dust cleared revealing that Carrick had been unseated. He rolled to his knees and was about to scramble to his feet when his frightened horse kicked out catching him full in the hip. His mail did little to protect him from the impact and a crack could be heard from the terrace. Unable to rise, Carrick lay moaning in agony in the dust. His opponent dismounted and approached to see what damage had been done. Squires and servants surrounded the fallen earl but were afraid to move him because of his terrible pain. Finally, it was decided that he must be taken inside to be cared for and the extent of his injury assessed. Six men lifted him onto a stretcher amidst his howls of agony and carried him into the castle. Examination showed that his hip was badly broken; an injury that little could be done to help. The joust continued but the atmosphere was tense as thoughts remained with the injured Carrick.

News of Carrick's injury was carried to the General Council by his brother Fife. He pressed them to give him the role of lieutenant to his father, in place of his brother. They were reluctant to do so choosing to wait and see to what extent Carrick recovered.

⚜

On the border between Scotland and England, skirmishes continued. Lord Neville and Henry Percy, Earl of Northumberland were at odds with each other and James, Earl of Douglas, saw it as an ideal opportunity to lead a raid into England. Gathering a force of trusted men, he led a raiding party towards Durham whilst his main force he sent towards Carlisle. Northumberland sent his sons, Sir Ralph Percy and the impetuous Harry, known as 'Hotspur', to Newcastle to cut off the Scots' retreat.

The forces met and there were skirmishes around the walls of the town, during which Harry Percy was furious to see his pennon captured by Douglas. He vowed to re-capture it and set off in pursuit of Douglas, spurring his horse forward furiously and leading his men onwards with but one thought in his mind – he must recover his pennon.

It was not until they had attempted, unsuccessfully, to take Otterburn Castle that Douglas set up camp. In spite of advice to continue their retreat, Douglas decided to remain there.

The Scots nobles had settled down for the evening and put on loose gowns for comfort when suddenly the alert was given by a scout. The English were upon them!

There was confusion in the Scots' camp as men rushed to arm themselves. The Earl of Moray even forgetting his helmet. Douglas responded quickly; not even waiting to secure his armour he charged forward with the cry, 'A Douglas, A Douglas!' A fierce and bloody hand to hand battle ensued in the moonlight, the ground slippery with blood, amid the shrieks and cries of the wounded. Douglas led a successful charge down the hillside towards Hotspur's right flank.

Although fierce fighting continued for some hours the English were gradually forced into a tighter and tighter section of the field and were now unable to use their long-bows, tired and hungry. The Scots forces began to prevail. Douglas was fatally wounded in the neck and knew that he could not survive. He beckoned one of his officers and pulled him close so that he could speak to him. In feeble tones, he ordered, 'Do not let the men know that I am killed. It will defeat their spirits if they believe their leader is dead. Fight on and I am with you. There is a prophesy that a dead man will win the field and I am that man.' With that, he gave up his last breath.

During the course of the night, Henry Percy and his brother Ralph were captured by Hugh Montgomery who was destined to receive a huge ransom for him from the Percy family.

Although the English were not routed the Scots took the field. They gathered up the bodies of Sir John Gordon, chief of his clan, and James Douglas whose body was buried with all honour in Melrose Abbey beside that of his father. Many other Scots lay amongst the dead yet no so many as the English.

Carrick's accident had left him physically unfit and unable to carry out his duties. His failure to bring the country under his control and to show any enthusiasm or aptitude for rule frustrated his ailing father who decided it was time to make his next eldest son, Robert, Earl of Fife, Guardian of the Kingdom.

Sir Thomas Hay was relieved. At last Scotland would have a ruler with some degree of competency and enthusiasm. He was to live to regret Robert's appointment as he discovered the man to be one of the most ruthless and cunning that Scotland had ever seen.

❧

On his return to Slains, Thomas was surprised that Elizabeth's welcome seemed rather distracted. He had much to tell her and was disappointed and angry that she appeared uninterested. Eventually he challenged her. 'Madam, I cannot insist that you listen to my tales but I would consider it your wifely duty to at least favour me with your attention.'

Shaking her head to clear it she explained that there had been some odd occurrences of late which she was concerned about. She had sent for one of her ladies a few nights ago only to be told that she was nowhere to be found. Enquiries had revealed that several of the women were missing and no amount of searching or questioning had unearthed their whereabouts.

Thomas shrugged it off telling her that they were probably meeting their lovers but Elizabeth was sure this was not the case.

Eventually, Thomas promised to look into the matter. He sent for Elizabeth's other maids who stood before him with their heads bowed. At first, he put this down to maidenly modesty but he began to realise that they were uncomfortable with his questioning, glancing at each other under lowered eyes. Try as he might, he could get no information from them so decided upon a course of action and dismissed the maids.

That evening he changed into his darkest clothing and hid himself in the stables. Before an hour had passed he heard a whispered exchange. Two of the maids that he had spoken to were talking to the guard. After a few moments, the guard bent his head and stole a long deep kiss from one of the girls before unlocking the gate and letting them through. Thomas waited a short time before leaving his cover and approaching the guard.

'Why did you open the gate and let those maids out?' he demanded.

The guard was taken by surprise. 'Your job is to guard the gates after sunset and let nobody pass through except me or my family. Two maids alone!' he growled, 'They could be murdered...or worse!'

The guard tried to splutter a response but before he could make a coherent reply Thomas had hauled the gate open and was silently following the girls.

Although there was a full moon and a clear sky it was still difficult to travel the rough road in darkness so Thomas' progress was slow. Not, however, as slow as the maids in their long gowns. It was not long before he heard them and then caught sight of them. Thinking that they were alone now they didn't worry too much about keeping their voices down. From their conversation Thomas gathered that they knew where to find the missing maids but were nervous about going there.

Thomas followed them for almost an hour before they stopped and concealed themselves in a copse. Keeping his distance he watched and waited.

It was not long before he heard voices; a deep male one at first then female voices. A procession of figures emerged from the other direction and left the road. The girls he had shadowed moved silently to follow at a distance. As he watched, the procession entered a stone circle and each person took up a position; one at each stone. The man whose voice he had first heard held something in his hands and approached each of the others, in turn, presenting it to them and chanting some strange words. It was clear that he held the girls in a trance. They each responded to his words and bowed their heads to him.

When he had completed the circle he returned to the first girl he had approached and led her by the hand into the centre of the circle where there was a large flat stone which seemed to be some sort of altar. Pressing the girl back against the stone he began to undress her. Thomas was in no doubt as to his intentions. He sprang from his hiding place and grabbed the man by his clothing dragging the scoundrel around to face him. Without hesitating, he pulled back his arm and landed a stunning punch on the man's nose sending him sprawling across the circle.

The girls, as if released from the spell, screamed in terror. The one who had been held in the centre of the circle fled, sobbing, into the arms of another. Lifting the bloodied man to his feet by the front of his clothes, Thomas took control of the situation demanding silence and gathering the girls to him. He bound the felon's hands with twisted grasses and demanded that they all return with him to the castle.

Many of the girls were tearful and supported each other through the dark pathways as they stumbled over roots and stones.

When they reached the castle gates Thomas roared to the guard to open up and led the group into the hall. His guards had sprung to life when they heard his voice and he thrust his captive at them with orders to throw the bastard into the dungeon until he was ready to deal with him.

Thomas ordered wine to be brought and given to the maids to warm and calm them. The noise had disturbed Elizabeth who was aghast when she took in the situation. Thomas explained to her what he had discovered and suggested it was best if she spoke to them to discover if any harm had befallen them. He strode from the room leaving her to calm the maids down.

Elizabeth's enquiries discovered that the felon had visited the castle some time ago and enticed the maids to join him at Collieston. When they reached the village he had told them stories of magic and how he could foretell who they would wed. Lured by his tales a number of them had planned to go and swore the rest to secrecy. They had intended to return the same night but he had given them a drink containing thorn-apple and they had forgotten about getting back; their passions aroused and enthralled by his hypnotic voice. None of them were aware that they had been away for days but it seemed that they were unhurt and none had been violated. It seemed that Thomas had arrived just in time.

The foolish girls were reprimanded and sent to their room.

Hauling the man none too gently from the prison, the guards dragged him before Sir Thomas. 'I have heard how you lured my maids away from the safety of Slains Castle and saw with my own eyes what you intended to do. Have you anything to say for yourself?'

The prisoner hung his head. It had been difficult to see him in the dark but now it was clear that he was in his late forties with straggling grey hair and, although he must have been quite handsome in his youth, the years had not been kind to him. A scar marred his face, running from below his eye to the corner of his mouth and two of his fingers were missing showing that he had once been an archer and had paid the price for being captured.

'You will be taken out and hanged. Your body will be left as a warning to others and your possessions will be given to the poor,' declared Sir Thomas indicating to the guards to carry out his orders.

He sent a messenger to Collieston to discover if he had any family in order that they might be told of his fate and to collect his possessions.

ᘓᘔ

1389

The ageing king was gravely ill and his son, John, severely restricted as a result of his injury. John's younger brother, Robert, Earl of Fife, continued to rule Scotland. Sir Thomas was often called upon in his capacity of Constable of Scotland and spent much time working with the king's sons.

Although Fife was the most motivated of the three, Thomas was beginning to realise that he was ruthless in his desire to advance himself and would let nothing and nobody stand in his way. More than once Thomas exchanged heated words with him but knew to beware of Fife's temper if he wished to keep his life.

The next year, news of the old king's death at Dundonald Castle came as no surprise. He had been ailing for some time and at seventy-four years old he had not been expected to recover.

His eldest son, John, was now to be crowned king but aware of the strength of feeling against the hated John Balliol, he was wary of becoming King John and so took the name Robert III, hoping to be likened to Robert Bruce. Fife stormed about the castle, furious at his brother's choice of name as he had hoped one day to become Robert III. His older brother was weak in body and spirit, presenting Fife with no difficulty in retaining control of Scotland and in spite of his brother's coronation he retained the title Guardian of Scotland.

When Robert II was buried at Scone Abbey, Albany led the mourners followed by Sir Thomas Hay. The new king travelled in a carriage due to his disability and was totally eclipsed by his younger brother who wore the finest clothes he could buy and wore a spectacular gilt sword embellished with jewels. He rode upon a jet black horse and presented a formidable figure.

On their return from Scone, Thomas was required to stay in Edinburgh with the king and his brother, the Earl of Fife.

Knowing that Fife hated him for his loyalty to the king, Sir Thomas was always on his guard but he never expected the course of action that Fife would take.

༺ঌ৵৯༻

Following the new king's coronation, Thomas took the opportunity to return to Slains Castle for a while. Having been away for so long he was eager to get home and did not stop to refresh himself on the way but merely took a drink from his riding flask. The contents tasted foul but in his hurry he had gulped some down. Spitting and wiping his mouth with the back of his hand, Sir Thomas swore and throwing the flask aside continued his journey. It was only when he arrived and was awaiting supper that he began to feel nauseous. Excusing himself he stood to make his way from the hall. He had not reached the door before he fell to the ground trembling. Fearing another outbreak of plague, Elizabeth ordered servants to take him immediately to his chamber and report on his progress.

Before an hour had passed, the servant returned begging Elizabeth to come to Thomas' chamber as he was convulsing and she feared for his life. On opening the door, Elizabeth was shocked by the silence. She entered to find him lying still on the bed. His breathing was shallow and he was not moving but a look of horror in his eyes drove fear into her heart.

Kneeling by his bedside, Elizabeth took his hand and pressed it to her lips. It felt cold and limp and she looked up in shock. She was appalled that Thomas had just returned to her and, with no prior ailment, would now die. She put her head on the bed and sobbed her misery.

Thomas was horrified. He could not move and could barely breathe. His mind raced but his body would not respond no matter how hard he tried. Now he could not even open his eyes yet he could hear all. He could not understand what had happened to him but knew from the words being spoken that they believed him to be dead.

Four manservants came into the room and lifted Thomas into a coffin. They carried it down to his hall and he was aware that many people entered the room and approached the coffin to pay their respects. He wanted to cry out and tell them he was alive but no sound would come, nor would his lips move.

The coffin was carried out of the castle and placed upon an open cart. He heard the horses' bridles jingle and their hooves on the stones. He heard weeping and voices but still he could not tell them that he lived. The cart began to move. It bumped along the roads jolting when it hit stones and wobbling when it passed over ditches. He felt sure that he would fall and then perhaps they would find he was alive but the coffin did not fall and they travelled on to Coupar Angus.

Thomas heard voices but they were too far away to make out what was being said. He knew from the tone that people were offering their sympathy to his wife and children.

A bell was tolling and he suddenly realised it was for him! The monk's voices, raised in song, drifted out from the abbey church and Thomas felt panic overtake him. As he was carried into the church the singing grew louder. He heard Abbot Walter speaking about him and extolling his virtues and those of his ancestors. He could see a glimmer of light through a crack beneath the casket's lid; perhaps his last glimpse of light.

When the service was ended the monks carried the wooden coffin to the tomb where he was to be placed with his ancestors. A stone coffin had been prepared and he would be lifted out and placed into it. As four pairs of hands slipped underneath him he heard a roar of fear and astonishment. 'He's still warm!' cried a voice. 'A miracle!' The hands withdrew in horror and Thomas was dropped back into the wooden cask. With a huge effort, he managed to prise open his eyes a little. A scream came from Elizabeth as she swooned and people pushed to see what was happening. Abbot Walter took control and ordered two brothers to take Elizabeth to his house whilst four more were directed to take Thomas. As time went on he began to be able to make slight movements but still did not recover his voice. Brothers were gossiping in groups and the words, 'curse' and 'witchcraft,' could be heard.

The Abbot sent for Brother George, the abbey infirmarian, to care for Thomas as he recovered. When he was sure that all had been done that could be to make Thomas comfortable, he asked him for his opinion of the ailment.

'I have heard of a deep sleep such as this but never seen such a case. The victim suffers paralysis and appears to be dead yet still lives.'

'Brother, you used the word victim, are you saying Sir Thomas has been poisoned?'

'Well I cannot be sure but this, if I am correct, is caused by hemlock.'

'Could he not have eaten it by accident?'

'I think not. Its odour is most disagreeable so it would not be eaten in mistake for food.'

The abbot left Brother George to care for the patient whilst he led Elizabeth away and gave her a glass of wine. 'It would seem that somebody does not like your husband, my lady.'

'But he had only just returned from the king's court. He did not stop on his way home and. As far as I know, he met nobody on the way.'

'We must leave him to rest. He has a long recovery ahead of him and we must thank God that he lives.'

The abbey bell was ringing to call the brothers to the next service of the day. Abbot Walter invited Elizabeth to join them and give thanks for Thomas' recovery which she gladly agreed to do.

When Thomas was fit to leave his bed he sat with her and discussed what had happened. They puzzled over who might have wished his death when suddenly it occurred to Thomas that the only person at the Royal Court with whom he had had disagreements was Robert, Earl of Fife. Was he capable of murder? Thomas believed he was.

There was no proof of Fife's guilt and Thomas knew that it would not serve him well to accuse him unless he could prove him guilty but he knew now that he must beware of this dangerous enemy.

1398

King Robert III was now so restricted by his injury that it was nigh on impossible for him to carry out his royal duties. The Scottish Parliament, encouraged by Queen Annabella, appointed his eldest son, David as first Duke of Rothesay to be Lieutenant of the kingdom and rule in his father's place in an attempt to ensure that David succeeded as king after his father. Thomas was appointed as an advisor to David. At the same time, they made Robert, until then Earl of Fife, the Duke of Albany.

Sir Thomas hoped that Scotland might now have a ruler who would act in the interest of the people and country of Scotland but it was not to be so. Three years previously, David had married Elizabeth Dunbar, daughter of the Earl of March. However, the Papal dispensation needed because they were blood relatives was declined, and in 1397 the couple had separated. This did nothing to appease the unruly nobles. There was rivalry between the highlanders, his brothers and the lords of the isles. When David went ahead and married Mary Douglas, daughter of the third Earl of Douglas, some declared his marriage bigamous. Amongst these was his father in law from his first marriage who had hoped that his grandsons would eventually become kings of Scotland. In his fury, he decided to switch his allegiance to Henry IV of England who used this to invade Scotland and capture Edinburgh.

Thomas was working furiously to call up troops to defend the kingdom and successfully reclaimed Edinburgh in as short time as possible but he was concerned that this was just the beginning of a major attack on Scotland whilst its rulers were caught up in a power struggle of their own.

Queen Annabella was fearful that David's Uncle, now the Duke of Albany, would try to usurp the throne and she was justified in her fears.

When his mother died just a couple of years later, David felt free to make decisions for himself and although he was obliged to consult his council before doing so, like many young men he rebelled against the restriction that this put upon him and neglected to do so. Many of the barons felt that their positions were threatened by his decision to act independently, especially Albany.

In February 1402, David set out for St. Andrews. Just as he arrived outside the city there was a clatter of hooves and he found himself surrounded by soldiers led by Sir John Ramornie and Sir William Lindsay of Rossie, agents of his uncle the Duke of Albany. Taking him by the arms they hauled him from his horse and took his sword before arresting him and holding him prisoner in St Andrews Castle until further instructions arrived. Before long a rider brought orders to take their prisoner to Falkland Palace, Albany's residence in Fife. A guard was sent to bring him out and a hood was thrust over his head and bound around his neck. He was then bundled onto a mule, seated backwards and travelled like this for the entire journey.

By the time they arrived at Falkland Palace he was aching and humiliated. He was dragged down from the mule and thrown down into the dungeon. Furious at this treatment, David bellowed at his guards and demanded to be released. He demanded that Sir Thomas Hay be sent for to explain why he had been arrested but David's captors were acting without Thomas' knowledge.

The guards were under orders neither to speak to David nor to give him food or water. Hunger gnawed at his insides making him writhe with pain. Thirst began the first evening of his captivity. Calling for water he got no response from the guards. There was no sound of anybody being within earshot. The isolation closed in on him like the darkness of the coming night. He awoke; his head aching badly, sorely in need of a drink and with cramp in his legs. He struggled to his feet and threw himself against the door. Following the thud, the silence resumed. He began to talk about his captors. What he would do when he was freed. He told himself that his rescuer was on their way and gradually his ramblings became more and more irrational. Although he had nothing to drink nor food, it was salt that he craved most. His tongue was so dry that it clung to the roof of his mouth and yet, somehow he felt quite euphoric. It was two days before he lapsed into unconsciousness and within a very short time, he breathed his last.

Sir Thomas was shocked when he heard of David's death. He demanded to know why he had been arrested as no information about this had come to him. The Constable of Scotland was supreme judge in all matters of riot, disorder, bloodshed, and murder committed within a circuit of four miles of the King's person, or of the Parliament and Council representing the Royal authority in His Majesty's absence. The trial and punishment of persons committing such crimes and offences came properly within the jurisdiction of the courts of the Constable and his deputies. For an arrest such as this to be carried out without his knowledge was unthinkable.

Albany demanded a public enquiry into the circumstances of David's death, which he himself controlled. The enquiry exonerated him of all blame concluding that David had died, 'by divine providence and not otherwise,' and commanded that no one should, 'murmur against,' Albany and Douglas.

Sir Thomas took the news of David's death to the king who had retired to his lands in the west. King Robert was horrified and knew that Albany must be responsible.

The only remaining obstacle to an Albany Stewart dynasty was the king's remaining son, James. King Robert feared for James' life and asked Sir Thomas to arrange for him to be taken to France where he believed he would be safe.

The plans were swiftly put in place and James was escorted to Dirleton Castle until 1406 when he was to be taken to Edinburgh. Without warning, James was told that he was to be taken to France. Sir Thomas Hay and a small escort was already prepared and within the hour James was mounted and left the safety of the castle.

As they travelled the guards were on the alert for danger but were taken by surprise when James Douglas of Balvenie and his men emerged from the depths of the forest. Sir David Fleming of Cumbernauld was run through immediately and three of the guards were dispatched before they could draw their weapons. Sir Thomas grabbed James' bridle and galloped away with James still stunned and clinging on to his horse before taking control and riding independently. The Earl of Orkney escaped with them and the three rode hard for several miles before slowing. Thomas looked back and signalled to the other riders to stop. He dismounted and knelt down with his ear to the ground. It was impossible to see through the forest but horses following them would be heard through the earth from almost a mile away. It seemed that the pursuit had been abandoned. Considering what they should do, the men discussed the possibilities for escape. The Earl decided that, in the absence of further support, he would take James to the Bass Rock in the Firth of Forth where he would be safe while Sir Thomas made alternative arrangements to get James to France. They remained on the rock for a month whilst a ship travelling from Danzig, en-route for France, was bribed to pick them up. They boarded the vessel and within half an hour they had set sail. Thomas heaved a sigh of relief as he saw the ship sail away.

As the ship made its way south the captain was confident that all was well and retired to his cabin. Shouts and cries were not uncommon on ships but there was something about the tone which alerted him to the fact that something was amiss. As he reached to open the door it burst open and he was pushed back into the cabin. A hand pinned him to his bunk by the throat as a knife was plunged through his heart. Henry IV, King of England, was only too happy to take James prisoner.

His men had pulled their ship up alongside and boarded before the crew realised they were under attack. Most of the crew were thrown overboard; the rest were thrown in the hold and locked in. James was hauled up on deck and dragged aboard the English vessel which immediately set sail for London.

King Robert was horrified when he was given the news of his son's abduction. He knew that his cousin Albany was ruthless and feared that King Henry would arrange for young James to be dispatched as David had been. He felt sure now that Albany had killed David.

Sending for his wife the ailing king poured out his grief and frustration. 'My dear,' he said, 'I am an old man and will not be long in this life. I have been an absolute failure as a king. Scotland is in turmoil; the barons hate me and ignore me; one of my sons has been murdered and another in the hands of the English. They will write on my tombstone, 'He was the worst of kings and most miserable of men.' Nothing that she could say would comfort him and before much longer his prediction came true.

The king's body was taken to Paisley Abbey where it lay in state. Sir Thomas Hay, himself now an elderly man, was responsible for guarding the body and organising the guards and procession for the funeral. Thomas' wife, Elizabeth joined him at Paisley and was concerned to see how frail he had become. The time that he had spent serving the king by trying to preserve the succession had taken its toll. A hard life of fighting and travel around Scotland and England had also had its effect on the aged Constable.

The funeral procession passed along a road cobbled with rounded stones, one of which was raised and, absorbed with the proceedings, Sir Thomas caught his foot on it and stumbled. But for the swift reactions the two earls behind him, he would have fallen. Elizabeth gasped and was relieved when she saw him set safely back on his feet. She knew it was his responsibility to fulfil his duties and he would have been horrified if it were suggested that he rest from them but feared that his adherence to duty may cost him dearly.

The heir to the throne was a prisoner in England and Robert Stewart, Duke of Albany had been made Governor and Regent of Scotland. One of Albany's duties was to negotiate with the English for James I's release but not surprisingly there had been little progress. Sir Thomas had done his best to support the old king but could do nothing to help the captive James and would not support the murderous duke. Whilst this situation continued, there would be no coronation to attend which left him free to return with Elizabeth to Slains Castle. En route they stopped at Inchetuthel, to visit his cousin. He longed to see his sons again and would not linger long but be on his way north as soon as he reasonably could. William as his heir had been the master of Slains Castle in his father's absence and was capably looking after affairs there. Gilbert was at nearby Bowness Tower running the more northerly estates. David stayed with him as a nagging cough had troubled him for some time and it was felt that the air was just a little warmer at Bowness.

A week later Thomas' sons were shocked by the arrival of a message, telling them that their father was ill and near to death. They must come to Inchetuthel to say farewell and receive their father's blessing. Gilbert sent for their horses and without waiting for them to be saddled they threw themselves onto the horses and rode at a gallop to Inchetuthel.

When they arrived a groom took their horses and told them that William had already arrived. They ran to his father's chamber where William and his mother were beside his father's bed holding his hands. The exertion started David coughing and it took him some minutes to regain his breath. A priest stood nearby muttering prayers in the darkened room. Elizabeth stood back to allow Gilbert and David to approach their father who beckoned with his finger to draw them nearer. Gilbert bent his head close to hear Thomas' words.

'My beloved sons; I am proud of you and give you my blessing. Take care of your mother and sisters and be proud to bear the name Hay. A Hay, a Hay, a Hay......' and with that his last breath left him.

Sir Thomas had died an old man and William had been well trained in the role of Constable of Scotland. He organised his father's funeral and led the procession as they set out from Inchetuthel for Coupar Angus. His mother, Elizabeth, although also old and frail, preferred to ride on horseback than to suffer the journey over rough and bumpy lanes in a carriage. Thomas' daughters, Elizabeth and Alicia and their husbands would join the family at Coupar Angus.

They arrived safely at the abbey where the faint and exhausted Elizabeth was escorted to the Abbot's house. She gave the Abbot a purse of gold for the abbey and Thomas' tomb and a document bearing Sir Thomas' seal. Fearing for her health the Abbot put it to one side whilst he ordered brandy to be brought for her.

When she had drunk it he told the prior to escort her to her room to rest. Elizabeth was grateful and thanked him as she left. She recalled the last time they had been at the abbey when Thomas was almost buried alive. The thought was poor company and distressed her greatly as she lay on the bed and closed her eyes to shut out the memory.

When the guests sat down at the Abbot's table for supper, Elizabeth did not arrive. Alicia went to ask her if she would prefer a meal in her room. She tapped on her door but receiving no reply she gently pushed open the door. Elizabeth lay still. She stepped into the room to try to rouse her and let out a gasp as she realised that her mother had succumbed to the strain of losing her dear Thomas and the arduous journey to the abbey.

Rushing from the room she flew to the Abbot's dining room. It was apparent to those seated around the table that something was wrong. The men stood and followed the Abbot to Elizabeth's room where she lay so peacefully. One of the monks who had followed brought a candle and stood to one side as the abbot recited prayers for her soul.

When they left her chamber the Abbot suggested that he might bury Elizabeth with Thomas the next day. Their sons were sure they would not wish to be parted and thanked the Abbot for his kind offer.

When he remembered the document which Elizabeth had given to him on her arrival the abbot went to his study to read it. He unfolded the paper and read in silence. Sir Thomas had bequeathed a large plot of land to the abbey with a condition that prayers be said for his soul and those of his family. He added a request that, when the time should come, Elizabeth be placed in his tomb with him. 'One might say it was a message from the grave,' he mused.

⁂

The return journey to Slains Castle was a solemn one with hardly a word passing between the brothers. David's cough meant that they travelled slowly and, although he tried to hide it, William saw that his brother was spitting blood when he coughed. They had taken a sad farewell of their sisters, Elizabeth and Alicia, and promised to visit them as soon as they had settled matters at the castle.

William was now the Constable of Scotland and had duties to fulfil but was wary of what the usurping Albany might bid him do. He had not always agreed with his father's way of doing things but wished now that he could ask his advice.

Knowing that Slains would need a mistress to take charge of its keeping and he must provide heirs, he knew that he must make a suitable marriage as his sisters had. He recalled Sir Patrick Gray, of Broxmouth who held considerable lands including those of Longforgund in Perthshire and who had been a good friend to the family for years. Sir Patrick had a daughter, Margaret, who was most attractive. William had noticed her at the cathedral during a friend's wedding and awaited his opportunity to spend a moment with her. She accepted his invitation to dance with a smile, holding out her hand for him to lead her out. She moved gracefully and her eyes were like those of a doe. Her chestnut brown hair was braided at the sides of her head and fell loosely over her shoulders.

For the next few months, William visited Broxmouth whenever possible. He must make a suitable match but he was determined it would be one that would be to his liking. He found Margaret to be most biddable to her father's will and of an agreeable nature. Her laugh was full of joy and she seemed to be able to get on with everybody. He loved her sense of humour and she was capable in all womanly skills. She could converse on a level far in excess of that normally expected of a lady, as her father had permitted his daughters to join in their brother's education, claiming that if he was to pay for tutors they could as well teach seven children as four. William decided to offer for her hand and was shocked to learn that she had another suitor who had also requested permission to marry her although, as yet, nothing had been agreed.

Sir Patrick was a wise man and, quite apart from his desire to extend his lands, he wanted to see his daughters happily married if possible. William Hay's land adjoined his and a union of the two families would be beneficial. To marry the Constable of Scotland would be an excellent match and he approved with alacrity.

❧

William insisted that David remained at Slains with him. He worried about his cough and sent for the wise woman to fetch some herbs to ease it.

The woman brought a drought of herbs which she had prepared but as she approached his chamber he took another fit of coughing and turning to William she shook her head. 'This will saucht him a wee bit but there is naething tae cure that hoast. I've haurd the like afore and it's just a maiter o' time.'

William was shocked. 'I must get him to Edinburgh. We will find the finest physician.'

'Ye can spend yer clink on yer fine doctors if ye will and they'll take yer clink gledly, but none can cure what he haes.'

Stunned by the news, William showed her into David's room.

'What's this?' he asked.

'The wise woman has something for your cough,' replied William.

'That's kind of you, William, but she can't do anything for me. I know what ails me and I'll not last until the winter.'

'How long have you known?' William was shocked that David knew he was so ill and he had failed to notice just how poorly his brother was.

'I knew last year. I've heard the like before and know there is no hope.'

David's prediction was correct and within weeks he was confined to bed, unable to sit without help.

Fearing for his new wife, William would not let her nurse David, setting a serving girl to look after him but taking the trouble to visit him often and sit talking to him.

As William entered the room a week before Christmas, David began to cough so badly that William went to the door and summoned the girl to come immediately. He went to the bed where his brother lay; now a shadow of the man he had been. He put his arm behind David's shoulder to lift him and ease his breathing. As the bout of coughing grew stronger a gush of blood poured from David's mouth and his body became limp. William looked in astonishment at his brother lying against his arm. Tears rolled down William's face and he was unable to stop them. His dearly loved brother had been taken from him. He did not know how he could face life without him to laugh and joke with; to practice sword skills with and to share his joys and sorrows. Sobs shook his body. The serving girl quietly left the room to give him space to sob out his grief and to tell the squire to get a message to Gilbert.

Gilbert wasted no time in getting to Slains and sped to David's room to share William's grief.

It was agreed that David should be laid with their parents at Coupar Angus and a message was sent to Abbot John, telling him the news and the date they would arrive.

CHAPTER 15

1407

William Hay took his new wife to the castle at Slains and gave her the keys as a sign that she was mistress of the castle. He was a staunch supporter of the king but whilst Albany remained in power he had no choice but to obey him. In an effort to keep his interaction with the Duke to a minimum, William spent as much time as possible on his estates at Slains and Erroll.

Margaret bore him a son, Gilbert and a daughter named Elizabeth after his mother. Gilbert thrived but little Elizabeth was not a strong child and the exposed conditions at Slains Castle took their toll of her health. Before her first birthday, the child faded and died, leaving her parents distraught. William pleaded his daughter's death as justification for staying at Slains Castle a while longer but when he could resist no longer and must go to do Albany's bidding he took his wife to their private chamber. From his pocket, he took a ring which he showed to her. 'The front of the ring opens,' he demonstrated, 'within it, I will put a small quantity of poison.'

Margaret was shocked. 'Why do you give me such a ring?' she asked.

'There is much danger. Albany knows that I support King James and I will not always be here to protect you and Gilbert. Should it come to the worst and you are at risk, they would not treat you gently. It would be better to have a swift death than to suffer at the hands of Albany's men. Should the need arise you must give half of the contents to our son and swallow the rest yourself. I would not see you suffer.'

Margaret knew that what he said was true. She had heard of David's death by starvation and other tales of Albany's cruelty. She realised that what William was giving her was a kindness.

Before he left, his brother, Gilbert asked to see William alone. 'I know that you must answer the king's call,' he explained, 'but before you leave I must tell you that I have asked Elizabeth Reid to be my wife. We had hoped to wed in the summer but as you have to leave and we cannot say when you might return, I shall bring our wedding forward.'

William feigned anger at first, asking why Gilbert had not sought his permission, before slapping his brother on the back. 'Congratulations Gilbert. You kept it quiet, didn't you? I had no idea.'

'It's not so much that I kept quiet as you being too busy to notice!' laughed Gilbert, delighted that his brother was agreeable to the match.

That evening at supper, William called Gilbert and Elizabeth before him and offered his congratulations.

'Now, I suppose I must give you a gift for your wedding,' he mused. 'Well, you've done well at Bowness Tower and proved yourself a good steward. I think you might look after Dronlaw just as well. Take it as my wedding gift to you both. I will have the papers drawn up before your wedding day.

More good news was to greet William within the month. His sister, Alice, had been a child bride but her first husband had been much older than her and had died, leaving her childless. Within the year she had married Sir William Hay of Lochorwart and Yester; A noble branch of the Hay family who had land and power in the borders. The news that she had given birth to a daughter, who had been named Alicia after her mother, was a welcome pleasure to William and Elizabeth who decided they must visit them and see the new baby as soon as possible.

❧❧❧

William, arriving at Albany's court, was unclear why he had been sent for. He was kept at the court for over two years for minor duties and events whilst having to leave the duties of his lands to his brother and cousins.

The reason for his detention became clear when Donald, Lord of the Isles, gathered an army at Ardtornish Castle. His aim was to gain control over the lands of the Earldom of Ross. He then sailed around the north coast of Scotland, landing his forces at Dingwall where he defeated an army of 3,000 MacKays before moving on to capture Inverness. Albany did not want William and the forces he controlled in Aberdeen to join Donald and by keeping him at court he thought to prevent him doing so.

In an effort to draw Robert, Duke of Albany into open conflict, Donald, by now with an army of highlanders numbering some 10,000 men, marched east, into Moray, before turning towards Aberdeen. At Harlaw, Donald's army faced a force of 2,000 men, largely mounted knights, under the command of Alexander Stewart, Earl of Mar, a nephew of Robert, Duke of Albany.

The fighting was fierce and bloody but by nightfall, no clear victor had emerged. Overnight Donald withdrew towards Inverness, leaving the Earl of Mar waking the next morning to find that he controlled the battlefield. This left Albany able to claim a victory over the highlanders. He then led an army to re-take Ross which he later awarded to his son, John Stewart, the 2nd Earl of Buchan.

William Hay was furious that he had been prevented from being present but knew he was powerless to do anything about it if he wanted to be in a position to support the true king.

Eventually, William was permitted to return to Slains where he invited other supporters of the true king to meet with him. He knew it was dangerous and meetings must be infrequent but many of the barons felt strongly that Albany was dangerous and the true King of Scotland should be rescued from the English king.

Whilst in England James was receiving a good education as befitted a young king. He learned to appreciate literature and music and was becoming a well-respected sportsman. He absorbed the English method of governance and developed a deep respect for King Henry V. For a short time James even fought with the English army in France but the fact that there were Scottish soldiers supporting the French army which he fought against, caused some Scottish nobles to question his right to rule Scotland.

Murdoch Stewart, Albany's son and the king's cousin had also been held captive by the English since 1402 but in 1416 he was traded for Henry Percy whom the Scots had held since his capture at the Battle of Otterburn. James remained captive whilst the now ageing Albany continued to make little effort to free him. Many of the Scottish barons were not unduly concerned as Albany, in spite of his ruthlessness was making Scotland a more stable country and bringing the nobles under control. As a result, Albany continued in power until his death, at the age of eighty, in 1420 at which time his son, Murdoch took over from him.

CHAPTER 16

The war between England and France continued. The English king, Henry V had taken advantage of the internal division in France and a major battle at Agincourt had seen the English forces victorious and much of northern France was now in the hands of the English king.

In 1295 France had formed an alliance with Scotland built upon their shared interests in controlling England's aggressive plans. As a result of the alliance, many Scots found employment as mercenaries in the French armies.

The French king, Charles VI, having suffered bouts of insanity, his son took the title Dauphin – heir to the throne – at only fourteen years of age.

King Henry's victory at Agincourt had been a disaster for France which they could not afford to repeat. Under the guidance of his advisors, the Dauphin now looked, once again, to Scotland for help.

Twelve thousand Scots boarded ships bound for France waved on their way by wives and lovers. Each hoped to return with wealth and honours and strode proudly aboard to the swirl of pipes and rattle of drums.

Their reception was not so enthusiastic; 'Consumers of mutton and wine,' was the fairly dismissive description which met the Scottish soldiers who arrived in France in the autumn of 1419.

Their first great test came on Easter Sunday, 1421, at the Loire town of Baugé. King Henry had returned to England to take part in a royal progress with his wife, Catherine, leaving his brother, Thomas Duke of Clarence to lead the English army. The Scots were led by John Stewart, the Earl of Buchan. By the end of the day, the English army had been routed and the Duke of Clarence lay dead on the field of battle. As Pope Martin V observed upon hearing the news, 'the Scots are well-known as an antidote to the English'.

The Dauphin was quick to recognise the valour of his Scottish forces and had already created a personal bodyguard for himself made up entirely of Scots, the Gardè Ecossaise. Now Buchan was made Constable of France and therefore was in command of the French army.

News of the death of King Henry V of England came as a shock to England as to Scotland and France. He had succumbed to the flux soon after returning to France and died suddenly leaving his nine-month-old son as King of England.

1423

A messenger arrived at Erroll where William Hay was spending time with his cousins and stewards going over the estate affairs. The man carried a summons from the Scottish Parliament. William was to present himself as soon as possible to receive instructions about a mission he was to undertake but no further details were given. Curious as to the nature of the matter, he set out with all haste, curious to discover what his mission was to be.

Taking with him an escort of five knights, he made good time in reaching Edinburgh, where he made his way to meet with the Parliament. When he was called forward into the great hall, William found himself facing a select group of the Parliament who explained to him that, since King Henry V had died the previous year and England's king was a child, they proposed to try to negotiate with his advisors. As Constable of Scotland and a man in whom they put their trust, William was required to travel to England as the Commissioner to treat for the ransom of King James I. William was aware of both the honour and the responsibility which this task held. He was not to return to his lands but to go immediately and all that he would require for the journey had been made ready. The Parliament had appointed a company of Scotland's finest guards to accompany him but William demanded that at least three of his own men also join the party. The other two were to return to Slains and explain to Margaret where William was going. This was granted and the following day they set out at dawn.

The journey was eased by the safe conduct granted by King Henry's Council but the party faced numerous hardships along the way when they needs must stay at inns of doubtful quality and bad weather made roads muddy and dangerous.

Finally, they arrived and after several days awaiting an audience, William Hay was led into a meeting room by a stern-faced official in red robes bearing the royal crest. The man stood to one side bowing deeply before retreating. William barely noticed as he faced the king's guardians and the privy-council. The discussions were prolonged and numerous meeting took place before an agreement was reached that King James would be released if a ransom of £40,000 was paid and hostages delivered as a guarantee of payment. Messengers were immediately sent to Scotland with the news and a request that the required hostages be sent to England as soon as they possibly could.

Many Scottish nobles were required to send their sons as hostages and some were resentful but most, knowing that the boys would be well treated and educated, and mindful of the need to bring James back to Scotland, were happy to comply. When the hostages finally arrived, James was released into the care of William and the guards, with additional guards supplied by the English king, to ensure their safe passage as far as the border. They set off with all haste to deliver James back to his rightful position as King of Scotland.

During the journey, James confided in William regarding his concerns about returning. He had been in England for eighteen years, spending most of his youth there and becoming more familiar with the English court than the Scottish one. He was also acutely aware that many of the nobles would not welcome him back as a result of his fighting with the English army in France where some Scottish nobles fought with the French army.

William agreed that this was fact but argued that James would make the court his own and whatever form that took was his decision alone. He could not undo the fact that he had fought in France but the Scottish nobles must be made to understand why and accept that he was their rightful monarch. If he proved to be a strong ruler, most nobles would support him or at least accept him.

As it transpired, many of the nobles welcomed his return. King James had had to wait a long time to revenge the death of his brother, David, to whom he had been very close, and now that Robert, Duke of Albany was dead, his son, who had taken his place, would take the punishment.

James was grateful to William for his efforts in securing his release from England and his good advice during their journey home. In recognition, he knighted him amidst all of the celebrations at his coronation.

After his coronation, King James was merciless in imposing Royal authority. Feuding between nobles, the maintenance of their large armies was forbidden and he imposed the law and raised taxes to repay his ransom.

Soon after his coronation, King James I had Murdoch and two of his sons arrested and tried for treason. They were found guilty and executed.

James was proving himself to be a strong king.

With the Lowland barons partially suppressed, he turned to the Highlands. He summoned the Clan Chiefs to a parliament in Inverness to which about fifty turned up. When they were gathered he had them arrested. Some were immediately executed; others executed later, and still others imprisoned.

Alexander, Lord of the Isles, was one of those imprisoned. It was almost a year later that he was released and he promptly raised 10,000 men and burnt the town of Inverness.

Alexander's actions showed that the king's actions had been justified and he had no difficulty in raising an army which he marched north and trounced the rebels. Alexander stood before the king and begged for his life. James, aware of the fact that the Scottish nobles would be waiting to see how he reacted, imprisoned Alexander in Tantallon Castle.

The Scottish nobility continued their private wars and the King continued to punish their insubordination. He confiscated the earldom of Strathearn and imprisoned the young Earl.

Sir Robert Graham, Strathearn's uncle, denounced the King as a tyrant in Parliament and tried to have him arrested but his attempt failed and he was banished and deprived of his estates.

Unperturbed by this, many of the nobles backed Sir Robert in his attack against the severity of James's rule and, along with the King's uncle, Walter, Earl of Atholl, plotted to assassinate him and replace the King with his own grandson.

In France, the battles continue. There was fear that if Orléans fell, France would fall and in a desperate attempt to raise the spirits of his troops, the Dauphin chose to accept the claims of a young peasant girl, Joan of Arc, that she had received visions of the Archangel Michael, Saint Margaret, and Saint Catherine instructing her to drive out the English and bring Charles to Reims for his coronation.

The Battle of Verneuil in Normandy in 1424 cost Scotland the life of Buchan, commander of the Scottish forces.

King James sent for Sir William and explained that Buchan's death meant that he needed William and his brother, Gilbert, to join the Scottish forces in France. He was aware of Sir William's military prowess and felt that he was the right person to replace Buchan. 'This is a great responsibility which you will undertake,' James acknowledged. 'It is important that our men are led by a noble whom they know I trust and respect and therefore I am going to elevate you to the rank of Lord Hay of Erroll. Do well and I shall reward you handsomely. The honour of Scotland is in your hands.'

'You are most gracious, your majesty. You do me a great honour. I shall do my utmost to justify your faith in me,' William replied.

He had little time to prepare as he was to sail within the week.

In his chamber that evening, William sat down to write to Margaret and explain that he was to be sent to France but would return to her and their son, Gilbert, as soon as he possibly could. He made much of being created Lord and understated the risks he would face so as not to alarm her. He asked her to write to him saying that her letters would bring him joy and explained how she could get the letters to him.

The following day, William set off for Dronlaw to meet his brother in order that they might travel together to France. Between them, they had a retinue of over thirty knights and men making the journey safer.

Their arrival at the court of the King of France was greeted with relief. The French had suffered from a lack of numbers since the plague had devastated the population and those who remained and were fit to fight were demoralised by a series of humiliating defeats.

Two weeks later Sir William was surprised to receive a basket from Slains. In it was a pigeon and a message was attached to the pigeon's leg. Removing the paper he read, 'My darling William, Gilbert, with the help of the falconer, has been training this bird, Valiant, to return home. I pray you, take it with you and when the king of France is crowned, attach a letter to its leg as I have done and set it free. The bird will, I trust, return to us and I shall know that you are safe. I cannot bear to wait until you return to me, not knowing that you are well. My love to you always, M.'

Lord William Hay and his brother, with sixty Scottish men-at-arms and seventy Scottish archers led by Sir Patrick Ogilvy of Auchterhouse, escorted Joan of Arc into the besieged city of Orléans on April 28th, 1429, to the celebratory skirl of the Scottish pipes playing 'Hey Tuttie Taiti'; the same tune that had marched Robert the Bruce into battle at Bannockburn a century before.

Her standard, depicting God as King of Heaven, had been made a few months previous by Hamish Powers, a Scotsman living in the city of Tours.

The French troops cheered believing that their leader was sent by God. The English, hearing that God had sent a leader to defeat them, feared defeat. To the French, it was the encouragement that they needed and just nine days later the siege was lifted.

Victory after victory ensued. The military procession to Rheims continued with the Garde Ecossaise providing an escort for both Joan and the Dauphin. And so, in the July, King Charles VII was crowned. Lord William Hay had been slightly wounded during the fighting and was recalled by King James but his brother, Gilbert, attended the ceremony. Before he left France, William sent for the basket that his wife had sent to him and attached a message to the bird's leg. He lifted the bird swiftly, offering it flight. With a rush of wings, the bird rose into the sky and after a moment's hesitation flew away.

On his return to Scotland, Lord William reported events to the king and as soon as he was excused he set off to Slains.

Forgetting herself, Margaret ran out to meet him, throwing herself into his arms as he dismounted. He hugged her and held her at arms-length to look at her before folding her in his arms and kissing her.

'It was good to hear that you were safe,' she laughed. 'I had heard that you were wounded and feared the worst but Valiant brought me your message and it was here the day after you wrote it.'

'He made good time then. How clever of Gilbert to train it to come home.'

'It is always hard waiting when you go to away. When I know you are in a battle it is even worse. To hear that you are alive and well means everything to me.'

When William heard that Joan of Arc had been captured and handed over to the English he was shocked. He knew that they would show her no mercy. His worst fears were realised when news arrived telling them that, following a mock trial, Joan had been burnt at the stake.

William was aware that the years were telling on him. When he woke in the morning he ached from old wounds and his joints were stiff. He knew that life was unpredictable, especially for a man of his standing. He knew that succession was important and worried that his son, Gilbert, had not yet chosen a wife.

Duties in Scotland and France had meant that Gilbert had been kept busy running the estate and standing in for his father in numerous roles. Now it was time to find him a wife; and William had just the bride in mind. His sister, Alice, had a daughter, Alicia by her second husband. William believed she would make a good wife for Gilbert and reinforce links between the Hays of Erroll and of Yester. He broached the subject with his son and it was decided that they would call at Yester for Gilbert to renew his acquaintance with Alicia. William was looking forward to seeing Alice again. It had been years since they had last seen each other.

Gilbert remembered his cousin as a rather giggly little girl who liked to join in with the boys' games when she was free from her mother's bidding. He was stunned when he met her. She had grown into a self-confident young lady. She was skilled in music and stitching and could even read, write and keep figures. Gilbert was impressed. In spite of her skills, she was demure and kept her head down in the company of men, speaking when she was addressed and keeping her counsel at other times.

William hugged his sister, kissing her on the cheek. She looked weary having been in despair since the death of her eldest son, Thomas. Her husband having died a few years earlier, Alice and the younger children had continued to live under Thomas' protection but since he had been succeeded by his younger brother, David, they had not been welcome. Sir William reassured her of his support and put his proposal to her. Alice was relieved at the suggestion that her daughter marry Gilbert and reside at Delgatie Castle and as the young people got to know each other again, William and Alice discussed plans. Alice's father had left a goodly sum for her dowry which had been confirmed in his will.

At the end of the day, William asked Gilbert if he was happy to offer for Alicia's hand. His response was a relief to William. Gilbert was quite taken with Alicia and was happy to take her as his wife.

Whilst they were talking, Alice was telling Alicia of their proposals.

Alicia was aware of her duty but more than this; she liked Gilbert. He was an intelligent man and had delightful manners. She knew her marriage would be a good match for her and her agreement was not necessary but she was happy to accept the proposal.

❧❧

Their marriage was swiftly blessed with two sons, William and Gilbert who loved to romp around the castle grounds; a pleasure only possible at Slains Castle under close supervision. Gilbert's grandfather, Thomas Hay, had had a great deal of restoration work carried out at Delgatie Castle which had been badly damaged by Robert Bruce's men during the Harrying of Buchan. It was now a comfortable home as well as being strongly defensive. Being inland, Delgatie was less exposed to the weather than Slains Castle and Sir William spent time with them whenever he could in order to avoid the haar and the cutting wind on the coast.

Gilbert was concerned that his father seemed frailer each time they met and prepared himself for the fact that he might soon step into his father's shoes. His sons were growing fast and he was negotiating with James Douglas 7th Earl of Douglas to take them into his household at Abercorn Castle in Linlithgowshire, to train as pages and then stewards. Gilbert admired Douglas' record in deputising for his brother when he had been held captive after the Battle of Homildon Hill in 1402 and believed he would be a good role model for his sons. Douglas wanted to increase the status of his family and links with the Hays would be useful indeed.

The placement was agreed and Sir William and Margaret set off for Delgatie to see their grandsons before they left for Abercorn Castle. William was well clothed against the weather but his chest troubled him none the less. With them, they took two highland ponies as gifts for the boys.

On their arrival at Delgatie Castle, Sir William and Lady Margaret were greeted by the boys rushing out to meet them. When they showed them the ponies which they had brought the boys could not wait to show their father.

'What are their names?' young William asked.

'That is for you to decide,' his grandfather told him.

'I'm going to call mine Tempest!' declared William after a moment's consideration.

'Mine will be called Jester,' his brother decided.

Gilbert stepped out to meet his parents and thanked them heartily for coming and for the ponies. Telling his sons to lead them to the stables and to ask the groom to show them how to care for them he turned back to his father. In their excitement, young William and Gilbert begged their father and grandfather to come with them and watch them brush their new mounts. The men happily agreed, taking the opportunity to compare news as they walked.

Arriving at the stable, they saw that the blacksmith was at work and young Gilbert asked him to look at his pony's shoes for him. Smiling indulgently Sir William nodded to the smith. As young Gilbert led his pony across, a spark from the forge flew into the air. Gilbert's pony whinnied and shied. His father stepped back to avoid the animal's feet and yelped with pain. He had stood on a discarded nail from a shoe which the smith had taken from another horse. Sitting on a nearby bench, he pulled out the offending nail and removed his fine leather shoe to see what damage had been done. As Margaret overcame her shock, she took Gilbert's foot in her hand to see the wound. 'There is not too much blood but the nail has penetrated quite deeply into his foot,' she reported. He replaced his damaged shoe but the pain was enough to make him limp back to the castle and sit down. Hot water was brought to bath his foot and an ointment to soothe it. Although the wound throbbed he assured his family that he was not badly hurt.

Satisfied that there was no real harm done, the boys gathered around their grandfather to hear stories of his battles and dealings with the king.

The following day, Gilbert took his sons, as planned, to Abercorn Castle and handed them into the care of James Douglas. The rotund figure seemed quite fatherly to the boys so although they were on their best behaviour and knew that strict obedience was expected of them, they were not afraid when, a few days later, their father bade them farewell and left.

By the time Gilbert arrived back at Delgatie Castle he was feeling stiff and felt feverish. His throat felt tight and he felt sure he was suffering from an ague. Alice insisted that he go to his bed and gave orders for an infusion to be prepared. She would not let the servants help him and insisted on tending him herself in spite of his protests that it might be contagious.

When Alice realised that his condition was worsening, she called upon Lady Margaret to advise her. Time after time they replaced the bed sheets as they became soaked with sweat. Alice tried to feed him with broth and give him sips of water but it was becoming increasingly difficult for him to swallow. Gilbert was becoming delirious and nothing which they could do seemed to help.

Lady Margaret slipped from the room and found William. Sharing her fears with him she asked him to send for the priest as she believed their son to be close to death.

The priest came with all haste and administered the Last Rites as Sir William and Lady Margaret stood holding each other whilst Alice sat at her husband's side, holding his hand. As the priest turned from the bed Gilbert's throat rattled with the sound of death and he breathed no more.

Distraught, Alice sobbed and threw herself onto his body. He had been a good husband for the short time they had been married and she loved him dearly.

Sir William and Lady Margaret could not believe that their only son was dead. Just a few days ago he had been hale and hearty, laughing with his children and looking forward to organising more building at the castle. Now he was gone, leaving his seven-year-old son as his grandfather's heir.

Abbot William at Coupar Angus expressed his sympathy to Gilbert's wife, Alice and his parents when they arrived with his body for burial. The brothers chanted the requiem mass and Gilbert was laid to rest with his ancestors.

The abbey bell continued to toll as they left the church building and made their way, with the Abbot to his house.

As generous benefactors of the abbey, the Hays were always welcome guests there. Sir William knew that it would not be long before he joined his son and was sure to make a generous gift of land and money and arrange for a suitable tomb to be carved for his son before they left to return to Delgatie Castle with Alice. Her sons had joined them for the funeral but must now return to Abercorn Castle to continue their training with James Douglas.

When William returned to Slains to mourn his son's death, he was greeted by a messenger who had ridden hard to tell him that King James was laying siege to Roxburgh Castle which was held by the English. William was required to go immediately to support the king and bring as many men as possible with him.

William immediately set about preparing to support the king. He gathered men and weapons, horses and supplies and set out with as much speed as could be made but even so, the journey took over a week and by the time they arrived the siege had failed.

The strain of the journey in the hot August weather took its toll on Sir William, who, on his return to Slains, was confined to bed with exhaustion.

CHAPTER 17

In 1436, King James and his court went to celebrate Christmas at his residence at Blackfriars in Perth. Sir William Hay, as Constable, was amongst the guests but aware that he was also responsible for the king's safety. They were still there on the evening of 21st February and James was enjoying a lively evening with his fellows. He had supper about nine o'clock after which most of his attendants retired but the king stayed up a little longer to enjoy some music and singing.

Sir William retired to his chamber. The evening had been long and had taken its toll on him. No sooner had he donned his nightshirt and lay down than he was asleep than a shadowy figure silently crept out of the darkness. Before William was even awake he was struck over the head. Bound hand and foot and with a gag in his mouth, William struggled even to breathe, much less call out a warning.

At midnight, the King called for a parting cup before going through to the bed chamber where the Queen and her ladies were talking. James changed into his nightgown and slippers and, placing himself in front of the fire, joined in their banter.

Suddenly there were the sounds of armed men in the passage outside. The Royal party hurried to push the bar through the brackets that secured the door, but it was missing, removed by Robert Stewart, the King's treacherous nephew. One of the Queen's ladies, Catherine Douglas, put her arm through the brackets while the King used a poker, which he found in the fireplace, to lever up some floorboards so as to slip below into a cellar that doubled as a sewer. Normally he would have been able to crawl through to safety, but the drain had been blocked a few days earlier. The boards were replaced hiding the king before the assassins burst into the chamber, breaking Catherine's arm.

They threatened the Queen and her attendants but could find no sign of the King. They searched the chamber throwing chairs about and throwing open a kist. When they did not find him they went on to other rooms in the palace. Assuming that the silence above meant that the danger had passed, James called out for assistance in escaping from his refuge. The killers heard his cries and returned to the bedchamber where they found the king with his hands braced on the edges of the floor boards trying to lift himself out. He ducked back into the cellar desperately looking for an escape route. Two of them went down after him. In the confined space, the King took one by the throat and tried to wrest the knife from his hands. A thud behind him told of the arrival of Sir Robert Graham who joined the attack and the King was finally dispatched, receiving 16 stab wounds to his body. The conspirators fled. It was not until hours later that Sir William was discovered, as his attacker had left him, and untied.

The conspirators hoped for the queen's support but they had misjudged her and she immediately set about finding her husband's murderers. Within a month the young King James II was crowned and the leaders were caught. As punishment for his attack against the crown, the Earl of Atholl had a red-hot coronet placed on his head before he and his son were beheaded; Robert Stewart was tortured to death.

Sir Robert Graham was found cowering beneath a rock above Blair Atholl. He was captured by the Chief of Clan Donnachaidh and carried through the streets of Edinburgh in a cart, naked, with his right hand nailed to an upright post, and surrounded by men who, with sharp hooks and knives and red hot irons, kept constantly tearing at and burning his body, until he was completely covered with wounds. The following day he was forced to watch his son being disembowelled alive before suffering the same fate and his body quartered.

The young King James was taken to Dunbar Castle to live with his mother and sisters until he was old enough to rule independently. Reeling from the events which had occurred, just a week after returning to Slains Castle, Sir William Hay rode out to visit his tenants at Furvie. As he dismounted his head reeled and he stumbled backwards. The farmer he was visiting reacted swiftly and grabbed at William's tunic preventing him from falling to the ground. 'Pardon me, My Lord,' said the man bowing and stepping back swiftly, afraid that he had offended his laird by touching his fine garments. But as he looked at William he realised that he was unwell and putting an arm around him he supported him into his house, ducking as he helped him in through the low doorway.

Having only stools to sit on and realising that the Laird could not sit unaided, he lay him down on his bed which was within a cupboard at the end of the room with a shabby curtain across to keep the draughts at bay. In the gloomy light which struggled through the shuttered windows, he could see that William needed help.

As he struggled with the question of whether to stay with his master or go for help he heard a voice and raced to the door. A loon was coming up the lane chatting to his dog as he walked. 'Here lad!' he called in anguish, 'Take this horse and ride to Slains Castle. Tell them the Laird is in need of help.' The loon looked at him as if he were mad. 'Tac the laird's horse?' he questioned. 'I canna dae tha, I'd be skelped!'

'I'll skelp ye masel if ye dinna! The Laird's dyin' so dinna argie!' And with that, he grabbed the loon by the back of his neck and dragged him towards the horse almost lifting him into the saddle.

The lad drove his heels into the horse's flanks and rode as fast as he could, looking back over his shoulder at the farmer.

Arriving at Slains Castle he dropped from the horse calling for help. The castle people were wide eyed to see a loon riding Sir William's fine horse and shouting at the top of his voice. A squire appeared and grabbed his arm. 'What is the meaning of this? How did you come by Lord Hay's horse? Where is he?'

The boy spluttered out his reply cowering lest he should receive a blow for his troubles.

Realising that there must be some truth in the boy's words, the squire called instructions to send help and taking the horse himself, dragged the boy up in front of him to show the way.

Turning the horse around he rode with all haste to find William.

When they reached the cottage the farmer emerged apologising for having taken his laird into such a humble home and spluttering an explanation of what had happened. The squire placed a hand on his shoulder and reassured him.

When the farmer led him inside it took a few moments for his eyes to adjust to the darkness. As objects began to appear in the gloom he made out the bed and stepped towards it. William was very still and his breathing was shallow. He took his hand and felt the cold dampness of it. 'Bring wine,' he ordered. 'I hae nae wine,' apologised the man, 'I can fesh water.'

Realising how foolish his request had been the squire nodded his thanks. He took the water which was offered and moistened William's lips with it, afraid to let him drink it for fear of it being unclean.

As he heard horses approach, he went to the doorway to meet the riders and quickly explaining their laird's condition he led them inside. Lady Margaret swept into the cottage and approached her husband. The farmer brought a stool for her to sit but before he could offer it she had taken William's hand and let out a cry of dismay. His hand was cold and the stillness of death could be felt.

Falling across his body she wept.

William had succumbed to his ailments and was laid to rest with his son and ancestors.

CHAPTER 18

The young William Hay was just nine years old when his father died. His cousin, Edmund Hay of Leys, was appointed as his guardian and he was to go, with his brother, into Edmund's household. The boys were sorry to be moving away as they had settled at Abercorn Castle and knew the family and servants well. With eleven children in the family in addition to William and Gilbert, there were always ways to find entertainment and other boys to practice combat skills with.

James Douglas also had four daughters and William particularly liked Lady Beatrix who was quite accomplished for her age and fun to be with. Her long flaxen hair, plaited at the sides, ran freely down her back framing her heart shaped face and accenting her gentleness. He well remembered the time she had come to him cradling a wounded bird in her hands and begging his help. There was nothing to be done for the creature but she had tried to nurse it and wept bitterly when it died.

As the boys grew they both became skilled riders and swordsmen. Their uncle was a strict but fair master who praised their efforts but would accept no slacking.

Two years later, with the death of the Douglas regent, Sir Alexander Livingston of Callendar imprisoned King James' mother and her new husband in Stirling Castle, only releasing them when he was given custody of the king until he became of age.

William was shocked by the news brought to Erroll by a messenger from Edinburgh. Crighton and Livingstone who were joint regents with William, 6th Earl of Douglas until James, were furious at the power which the Douglases were gaining. They had invited Douglas to a meal at Edinburgh Castle.

During the meal, a black bull's head, the symbol of death was brought in and in the presence of the young king they had carried out a brief trial before convicting William Douglas and his young brother, David of high treason and beheading them within the castle precincts. People, the messenger reported, had already begun to call it the Black Dinner.

William had become very fond of James Douglas and to hear of the death of two of his great nephews in such a dreadful manner made the young William angry. His family's connections with the Douglases went back to before the Battle of Bannockburn. They had fought side by side in many battles since and were great friends.

William immediately requested that his uncle take him to see James Douglas to offer his condolences.

His arrival was greeted with relief by Douglas and his family. Their grief was immeasurable and James declared that the Douglases would have their revenge. He raged to William that it was Crighton and Livingston who were responsible. He had heard that the young king had tried to protest but to no avail.

'I cannot accept that James believed them guilty of treason. He is but a boy. Those bastards have used the king and abused their power!'

William and his uncle stayed for a week before returning to Erroll. William took the opportunity to spend some time with Beatrix and realised that his affection for her had deepened.

He and his uncle, Edmund, returned to Erroll and were surprised soon after their arrival to receive a message from James Douglas. The title Earl of Douglas was to pass to him and, although the Lordships of Annandale and Bothwell were to be retained by the crown, the other Douglas estates were to be divided between him and the late earl's sister, Margaret. What more proof could be needed that the king did not believe the charge of treason?

⁓

Finally, the time came when William was old enough to take on his role independently. He returned to Slains as laird and was not long in gaining the respect of his people.

William gave his brother, Gilbert, Delgatie Castle which had undergone numerous changes and repairs in the years of their absence and was in an excellent location for controlling the more westerly parts of William's lands.

In taking up his duties as Constable of Scotland, he spent much time at the king's court and enjoyed the admiration of many. His charm, good looks and wealth made him an attractive proposition to many a young lady and more than one offered up her charms to him in the hope of advancement. The result of one relationship was the birth of a girl child who was to be named Beatrice. Although William had no intention of being trapped into marriage in this way, he did acknowledge her as his own and provided for both her and her mother.

Recalling the happy times he had had at Abercorn Castle William returned from time to time to renew his friendship with the Douglases.

He was saddened when he heard of James Douglas' death in March 1443. William and Gilbert recalled being awed by his size the first time they were committed into his care as children but grew to love and respect him and took time from their responsibilities to attend his funeral and express their condolences to his family. Douglas' 18-year-old son, William, was to become the 8th Earl of Douglas.

William's friendship with Lady Beatrix Douglas had always been special and some time after her father's funeral, William sought out her brother, William to ask for her hand in marriage. William Douglas was delighted, not only that his sister would be marrying the Constable of Scotland, but that his good friend would become his brother by law.

On being told of the arrangement made for her, Beatrix was less than enthusiastic. She had long admired William and found him very attractive, dreaming of his embrace and longing to be his bride, but she knew of his earlier relationships and worried that he would prove to be unfaithful and put her aside if another took his eye.

Boldly she faced him. 'Sir, your seeking my hand is an honour but will you always honour me?'

William was taken aback. 'What mean you madam?' he asked.

'There is another Beatrice in your life,' she declared, 'How can I be sure that you mean to be constant when your child gives evidence of your roaming eye?'

'I am neither priest nor monk nor eunuch,' grinned William, 'but when you are my wife I shall need no other woman as I am sure you will provide for my every need.'

Turning away to hide her blushes, Beatrix bowed her head.

'Does that answer your question?' asked her brother.

She turned coyly to look at William from under her lashes and nodded briefly. In two strides William crossed the room and scooped her into his arms gently brushing her lips with his before deepening his kiss until her body melted against his. By the time he lifted his head she was glad that his arms still held her lest she be unable to stand unaided.

'Well that seems to be settled,' laughed Douglas. 'Now we just need to discuss details.' Beatrix realised she was being dismissed and holding her head high she made a valiant effort to leave the chamber with dignity.

CRUST

William was becoming a well-respected nobleman both amongst his peers and in the eyes of the nobility. Livingston still controlled the king but saw fit to have him attend such an important noble's wedding. Much of William's time was spent at court and so his wedding to Beatrix was to be celebrated at Holyrood. The wedding breakfast at Edinburgh Castle saw many of the barons who were supporters of the king gathered together to celebrate the union and enjoy the lavish feast.

Festivities lasted several days and at their conclusion, William begged leave to take his bride to Slains and introduce her to his people and the castle.

The young king gladly agreed but bade William return to his court within the month. King James enjoyed his company and valued his counsel. William was bound to be at Holyrood for the king's marriage to Mary of Guelders in July 1449 and there was much to organise in preparation.

CRUST

The ceremony and feast at King James' wedding was spectacular with Lord William playing a major role. His robes of black velvet with gold trim and fur edging was second only to those of the king himself. He sat at the king's right hand during the feast and enjoyed the confidence and respect of many nobles.

When William was finally free to return to Slains and his wife, he found her to be expecting their first child. His joy knew no bounds and he fussed around her until she forbade him to do so. Laughing she told him that bearing children was natural and happened every day but they both knew that childbirth was a dangerous event and every woman who bore a child risked her life in doing so.

When her time came to be delivered, William strode around Slains Castle restlessly, barking at anyone who dared speak to him and cringing as he heard her cries.

Finally, he could bear it no longer and taking the stairs two at a time he raced to her chamber and burst through the door. The midwife was about to reprimand him as she stood with their newborn son in her arms but Beatrix hushed her and smiled at her husband. 'You have a son, Sir,' she greeted him.

Taking her in his arms he hugged her as tears raced down his cheeks. 'My beloved, Beatrix. We shall call him Nicholas.' They had spent many an evening discussing names and Nicholas was the one she had favoured. 'Thank you, my lord,' she said softly.

William was then chased from the room and grinning like a simpleton he stopped every person he met to tell them that he had a son. The people of Slains smiled and nodded indulgently. Some congratulated him and all were delighted when he announced that there would be whisky for all to celebrate the birth of his son.

Nicholas was swiftly followed by another son, William and daughter, Elizabeth.

Beatrix was becoming used to William's absence as much of his time was spent either visiting his lands or at the royal court. Sometimes she would accompany him but with a young family to care for and not caring to travel when she was pregnant, she more usually remained at Slains Castle.

Now the king had need of William's services again. It was February and the roads held many dangers. Not only the winter storms and frozen roads but the hungry beggars and outlaws who haunted the forests and hills. Travelling with guards and arrayed in expensive attire indicated wealth and made him a target for hungry men who had nothing to lose by attacking.

William was relieved when he arrived safely at Stirling Castle to meet the King. He was surprised, as he dismounted, to hear the approach of another party of wealthy travellers at the castle and turned to see that it was none other than William Douglas, his wife's brother. They greeted each other warmly and exchanged news of their families before, making their way into the castle, William Hay asked his brother by law what brought him to Stirling.

'The King's command,' came the reply with a wry smile. 'I fear that James has a grievance with me as he granted me safe conduct here.'

'Ah, the Stewart's fear that you become too powerful. You would do well no to make too great a show of wealth whilst you are here. A humble attitude will serve you well.' But William Douglas was not the man to fear to display his power or his wealth. He loved to discomfort others by flaunting his family's titles and power and although he was well favoured by King James, there were many who would be happy to see him dishonoured.

King James sent for William Hay as soon as he heard of his arrival. Greeting him warmly he asked after his family. 'Well, MacGaraidh Mor!' declared the king, 'You have served me well and deserve to be recognised for this. I have decided to make you an earl. What think you of that?' he asked slapping William on the back. 'We will, of course, celebrate this evening and then I believe you would like to take this news to your family. You may leave the court for a month but then I would have you return.'

'Thank you,' replied William bowing, 'My wife will be looking for my return. She will be brought to bed of our next child within the month.'

'Then if it be a boy we will drink his health,' laughed the king.

Whilst they spoke, William was aware that, in spite of his words, James seemed pre-occupied. Although he seemed well enough in health there was clearly something troubling him. William had long been a confidante of the king and felt close enough to James to speak freely.

'Your Highness, forgive my forthrightness but I feel that all is not well with you. Is there any way in which I may serve to relieve you of your burden?'

The King sat abruptly in his chair. His silence hung heavily in the air until he leapt to his feet.

'William Douglas!' cried the King. 'The man is a fool. I give him my ear, I give him power and wealth and the idiot ever looks for more. His enemies grow envious and accuse him of many grave deeds.'

'So this is why you have sent for him,'

'He is here?'

'Aye. He arrived moments after I did. Would you see him now?'

'Nae. The fool can stew a while. We will talk when we eat. Go and take your ease, William. You have had a long journey and will need to refresh.'

Acknowledging his dismissal, Lord Hay bowed and left the king's chamber. Making his way swiftly to seek out William Douglas, he advised him of the situation and warned Douglas yet again to curtail his displays of power and wealth.

William's warning fell on deaf ears and William Douglas' arrival for dinner was loud and proud. His attire outshone even that of the king himself and there were loud murmurs of anger and hatred. The king arrived accompanied by his steward and bade Lord Hay sit on his right hand and William Douglas on his left. Douglas glowered believing himself greater even that the Constable of Scotland.

Conversation during the meal was of land and families but gradually, Douglas could not resist referring to his power and acquisitions. The tone of the conversation grew heated and voices rose until the king abruptly stood and ordered all to leave save Hay and Douglas. The king indicated to two of his bodyguards to remain at their posts.

Breathing deeply and struggling to maintain his control, King James turned to face Douglas and bellowed at him.

'I have shown you great favour and yet you continue to plot against me!'

Douglas grew pale.

'You consort with John MacDonald, and Crawford to destroy me!'

Unrepentant, Douglas boldly faced the king. 'Who says this?' he demanded.

'You do not deny it!' roared James, his attempts at reason dissolving in his anger.

'Many envy me. They would seek my downfall and say much of me that they would have come to your ears.'

James seethed at Douglas' arrogant attitude. Taking Douglas by the throat he pinned him against the wall.

William Hay strode forward. 'Sire,' he said firmly, 'Douglas is a fool. Let him beg your forgiveness and assure you of his allegiance.'

Douglas looked at William in horror having no thought of begging forgiveness.

The king caught sight of Douglas' face and roared in anger. Snatching the dirk from his belt he thrust it into Douglas' belly.

Abruptly the king stood back letting go of Douglas' robe and letting his writhing body fall to the floor. Blood seeped out forming a pool and draining the colour from Douglas' face. He reached out a hand to William but as he did so the bodyguards pushed Hay aside and with brutal blows ruthlessly dispatched the wounded Douglas.

King James stood in horror for a moment. Douglas had been a close friend for many years and his plan had been to reason with the man who now lay dead at his feet.

Recovering his composure the king turned and strode from the room leaving the guards to remove Douglas' body.

William Hay was shocked at what he had witnessed. As Lord High Constable of Scotland and therefore Chief Judge of the High Court of Constabulary, William had the power to judge cases of bloodshed and murder which occurred within four miles of the king but when the offender was the king himself and William had witnessed the deed he could not be called upon to sit.

❧❧

Having dealt with the aftermath of the evening's events, William was preparing to retire for the night when an urgent knocking on his door was answered by his steward. A liveried messenger stood imperiously at the door.

'The King commands your presence in his privy chamber immediately,' he declared.

William looked at his steward and shrugged before following the messenger.

When they arrived at the king's chamber the messenger tapped lightly and responded to the command to enter. William followed him into the room. The king indicated a chair and instructed William to sit before dismissing the messenger with orders that they were not to be disturbed.

James strode across the room three times before stopping before William and declaring, 'You saw it all. His behaviour was treasonous. I faced him with his plotting against me and he did not even attempt to deny it.' The king knew the strength of the Douglases and feared that his actions would serve them as justification for rousing others to challenge his kingship.

William did not answer immediately. His hesitancy distressed the king and his agitation grew as William got to his feet and stood face to face with James.

'Sire,' he began, 'William Douglas has been your friend for many years and served you well. He was brother to my wife and I knew him to be a good man.'

He paused and the young king found that he had been holding his breath. Now he sucked in air in response to the answer he perceived William to be giving but before he could give way to the storm of his response, William continued. 'But Douglas did not deny your accusations and had grown bold in his actions. There may have been some truth in the stories of his accusers. The important issue is that he did not deny your accusations.'

'As ever you give me good counsel, William. I loved Douglas well but he has betrayed me and suffered the consequences of his actions.

I bid you good night William.'

Recognising his dismissal, William returned to his chamber and in thoughtful silence allowed his steward to prepare him for his bed. He lay awake contemplating the night's events. He had sworn allegiance to the king and knew that many nobles plotted and conspired against him. He also knew that, in spite of some barons changing allegiance to support the king, the Douglases were growing too powerful for the king's comfort. And yet James loved William Douglas and had shown him many favours. The king's struggle to control the nobility of Scotland was becoming an impossible task. Perhaps his actions tonight would help to rein them in.

Whatever else came of the night's events, William Hay had lost a friend and would have to break the news to his wife that her brother was dead at the king's hand.

News of William Douglas' death stunned the court. Courtiers whispered in shadowy corners and serving girls huddled together to discuss the stories which were reaching them.

Douglas' brother was furious when he heard of William's death and raged to any who would listen. Finally, demonstrating the fearless confidence which the Douglases felt, he took the Safe Passage which had been given to William and rode through Stirling dragging it through the mud behind his horse.

Soon after Elizabeth's birth, William had been recalled by the King as a supporter of Alexander Seaton, 1st Earl of Huntly, who had been elevated to the office of Lieutenant-General of the North to oppose Alexander, 3rd Earl of Crawford. Crawford was seeking to avenge the death of the Earl of Douglas at the king's hands and was a threat to the king's peace. Huntly was to confront Crawford but William was to remain at Stirling with the king.

Huntly's forces outnumbered those of Crawford when they met on a level muir in the north east of Brechin but none the less the battle was undecided for some considerable time until Collossie of Bonnymoon, who had been upset during a conversation with Crawford the previous night, changed sides and went to support Huntly. Despite Crawford's best efforts, his men were dismayed by this defection and fled in all directions.

Huntly had lost two of his sons and five barons and during his absence, Archibald Douglas had devastated Strathbogie.

Crawford's brother and almost sixty men of rank along with many more of his men were slain whilst he himself fled to Finhaven. Railing against his defeat, Crawford swore that he would willingly take seven years roasting in hell to have the honour of such a victory as had that day fallen to Huntly. Infuriated at Huntly plundering the county of Moray, and razing Elgin to the ground, he attacked the estates of those who had refused to fight with him, blaming them for his defeat and taking them and their families as his prisoners.

The rivalry and power struggles between the nobles continued and King James was determined that it must stop, both for the good of Scotland and to establish his own control. On coming of age, one of his first acts had been to imprison Sir Alexander Livingston and forfeit his lands and he intended to continue to act to restrain the power of the nobles and restore the power of the throne.

For now, unrest amongst the barons continued. King James sought council from William who suggested that gaining the allegiance of Douglas' supporters would weaken him and strengthen the king's position. This could be done with gifts of land and positions of power. William's judgement was correct and those who had benefited in this way turned to the king.

❧⋆❧

The king retained William at Stirling for the next four months until Parliament sat on 12th June. William was torn between wanting to be with his wife and comfort her for the loss of her brother and wanting to keep the dreadful news from her, knowing that she would soon be giving birth to their next child and wishing to spare her the distress at this time. However, he had no choice but to obey the king's command which was tempered by James' disclosing to William that he was to be elevated to the rank of Earl in recognition of his sound counsel, whilst Sir William de Borthwick was to be made Lord Borthwick.

Knowing that Beatrix would never forgive him if she were not there to witness the ceremony, William decided to send for her and tell her of her brother's death himself. He sent a fine carriage and fifty knights to collect her from Slains Castle with orders not to tell her anything of events.

Beatrix was surprised to hear the group arriving unexpectedly and thought to find William in their midst. When she heard that she was to travel to Stirling Castle to join him and bring her finest robes she became excited to be visiting the royal court. Her maids carefully packed her robes, placing padding between them to prevent creasing and carefully rolling the most delicate items.

Eventually, all was made ready and Beatrix climbed into the carriage with two of her maids. Guards rode either side of her carriage and the party set off at a sedate pace in recognition of her delicate condition. The party stopped to rest at Erroll and William's people took great care to see that Beatrix was rested and well cared for before she continued her journey. The women folk fussed over her and delighted in discussing the forthcoming birth.

The latter part of the journey being somewhat shorter, they arrived at Stirling Castle by early evening. A messenger had been sent ahead to tell William of their approach and he was waiting in the courtyard as the party approached.

Stepping up to the carriage, William held out his hands to assist Beatrix in alighting. Although he was delighted to see her arrive safely, she knew from his demeanour that all was not well. After his initial greeting, William offered his arm to his wife and led her into the castle and straight to his chamber.

'What has happened?' she asked immediately. 'There is something amiss.'

Taking her hands in his, William led her to a chair and gently urged her to sit.

'There is something which I must tell you that I did not wish you to hear from another's lips.'

'What so dreadful that you must tell me yourself?'

'When I arrived at Stirling I met your brother, William. He was here at the king's command.'

'I must see him. It is long since we spent time together.'

'Please, Beatrix, let me finish.' She leant back and looked into his eyes as he continued.

'The king had heard of William's dealings with John MacDonald and the Earl of Crawford. He tried to reason with William but the man was an arrogant fool and pushed the king's patience to breaking point. My love, I must tell you that your brother was a victim of his own power-seeking and arrogance. He challenged the king's authority and would challenge for his throne. In his fury, James stabbed him and his guards dispatched him.'

Beatrix gasped, her hand flying to cover her mouth as she desperately struggled to draw breath. Seeing her distress, William drew her into his embrace and held her hoping to comfort her until her sobs subsided but he became aware that her distress was such that she could not draw breath and bellowed for her maids to enter. Rushing into the chamber, Beatrix' ladies loosened her clothing and fanned her to no avail until one drew back her hand and, to William's horror, slapped Beatrix sharply across the face. The shock broke her panic and she drew in a gasping breath. As the ladies fussed to calm and sooth their lady, William stood aside feeling helpless. Suddenly Beatrix doubled in pain. Her ladies were horrified to realise that the shock of the news had brought on her labour. Behind cupped hands, they whispered that it was too soon. The child was not due and would be too early.

William was ushered from the room and a midwife sent for.

The child was a boy. He survived the delivery but was small and weak being not yet ready to be thrust into the world. Beatrix suffered, not only from the childbirth but her distress at the news of her brother's death. She asked for William who came immediately and knelt by her bed. He tried to comfort her with words of hope for the child and regret that he had been unable to save her brother's life. Beatrix reassured him that she didn't blame him for William's death and thanked him for his thoughtfulness in ensuring that she did not hear the news from another.

The baby lived but was so frail that it was decided to baptise him as soon as possible. The king suggested it be done at Stirling as neither the child nor its mother were strong enough to undertake a journey, no matter how short. Gilbert was to be his name in honour of William's brother.

❧⚮❧

On 12th June 1452 the king fulfilled his promise to elevate William Hay to Earl. Red robes trimmed with ermine were provided for William and matching bonnet which was bejewelled with precious stones and embroidered with spangles. The ceremony was attended by powerful barons from throughout Scotland, some true to the king and others known to be supporters of the Douglases. King James wished to show his people how highly he regarded those who supported him and reward William for his true and wise counsel. He hoped that this would in some way discourage the Douglases from their relentless plotting against him. In this, he was to be disappointed.

Following the ceremony, James assured William that he would give him a charter giving him the territorial Earldom of Erroll and Lordship of Slains as soon as his scribes had drawn it up. He would have it delivered to Slains as he knew William would be anxious to return with his wife and new son.

As soon as Beatrix was able to travel they prepared to leave Stirling Castle and she huddled in the carriage with Gilbert clutched to her. She still mourned the death of her brother and feared for the frail life of her new son. She longed to get home to care for him.

Their stop at Erroll was brief. William knew that his people would wish to celebrate his elevation and hear of the events which had occurred at Stirling and he would not disappoint them. They would not yet know of Gilbert's birth and the ladies would wish to fuss him but William was conscious of his wife's distress and kept their stay to a minimum but left behind a substantial quantity of whisky for the celebrations.

As promised, the king sent a messenger to Slains the very next month bearing William's charter. William invited him to join them at dinner and took the opportunity to speak with him about events at Stirling Castle since he had returned home.

❧

The following year Beatrix gave birth to twin daughters, Isabelle and Margaret who were both strong and healthy but Gilbert continued to be a sickly infant and did not thrive as the others did. His mother kept him close and fussed over him, keeping him indoors and ordering cook to prepare simple dishes for him, yet, in spite of her efforts, she knew he was fading.

Before he reached his third birthday Gilbert was confined to bed. Every hour Beatrice would creep up to his cot to watch and see if he was still breathing and sit by his side rocking and crooning. He lasted but a month before his little body gave up the struggle to survive. His parents were distraught. Many a child died in infancy but it did not make it any easier to bear. They wept and comforted each other as they mourned his loss. So many times Beatrice would think she heard his voice and turn to find he was not there. In her dreams she would see him playing with the wooden cart which the carpenter had made for him; she would turn to speak to him and realise he was not there. She felt she would never get over the loss but as time went by the hurt began to heal. She could not say she got over his death; she never would, but with time it became easier to bear and was eased somewhat by the birth of their sons Nicholas and William.

William was a well-respected man, both by his friends and others. Even those who did not share his allegiance to the king could see that he was a just and honest man and many came to give their Bond of Manrent to him. He spent as much time as he could with his family but his duties and his land often took him away. He bought the lands of Petilyel and others adjoining his land at Erroll, sharing his fortune with family members and advancing his brother.

Just as William and his brother Gilbert had been trained, firstly as pages and then as squires, by Douglas, his sons, Nicholas and William went to the Earl of Huntly and their older sister, Beatrice was sent with them to be brought up as a lady, whilst avoiding embarrassment to William's wife. Huntly had now adopted his mother's name of Gordon rather than Seaton when he inherited his grandmother's lands in Aberdeenshire and he was now a very wealthy man.

As Earl of Erroll, there were many noble families who sought William's daughters' hands in marriage but of all the suitors he favoured the Gordons and during their early years the two families became close. In due course, the young Beatrice was betrothed to Alexander Gordon, Huntly's son by Egida Hay. His parent's marriage had been annulled thereby rendering him illegitimate as she was.

Alexander had developed a great affection for Beatrice in spite of her being base born and he swore that he would have no other bride than her. She was five years his elder and he had worshipped her from his earliest memory. His father, having a great affection for Alexander and also in the knowledge that William would settle a great dowry on his daughter, gave way to his son's demands. Beatrice knew that the marriage was a good one and had a liking for young Alexander so was happy to comply and thanked her father for providing such a fine dowry for her.

William wanted nothing more than to be with Beatrix but a summons from the king could not be ignored. The Douglases continued to grow in power and to be a threat to King James. He had been at war with them for years taking lands from them only to return them later. Many saw this as weakness and the time had arrived for James to establish his authority or risk assassination. William was ordered to rally the king's forces and see them assembled for battle.

Beatrix sobbed as he rode away; her maid-servant supporting her for fear that she collapse. A potion was sent for to sedate her as she was led to her chamber and was helped onto her bed to rest.

❧

The king's forces under George Douglas, head of the Red Douglas family, and William Hay met James Douglas' supporters at Arkinholm. William was surprised to find that both combatants had very limited numbers of men yet it was to prove to be the decisive battle in a civil war between the king and the Black Douglases. The king had already taken the Black Douglases castle at Abercorn and their supporters, the Hamiltons, had defected.

James Douglas himself headed to England to seek support for his army; his brother Archibald Douglas, Earl of Moray was slain in the battle and his head presented to the king, while Hugh Douglas, Earl of Ormonde was seized and executed. John Douglas, Lord of Balvenie fled south.

The Black Douglases were finished and James destroyed Abercorn Castle as a sign that their power was ended.

In the aftermath of the battle, the lordship of Douglas along with the original possessions of his ancestors in Douglasdale were given to George Douglas, 4th Earl of Angus

CHAPTER 19

In 1457, when he was eight years old, Nicholas Hay was contracted to marry Margaret, Huntly's daughter. Margaret was several years his elder but as Huntly's eldest daughter William Hay saw her as the perfect match for his son and heir. Nicholas was furious. He had never seen eye to eye with Margaret and as she was Huntly's natural born child he did not think her worthy to become his wife. The marriage would not take place until he was a little older but the boy nursed his resentment of the match and was determined that the marriage would never take place.

Alexander Gordon, Earl of Huntly, was ambitious and how better to improve his family's wealth and status than to find an advantageous marriage for his son and heir, George Gordon. George was married by contract to the wealthy heiress Elizabeth Dunbar, daughter of the Earl of Moray and widow of Archibald Douglas. As she had been joint heiress of her father, Huntly saw her as an attractive match.

A papal dispensation had to be attained for their marriage to take place because they were related within the forbidden degrees but in spite of it being granted and the marriage taking place, the attraction rapidly faded when the opportunity arose to make a match with Annabella Steward, daughter of the late King James I and former wife of Louis of Savoy, Count of Geneva. A divorce from Elizabeth was arranged and at eighteen, George found himself married to Annabella.

The wedding was a splendid affair. Alexander Gordon wanted the Scottish barons to see the importance of his family and marrying his son to a princess gave them considerable status. No expense was spared and the gathering extended to over a thousand guests. The king himself, the bride's brother, was present and William Hay, Earl of Erroll was seated beside him. Many of Erroll's family accompanied him and his son Nicholas was seated beside Margaret Gordon whom he was contracted to marry. With childish pique, he pointedly ignored her and made play of enjoying conversation with those around him until his eye fell on Elizabeth, Margaret's younger sister. Elizabeth had grown into a young lady of remarkable beauty and had a ready wit. Even at his tender age, Nicholas had an eye for a pretty girl and during the evening he monopolised her, glaring at any other young men who approached her and pointedly avoiding Margaret.

In 1460 William's death was a shock to all who knew him. Apparently in good health, he left Slains bidding farewell to Beatrix and leaving orders for work to be carried out in the castle in his absence. He set out with his squire, Logan, a young man of serious countenance and steady confidence. With them went a number of knights and retainers, to attend the King who had sent orders for troops to be gathered to support him in England. Chatting cheerily as they travelled, the group were taken by surprise when William suddenly slumped forward in his saddle and lurched sideways to hang, head down over his horse's neck. Most of the group were stunned into immobility but Logan leapt from his horse to attend his master. 'Help me get him down!' he ordered as the men sat stupefied.

Spurred into action they rushed to remove William's feet from his stirrups and lower him to the ground. He was still breathing but not conscious. The left side of his mouth seemed to droop and he was quite unresponsive. It was decided that the best course was to return to Slains Castle where his own people could care for him.

Arriving at the gatehouse late into the night, Logan hammered on the door with his fists.

'Hold fast,' came a voice, 'we will not admit rowdy men.'

'You will admit the Earl of Erroll!' declared Logan. His words were met with a gasp and the sound of the gate being hurriedly un-barred.

Seeing that the earl was ill, the gatekeeper immediately sent for help and William was carried up to his chamber.

Beatrix was almost swept off her feet as Nicholas and William raced past her with little Elizabeth calling after them. Their boisterous play was a joy to her but a worry as they broke free of their nurse and scampered too close to the steep stairs in the castle. She had not looked to see the return of the party, who left with her husband, for some weeks and was shocked when she heard familiar voices in the court-yard. Her first thought was that a section of the party had been sent back to fetch some forgotten item.

Fear struck her heart when silence fell over the ostlers who raced forward to take the horses. Something was wrong.

Almost tumbling down the stairs, Beatrix tried to retain some semblance of dignity as she rushed to discover what had happened.

She reached the courtyard and stopped in her tracks. Her eyes met those of William's squire and registered the sadness there. Her hand flew to her mouth. The silence seemed to last an eternity before a wail broke the air. Starting as a thin keening it grew in strength and volume, rising to a scream as nobody denied her fears. Tears coursed down her cheeks and she stood rocking and wailing. Her maid, Shona, arrived at her side and held her in her arms. The children, who had appeared in the doorway, stood silently, shocked to witness their mother's distress. Their nurse gathered them with her arms and bustled them away, Elizabeth crying and reaching out for her mother's comforting arms.

Beatrix fought back her tears and examined William. She shook her head with tears in her eyes. 'I have never seen aught like this,' she declared. 'I don't know what is to be done for him.' Her words broke on a sob and her lady's maid took her in her arms. 'We will send for the Wise Woman,' she said.

'That witch?' asked a shocked servant.

Those gathered were horrified, some at the thought of their beloved master being treated by a witch and others at the woman who was so skilled in healing being referred to in such a way. All feared the power of witches but most knew that they needed the skills of the Wise Woman when they fell sick or wounded.

'Fetch her,' ordered Beatrix, 'She is our best hope if William is to recover.'

Logan fled the chamber and raced down the turnpike stairs to do Beatrix' bidding. He bellowed to the guards to get a boat ready and accompany him to fetch the Wise Woman. Holding a lantern aloft, the men hauled the small craft into the sea and dragged the oars to find their places in the rowlocks. Pulling as hard as they could they sped the boat towards Whinnyfold.

Within the hour they returned. The wise woman lifted her skirts as she stepped out of the boat and waded ashore, indicating to the men to bring her basket of herbs and jars of potions. They had told her of their lady's distress and she had added calming herbs and poppy juice to her basket.

They entered William's chamber to find Beatrix on her knees, weeping at his bedside. He still had not woken, nor shown any sign of recovery.

After a brief examination, the Wise Woman slowly stood upright and announced, 'I could bleed him but it would be to no avail. The problem lies within his head and cannot be repaired.'

William's people were shocked. 'We can't just do nothing!' declared Beatrix. Murmurs of agreement came from the others.

'I have seen cases like this before,' the woman told them. 'Bleeding is to no avail. Sometimes there is a degree of recovery but always there is damage. We do not know why but one side of the body or the other is affected. More rarely both but in these cases, the victim often does not regain consciousness. I have studied much and talked with those who have travelled far and seen doctors perform an operation to treat similar conditions but it is dangerous and I have never carried out such an operation myself.'

'But you have seen it done?'

'Nay, I have only heard of it.'

'Is there aught else that can be done?'

'No.'

'Then you must try.'

The woman bowed her head and stood in silence for what seemed an eternity.

'I have never done this operation. I am not a surgeon. You'd best send to the abbey and ask for the infirmarian to come and help. We will let him rest until tomorrow.'

'Should we not take him to the abbey?' asked Beatrix.

'He should not be moved,' replied the old woman. 'It is best that the brother is brought here.'

Logan insisted he be the one to ride to the abbey and set off immediately in spite of the sun not yet having risen.

His arrival at the abbey caused a stir; the brother porter being surprised at his arrival wearing the Hay arms but unexpected. The good brother was elderly and struggled to open the gates with haste in order to admit him. Hearing the noise, others of the community had approached to discover the cause of the uproar and it was not long before Brother Gilbert, infirmarian at the abbey was standing before them. He beckoned Logan to follow him as he rushed towards the infirmary.

'I will prepare the instruments that I will need and discuss the procedure with Brother Paul who will assist me. And, of course, I will need permission from the Abbot. But, in the meantime, he is dangerously ill and for the sake of his immortal soul we must administer the Last Rites.' With this, he led Logan across the cloister.

Having prepared his pack, Brother Gilbert led Logan towards the Abbot's house. Seeking an audience he spoke to the prior explaining the need for him to go to the aid of their benefactor, William Hay.

The prior, a lean figure who jealously guarded his access to the abbot, pursed his thin lips whilst considering before he knocked softly on a door and, receiving a muffled response, opened the door just enough to slip through and close it behind him. Time stretched out as Logan and Brother Gilbert awaited his return, but when he finally emerged from the abbot's chamber they were relieved to be told that permission was granted to attend the stricken William.

Horses were hurriedly prepared for them and they set off with all haste to return to Slains Castle where a lookout had been posted to herald their return. As soon as they had dismounted, the men were rushed to William's bedside, Brother Paul turning to retrieve the satchel which contained Brother Gilbert's medicaments.

Brother Gilbert greeted the Wise Woman with an inclination of his head. They had met before and he admired her skills as a herbalist and her courage to admit when she could not help.

He dismissed Beatrix and Logan from the room whilst he examined William and shook his head. When he had completed his examination he sought out Beatrix.

'My good Lady Erroll,' he began, 'Earl William is not suffering. He does not feel pain, neither can he hear or see. Although he yet breathes, his brain has ceased to function. I fear he will not recover. I am so sorry.'

Just after dawn, a long low moan stirred the castle's inhabitants as Beatrix witnessed William's last breath. His body lay still and as she threw herself across him willing him to live her moans turned to uncontrollable sobs

William's men were devastated. He was just thirty years old and had seemed perfectly healthy when they set off. Now their master was the young Nicholas who, at eleven years old, was now the Earl of Erroll.

The Wise Woman brought herbs to sedate Beatrix.

Opening the door to admit the Wise Woman, Shona permitted her to approach the sobbing figure on the bed. Sitting beside Beatrix, the woman placed her hand on the countess' back and gently rubbed. At the same time, she crooned a tuneless yet soothing sound. No words were spoken, yet, with time, Beatrix's sobs subsided and she was able to gasp out her husband's name.

'It's aw right hen,' crooned the wise woman as she offered a cup to her lips and gently tipped some of the contents onto her tongue. The poppy juice swiftly carried her into a blessed oblivion.

'Time eneugh fer her tae ken o' the laird's death when she has over the furst shock.'

It was through a mist that Beatrix heard the story of William's death. Thinking it to be a bad dream she shook her head to try to throw off the words. Gradually the poppy juice wore off and she emerged from her sleep enough to realise that it was true. William was dead.

Her maid passed her a cup of wine into which the wise woman had sprinkled soothing herbs to ease her through the trauma.

It was three days before Beatrix was able to leave her chamber and seek out her children to comfort them. With the resilience of youth, after the first shock in learning of their father's untimely death, Elizabeth had returned to her daily routine, the loss being beyond her understanding. William was subdued and welcomed their mother's comfort but Nicholas keenly felt his new role and was unsure if he should accept a mother's hugs and tears or stand alone and dignified.

⁂

The funeral of William Hay, first Earl of Erroll was spectacular.

Following his death, his body was put into a chamber and watched for three days. When preparations had been made the procession set out from Slains Castle led by twenty-five poor-ons carrying staffs with the Hay arms painted on buckram. They were followed by his lordship's master stabler riding on horseback in full armour carrying on a spear's point the colours of Erroll with gold fringing. Behind him came two lackeys in livery and coats of black velvet with crests of goldsmiths' work on the breast leading a horse covered with a rich foot-mantle. Three trumpeters followed and behind them came the Slains Pursuivant. The master of the household came next carrying the Constable's baton and he was leading four gentlemen carrying the arms of the Hay houses and a pinsell and standard which had painted on it the Earl's achievement. Eight trumpeters came next preceding a servant carrying a mace covered by black crisp. Next was William's steward carrying the Constable's robes of red velvet lined with gold silk with sleeves edged in ermine.

William's brother, Gilbert, followed carrying the Earl's sword and vest and was followed by his son bearing a gold coronet on a velvet cushion.

William's corpse was carried behind them in an oak casket covered with a black velvet mortcloth embroidered with his arms.

Many of William's cousins took the role of coffin bearers, taking turns due to the distance they had to travel.

A rich pail of black velvet was held above the coffin by four more cousins and was followed by innumerable barons, knights, esquires, gentlemen and burgesses conveying the corpse from Slains to Coupar Angus.

❧

Following a mass and a sermon by James Kennedy, Bishop of Dunkeld, William's coffin was carried to its burial place to be laid with his ancestors.

❧

Parliament decided to appoint Alexander Gordon and Sir Edmund Hay of Leys as guardians to Nicholas and Nicholas was to live with Alexander Gordon as squire at Strathbogie. His brother William would accompany him whilst his sisters remained at Slains Castle in the care of their mother.

The parting was a tearful one. Beatrix had lost so much and now her sons were to leave her. She took them into her chamber and spoke to them tenderly reassuring them of her love and reminding them to behave as was fitting for their rank. As she spoke the door burst open and the girls, who had escaped their nurse, tumbled into the room begging Nicholas and William not to go. Beatrix clutched them to her, wiping away their tears she tried determinedly to stem her own.

'We will sew fine shirts for Nicholas and William and at Christmas we shall visit them and take our gifts,' she promised. 'I will give you gold thread to use and they will be the finest shirts in Scotland.' The girls were somewhat mollified by this as they had never been permitted to use the expensive gold thread before and a visit to Strathbogie was to be looked forward to with great excitement.

Sir Edmund Hay of Leys arrived to accompany the boys on their journey and Nicholas sat proudly in the saddle, his horse caparisoned in his arms, as his standard bearer led the procession out of the gates. He had yet to understand the extent of his power and position but he revelled in the splendour of pageantry.

As he had prepared to mount, his mother had drawn a gold pin shaped like a falcon from the folds of her cloak and fastened it in his bonnet. 'It was your father's,' she told him and turned away to conceal her grief. Nicholas put his hand on the hilt of his sword to reassure himself and spurred his horse forward.

Their departure was abruptly halted by the arrival of a messenger who, by his dishevelled appearance, had ridden hard to deliver his news. Almost falling from his horse with exhaustion he blurted out, 'The king is dead!' Beatrix's hand flew to her mouth as she crossed herself with the other one.

'Bring the messenger into the castle,' commanded Beatrix. 'Fetch refreshments,' she directed the shocked castle dwellers and led the way into what had been William's chamber.

When he had recovered a little, the messenger revealed that King James, who had a great passion for artillery, had been leading the siege of Roxburgh Castle which was in the hands of the English. This is why he had sent to William Hay to supply troops. He was standing near one of his prized cannons and ordered it to be fired. The gun had exploded and the king was killed. His young son, now King James III, was but a seven-year-old child, leaving Scotland in danger of returning to the power struggles between barons which it had been torn apart by for so long before James brought them to heel. There was a stunned silence.

❦

The king was to be buried at Holyrood Abbey and the coronation of his son, King James III was to take place at Kelso Abbey. He was just nine years old and his mother aided by the aged Bishop Kennedy of St. Andrews, was to be regent.

Sir Edmund and Beatrix knew that it was essential that Nicholas attend both the funeral of the dead king and the coronation of the new one. It was decided that he should go with all haste to Erroll where tailors from Perth could be sent for to prepare robes which befitted his status as Constable of Scotland and Earl of Erroll. A suit of mourning would be required for the funeral. Black damask trimmed with ermine and a chaperon embroidered in silver for his head.

For the coronation, he was to be robed in red, bedecked with spangles and trimmed with the finest mink.

Whilst Nicholas and his party were en-route to Erroll, a rider approached at great speed. The guards drew their swords and Sir Edmund drew Nicholas into the cover of the forest, drawing his own weapon in readiness to protect the boy. As the rider drew close he gasped out, 'Sir Edmund, I bring news!'

Edmund urged his horse forward followed by Nicholas. 'What news, man?'

'Sir, the king has been taken prisoner at Linlithgow. Sir Alexander Boyd and his brother Robert have taken him to Edinburgh Castle with the support of the Flemings, Hepburns and Lindsays. The King was made to appear before Parliament and forced to state that they had acted on his approval. Robert Boyd has had himself appointed the king's guardian and has raised his son, Thomas, to the position of Earl of Arran. He plans to have Thomas married to the King's sister Mary.'

'By God he does!' exclaimed Sir Edmund. 'I must go to parliament immediately and represent Lord Erroll. I must try to stop Boyd and his cronies but I fear he will already have too much influence.'

Sir Edmund sent his manservant to prepare for his departure. He would take Nicholas with him to be left at Erroll in order that he might be fitted for his new clothes.

Sir Edmund was reluctant to leave so soon but knew that he must petition parliament against Boyd. He spent many hours closeted with Huntly discussing plans for the boys training and futures. They agreed that in a few years William should be sent to the Abbey at Coupar Angus to be trained for the church. Nicholas' future was more complex.

They had both observed Nicholas' behaviour towards his betrothed and Sir Edmund was concerned at pushing the boy into a marriage which he so clearly resented. He was also reluctant to have the boy wed to Margaret as she was Huntly's natural daughter. Much better he marry her half-sister, Elizabeth. Sir Edmund put his proposal to Huntly who was reluctant to withdraw from a contract which had been agreed with the boy's father, however, he decided to consider carefully before making a decision.

Having been summoned, the couple met in the doorway. Nicholas held the door open for Margaret as was expected of him and she flounced through sneering as she passed him. Huntly and Edmund looked at each other with concern. Although Nicholas followed Margaret into the room he stood facing his guardians and ignored her.

Huntly addressed Nicholas welcoming him to Strathbogie and explaining that he would be trained in the skills and duties which he would need as Earl of Erroll and Lord High Constable of Scotland. Margaret was instructed to obey her betrothed in any request he might make of her. She bowed her head in apparent obedience but looked sideways at Nicholas with hatred in her eyes as she did so. She had no intention of obeying this child!

When they were dismissed, Huntly and Edmond exhaled loudly. It was clear that neither Nicholas nor Margaret wished the match. Huntly was convinced and withdrew the contract from his desk giving it to Edmund to destroy. 'I shall have a new contract drawn up agreeing the betrothal of Nicholas to my daughter Elizabeth.'

The following day Nicholas was told of the decision and, although he merely acknowledged the arrangement in their presence, he was thrilled to be free of Margaret and betrothed to her comely and sweet-natured sister Elizabeth.

Elizabeth received the news with a clap of her hands before she stopped herself and took a more demure pose. She had secretly admired Nicholas in spite of his youth but he was betrothed to her elder sister and she had not dared to hope that this would change.

Beatrix was, in due course, told of the change of betrothal and greeted the news with the announcement that her hand had been sought by Arthur Forbes who had the king's permission to wed her. The wedding would take place within the year leaving Sir Edmund as sole guardian of her children.

Celebrations had been planned for the birth of Alexander Gordon's grandchild, Isabela, daughter of George Gordon and the princess Annabella Stewart. It was decided to make it a joint event to also celebrate the marriage contract of Nicholas and Elizabeth. The king and his mother would be present for the child's baptism and Sir Edmund Hay saw this as an opportunity to impress him.

King James was in high spirits when he arrived at Kildrummy Castle for the event. He had been advised that the support of Hay and Huntly were vital in his efforts to control the barons of Scotland and he had installed George, Huntly's heir, as keeper of, not only Kildrummy but also Kindrochat and Inverness Castles.

The celebrations were on a grand scale with both families delighted with the marriage contract and the fact that Annabella had proved her ability to bear children. The Royal Standard was flown alongside the arms of both Hay and Gordon and musicians entertained whilst the feasting began. Whisky and good wine flowed freely as the night wore on. Dancing began quite sedately but as time passed it grew faster and more intimate. George Gordon was enjoying the festivities to the full and danced with many a pretty young lady to his wife's disgust. When he slipped away with his arm over a buxom lass's shoulder, Annabella was furious. Flouncing over to her brother, the king, she took him by the hand and followed the couple to the chamber she shared with George. Bursting through the door she discovered her husband lying atop the girl with his hands exploring beneath her dress. Furiously she strode across the chamber and dragged him off her. George staggered to his feet and raised his hand about to lash out at her when he saw the king standing in the doorway.

James struggled to conceal a grin which threatened to spread across his face at George's being caught with his bare backside in the air. When he saw George's hand raised to strike his aunt the humour left his face immediately.

A number of guests had noticed Annabella lead the king from the festivities and had followed to see what cause her agitation. One or two of the bolder men peered into the room past the king's shoulder and roared with laughter. Sir Alexander Boyd, who was never far from the king's side, sneered and whispered in the king's ear. Word spread rapidly through the gathering crowd before the young king ordered silence and sent them away with orders not to speak of what they had witnessed.

James told the girl to leave George's chamber and the castle immediately and ordered George to attend him the next morning. For the present, he took Annabella to his own chamber and sent for her ladies.

'I know you are hurt and upset catching George with the girl but you must understand that he is a healthy young man with an appetite...'

'Appetite? I know all about his appetites!' she threw back. 'This is not the first slut he has...'

'Come, come, Annabella. Men have their needs.'

'As do women...'

'Annabella!' James was shocked and embarrassed that she should suggest such a thing. 'Go to your room with your women. I will speak to George tomorrow. I can understand his dalliance with a pretty maid but I will not have him strike you.'

Appalled that he could see no wrong in her husband's philandering she flounced away with her ladies pattering after her.

Young James preened himself, pleased with the way he had dealt with these adults and enjoying the power which he held.

Naturally, it was not long before the events of the evening came to the ears of Elizabeth Gordon. Knowing full well that stories developed as they passed from lips to lips she believed that it had been embellished many times before her hearing but when she mentioned it to Nicholas, his embarrassment to discuss the matter with his bride gave her to believe that it was closer to the truth than she had thought.

Nicholas and Elizabeth each returned to their home; Nicholas to the care of his guardians and Elizabeth to her father until Nicholas should reach the age of sixteen. They would, of course, spend time together but their lives as man and wife must wait.

Alexander, Earl of Huntly, was furious with his son's behaviour. Not that he denied a man's needs, but that he should flaunt his affairs before the king and in the presence of his wife was unacceptable. He raged at George for betraying the king's aunt so publicly and risking the king's favour towards the family rather than for the betrayal itself. But George was unrepentant, insisting that he would do as he wished.

❧

When Nicholas was at Erroll hearing reports of his lands and property in the area, news arrived that the Queen Mother had died leaving Kennedy and his people in control of the king. Amongst the Council of Regency was the 'Red' Douglas,

Earl of Angus and the power struggle for control of the king had resumed. Robert Boyd and his son Thomas, now the Earl of Arran, were draining revenues for profit and using their power to elevate their friends. The king was angry but powerless to intervene.

⚜

Although Annabella was a princess, she brought little to the power hungry Gordons and was proving to be irritating in her attitude to George's affairs. He grew tired of her complaints and was embarrassed when she, in retaliation began flirtations with other men. Their life together became tempestuous and George continued to look elsewhere for women to satisfy his needs.

Eventually, the situation between George Gordon and Annabella grew untenable and, as she had borne him only a daughter, his thoughts turned to looking for a new wife.

The Hays were considered to be one of the most advantageous marriages to be had. George's half-brother had married the Earl of Erroll's first daughter, Beatrix; ten years ago Erroll's heir, Nicholas had married George's sister Elizabeth and now George himself saw the advantage to be had by marrying Elizabeth Hay, sister of Nicholas who was now the Earl of Erroll. He approached Nicholas to negotiate a betrothal with the nineteen-year-old beauty. Nicholas had received numerous offers for his sister's hand but had held back, looking for a match with a family of appropriate standing. The Earls of Huntly were wealthy and powerful and they had been close friends since childhood. He knew that George had always cared for Elizabeth and had witnessed him trying to steal kisses. Many times Nicholas had come to her rescue and sent George away with a polite but stinging rebuke.

In spite of his youth, Nicholas was not about to let Huntly deflower his sister before their wedding night. He extracted an exceptional control agreement from Huntly for the betrothal. In order to protect Elizabeth from George's passion, Nicholas insisted Huntly swear an oath on the gospels that he would have no, 'actual delen,' with Elizabeth until after the marriage. The older man baulked at the condition but Nicholas insisted on the oath and he himself swore that he would see Huntly hanged if he broke his oath. 'This is a high price indeed,' laughed Huntly. 'We must set an early date for the wedding lest I disgrace myself in waiting.'

Unsure that George would be able to achieve the divorce and knowing that Alexander Gordon was against it, Nicholas, wishing to bind the two families together even further, made a further request of George.

'Your wife Annabella has given you a daughter, George. I would have you betroth her to my brother William.'

'Ha! She is yet a child. Surely your brother is looking for a bride he can bed without waiting over ten years.'

'Well if you can wait for Elizabeth…..'

'Agreed then but the same conditions apply.'

Nicholas was proving to be a wise and honest man, dealing fairly with nobles and peasants alike and was quite a favourite at court. His wife, Elizabeth had finally come to live with him at Slains Castle and enjoyed entertaining his guests who regularly came to visit the young couple.

Nicholas and George, Elizabeth's brother, had become close friends and had great trust in each other. Knowing that many nobles envied their power and status and would wrench it from them if possible, they decided to pledge their support to each other in a bond of alliance in which they agreed to defend each other against all living men.

'And, if it seems to be advisable to either of the Lords or their counsel to add to or reform this agreement, they shall be ready to put it in the best form without fraud or guile, for the honour and advantage of both the Lords.'

When he was not at the Royal Court Nicholas enjoyed spending time hunting and was frequently invited to visit other nobles who enjoyed his light-hearted company and admired his skills as a huntsman. He was often invited to take part in hunts with other nobles and looked forward to taking up their invitations whenever he could be spared.

Leaving Slains for Killimuir, Nicholas took his leave of his people and set off with Elizabeth, Logan carrying Nicholas' pencel, Malcolm his falconer, carrying Nicholas' favourite falcon, ten retainers and his hunting dogs running at his horse's heels. He left his brother, William, to care for his estate in his absence.

The party broke their journey at Strathbogie where Elizabeth was to stay until Nicholas returned enabling her to spend a week with her family. Moving on the travellers made good time, arriving the next day at Killimuir. The weather was fine and plans were made for the next day's hunting. That evening the guests were wined and dined in fine style, consuming the finest wine and whisky long into the night and entertaining each other with anecdotes.

By the time they retired the sun was rising and servants were yawning as they cleared the hall in readiness for the next day.

One by one the guests arose and, having broken their fast, took to the courtyard to find their horses made ready. Each took a stirrup cup before they set out, many still suffering the results of their indulgence the previous night.

Dogs barked in excitement as they wandered between the horse's feet. Hawks were brought out, hooded and sitting on heavy gauntlets. They were passed to the lords in readiness as a horn sounded. The men spurred their horses into action in pursuit of their prey. There was laughter and rivalry between the hunters and Nicholas was determined not to be bested by the older and more experienced lords.

With his hawk on his hand, he rode ahead to flush out the prey.

Suddenly a brace of pheasants rose into the air. Nicholas commanded his hawk to attack and in an instant, it soared into the air. He spurred his horse on to follow and breaking into a gallop it carried him through the rough grass, breaking cover and following the hawk.

Within moments the hawk brought its prey down and Nicholas slid from his saddle with his dirk in his hand to see that the bird was dispatched. Others of the party had followed and several of them dismounted to see the first quarry. Two stepped forward unsteadily and bent forward to look over Nicholas' shoulder laughing and reeling with the last night's drink still dulling their senses. There was a curse as one of the nobles stumbled over a dog and thrust out his hand to stop his fall. He lurched forward over Nicholas and falling onto him was jeered by his fellows who laughed and clapped at his antics.

Nicholas collapsed to the ground and lay still. Guffaws and cheers greeted this and he was grabbed by the back of his surcoat and lifted back to his feet. His would be helper realised by the dead weight that all was not as it seemed. He slowly lowered Nicholas back to the ground turning him over as he did so and stepping back as he let go. The laughter stopped with the sobering sight which met the men. Nicholas' own dirk was buried in his chest.

The silence was broken by an oath from a bearded man who stepped forward to examine Nicholas more closely. He knelt on one knee and placed his hand on Nicholas' chest. Rising he shook his head and beckoned two of the falconers forward. 'Help me to get him over his horse,' he instructed. 'We must return to Killimuir.'

Even the dogs were silent as they arrived back at Killimuir. Servants came down the steps to see what had brought them home so soon and shocked faces took in the scene as Nicholas' body was slid from his horse and carried in. The body was placed on a table and a priest was sent for to pray for his soul.

A messenger was sent to Strathbogie to carry the news to his young wife; another to Coupar Angus Abbey to William, Nicholas' brother was being educated for the church, asking for him to come swiftly. A third messenger was sent to fetch the coroner.

The coroner was first to arrive and, having questioned those who had been with him, agreed that it had been an accidental death with only the knife to blame. Leaving, he promised to send to Coupar Angus to ask the good brothers to pray for his soul and prepare for his burial.

Elizabeth and her brother, George, arrived before night-fall. Elizabeth needed to see with her own eyes that her husband was indeed dead. Shaking her head in disbelief she laid her hand on his chest and wept. Her brother put his hands on her arms and turned her towards him, pulling her close and holding her as she sobbed. 'Elizabeth,' he coaxed, 'we must leave the servants to prepare his body.'

'No!' she exclaimed. 'It is my place to bathe him. No other shall touch him.' George was reluctant to permit her to lay out her husband's body but seeing her determination decided not to distress her further by his refusal.

Whilst Elizabeth was about her task, William Hay arrived.

'It seems you are now Earl of Erroll, William,' George greeted him.

'Would that I were not and my brother yet lived,' he replied. 'This is a sad day for Scotland.'

'With your permission, I would like to take Nicholas to rest at Huntly for a night. My father ails and could not travel but I know he would wish to pay his respects.'

'Of course. We can stay a night as we make our way to Perth. I would like the chance to see you, father, again. He is a good man.'

A coffin was prepared and Nicholas' body laid in it in readiness for the journey. A solemn party left Killimuir the next day and made their way to Strathbogie where a feeble Alexander Gordon greeted them sadly.

Taking the body to the chapel, William Hay and George Gordon knelt side by side to mourn him. A silent figure slipped in beside them and Alexander, unable to kneel, took a seat nearby to pray with them.

Elizabeth Hay was being comforted by Huntly's wife when a small child of about six years burst through the door. 'I want to see the lady!' she demanded.

'Isabella! Do not run and be silent. There is grief in this house and you will respect our visitors.' The child stopped and seeing the tears in Elizabeth's eyes, she took her hand and bade her not to cry. 'My nurse says it is not fitting for a lady to show emotion,' she explained.

'And she is quite correct,' agreed Elizabeth drying her eyes and struggling to control her tears. The child seemed satisfied that she had reminded the lady how to behave and took Elizabeth's hand giving it a gentle squeeze. 'I must return to my needlework now or I shall be in the most dreadful trouble,' explained the child as she curtsied and went on her way.

As the procession approached the Abbey of Coupar Angus, the abbey bell could be heard tolling. A column of white-robed figures processed out to meet them and fell into line behind the mourners.

Nicholas' body was taken directly to the chapel as the frail and stooped figure of Abbot David Bane greeted William and Elizabeth. Taking them to his guest house he offered them refreshments before they returned to the chapel for Nicholas' burial. William approached the abbot whilst they drank wine.

'Father Abbot, a word if you would.'

'My son, this is a difficult time for you and you mother. Whatever I can do to help you need only ask.'

'I had never expected to be Earl of Erroll and Constable of Scotland. I am not prepared for the role. Even as a child, I had hoped in due course to enter the church. My father would not hear of it and had me betrothed but when he died I thought my way was clear to follow my calling. Now I must take on this most daunting role.'

'My son, the Lord makes our paths clear to us. You felt he had called you to take vows, now you see he has another path for you. He has called you to take an oath to the king and to guard our most precious sovereign and land of Scotland. It is not for us to question God's decisions. You may serve him by serving Scotland. He will guide you and support you as He has chosen this great role for you.'

'Father Abbot, your wisdom is great and I thank you for your words. Would it be too much to ask the brothers to pray every week for five years for my brother's soul? I wish them to say masses for him every Sunday this year and next and to pray for my ancestors who are also buried here. For this kindness, I will make a donation to the abbey of lands and silver and I will come and join their prayers whenever I can.

My brother was dear to me and I fear that having died unshriven, his soul may suffer.'

'Bless you, my son you are very generous. The brothers will do as you request and gladly so. Your brother was a good man and deserving of our prayers. Now we must lay him to rest and say our farewells to him.'

Abbot Bane nodded to Elizabeth to indicate it was time for them to make their way to the chapel and led the mourners into the cloisters. As the bell tolled, the brothers made their way towards the chapel, walking in twos, and chanting as they progressed.

Nicholas' body lay before the altar with candles at each corner. Elizabeth stifled a sob as she saw it. The brothers' procession split into two lines and each progressed to take up their positions on either side of the coffin. The Latin chant was beautiful and the sound of their voices soothed the mourners. Elizabeth did her utmost to remain outwardly calm as befitted her status but her love for Nicholas was such that she grew faint and William was obliged to put his arm around his mother to support her.

Following the service, the coffin holding Nicholas' body was carried down into the crypt below the altar and laid to rest with his ancestors.

William helped Elizabeth out into the fresh air and led her to a seat within the cloisters. The frail abbot stood before her to offer final condolences before their departure.

'Father Abbot,' Elizabeth breathed, 'I make one further request of you.'

'If it is within my gift you are assured,' he replied.

'I ask that, when my time comes to meet the Lord, I be laid to rest with my beloved husband.'

'But my lady, it may well be that you re-marry before that time. You are yet a young woman and your son is betrothed to Isabella Gordon. Surely you would be laid to rest with your new husband.'

'I have no wish to re-marry but your words bear wisdom. In the fullness of time, I will no doubt be required to marry again. Even so, I fear I shall never love another as I love Nicholas and would have your assurance that my wishes will be honoured.'

'My lady, I shall see that your wishes are carried out but pray that it will be many years yet before we look to do so.'

Elizabeth inclined her head in gratitude and followed William to the courtyard where their horses awaited them.

Seeing where his duty lay, William Hay, now third Earl of Erroll, took Isabella Gordon into his household to live at Slains residing with the ladies until she should be of age for their marriage to be consummated. His mother was sent to live at Erroll until she could be cloaked with a new husband.

Elizabeth arrived at Erroll to find the old castle in need of some urgent repairs. She wrote to William advising him of the problems and suggesting that he might consider replacing the old structure with a new building more in keeping with the status that the family had now risen to.

CHAPTER 20

It was not long before Nicholas Hay's worst fears became reality and news that James was taken captive at Linlithgow and taken by force to Edinburgh Castle by Sir Alexander Boyd, along with the Flemings, Lindsays, Hepburns, and others came to William's ears. The powerless young King was made to appear before Parliament and forced to say that they had acted with his approval. Boyd, an ambitious man, had then been appointed the boy king's guardian. He raised his son, Thomas, to the position of Earl of Arran and married him to the King's sister Mary. William was horrified. The idea of Boyd having such control over the king was unthinkable. He knew that King James would be furious at being treated in this way and feared what else might come to pass before James came of age. He did not have long to wait.

It was whilst William was in the mews inspecting his hawks that the clatter of horses hooves announced the arrival of visitors to Slains Castle. Peter Hay of Megginch's arrival was unexpected causing William to believe there must be a problem at Erroll. He was surprised to find that the news he brought was not of Nichols' estates but of the king. A marriage had been negotiated for the young King James. His betrothed was Margaret of Denmark, daughter of Christian I and Dorothea of Brandenburg. Her dowry was to be 60,000 florins; an offer the Scottish Parliament could not refuse but William was stunned at the audacity of the king's guardians. Orkney and the Shetlands which were rented by Scotland from Norway were to be collateral for Margaret's dowry. The Scottish government was in arrears and in danger of losing the Islands so the approval of parliament was assured and the following year James and Margaret were married. She was just thirteen and James was seventeen.

After his marriage, the King was determined to destroy the Boyd regency. He took control of his government while Robert and Thomas Boyd were out of the country forcing them to remain in exile. Thomas Boyd's marriage to James' sister was declared void and James began to show favour to artisans whom he trusted rather than the barons. Amongst these were Thomas Cochrane - a mason turned architect, William Roger - a musician, James Hommyle - the royal tailor, Torphichen - a fencing master, Dr Andreas - an astrologer and Leonard - a shoemaker. The king made this disparate group his advisors and councillors in place of the Lords, but as they lacked the power of the Lords, the country was becoming lawless and out of control.

William Hay was greatly concerned that he had not yet found a suitable wife for his sister Margaret. Now a beautiful seventeen-year-old and with a handsome dowry and powerful family, she was an exceptional match for any nobleman. He had decided to travel to Erroll to assess the repairs needed to his property there. He arrived in driving rain and made haste to get indoors. What he found upon entering proved Margaret's concerns correct. He greeted his mother and expressed his shock at the obvious problems. Sections of the roof were leaking and much of the woodwork was springing apart.

Sitting down with his steward, Cameron, they discussed the options available. William made it clear that he placed no blame on Cameron; it was simply the passage of time which had taken its toll. Taking all into consideration, William decided it was time to replace the old bailey with a new house which would be known as Erroll Park. An architect from Perth was sent for and he was given proposals to work from.

Whilst William stayed at Erroll, Alexander Fraser, fourth of Philorth, approached him with a request for his daughter Margaret's hand and, although he was by far her senior, William knew him to be a kind and honest man. Looking to avoid having to refuse more eligible but less desirable suitors, William decided to accept Alexander's offer.

Margaret was an obedient sister and in spite of her distaste at marrying a man who was as old as her father would have been, she submitted to the marriage and was soon with child.

Her pregnancy was not without its difficulties and five weeks before her time she gave birth to a son who was swiftly baptised for fear that he would not survive. He was to be named Alexander after his father and, in spite of his early delivery he survived.

As the child grew, Margaret could not help but compare him to the lusty children of others and it was clear that his development was slow. He lacked the energy and alertness of his peers and lay silently in his crib. As the years passed it was clear that the boy was feeble-minded but he was a pleasant young man and loved by his family and servants. His father encouraged him to study without criticising his lack of progress. The boy loved to work with horses and in spite of his lack of academic prowess, he was a superb horseman.

When his father Alex Gordon died in 1470 leaving George as the new Earl of Huntly he wasted no time in securing a divorce from Annabella. He had found that his liking for Lady Elizabeth Hay grew beyond his expectations and he was keen for the marriage to go ahead as soon as possible. Although George was fifteen years her senior, Elizabeth found him very attractive and his closeness to her family meant that she knew him well. She loved his charm and was a very willing bride.

As soon as his divorce from Annabella was confirmed, George rode with all haste to visit William Hay to set a date for their wedding. He found William going through the estate accounts with his reeve and checking that the payments from his tenants were correct. William looked up and, seeing the grin on George's face, bade the reeve leave them. The fellow bowed and left closing the accounts book and taking it with him.

William stood and took George's proffered hand. 'Good news,' George announced, 'I am free to marry Elizabeth.'

'Good news indeed but you must stand by the agreement you made with my brother yet a while. We will arrange the marriage as soon as possible and it can take place at St Machar's in Aberdon.

William sent for Elizabeth who arrived in a state of suppressed excitement.

'Behold your betrothed,' he announced.

Elizabeth could restrain herself no longer and threw her arms around George's neck. He covered her lips with his and William stepped forward to part them, shaking his finger at George in reproach whilst grinning at their enthusiasm.

'Tell your ladies to prepare for the arrival of your dressmaker, Elizabeth. I shall send for him immediately and whilst you are with him I shall ride to Aberdon and arrange a date for your wedding.

⟡

William paid the priest handsomely to find an early date to marry the couple and returned to report his success and Huntly set off with all haste to prepare himself for his wedding and to invite the most powerful barons to attend the ceremony.

⟡

Now that he was of age King James was determined that he would choose his own advisors. The Scottish Parliament was greatly concerned by his lack of interest in the mundane issues of government and the numerous suggestions he was making for irresponsible schemes and looked to William Hay whom they appointed to the Privy Council along with George Gordon and between them they attempted to advise the king. William was sent as Commissioner to treat with the English at Alnwick for mutual redress of wrongs committed on the borders and for truce, peace and confederacy between the kingdoms and to consent in their master's name to any matrimonial contracts which might help to secure the continuing peace.

⟡

When William and George returned to Scotland having secured a peace, they went directly to Stirling Castle where the king was residing, awaiting the birth of his first child. There was an atmosphere of tension. Childbirth was always dangerous but should the queen be delivered of a son, it would be a matter for great rejoicing.

As they entered the castle forecourt a squire ran out shouting, 'It's a boy and all is well!' and darting back and forth to deliver the news to all within the castle precincts. George turned in his saddle and remarked that this could be a child to seal the peace with England.

Before the child, James, was two years old it seemed that the Earl of Huntly's prediction would be proved to be correct as a marriage contract between him and Cecily, third daughter of Edward IV of England was announced.

CHAPTER 21

George Gordon's efforts on their wedding night had resulted in the birth of a son whom George named Alexander after his father. Two years later Alexander was followed by a sister, Catherine. Sons William and Adam followed soon after along with sisters Agnes and Eleanor.

William Hay and Isabelle had also been blessed with a family and their children, William, Thomas, John and Beatrix grew strong and lusty. The sound of their laughter rang throughout the castle and their nursemaid and tutors were hard put to prevent them playing too close to the cliff top and risking falling onto the rocks below. William and Isabelle were delighted with their young family and spent many happy hours playing with them and preparing them for the important roles they must play in the future.

William took time to visit his family and properties in Erroll. The new house was finished and was everything that William had hoped it would be. The exterior was built of sandstone and glowed in the sunshine. Towers topped by bartizans stood at either side above the doorway which was topped by an imitation portcullis suspended above the front door. As he looked up at the stepped gables he saw a figure pass one of the small lancet windows in a tower and realised it was his steward, Cameron, as the figure moved on and passed by one of the large bay windows which was glazed with plate glass. Above the window, the roof was adorned by pinnacles and crenulations giving the effect of a mock castle.

As he approached, under his feet were enormous flag-stones which continued inside the building. Cameron had seen his master's approach and opened the door.

William greeted him warmly as he stepped inside and looked about him. Much of the stonework had been left exposed at William's request but oak panelling to the lower walls in some rooms gave warmth to the atmosphere. A large stone fireplace in the entrance hall was supported by pillars and contained a glowing blaze.

From the hall, an enormous oak staircase swept up to the first floor with wood panelling on the wall and arched opening in the bannisters, each with a group of three shields set into it. At a turn in the staircase, a bay window looked out onto sweeping gardens bordered by hedges and studded with fir trees.

Entering a bedroom he was delighted with the beautiful panelled ceiling with his arms displayed diagonally across in panels from corner to corner. Panelled wooden shutters, carved with mistletoe, sat at either side of each of the five windows around the room and light flooded in to reveal a pink marble fireplace.

Satisfied with all he saw, William went back down the stairs and passed through the wide oak door into the library. The walls were panelled from floor to ceiling, incorporating bookshelves lined with leather bound volumes.

He was about to enter the dining room when a servant coughed behind him. 'My lord, there is a messenger who brings news from Edinburgh.'

William told the girl to bring the messenger to the library where he would see him in private. Here he received the news that the king had imprisoned his brothers Alexander, Duke of Albany in Edinburgh Castle and John, Earl of Mar, who was accused of sorcery against the king had been taken to Craigmillar where he was dispatched. James had been convinced that they were plotting against him and lacking the advice of experienced councillors he had acted in panic.

Information that Mar had died of a fever reached William Hay's ears before long. Albany had managed a daring escape into England and it was feared that he would try to persuade Edward to support him.

Wherever he went, William heard grumbling from rich and poor alike against the king. Harvests had been poor giving the people little to eat and this, accompanied by high prices and outbreaks of plague were nurturing resentment against his government.

When William received a summons from the king he wondered why he was needed fearing rebellion amongst the people. He rode straight to Stirling and was received into the king's presence immediately.

'Ah, Erroll,' sighed James, 'My brother Albany has returned to Scotland with forces supplied by King Edward. Edward's brother, Richard, Duke of Gloucester, leads his army. You must rally the barons and form an army for me to destroy him.'

'Sire, I will do my best as my duty demands but I fear the barons resent your choice of advisors and will hesitate to send men.'

'Resent my choice of advisors!' roared James, 'Who are they to resent? They have sworn allegiance to me and are bound to supply knights and men to support me! I shall choose whom I like. In my experience, the nobles of this land seek their own wealth and power rather than mine. Tell all who falter they shall suffer if they fail me.'

William Hay knew that it was his duty as Constable of Scotland to gather an army for James but try as he might, some barons failed to fulfil their obligations and William was troubled at the king's stubborn refusal, even now, to renounce his unpopular favourites. Rumours that some of the lords were rebelling were confirmed when six of the king's advisors, including the much despised Robert Cochrane, were taken and hanged and James himself was arrested at Lauder Bridge and carried off to Edinburgh as a prisoner.

Albany and his ally Gloucester were now in pursuit of the captive King. On their arrival at Edinburgh Castle, Albany claimed the throne as Alexander IV. Albany's mistrust of the barons equalled that of the king. He realised that he had put himself in a dangerous position having alienated both James and the barons. Realising the danger he had put himself in, he released his brother and restored him to the throne.

Furious at his brother's behaviour, James ordered Hay to gather a force to pursue Albany who had fled to his estates in Dunbar and bring him to justice, but by the time William's men reached Dunbar, Albany had gone from there to France. William, Earl of Erroll was able to stand down the army, such as it was, and return to Slains for the time being.

Visitors to Slains Castle were always welcome and many minor nobles came to sign bonds of manrent, to seek marriage contracts for their children or to negotiate for a son to be taken as a page. On the 17th of April, 1483, Alexander Irvine of Lonmay, son and heir-apparent of Sir Alexander Irvine of Drum,

'became true man and servant to a noble and mighty lord, William, Earl of Erroll, Lord the Hay, and Constable of Scotland; in true man-rent and service, in peace and in war, with my person and goods against all that live or die may, my allegiance to the King only excepted. And, if I see or hear of any hurt or peril to his person, friends, goods, or heritage, I shall warn him thereof, and to the utmost prevent it. If he asks me

any advice, I shall give the best I can; and if any counsel be shown to me, I shall conceal it without fraud or guile . . . At the end of seven years my fee to be considered and modified by the persons undernamed:— Mr Gilbert Hay of Ury, Mr David Hay, Mr John Hay, prebender of Cruden; Alexander Fraser of Durris, Robert Blynsall, alderman of Aberdeen; and Alexander Irvine of Belte, or such-like persons.'

He was one of many who sought the protection of such an important noble as the Earl of Erroll. William insisted that his sons be present to witness bonds of manrent and explained to them that they were important in assuring support in times of need and enabling him to demand knights and men when they were required for battle. Young William listened solemnly to his father's words as he did to every advice that his father gave him in preparation for his role as Constable in due course. William was painfully aware that life and death were unpredictable and God might call any of them to account at any time.

Noble lords brought their offspring to show how accomplished and eligible they were. William's family enjoyed the distraction of these visits and welcomed the opportunity to play with other children. Although there were times when they must be restrained and display the charms expected of the children of an Earl, there was always time for fun.

Alexander Burnett of Leys was one such visitor who sought a position in William Hay's household for his son, also Alexander.

The child seemed listless and William doubted that he would ever make old bones, still less a noble squire. Standing silently beside his father the child answered questions without enthusiasm. Eventually, William decided to send the child to play with his own offspring whilst he told Alexander that he would not take the boy on as a page.

As soon as the child had been taken from the room, William started to explain his concerns only to be interrupted by Alexander Burnett; although an immensely wealthy man, he was known for his thrift so when he offered to pay handsomely for the place, William knew he was desperate. He had known the man for a good number of years and valued the support of the Burnetts when gathering forces for the king. In order to soften the blow, William agreed to take the boy for a month to see how he fared.

Alexander dined with William and took his leave the following day. The children were sent for to bid farewell to their guest. Young Alexander looked pale and as his father rode through the gates he vomited.

William took this to be fear at being left in a strange place and felt it confirmed his doubts about the boy's suitability. However, not an hour had passed before a servant was sent to tell him that the boy was ill. William, concerned that a boy in his care was unwell, made his way to the nursery. Isabella was already there and turned as he entered. Her face told William that she was afraid. 'William, the boy has measles!' She pointed to the tell-tale rash. 'I've seen it before,' she told him. 'William what if our children catch it? They may die!'

'Move the children to our room. We must isolate Alexander and let his father know.'

'Close the curtains,' Isabella told a servant. 'Light is not good. It can blind a child who has measles.' Obeying her mistress the maid drew the curtains and sent for a bowl of cool water to bath the child's brow.

Alexander Burnett of Leys returned as soon as he received the news. William invited him to stay until the child was well again.

Two days later, William's children bore the same rash. Isabella was beside herself with worry. She refused to leave the nursery and slept fitfully in a chair beside their beds. As their fevers rose she bathed them, gave them sips of herbal infusions and soothed them, praying that the fever would break and her children would recover.

The next night the fevers rose to a climax. The children's bodies were soaked with sweat and they rambled as their minds were confused. Alexander had started to recover and Isabella was encouraged by this to believe that all would be well. When first William and then Thomas finally seemed to be sleeping peacefully she was relieved. Young Beatrix also seemed to settle as the fever broke but John's temperature soared and he thrashed around crying out and moaning.

Exhausted through lack of sleep and endless worry, Isabella finally succumbed. He head lolled on her chest and she slept deeply. When she awoke she became aware of the stillness in the room. In panic, she reached out to John but recoiled as she saw his face. The infection had done its worst.

She heard a scream but was oblivious to the fact that it came from her own lips. Her hand flew to her middle as she desperately tried to breathe. Running footsteps approached up the stone spiral stairs. By the time William entered the room, she was clutching John's lifeless body to her and rocking to and fro.

Isabella would not let anybody take John's body from her and for twelve hours she held him to her. Finally, William decided he must intervene. 'Isabella, my love, the child has been taken back by God. He was only leant to us for a short time but we loved him dearly. Please, help me grieve for him.'

Isabella stopped rocking.

'We have our other children to care for,' he continued. 'They need you to help them to understand what has happened.'

She let William take John's body from her and turned to clasp him tightly and weep on his shoulder. Gently he led her away soothing her with gentle words and stroking her hair.

෧෭

Scotland had been true to the peace which had been negotiated with England. The ongoing battles between the houses of York and Lancaster gave England enough to deal with and made it an easy target should Scotland renege. When Edward IV, known for his excesses, died suddenly in 1483 leaving his twelve-year-old son as his heir, Richard Duke of Gloucester had the young king and his brother housed in the Tower of London for safety.

෧෭

It was just a year after John's death that Isabella told William that she was carrying their fifth child. He was delighted and promised her that, should it be a boy, they would call him John. Isabella hoped that it would indeed be a boy but she feared the delivery which was always so dangerous.

She prided herself in the smooth running of the castle and her personal care of her children. She had always watched closely over them and became almost obsessive since John's death. Their energy often led the boys to challenge each other to fighting competitions and tilting was one of their favourites. In order to excuse her presence, she would sometimes hold the hoop for them as they rode their ponies with wooden lances in their hands. Armour made from boiled leather was specially made for them and they loved the excitement of riding full tilt at each other.

William had challenged his brother and they hurried the stable boys to saddle their mounts, calling to them to hurry and struggling into their armour. Thomas was mounted first and turned his pony away, taking his lance from the stable hand. William was soon ready and they kicked their mounts on to take up their positions at the end of the practice tilt which their father had had made just outside the castle walls. Isabella held a rope which hoisted a ring into the air for them to try to catch on their lances. William went first and caught the hoop without difficulty. Thomas prepared to take his turn. He hefted his lance under his arm and spurred his pony forward. The animal was courageous and leapt forward carrying its young rider towards the hoop. He lowered his lance ready to thrust it through the hoop but as he did so his saddle began to slip. In his haste to prepare the beast the stable boy had not re-tightened the girth and before he could right himself, Thomas was slipping down the side of his mount. In panic, he gripped his lance tighter and struggling to regain his position he did not see Isabella step forward to help. As he reached her he felt a thud and heard a scream as his lance struck his mother full in the middle piercing her and the child she carried.

The children's screams of horror brought the castle people running. The women sobbed to see their mistress so terribly killed by her own son. William jumped down from his pony and ran to his brother to rescue him from his misplaced saddle before turning to his mother's prone body, the lance still piercing her middle.

The baker's wife put her arms around the boys and turned them in towards her; William struggled to turn back but she held him fast whilst the armourer broke off the shaft of the lance.

Isabella's body was laid gently on the bed in her chamber and William knelt by her side. Young William holding his brother's hand stood in the doorway.

'Father, it was not Thomas' fault. His saddle slipped and he tipped…'

'Go,' said William the suppressed anger in his voice casting fear into their little hearts. 'I shall speak to you later,' he told them more gently.

It was many hours before he could leave Isabella's side and face his children. Beatrix's tear stained face was being wiped by her nurse and William and Thomas stood courageously before him. William stood, his great height looming over them. A myriad of emotions passed over his face. Sorrow, anger, despair, love and pity vied to control his features. Eventually, he held out his arms to them all. 'We have all suffered this day,' he told them and clutched them to him.

❧

Young William grew more like his father every day. He favoured him in looks having a mop of auburn hair and dancing chestnut eyes; he excelled in battle skills. He was a fine horseman and was becoming a swordsman to be reckoned with.

Isabell's death had been a blow to William and the children and he mourned the child who was never born, yet he must consider his own needs and those of his children. He was just thirty-five years old. He must find a new mother for them and make a marriage for himself which would be advantageous.

The Leslies and the Hays had historic ties and were growing in power through marriages and royal favour. William set his sights on Elizabeth, daughter of George Leslie 1st Earl of Rothes and in 1485, with the king's permission, a marriage contract was drawn up by William and George Leslie and their union was soon blessed with children; William had promised that his next son would be called John and he was true to his word. John was soon followed by William and Elizabeth.

The following year, William Hay found a second husband for his sister, Margaret, in the person of Gilbert Keith. She had been widowed for some time and he saw the opportunity to strengthen the bond between their families and advance his standing amongst the nobility.

Her son, the feeble minded Alexander, was to have Sir Walter Ogilvy of Boyne and John Fraser of Ardglassie as his guardians. Sir Gilbert Keith was dismayed that parliament should give his wardship outside the family as he had taken a liking to the boy and had plans to find him a good marriage. The boy's mother was his wife and he saw no reason for other guardians to be appointed. Although Gilbert was much older than Margaret, having been born long before her father had, he was a good and kind man who respected Margaret for her intelligence as well as her beauty. He would discuss the feuds between barons and the actions of the king. When the currency was debased by issuing copper coinage he valued her opinion on the likely implications.

The king had agreed peace with England and a marriage alliance between his eldest son and King Edward's daughter, Cecily of York, which many nobles resented. Scotland and England had been enemies for many years and numerous Scottish families had lost menfolk in battles against the English; they were not ready to provide additional taxes to pay for a wedding which united them with an old enemy.

William's visit to his sister was primarily to tell her and Gilbert of his forthcoming marriage but when he arrived he was surprised not to receive the usual enthusiastic welcome from his nephew. Hearing that Margaret's son, Alexander, had been given into the care of Walter Ogilvy and John Fraser, he understood his sister's distress.

Before he left, William agreed to request the king to intervene with parliament to have the boy made his and Gilbert's ward.

'When he is in our care we can arrange a suitable marriage for him for his benefit and not for gain,' he promised. 'I will pay whatever it takes to secure his wardship.'

King James III was disinterested in the affairs of the clergy and the nobles and seemed almost to delight in antagonising them but he had a liking for William and sold him Alexander's wardship without a second thought.

William wasted no time in securing a marriage contract for him with Marjory, daughter of the Thane of Cawdor. The thane was delighted at the prospect of his line being linked with such eminent families but his daughter was horrified at the prospect of, not only being wed to a feeble minded youth, but also of her offspring bearing the same characteristics. 'I shall not wed that slobbering half-wit!' she declared. 'I care not what title he may have or what land our family might gain. Father you cannot really mean to sacrifice me like this!' Her father was furious and presented her with an ultimatum; Marry Alexander or be sent to a convent. She chose the latter.

CHAPTER 22

Intermittent warfare continued along the border between England and Scotland and William Hay was repeatedly called upon to provide troops and rally support for the king. The English had laid siege to the well-defended fortress at Berwick upon Tweed but with little success and William had called upon Sir John Hay of Yester and Sir William Hay of Lochloy to accompany him, bringing knights and supporters with them. Staying at Yester they discussed ways to remove the English and relieve Berwick.

In 1482 Albany, King James' brother, had returned to England and signed a treaty at Fotheringay, in which the English promised to support his claim to the throne in exchange for Albany taking the title of Alexander, King of Scotland. He would acknowledge that he held it as the gift of the King of England and agree to pay homage to him. He must also break the Auld Alliance with France. England would receive Berwick and other border towns. Albany must marry Lady Cicely, one of King Edward's daughters. To do so he must first divorce his current wife and Cicely must break her betrothal to King James III eldest son, James.

The treaty having been signed, the English sent a force of almost 20,000 led by Richard, Duke of Gloucester, to attack Berwick. In the face of such forces, the gates were opened, yet the garrison sat tight in the castle and the English forces moved north leaving them unmolested.

As the English crossed the border into Scotland, William and his men hastened to Edinburgh to swell the king's numbers. Erroll, along with Huntly, advised the king to open negotiations. Realising the danger of the situation King James followed their advice and signed an agreement.

The Earl of Buchan gained an audience with the king and through his skills of persuasion, turned the king's mind causing him to violate the agreement. Erroll and Huntly, furious and frustrated finally abandoned the king's forces and retired to their estates.

King James, having gathered what remained of his forces, gave the nobles the opportunity that they had long awaited. While the Scottish army was encamped at Lauder, a band of nobles, who had been furious to find that the king had put Cochrane in charge of artillery, met to discuss what course of action they might take. Lord Gray suggested that they must get rid of these familiars and hangers-on in whom James had such faith, especially Cochrane. 'He plays with the king as a cat might play with a mouse,' he declared. Archibald Douglas fifth Earl of Angus offered to 'bell the cat'.

They called Cochrane to a meeting in Lauder Kirk, at which he duly arrived decked out in his splendour. He was held there while the others went to the King's tent and arrested the rest of the group. All of the king's familiars were taken to Lauder Bridge and hanged; Cochrane first. James himself was taken as a prisoner to Edinburgh Castle by his uncle the Duke of Athol.

King James, now without his chosen advisors, turned to the nobles whom he felt would give true support and once again Erroll was commanded to attend the Royal Court.

There was no organised defence against the English and William was forced to send to Sterling, Perth and Glasgow for men to support the city against the advancing English.

Albany yet again demonstrated his mercurial character by accepting the promise of the restoration of his lands and appointment as Lieutenant-General of Scotland rather than pressing his claim to the throne.

Richard of Gloucester could not believe what was happening. At great expense, he had brought thousands of men to support Albany's claim and was now told that the claim was not being pursued. Furious, he met with his generals to discuss whether they should sack Edinburgh and take the city for England or return with his forces intact.

Realising that Edinburgh Castle was almost impregnable and that Edward IV was ailing back in England, he decided to accept a written assurance from Albany that he would honour the treaty of Fotheringay. He also demanded a guarantee from the citizens of Edinburgh that any monies paid by the English for a proposed marriage between the Duke of Rothesay, James III's heir, and Edward IV's daughter, Cecily, would be reimbursed.

The death of King Edward IV was to be the undoing of Albany. Richard, Duke of Gloucester abandoned him to travel south and, having secured Edward's sons, pronounce himself Protector of the Kingdom. Lacking the aid he expected from England, Albany retreated to the borders. Leaving his castle in the hands of the English and was finally killed whilst watching a tournament in Paris.

'It is most embarrassing,' William Hay confided in his family 'to witness the king's railing at his wife and have to behave as though I were deaf to it all. I fear it will not be long before he sets her aside. They argue about anything and everything but most of all his male companions. She says he prefers them to her. Their sons are another point of contention. James clearly favours his second son, James Duke of Ross and Margaret supports the elder James. He sends me to administer justice where it should rightly be his role but I cannot refuse as my duty as Constable of Scotland includes sitting in judgement.'

William's prediction was fulfilled when the news came that the king and his wife were estranged.

Whilst at Stirling, William was called upon to attend as witness as the king conferred a dukedom on his intimate friend, John Ramsey. William was shocked and tried to approach James to advise against it before the deed was done, but the king turned his back on William as he approached, dismissing his attempt at conference. None the less William spoke. 'Sire, when news of this reaches the ears of the barons there will be rebellion! Without their support, your position is in danger.'

'You dare to threaten me Erroll?'

'Nae, Sire. I seek to give you true council.'

'I need no advice from the likes of you!' exclaimed the king, knowing that William's words were true but choosing to deny them.

Finally, King James tried to find some favour with the barons by elevating four lairds to full Lords of Parliament but this was to no avail as other, more powerful nobles supported his eldest son who feared being supplanted by his younger brother and became the figurehead of the opposition.

Now was the time when James realised he needed true council and he turned to William for support. Advising the king to rally troops in the north, William, knowing which lairds were true to the king, accompanied him and secured an army of supporters.

The king's troops met his eldest son and the rebel lairds at Sauchieburn near Stirling. Battle commenced and many men both young and old lost their lives that day.

King James had been unable to control the nobles and now he was unable to control his horse which bolted from the battlefield as a knight swung at him with his sword breaking the king's arm and ribs with its force. James fell to the ground. Struggling with the weight and unwieldiness of his armour, he pushed himself to his feet, staggering as he did so. The battle raged around him with men and horses screaming and the clash of metal ringing in his ears. As he pushed off his helmet he looked for a means to escape. Seeing a copse of trees, he lumbered off towards it gasping for his breath. He lay wounded and exhausted looking westwards towards a distant village. As the clamour of the battle faded to be replaced with the groans of the dying, James drifted into unconsciousness. Hours later he opened his eyes to see an old woman peering at him through short-sighted eyes.

'Help me, woman; I am your king,' ordered James arrogantly. The woman raised an eyebrow at his tone but began to unfasten his armour straps to enable him to rise and walk more easily. He winced as his arm was released and held it closely to his body. Helping him to his feet she indicated that he should follow her and led him to a nearby mill to rest. Realising that he had been wounded and injured in the fall from his horse, she offered to fetch a priest.

On the way to the village, the woman stopped at the ale house to refresh herself and, unable to resist a chance to gossip and become a celebrity, she told the innkeeper that she had the care of no other than the king himself. She talked on about his fine armour and arrogant ways.

The inn keeper's eyes lit up at the thought of selling such information to the rebel army but as he dwelt on it, he realised that he would gain nothing from betraying the king, whereas his armour would fetch a fabulous price were he to take it to a tournament and sell it.

With this thought, he made an excuse of re-filling the ale jug and slipped out of the back door. Making his way to the church he crept in and searched for some vestments to disguise himself as a priest.

His luck was in that day as, hanging on a peg, was a set of robes. Slipping them over his own clothes he made his way at a solemn pace to the mill. The king lay with his eyes closed and as he leant over him, he reached beneath the vestment and drew out his knife. Catching a whiff of the man's foul breath the king opened his eyes just as the knife was plunged into his neck killing him instantly.

CHAPTER 23

King James IV was crowned at Scone Abbey and, unlike his father, surrounded himself with advisors from the aristocracy. When his first chancellor, the Earl of Argyle, died, the post was given to Archibald Douglas, Earl of Angus.

Over many hours spent playing cards and dice the two became remarkably close which, in turn, proved to be advantageous for Archibald's family. His niece, Marion Boyd, was found a place at court and it was not long before the amorous king was casting glances her way and, flattered by the attentions of the handsome young king, she willingly became his first mistress.

William Hay, as the Earl of Erroll, felt keenly the need to not only maintain his family's status but to unite them with other powerful families. The reign of King James III had shown only too clearly what damage could be done to Scotland by rebel lairds and William had been away from Slains so much in recent years that he had not yet procured brides for his sons.

Many minor lairds still came forward to sign bonds of manrent to him but he knew that, in comparison to the more significant families, these men were trivial whereas a good marriage could add to his lands and secure his position. He had two sons and intended to use them well.

A succession of eligible young ladies and their families were invited to Slains Castle, each spending a month there whilst William's sons assessed their suitability and their fathers negotiated possible marriage contracts with William.

Eventually, it was decided and agreed by the king that William's eldest son, William, was to marry Christian Lyon, a daughter of Patrick Lyon, 1st Lord Glamis, and Thomas was to marry Margaret Logie, daughter of Lyon Logie of that Ilk. Their marriages were celebrated in due course and the family links duly forged.

Another marriage was to attract much more attention and gossip in both Scotland and England.

When Edward IV of England died, the Titulus Regis Act, which declared the marriage of Edward and Elizabeth Woodville invalid and their children, therefore, illegitimate, was used by Richard Duke of Gloucester to claim the throne of England as King Richard III.

On 22nd August 1485, Henry Tudor had defeated King Richard III of England at the Battle of Bosworth and claimed the English throne for himself. To secure his right to the throne he had married Elizabeth, daughter and heiress of Edward IV, reversing the Titulus Regis and uniting the red and white roses.

Now a young man arrived in England claiming to be Richard, the younger son of King Edward IV. If Edward IV's children were to be accepted as legitimate Prince Richard had a stronger claim to the English throne than Henry and was, therefore, a threat to his rule. Prince Richard and his brother, Edward V had been held in the Tower of London by King Richard III but Perkin Warbeck claimed that he had been rescued when his brother was murdered. In his support, Margaret of York, the boys' aunt recognised him publicly.

When Warbeck landed in Kent with a small army, he was routed and many of his troops killed. He retreated to Ireland and from there fled to Scotland.

In 1495 King James welcomed Perkin Warbeck to court at Stirling. Calling his advisors, James discussed how best to make use of, 'Prince Richard,' as he referred to him. William Hay suggested that the best way to display his recognition of the man as the prince he claimed to be, would be to marry him to a Scottish noblewoman. This would show that Scotland challenged Henry's right to the crown of England. Henry hoped to marry Katherine of Aragon to his son, Arthur, but the Spanish king would not permit this until Henry's position as King of England was secure meaning that the Scottish recognition of the pretender must be negated by a treaty between the two countries.

George Gordon had brought his daughter, Lady Catherine Gordon, to court in the hope that her beauty might catch the king's eye. Knowing the likelihood of great advancements for his family if she were to become the king's mistress, George was more than willing to offer her. William Hay was horrified at his niece being used in this way and sought to protect her. He was quite taken aback when the king chose her to be Warbeck's wife. George Gordon was thrilled that his daughter was to marry a man who might become King of England but William was gravely worried.

The marriage between Warbeck and Catherine was celebrated in Edinburgh with a tournament. Warbeck wore wedding clothes which the king had given to him and armour covered with purple silk for the tournament. In September 1496, James IV prepared to invade England with Warbeck. A red, gold and silver standard was made for Warbeck as the

Duke of York and James's armour was gilded and painted. William was told to muster the forces and have them in readiness to attend the king with arms and provisions for twenty days.

The Scottish forces assembled in Edinburgh and James IV and Warbeck offered prayers at Holyrood Abbey.

They crossed the River Tweed at Coldstream but, although they destroyed the fortified towers of Northumberland, the support they had hoped for failed to materialise and after four days they were forced to retreat to Scotland.

Seeing that there was no support for the pretender, King James decided to be rid of him and put him on board a ship bound for Ireland.

Marion Boyd, having born the king two children, Alexander Stewart and Catherine, now found her place in the king's bed taken by Margaret Drummond. By way of compensation, James gave Isabella the ward of the Laird of Rowallan, John Muir, whom she married, and the lands of Warnockland as a wedding gift.

The very beautiful Margaret, daughter of the first Lord Drummond, one of the royal justiciars, was known in the Royal Court as, Margaret the Fair. James was enraptured of Margaret, his Diamond of Delight, and installed her in Stirling Castle.

Margaret hoped to make her position permanent by becoming the king's wife and charmed him with her ready wit and obliging behaviour until, finally, he was persuaded to enter into a form of marriage with her.

Entering the chapel of Stirling Castle under the darkness of night and with Margaret on his arm, James led her to the altar two of James' closest friends awaited them. Before these witnesses, James and Margaret became handfast. It was at the castle that she bore him a daughter whom they named Margaret, but by the following year, under pressure to marry Margaret Tudor, and the desire to pursue a new lover, he sent her back to her father with a generous reward for her services.

James' next mistress, Jane Kennedy, was to be provided by Archibald Douglas. She had been his own mistress until the king's eye fell on her and he was unwilling to give her up without a fight. Storming into James's throne room, he challenged the king to admit he had stolen her from him. James was furious but kept his anger in check, merely summoning his guards and ordering that Douglas be taken away. The royal writer was summoned and a document drawn up immediately dismissing Douglas from his post as Chancellor and ordering that Douglas be put under house arrest on the Isle of Bute.

❧❧

The next year Warbeck made another attempt to press his claim to the English throne, landing in the south of England. Initially, he found some support but when he heard that the king's scouts were at Glastonbury, he panicked and fled. Finally, he was captured and imprisoned in the tower of London before being paraded through the streets to be mocked.

At first, Henry treated him well, even allowing him to be at court although forbidden to sleep with his wife, Catherine but after his second attempt to escape Henry felt he was too much of a threat and had Warbeck drawn to Tyburn on a hurdle and hanged.

Catherine returned to Scotland and rather than return to Strathbogie and her parents whom she felt had used her badly, she resided with her uncle, William Hay, at Slains Castle. In the evenings she would regale them with stories of her life at the English court and the horror of her husband's death. Whilst they attended the marriage of William's sister Margaret to Sir Robert Douglas of Lochleven Catherine begged William to intervene with her father not to marry her again to a man of high estate. She would be content to remain unmarried in future or to marry a humble but honest man.

It was a sad day when the news came to Slains Castle of the death of Elizabeth Gordon, wife of William's deceased brother Nicholas. Since Nicholas' death, she had married Lord John Kennedy, but John respected her wish to be buried with Nicholas as she had requested and arrived in person at Slains Castle to bring the news of her passing. William received him with gratitude and commiserated with him for his loss.

'Elizabeth was a fine woman and a good wife,' John declared, 'but I know that Nicholas was her true love and it would grieve her soul not to be reunited with him in death.' Nodding, William shook his hand and proffered a glass of whisky.

'You are a good man, John. Nicholas would be happy to see how well you cared for her.'

The brothers at Coupar Angus Abbey made good their promise and received her into the chapel to be laid to rest with Nicholas. As the brothers ceased their chant and turned to file out as the service concluded, the door of the chapel swung open on a gust of air and a beam of sunshine speared through the stained glass window above the altar. The brothers and many of the family crossed themselves and whispered voices shared the belief that Nicholas was happy to be reunited with his love.

CRIME

James had received a letter from the king of England. Reading the content he wished to consult with his advisors and sent out orders for them to attend him.

As soon as they received the summons Erroll and Huntly hastened from the hall towards the stairway followed by a number of courtiers. Deep in conversation whilst descending, Huntly was bustled by a crush of giggling ladies as they hurried to attend one of the king's mistresses. Distracted by their beauty and chatter, he missed his footing and fell back upon the wall. Unable to regain the step he hurtled backwards down the stairs tumbling over and over as he descended.

There were screams from the ladies as he went past them knocking one off her feet and into another. His head spun as the walls rushed past him and he tried in vain to grab anything to halt his fall.

Lying prone at the foot of the stairway a trickle of blood escaped his ear and his eyes were fixed. Ladies screamed and fussed covering their faces and sobbing. The noise brought the king himself to find the cause and seeing that the earl was dead he indicated to his guards to guide the ladies away whilst the body was removed.

George Gordon 2nd Earl of Huntly was seventy-five years old when he passed away. Elizabeth Hay, William's sister, had been his third wife and he had seen many historic events during his lifetime, not least the marriage of his daughter to a

pretender to the throne of England. Catherine found it difficult to forgive her father for giving her to be used by the king
in exchange for being made Chancellor of Scotland and
refused to attend his funeral but many nobles, including
William Hay, knew him to be a good man and mourned his
loss.

His son Alexander became Earl of Huntly on his death
and in sympathy with his sister's protests at having been used
by her father for his aggrandisement, permitted her to choose
her second husband herself.

CHAPTER 24

James IV was proving to be a strong king in Scotland and began to construct magnificent buildings at strongholds throughout the kingdom. His court was becoming famous throughout Europe as a centre for the arts and science. He was dedicated to education and founded King's College in Aberdeen and a surgeons' college in Edinburgh which was to be given the body of an executed criminal once a year on which to practice anatomy. He commissioned the fabulous Holyrood Palace in Edinburgh and a Royal Chapel and Great Hall at Stirling Castle with beautiful stained glass windows bearing the arms of the greatest nobles in Scotland.

After so many years of conflict, Scotland was being brought under the control of the king.

James had been fifteen years old when he ascended the throne. He had been used, against his will, to bring down his father and realising he had played a significant part in his father's death, he wore a celice – an uncomfortable metal chain – about his waist as penance, adding links to it each year to increase the weight.

On 8th August 1503 at the age of thirty, James by proxy – the Earl of Bothwell standing for the king – married the twelve-year-old Margaret Tudor, daughter of King Henry VII of England bringing Scotland and England together. Margaret's dowry was to be £10,000 and her allowance was fixed at £1,000 Scots. As a marriage gift, she would receive Ettrick Forest, the castles of Doune, Newark and Stirling, the palaces of Methven and Linlithgow, the Earldom of Dunbar, the shires of Linlithgow and Stirling and other pieces of land.

King Henry VII of England's priority was securing his crown and dealing with conflicts with France. The constant diversion of attacks on his northern border from the Scots was a distraction and expense he could well do without. Peace with Scotland would solve many of his problems.

James and King Henry had agreed on a pact of perpetual peace the previous year and the marriage sealed the agreement. Henry believed that, as a result, England would eventually control Scotland through the children of this marriage and James hoped to bring an end to the continual fighting between the two countries which was draining the economy and costing so many lives.

The barons of Scotland had been brought under the control of the crown and the country could look forward to a period of peace and prosperity.

Although the marriage had taken place by proxy, the couple were not to meet for some years. King James was considered to be highly sexed as he already had a number of bastard children and King Henry was painfully aware of the risks not only of childbirth but also in sex. The death of Katherine of Aragon's brother had been put down to an eagerness to procreate putting a fatal strain on his weak constitution and just two months after the betrothal of James and Margaret, Henry's son, Prince Arthur, had died. Henry blamed himself for giving the boy premature sexual experience which he saw as causing the boy's death.

When finally the couple met, the arrival of Princess Margaret was an event to be remembered for generations. The party had travelled through York, Durham, Newcastle and Berwick, led by the Earl of Surrey. Margaret's ladies rode on palfreys or were drawn on litters and were escorted by gentlemen, squires and pages.

They were greeted by the Archbishop of Glasgow as they crossed the border into Scotland to great clamour from the drummers, trumpeters and minstrels who accompanied them.

The archbishop was accompanied by a thousand Scottish lords and gentlemen bedecked in fine jewels and gold chains and heralded by a hundred pipers.

When they arrived at Dalkeith Castle, King James made a grand entrance wearing a jacket of red velvet and accompanied by forty of his gentlemen. William Hay was amongst them and was stunned by Margaret's beauty. She bowed to her future husband and James bowed low before they kissed in greeting. James offered his arm and Margaret placed her hand on it for him to lead her into the Great Hall which adjoined the tower castle. Leading her to the high table where two ornate oak chairs stood side by side, they took their places together.

Later in the evening he silenced the minstrels and sat before the clavichord which he played for her to her great delight. Taking up a lute he continued to demonstrate his skills as a musician and impressed her with his musicality.

When Margaret retired to her room, she found her ladies gasping in admiration over a fabulous dress and robe of cloth of gold trimmed with black velvet and black fur. It was a gift from James and matched his own outfit so that they could dress alike for their entry into Edinburgh. Margaret was delighted and held the dress against her looking in the mirror and twirling around whispering, 'Queen Margaret of Scotland.'

Their entry into Edinburgh was greeted with cheers. The church bells were ringing throughout the city and rich and poor alike turned out to see the spectacle. Margaret rode pillion behind James and they were escorted by two hundred knights.

The king wore a jacket of cloth-of-gold bordered with purple velvet, a doublet of violet satin and scarlet hose. William Hay was responsible for the king's safety and riding immediately behind the king he scanned the crowds for possible risks. Amidst the milling crowds, it was a real possibility that an assassin could lurk, concealed by the huge number of people. Although the union was expected to be to the benefit of Scotland, there were still those who had suffered as a result of the king's bringing order to his kingdom. A shout from a window of one of the high buildings which lined the route proved to be no more than an enthusiastic drunk toasting the couple's health and shouting lewd remarks but William was alert to any threat which may occur.

As the procession made its way through the city, they stopped to witness the numerous pageants which were being performed in their honour.

The next morning the union of the thistle and the rose was celebrated in the chapel at the Palace of Holyrood. The bride wore a gown trimmed in crimson, a gold collar encrusted with jewels and a long coif below the crown made from thirty-five coins. James was magnificent in white damask with sleeves of crimson satin and black cuffs, a doublet of cloth of gold, scarlet hose and a bonnet of black cloth in which there was a rich ruby.

Margaret entered the abbey and stood near the font, with the Archbishop of York on her right hand and the Earl of Surrey on her left. The king was accompanied by his brother, the Archbishop of St. Andrews, by the steward, the chamberlain, William Hay the constable, the marshal and their staffs and by many other nobles, knights and gentlemen.

The ceremony was carried out by the archbishops of both Glasgow and York with James having his arm around Margaret's waist for much of the time.

The wedding feast was sumptuous with dishes of roast crane, roast swan and many others followed by dancing and entertainment until finally, James whispered in Margaret's ear. She looked at him with laughter in her eyes as he suddenly took her hand and they dashed away to his chamber leaving those who would witness the bedding to follow on their heels. On reaching the room he swept her through the door slamming it and shooting the bolt before even the nimblest of courtiers could follow. Laughing, the royal couple fell onto the bed exhausted.

When they had recovered their breath James took Margaret's hand and held it to his lips. 'My love, you are yet but a child. I shall not take that which is mine by right tonight but wait a while until you are a little older.'

'But sir, what will people say if our marriage is not consummated?' she asked nervously.

'Have no fear, the secret will be ours.' He took out his knife and placing it in the fold of his palm he drew it out slicing through the skin and rubbed the blood upon the sheet. 'There, they shall be none the wiser.'

Margaret was relieved and thanked him. James blew out all but one of the candles and then helped her to undress. Holding back the sheets he swept a bow to her inviting her into the bed before undressing himself and lying beside her.

The following morning, James gifted the borough of Kilmarnock to her as a morrowing gift. Edinburgh was lit up by bonfires and days of celebration and festivities followed.

In the following weeks, James took his new bride on a tour of his realm accompanied by many of the Scottish lords. When they arrived at Stirling Castle, Margaret was shocked to find a nursery of James' bastard children. He loved his children and recognised all of them. She was further affronted to find many of his mistresses at court and openly flirting with him but in her youth, she was at a loss as to how to deal with it. Finally deciding to face him about the situation Margaret spoke her mind. 'Sire, you have many children already. I trust that ours will not find themselves at odds with them in future years.'

'You have nothing to fear my dear,' he assured her with a gentle smile. 'We will have many children and none will surpass them. If it will put your mind at rest I will have my lords swear to support our children before all others both in my lifetime and ever after.'

'I demand that you also remove your bastards from Stirling!' she responded with surprising command for a lady of tender years.

James was happy to comply with her demands on this count but made no comment about setting aside his mistresses. In 1501 Janet Kennedy had born the king a son, James, Earl of Moray. Jane was a great influence on the king and in spite of his new wife's beauty and youth, Janet continued to entertain him for a further two years after his marriage, only to be replaced, then, by the young and comely Isabel Stewart of Buchan.

Even with a wife and acknowledged mistress, the king was not satisfied. His appetite was renown throughout the court and was the envy of many nobles who gave the more outrageous of his conquests nick-names, 'Janet bare ars' being one of the more popular.

CHAPTER 25

William Hay, 3rd Earl of Erroll used his influence to find places at court for many of his family, primarily the ladies who entered Margaret's household as ladies in waiting and advised her as she grew.

When William passed away, he was mourned not just by his family and friends but by the king and by many who knew him to be a good and honest man. Those who had pledged themselves to him had never regretted doing so. The brothers at Coupar Angus, who had benefitted greatly from his generous donations, were happy to repay his kindness in any way they could and assured his family of their prayers for his soul.

William's sons had families of their own. His eldest, William now the 4th Earl of Erroll, had had two children, William and Elizabeth, and his younger son, Thomas, had George and Beatrix. Thomas was now the Laird of Logie through his wife and William had been prepared by his father to take over the exceptional role which he inherited as Constable of Scotland. The brothers were close and took every opportunity to spend time together at Erroll, Slains or at Delgatie Castle in Turriff with Gilbert. The extensive lands which they and their cousins now held gave them power over vast swathes of Scotland and their support for the king meant that they, in turn, could be confident of his support.

Young William was flourishing in his new role and, when he was not required at court, spent many weeks visiting his lands and supervising their use. He excelled in his duties both judicial and martial. He presided over tournaments and enjoyed participating in them.

As he prepared to face yet another opponent at the tilts in Edinburgh, Donald, his herald, was called aside by a messenger. William noticed the frown on Donald's face and approached to discover what was amiss.

'My Lord, this man brings grave news. Your wife has lost the child she carried and is gravely ill.'

William instructed Donald to call the tournament to a halt and sped away to prepare for his departure. Leaving Donald and his grooms to care for his destrier, William mounted his second horse and rode furiously back to Slains Castle. As he rode the weather closed in. The wind howled and rain lashed him soaking him to the skin and making it almost impossible to see. In spite of the conditions William pressed his mount on. He slid from his saddle and stumbled towards the steps dripping and exhausted. His arrival was too late.

Christian had followed their child to the grave and lay serenely in their chamber. William hugged his children to him as they stood beside her body grieving. Finally, the children's nurse came and with a look of sympathy, she gently took the children away leaving him to say his farewells to his beautiful wife.

William's brother Thomas had followed him from the joust as soon as his steward had removed his armour for him. Racing after William he arrived at Slains Castle and slid from his horse before racing in to find his brother.

The stillness as he entered the hall told him the dreadful news. Taking the stairs two at a time he met William in the doorway of his chamber. He tried to speak but William brushed past him and strode away, leaving Thomas to nod consent to Christian's maid proceeding to lay out her body.

William sat in his chair. He held his head in his hands and sat motionlessly. Thomas approached and sat opposite. Neither spoke for over an hour. Logs cracked on the fire and voices called in the bailey but the silence in the room was unbreakable.

Finally, Thomas rose from his chair and placed his hand on William's shoulder. William turned his head to look at his brother. Slowly he stood up and put his arms around Thomas' neck. The men held each other in silence as each shared their grief.

The people of Scotland were growing to love their new king. James travelled throughout his kingdom making himself known to his people. He spoke Gaelic which endeared him to the highlanders and made it possible for him to speak to them directly. Although he had always worn his hair and beard long before his marriage, he was distressed when Margaret shied away from his kisses. She made little of it and would not confess to him of any dislike of his attentions but when James questioned her maid, he discovered it was a dislike of his beard. The Countess of Surry offered to remove the offending whiskers and was rewarded with fifteen ells of cloth-of-gold costing £330 and her daughter the same length of damask costing £180 for doing so. Margaret was delighted when she saw the results of what he allowed her to believe had been his own decision.

He was temperate in all that he did eating only as he needed to and dressing in great finery only when the occasion called for it. His care for his people was well known and when he was approached by a poor child, who took his hand in her simplicity, he waved away those who would have struck her to the ground for her insolence and instead gave her three shillings. Tales of his kindness drew support from his people and admiration from the wise.

James impressed his nobles with his courage, always being first into an affray without thought for his own safety and expecting courage and fearless support from his soldiers.

The king was to spend Christmas at Linlithgow and had spent the last month in Edinburgh whilst Linlithgow Castle was cleaned and prepared for the great festivities. Many nobles and their wives had received invitations to the festivities and as William and Thomas Hay arrived they met John Hay of Yester, Edmund Hay of Megginch, his cousin Edmund of Leys and Alexander of Delgatie on the approach to Linlithgow. 'Well met cousins!' William greeted them. 'We must find time to talk during this holiday.'

As they rode towards the castle they shared the road with carts full of tapestries, silver vessels and furniture which had been at Edinburgh and was returning with the king for the festivities. Even windows fitted with glass were to be found on the carts. The noise made conversation difficult as carters struggled on the muddy lane and called to each other in greeting or for help to extricate a cart which had become stuck in a pot hole. Minstrels played as they walked to show off their skills in the hope of employment yet knowing full well that they would receive a warm welcome to the festivities. There was much mirth when a tumbler slipped in the mud and measured his length, rising muddied from nose to heel he milked the opportunity to entertain and was thrown a small purse for his troubles.

Appetising smells were already coming from the kitchens as the guests arrived and everybody knew that, although King James himself ate little, he would offer a table groaning with good food.

The immense fireplace was glowing with a fire which warmed the whole room and guests warmed themselves as they came in from the bitter December weather. The floor was freshly strewn with rushes and sweet herbs and the tapestries swayed gently in the draughts. The hum of conversation grew louder as more guests arrived creating an atmosphere of cosy bonhomie. The king, wearing a crimson satin side gown and long gown of velvet lined with damask, sat in a chair which was covered with red velvet and fringed with silk.

The castle was alive with colour; members of the court were dressed in their new liveries which the king had presented them with for Christmas and guests displayed their wealth and importance by wearing their finest clothes and jewels.

On Christmas morning, the Chapel clerks sang a carol for the king as he, followed by the heralds, pursuivants and his guests, went to high mass. The Christmas meal began with the entry of the boar's head which was held aloft by the cook and accompanied by a small boy singing the Boar's Head carol in a high piping voice. The procession from the kitchen continued with delicacies of all kinds and fine French wines.

Following the meal the tables were removed and benches drawn close to the fire so that the company could enjoy the entertainment of harp and fiddle music. Mummers performed dances and the court fool made fun of the king's fine guests. Finally, Watschod, the tale-teller, entertained them with stories of heroism and adventure accompanied by the minstrels who had arrived with the guests.

Much of the conversation was about the king's interest in surgery and his attempts to operate on wounds and bad teeth. He had recently appointed an alchemist, John Damien, to discover the quinta essencia in order to turn base metal into gold. John was present at the feast and some nobles questioned him in mock respect about his experiments. Nobody took him very seriously since his attempt to fly by jumping off the battlements of Stirling Castle had culminated in his landing at the foot of Castle Rock with a broken leg.

As the evening drew on the guests began to grow weary. The king stood to leave the festivities and retire to his bed, bidding the company to continue if the wished. The company bowed as he made to leave the hall and William Hay felt himself held by the arm as the king passed and guided him out of the gathering. 'I would speak to you, Lord Erroll,' James declared. 'I have a new wife for you.'

'Your majesty is most generous but I do not look to wed.'

'It is my wish that you wed, William. You have seen your bride this day. She is Margaret Kerr. You danced with her earlier and a handsome couple you made. You will wed this spring. It is my command. And I shall create you, High Sherriff of Aberdeen, as my wedding gift to you.'

It was just four weeks before William's marriage that King Henry VII died. His son, Henry VIII was to prove to be quite a different man to his father. Whereas Henry VII had been anxious to avoid war, Henry VIII was hot-headed and impulsive, eager to prove himself as a soldier and to win back Gascony from France. William was concerned that Scotland's alliance with France would mean they were called upon to defend against English attacks.

Although William's marriage to Margaret took place as planned, he was soon re-called to the privy-council and sat with the king and his advisors, in Edinburgh, to discuss the possibilities should France call upon Scotland to support the Auld Alliance. He had been surprised to find himself quite taken with his new wife who was a skilled castellan and attentive to his every need. She in her turn found William to be a kind and considerate husband. He was of a fine body which, unlike many men, bore few scars of battle, and of handsome countenance. She set about stitching a fine shirt for him with a border of red shields intertwined with mistletoe and promised to have it finished when he returned from the king's court as, this time, she was not to accompany him being already with child.

It was 1512 when an ambassador from France arrived to ask for Scotland's help. The privy-council agreed that Scotland, by the terms of the treaty of 1502, could help but not actually invade England. Had James merely sent ships to help, as they advised, all might have been well. Instead, in his fervour to uphold the auld alliance and in the face of Henry's ambitions in France and knowing that the ships he had sent could not possibly reach France in time, he found himself in an impossible situation. He had to decide which treaty to uphold. Inducements by way of gold, arms and gifts of jewellery from France along with the offer of military advisors, helped to sway his decision.

The relationship between Scotland and England had deteriorated following English attacks on Scottish ships and James decided to order William to muster his army as he had decided to invade England.

Queen Anne, wife of Louis XII, had asked James to, 'take one yard of English land', in the hope of forcing Henry to send some of his troops back to defend the borders.

By 24th July, William Hay had gathered men from all parts of Scotland in the name of the King and six of James' ships were sent to France to support Louis. Edmund Hay of Leys was given command of one of the ships, taking some of his clansmen with him to serve on board. William's own son was furious that, having taken a fall from his horse whilst out hunting, he had broken his leg and was unable to join the gathering forces.

Scotland witnessed fevered activity throughout its length and breadth as noblemen, gentry and burgesses hurried to assemble men and equipment. Over 40,000 men assembled at Boroughmuir outside Edinburgh.

The Scottish Lyon Herald was granted an audience by King Henry on 11th August at the English camp outside the besieged town of Therouanne and proceeded to deliver the news of James' intention to attack England.

At the king's command, William sent out a proclamation through all the realms of Scotland, that all men between the ages of sixteen and sixty should be ready within twenty days with forty days provisions.

William Hay knew that the king was held in high regard throughout Scotland, including the Highland chiefs, and had little difficulty in persuading them to muster. Every town and village was a flurry of activity as families gathered supplies for their menfolk to take with them. Smiths and armourers worked long hours to make weapons from ploughshares and farm tools to equip the ordinary soldiers and provide the nobility with appropriate weapons for their rank.

Wives and sweethearts waved to their menfolk as they left, some with tears and others in the hope of their men returning with plunder or honours. Some womenfolk chose to go with the men to serve the gathered forces in whichever way it paid them to do so.

Whilst the preparations were underway, Alexander, Lord Home, Chamberlain of Scotland, took the opportunity to take advantage of the ruined towers which the Scottish forces had destroyed a few years earlier, and, mustering a force of 7-8,000 men, led a raid on Northumberland. They met with great success and were making their way back to Scotland with their plunder when they were ambushed by Sir William Bulmer. Bulmer's archers killed over five hundred of Home's men and took 400 hostages, along with Home's standard and the plunder they had gathered.

The Scottish army was ready by 19th August and, gathering men as they went, reached Coldstream ready to invade an undefended England.

Although the most wealthy and powerful had fine armour, weapons and horses, the common soldiers carried whatever they could find to fight with. Some carried farm implements and others improvised spears or swords, claymores and battle axes, but a supply of thousands of eighteen foot long pikes with lethal spikes was made available by France.

The French officers sent to train the Scottish soldiers, began by forming them into schiltrons – tightly packed formations and strictly disciplined. The front ranks were to be supplied with steel armour but those further back were less well protected.

Under James' orders, William gathered an artillery train of seventeen medium to large cannon and a number of smaller weapons. The largest guns fired iron balls weighing sixty-six pounds, necessitating hundreds of horses and great carts to transport the ammunition. The guns travelled frustratingly slowly, at about two miles per hour, with thirty-six oxen needed to pull each of them and men with spades to level the road before them; blacksmiths to maintain the gun carriages and teams of gunners. The site for firing the guns needed to be prepared and levelled and even then they could only be fired about every thirty minutes as they would quickly overheat.

On 24th August James held his last parliament at Twizel Hough. An Act was passed stating that the heirs of any man who was killed, or died serving in the army, would come into their inheritances exempt from paying wardship, relief or marriage.

∽∾

Thomas Howard, Earl of Surrey, although in his seventies and crippled with arthritis, had great military experience and was well favoured and trusted by King Henry. His disappointment at not being included in the French campaign was made up for by being appointed as Lord Lieutenant of the Northern Marches.

He began his preparations for war immediately by commandeering ships to transport supplies to Newcastle and gathering forces and money from Yorkshire, Lancashire, Cheshire, Cumberland, Westmorland and Northumberland.

Surrey's army was less well supplied. The king had taken his pick of the men and weapons with him to France leaving the defenders with about eighteen small calibre field guns which fires shot weighing about a pound. Unlike the Scottish balls, the English ones travelled quickly and could break into small pieces on impact causing damage all around them. They could be fired relatively rapidly and were lighter to manoeuvre.

The English forces also consisted of their fearsome archers and common soldiers armed with billhooks which were in effect hedging tools on 8 foot long poles.

Both armies were supplemented by men and women supporting them with food, supplies and entertainment.

The baggage trains carried not only the beds and fine comforts that the nobility expected but also the basic requirements of small beer, fodder for the horses, weapons and food.

The moving armies stripped the land of supplies to feed their numbers leaving farmers and their families to starve. Surrey's supplies were delivered to the port of Newcastle but even so, the fifty miles to be covered in order to reach the army made it impractical to continue to use the port. Using Berwick on Tweed as a supply port meant shorter delivery routes and gave Surrey a distinct advantage.

James always led from the front and was quick to lead the attacks on Norham and Etal Castles. Having taken them with ease he next attacked the nearby Ford Castle. Ford was held by the beautiful Lady Elizabeth Heron whose husband, Sir John Heron, was a prisoner of the Scots, as hostage for the murderous deeds of his brother, the Bastard Heron who had killed Sir Robert Kerr.

Elizabeth soon surrendered the castle to King James who made it his headquarters. The Lady Elizabeth knew that she could not hold the castle against the might of James' artillery but, knowing of James' weakness for women, rightly believed that she could hold James himself through her womanly charms.

Taking control of the castle James gave orders to his officers to restrain the castle soldiers but, fearing no danger from the women folk, he allowed those who would, to leave and others to provide for the needs of his men.

Elizabeth was respected as a noblewoman and treated as such, eating with the king and allowed her freedom within the castle precincts. That evening James was not surprised to find a naked female in his bed as he believed it to be a servant, warming it for him as was the practice. He was, however, surprised to find that it was none other than the Lady Elizabeth waiting to attend to his every desire. Slipping from the bed she helped James to disrobe taking every opportunity to touch him as she did so until he could restrain himself no longer and partook of all that was offered to him.

The following morning James gave his orders but lingered within the castle taking every opportunity to be near Elizabeth. So taken with her was he, that it was all his advisors could do to gain an audience with him.

Whilst the soldiers plundered the local area, William Hay and the king's other advisors urged him to move against the English before they were able to gather greater forces.

When the king finally left Ford Castle Elizabeth found that her sacrifice was in vain when William advised the king that to leave Ford standing was madness; the English could use it to their advantage. Realising the wisdom of his words James clapped William on the shoulders with the words, 'Away to it then, Lord Erroll, but spare the women,' and gave Elizabeth a wry smile as burning torches were brought and barrels of gunpowder taken into the hall, that her castle might be burnt to the ground.

Ever since the Scots had been on English ground the weather had been against them. There had scarce been a dry hour ant the cold wind chilled them through. James and his commanders had found the perfect position to camp their troops, on the hill known locally as Flodden Edge. It took time to prepare the positions for the guns but the English had far to travel and time was on their side.

Resources were dwindling and some of the nobles chose to send a few of their men home to take much of the plunder they had acquired to safety and return with fresh supplies.

This meant that numbers were reduced a little but still left the largest Scottish army that had ever mustered, camped on Flodden Edge.

King James exchanged messages with Surry through their heralds; Surrey wrote asking James to come forth and give battle on Milfield Plain north of Wooler. James responded - 'It beseems not an Earl to handle a King after this fashion,' suggesting that it was not for an earl to make demands of a king. Each held the other's herald for some time before permitting them to return to their camp when battle was agreed. When this was done, King James sent for his advisors to brief them on the exchange.

Arriving at the king's tent the nobles heard what they took to be a scuffle inside. Throwing open the tent flap they were taken aback to find the king just finishing with a camp follower. 'The cannon was loaded so I thought I'd try a test fire,' he grinned. Tossing the woman a coin he straightened his robes and became more serious.

'We hold a splendid defensive position,' James explained to his nobles. 'We are on high ground with our right flank protected by marshland; the land slopes away steeply on our left towards the River Twill. The English can only come at us head on, up the hill, and we have our artillery positioned to prevent this.'

His Scottish military advisors were concerned. They had never seen this entrenchment tactic previously and were reluctant to submit to the advice of the French advisors.

'The plan is to form up the men into pike columns which will roll down the hill onto the English,' explained the French.

In the English camp, Surrey was worried. He knew his only approach would be a costly frontal attack. 'We must seek an alternative way to attack. I will not have this Scottish king best me through his irregular and un-chivalric behaviour!' he declared.

That evening, as Surrey strode amongst his men, he heard a disturbance off to his right. One of the camp followers had crept up behind one of the common soldiers and clapped her hands over his eyes. He leapt up and grabbed her sweeping her off her feet and kissing her soundly. Surrey stopped suddenly. 'My tent!' he ordered his advisors abruptly.

When they had all gathered in his tent he explained his idea. 'That whore reached her man by creeping up from the rear. She reached him without being noticed. If we follow her example and manoeuvre around behind the Scots forces we can take them by surprise!'

A scout was sent out to see the lie of the land and came back with the intelligence that they could certainly get round behind the Scottish camp. Surry thought it worth a try. At least they might be able to get James to come down and fight on ground more favourable to the English.

Surrey was desperate. 'The men are drinking water,' he was told. The risk of disease from water was well known and this told Surrey that he needed to force James to come out and fight soon before his men were ill or deserted through hunger and thirst. He discovered that it might be possible to get behind the Scots, as he had hoped, and attack from the rear at Branxton Hill. It was risky but Surry was desperate.

In King James' camp, there were heated discussions about what the English were up to.

'So, my lords, ye may understand by this you shall be called the merchant, and your king 'a rose nobill', and England a common hazarder that has nothing to jeopardy but a bad halfpenny in comparison of our noble King and an auld crooked Earl lying in a chariot,' declared Lindsay, meaning that the English were risking an ailing old earl but they risked losing their king. He wanted King James kept safely away from the battle which was to come. When the king heard his words he was furious and threatened to hang Lindsay from his own gate. 'I shall fight this day with England,' swore James.

Friday 9th September the day broke dank and drizzly. to English army broke camp leaving behind their tents and carrying only their weapons. The vanguard marched over Twizzell Bridge the rear-guard using a ford to cross and they advanced towards Branxton Hill. The army had to cross the Pallinsburn stream which was, in itself, but a man's step over but due to the dreadful weather in recent months, the ground either side of it was marshy forcing them to divide.

King James, watching the movement of the English troops, sent out scouts to discover what the English were doing. Suddenly a breathless scout rode into the Scottish camp and leaping from his horse he fell on one knee before the king. 'The English have crossed the Till, Sire, and are preparing to attack our rear!'

James ordered his troops to break camp and for the rubbish to be gathered into a bonfire and burnt to create a dense smoke screen to conceal their movements from the English but preventing the Scots from watching the English movements.

James sprang into action giving orders for his army to be turned about and march to the top of Branxton Hill. Tents and baggage were left where they were but the guns needed to be turned around. The gunners needed the sites for their guns prepared which took time and there was no opportunity for surveying the ground.

There was still a feeling of confidence within the Scottish troops and any anxiety was overcome through the hustle and bustle of preparations for engagement. William Hay and his brother Thomas took the opportunity to drill their men. There had been little enough training in the new mode of fighting for commanders or their men, many of whom were inexperienced in combat of any sort.

The Scots still held the high ground and Erroll explained that as the English struggled up the hill they, in the close formation of the schiltron, would roll down towards them sweeping them away.

James and his commanders deployed the troops into their positions about a quarter of a mile up from the foot of Branxton Hill. All were on foot and the king gave orders for shoes and boots to be removed to get a better grip on the wet, slippery ground.

King James men took the centre with Earls Erroll, Crawford and Montrose on his left and the Earls of Lennox and Argyle on his right. The vanguard was led by Lord Home and the Earl of Huntly whilst The Earl of Bothwell led the reserve division.

When the smoke finally cleared the entire Scottish army had moved their position northward from Flodden Hill to the adjacent Branxton Hill. They could see the English vanguard on their left moving onto the flat ground facing Lords Home and Huntly.

The sound of the bagpipes stirred the blood of the Scots and cast fear into the hearts of the English.

A shot from an English gun began an artillery exchange. As William and Thomas looked on, the lighter English guns soon began to gain an advantage whilst the heavier Scottish guns were slow and suffering from being poorly bedded in after being hurriedly moved.

'I have my worries about our formations,' confided Thomas to William. 'Tightly packed as our men are we present a good target for the English guns.'

'Aye, our shots are lost in the soft ground,' agreed William.

Looking at his men, William saw that they were shocked by the tremendous noise from the guns. Mostly farm workers the common soldiers had never experienced the like and were nervous in the face of such smoke and noise.

Thomas nudged William and pointed. Home and Huntly's troops had started down the gentle slope at the western end of Branxton Hill facing the English vanguard. The English guns continued to fire and there were numerous casualties suffered as Home and Huntly approached but William and Thomas were encouraged to see that the soldiers stayed in formation and, outnumbering the English vanguard, had the advantage. The Scottish schiltron was proving successful and there were cheers from the Scots as many English fled the field. Howard was struck to the ground more than once and fearing a rout he sent to the Earl of Surrey for reinforcements. Now the Scottish pike schiltrons began to break up and Home and Huntly felt it wise to withdraw feeling that they had done their job and now needed to re-form their men whilst the remaining Scottish troops did their part.

'Why is Alexander Gordon taking his men from the field?' Thomas asked William.

'I hope it is merely to re-form,' he replied, 'it will be difficult to get them back into formation in the battlefield. We must learn from this.'

A messenger from the king stood before Erroll. 'The king commands you to advance.' They were the words he had been waiting for. All apprehension vanished as he indicated to Crawford and Montrose that the order had been given for them to take action. His pulse raced as the three earls roared to their men simultaneously, 'Forward!'

The tightly packed formation began to move down the hill. Erroll strode forward with his brother, Thomas, on his right and Gilbert Hay of Delgatie on his left. John Hay of

Yester was on John's left and many other Hays moved with them.

It was steeper than the western slope where Hume had been and men slithered on the wet ground as they struggled to hold formation in silence except for the occasional muttered curse as footholds were lost. As they reached the foot of the slope the front ranks found themselves knee deep in mud. Erroll found himself falling forward; the weight of his armour preventing him from regaining his balance and the press of men behind endeavouring to maintain the formation as they had been ordered to, pressing down on him. Thomas was aware that his brother had fallen but could do nothing to help as his own feet were held in the mud and sinking fast.

William was aware of arrows rushing into the ranks of men as he struggled onto his elbows to keep his head from being submerged in the mud. In his last moment, he felt a body fall on top of him driving him deeper into the suffocating mire. The breath was forced from his body as images of his family and Slains misted in his mind.

Thomas Hay found himself unable to withdraw his feet from the mud. His movement restricted by the armour which should have protected him, he struggled to free himself as arrows rained down from the English bows. He saw a few of his men break free of the mud and move forward but their long pikes were useless in close quarters and they were hacked by the English billhooks. Their screams rang in his ears as they met their deaths. Men who were his kin and those he had known all of his life were meeting a grotesque and untimely end and he was powerless to help.

Knowing that he was trapped his only hope was that the English would spare his life to extract a ransom for his release but it was not to be. The English hacked their way through the Scottish soldiers.

He was aware of their approach and time seemed to slow as the distance between him and the enemy shortened. Seeing that the English were sparing none, he struggled frantically before being pressed down by a body falling across him. Pain tore through his shoulder as a billhook found its mark. Within seconds the pain was obliterated as the next blow ripped out his throat.

The English forces raged through the trapped Scots destroying them with no account of rank. All of Erroll's kinsmen died upon the field that day, either during or after the battle. Eighty-seven Hays lay dead by the end of the day leaving none to take the dreadful news to their loved ones.

King James knew that his only hope was to kill or capture Surrey, but Surrey showed no sign of advancing up the hill towards him. James had a reputation for being impetuous, and, true to character, he led from the front taking his division down the hill towards Surrey and into the same boggy ground which had cost the lives of Erroll and his men.

The Earl of Surrey was surrounded by his bodyguards and James now found it impossible to see what was happening to his soldiers, being, as he was, in the thick of the fighting. All around him, the English billhooks were destroying the pikes held by the Scots and ravaging his men. James himself was a vulnerable target.

The Earls of Lennox and Argyle had command of the highlanders in their leine croich; the saffron colour, achieved by soaking them in horse urine, giving them a distinctive and eye-watering smell. These were covered by deerskin or cowhide jerkins, waxed to make them waterproof and giving protection from the elements which the English lacked. They would fight with battle axes and claymores which were much more useful in hand to hand fighting than the long pikes.

Seeing the king's difficulty they advanced down the hill but having little in the way of body protection against arrows, they fell victim to the English bowmen. Some tried to flee and the battlefield became a seething mass of confusion.

King James fell and was slain amongst his people just a few feet from Surrey. His body was trampled beneath feet and his death went unnoticed as the battle raged. It was only after the battle had finished that his remains were found, the iron belt still around his waist, and taken to London.

∽∾

As night fell, the battle, which had lasted for four hours, left a scene of carnage. Ten thousand Scots lay dead beside their king. Nine earls, fourteen Lords of Parliament and seventy-nine gentry would not return to their families. No noble family in Scotland escaped loss.

News of the defeat was quickly taken to Edinburgh but was met by disbelief. It was only as the truth became apparent that there was panic and the inhabitants set about building a wall to keep out the English forces that they feared would advance on the city; it was not to be.

The surviving Scottish soldiers made their way home taking stories of the carnage as they went. The horrors of the battle were told in towns and villages and women who had so recently waved to their menfolk as they set off in hope of battle honours and plunder, wept openly in the streets. Every area of Scotland was affected leaving families without husbands, fathers, sons, brothers and friends. Following on the ravages of plague the population of Scotland was so depleted that there were not enough people left to gather the harvest. Many families had lost every man and women were left to fend for themselves without hope of re-marrying because there were so few men left.

Queen Margaret waited in Linlithgow Palace for James' return. She had born James six children but only the seventeen-month-old child, James, who she now cuddled, had survived.

When the news was brought to her she was at first incredulous; James had promised to return. It could not be that he would not keep his word. Slowly the truth penetrated her mind and she suffered just as every other woman in the land, sobbing and wailing until her ladies sent for herbs to bring on sleep.

At Slains Castle, Margaret, Countess of Erroll, waited with Thomas Hay's wife, Margaret. When finally news came of the deaths of both William and Thomas they were inconsolable. Every woman in the castle precincts had lost their husbands and sons and their grief was unbearable. Every Hay who had gone to the battle had been slain. It would be impossible to run the castle without men folk. Food was needed and wood for fires and buildings. Weapons were needed to defend them….but what use without the men to use them. Horses to be cared for; fish to be caught; there were so many jobs that they relied on the men to do. It seemed impossible that, left with boys and old men, they could survive. And yet they knew they must go on.

William's son, also William, was now the 5th Earl of Erroll and would need support. At almost eighteen years of age, he and his cousin George were the only young men left to them and would carry a heavy burden.

Their grieving and worry was interrupted by the arrival of an old man riding a horse which was clearly above his station. He was helped down by a young stable lad and supported as he stumbled. He had clearly ridden hard and was exhausted. Margaret indicated for him to be brought inside and she descended from the hall to find the cause of his arrival.

When he had recovered sufficiently to speak coherently he explained that he had ridden from Huntly. George Gordon had died twelve years ago leaving his wife, Elizabeth, William Hay's sister, a widow. Now she had lost her third son, William, and shared with Erroll's wife the loss of William and Thomas her nephews. Lawrence Oliphant, her sister's son had also been slain. As if this was not enough, people were now accusing her eldest son, Alexander, 3rd Earl of Huntly of running from the battle and abandoning his countrymen to their fate. She was beside herself and terrified that she and her son would be murdered by the mob.

Margaret realised that, great as her loss was, others had lost much more. It could not make her suffering any less but her sense of duty made her react instinctively.

'William,' you must go directly to Huntly and speak to the people. 'You have lost your father and uncle and you have authority. People will listen to you.'

'You ask much of me, Margaret, yet I know my duty and will not back away from it.' And, still reeling from his own loss he sent orders for his horse to be made ready. His elderly manservant prepared his fine robes and helped him to dress. He must present a figure of authority.

Within the hour he was mounted and ready to ride to Huntly. His damaged leg was agony in the stirrups but it was a pain he must endure.

As he arrived the castle gates were opened to admit him. Women and old men crushed against him as he rode through and had to be restrained by fresh-faced guards who looked like children playing at being knights.

Finding his great uncle, Alexander, he shook his hand firmly. 'Welcome William,' he was greeted. 'My condolences at your loss.'

'And mine to you, cousin,' replied William. 'These are dreadful days. We must stand together for the good of

Scotland. Tell me of your experiences later; just give me a brief account of the battle for now. Our first priority must be to calm the people.' Alexander was clearly shocked and struggled to explain the events of the battle.

The two earls went out onto the steps of the castle, William limped badly and was supported by Alexander. William held up his hand for silence. Women still wept and stumbled from weakness but their noise quietened at William's authority.

'Good people,' he began, 'We have all suffered greatly through loss of our loved ones. I myself have lost my father, the Earl of Erroll, and four uncles. Every one of us sent our brave menfolk to fight and fulfil their honourable obligation to support our fine king and country. They went with love in their hearts and with courage. They were the very flowers of the forest. No man faces the battlefield lightly and Alexander Huntly along with Home was the first to lead his men into the battle to face the English. This man is no coward! He played his part and followed the king's orders. Had he not withdrawn his men when he did, they would all have been slaughtered. Some of you are fortunate in that some of your men have returned. You have your laird to thank for that. Our queen stands a widow just as many other women throughout our land. Your laird had lost a dear brother. I have lost my father, four uncles and many more of my kin. As you, I do not yet know the full extent of my loss. But we must all stand together for Scotland. We will mourn our dead – it is right to do so - and will always remember them as heroes, but we must also rebuild our lives and help each other. We have done so before and will do so now. The king is but a babe in arms and there might yet be conflict in our land between those who seek power for themselves. We must be prepared for this and not fight amongst ourselves. Your

Laird will support you and you must support him if you wish to survive. He is a good man and you will do well to heed him and thank him for bringing some of your men home.' And with this, he stepped inside.

Although many people still wept openly, there were murmurs of agreement and one or two people started to drift away. Gradually the yard emptied and silence fell.

William stayed the night with his Aunt Beatrice and Uncle Alexander but returned to Slains the next day knowing full well he would be needed there.

❧ ❧

Queen Margaret sat in her chamber in Linlithgow Palace. Still weak from having recently given birth to yet another child, who had lived but a few hours, she was already pregnant again. She held the infant James, her only surviving son, in her arms and rocked back and forth. 'Why?' she asked over and over again. 'Why did he ignore his advisors and put himself in the front line?'

A gentle voice of a courtier behind her replied, 'It was ever his way. He was a great and chivalrous king and would not ask of his people what he would not do himself.'

'What good is that now that he is no more?' asked the queen, stirred from her grieving by the voice. 'This child will now be king and Scotland will once again have but a child as monarch.'

'The king was prepared for such an event and has named you regent for the prince on the condition that you do not re-marry. He feared a future husband might seek to control the boy.'

'You speak to me of marriage when my husband's body is not yet cold! How could I think of such a thing? The king's body has not yet been brought home….'

291

'I fear it will not be, Your Highness.'

Margaret buried her head in her hands and sobbed. James had been a charismatic man, full of energy, who exhausted his nobles by travelling around Scotland to visit his people, playing golf and hunting. She had loved him dearly and was bereft.

'Your son must be crowned. Preparations must begin right away. Scotland must have a king.'

She knew that this was true and on 21st September, in Stirling Castle, the one-year-old James V was crowned.

In April of the following year, the queen gave birth to another son, Alexander, who was created Duke of Ross. She wept to think how James would never see his new son.

Seeking to find political allies amongst the Scottish nobles, Margaret found herself attracted to Archibald Douglas, 6th Earl of Angus, whose father had died at Flodden, and who used this as a common wound to link him to Margaret. Letting her heart rule her head, she secretly married him in Kinnoull Church near Perth that August.

The couple took her sons, James and Alexander to Stirling Castle.

'I shall not let them take my sons from me,' she declared. I am regent and have sworn to keep them safe. They are my own blood and that of by beloved James. I lost him to Scotland's battle with England but as a princess of England, I shall see my son rule Scotland.

By the terms of the king's will, she had forfeited her right to act as regent for her son by marrying. Archibald Douglas saw the infant king as a route to the Douglases regaining the power they held under James III and was determined to keep the boys under his 'protection'.

The Privy Council called an emergency meeting to discuss the situation.

'The Douglases again seek power. We cannae allow Scotland to be dragged down as it was before by them once agin acting as regent for an infant king.'

'Aye, we canna have them back snatching power and ruling Scotland by threats and violence.'

'If we were to invite Albany to become Regent,' suggested Erroll, 'being born and brought up in France, the people of Scotland would see him as representing the Auld Alliance; and he was the King's brother.'

At twenty years of age, William Hay was the youngest member of the Privy Council, yet he was a very serious young man of great learning being given more to books than the hunt, and well respected for his wisdom.

Nods of agreement met this suggestion and the meeting concluded with the decision that Albany be invited to return to Scotland and become regent. The Council decided that, as Erroll had presented the plan to call upon Albany, he should be sent as Envoy to France to present their invitation.

◇◆◇

In 1515, Albany arrived from France and Margaret was forced to hand over her sons. Although she was pregnant with Douglas' child they were forced to flee to England, where her brother had her lodged in comfort at Harbottle Castle. Within a short time, Margaret was delivered of a daughter, Margaret. The birth was difficult and Margaret lost a lot of blood leaving her weak and ill.

Whilst Margaret lay in her bed, so weak that she relied on her ladies for her every need, news came to Harbottle that her youngest son, Alexander, had died.

'Do not tell my wife of this,' instructed Douglas, fearing that without Margaret he would be unable to gain access to the power he desired. 'She is too weak and the news will distress her so that she might succumb to her suffering.'

As Margaret, The Queen Mother gradually recovered from her ordeal, she decided to travel to London to stay with her family in the hope of gaining their support.

'That is an excellent idea,' approved Douglas. 'I shall return to Scotland where I can be on hand to support James, should he need me.'

Although Margaret was disappointed that he would not be with her, she had not the influence over Douglas to sway his mind and must needs go to London without him.

Archibald Douglas lost no time, when he arrived in Edinburgh, in seeking out Albany and manoeuvring to gain favour with him, suggesting that Margaret had held sway over him in keeping the princes at Stirling Castle.

By the time Margaret returned to Scotland in 1517, she found Douglas had been living with one of his former lovers, Lady Jane Stewart and supporting her with the revenues from Margaret's land.

CHAPTER 26

There was much to be done at Slains Castle and throughout William Hay's lands. So many of his family had died at the Battle of Flodden, that he had to rely on the wives of the fallen and trusted servants to run the estates. Many of his tenants and those who had signed Bonds of Manrent to his father had been killed and their families would starve if he tried to claim the rents which were due to him.

William, like so many other barons, must look to the future, and support his tenants in this dark hour until they could regain their ability to support themselves. By working together his people managed to gather some of the crops to see them through the winter and William insisted they work hard. That summer had seen appalling weather and many crops were lost. Should the next year be similar they would need supplies. He insisted they gather more than the now reduced population needed as insurance against a bad harvest to come.

William made sure that ewes were put to the tups so that there would be lambs the next year. Sales of wool would help to pay for labour and there were always people who would come to Scotland to work if the price was right.

Fully aware that some of his people regularly rowed out to ships which anchored offshore and returned with illicit brandy and wine, he now decided to take advantage of this.

Although it was past midnight, the moon was full and cast its river of light on the sea. A ship in full sail came into sight and sails were lowered as was the anchor. William himself with a crew of youths rowed out to the ship. The captain had set sail without knowing of the devastation which had beset Scotland and carried a hull full of barrels to be sold at a favourable rate to the men of Slains.

When the sailors saw who was aboard the board they made to hoist the sails and up anchor but William's cry of, 'Hold fast!' stopped them in their tracks.

The ship's captain approached. His hand hovered over the hit of his sword.

'I know your business,' William announced. 'I have always chosen to ignore your trade but now I have need of you. I will purchase your cargo and you will take the wool I have and sell it in France. When you return, you will bring more brandy and wine and our deal will be repeated.'

The captain saw an opportunity to make a handsome profit and readily agreed. The barrels were loaded into the tiny craft and rowed ashore.

Wood was needed for the winter, but, with the scarcity of strong labour, he set the women and children to gathering fallen branches and small trees to store. Fresh meat would be in short supply with few men to hunt but women could fish and the catch could be salted for months to come.

There were so many preparations to make for the winter that he was glad of his mother's help in organising the Castle of Slains whilst he went to Erroll to oversee his estates there.

On arriving at Erroll he was glad that he had sent Edmund Hay of Leys with the fleet to France. He had now returned with some of his men and, along with Peter Hay of Megginch, had already set about making preparations for winter.

The most vulnerable families, some of whom had lost all of their menfolk, had been absorbed into the Hay households as servants and were grateful to their lairds. Some of the loons were old enough to have some knowledge of farming and other necessary occupations but others were in need of guidance. Setting the older ones in positions of responsibility gained their respect and most rose to the challenge, although some saw Scotland's disaster as an opportunity to advance themselves and left the land to seek their fortunes.

❧☙

It was almost five years before William took time to find himself a wife. There were many widows with whom he could make a very profitable match but it was Elizabeth Ruthven whom he sought.

Her father, William, 1st Lord Ruthven, sat on the Privy Council with him and had been impressed by Erroll's mature character, not to say fortune. William Ruthven was also one of the four guardians of the young King James V which Erroll thought might prove invaluable. It certainly meant that he had no problem in securing permission for the marriage and a contract was agreed.

Within the year Erroll and Elizabeth had a fine healthy son whom they named William in honour of William's father.

❧☙

In the wake of the losses at the Battle of Flodden, men flocked to sign Bonds of Manrent with William, as a security for lands. William was desperately in need of men to control his lands throughout the kingdom as so many of his family had died alongside his father.

As a member of the Privy Council, it was necessary for William to spend the greater part of his time in Edinburgh. The Scottish Parliament had much experience of noblemen seeking to control the kings of Scotland in their minority and were wary of history repeating itself. The queen mother had returned to Scotland and, in the face of her husband's infidelity, sought to associate herself with Albany. There had been rumours that she intended to become Albany's lover and he planned to murder the king and put himself on the throne of Scotland.

William was in the midst of composing a letter to his wife asking after her and the child when he began to feel unwell. His head and back ached and he decided to complete his task later. Taking to his bed, William fell asleep only to wake an hour later to vomit. He was feverish and threw back the blankets trying to rise and take a glass of wine. Gulping down a second glass he began to shiver and returned to the bed, wrapping himself closely and pulling the sheet about his neck.

His maid mopped his brow and bathed him with cool water, bringing him wine and broth when he could take it. The fever lasted for three days until, on the fourth day, he felt able to rise. The maid threw open the curtains and turned to ask his will. He was startled when she looked at him and screamed. Holding her hands over her mouth she fled the room.

Bewildered by her behaviour William rang the bell to summon a servant to help him dress. As time passed he grew impatient and then angry that nobody arrived. Striding towards the bell to ring again he passed the looking glass and stopped in his tracks. The reason for the girl's behaviour was clear. A rash covered his face and as he looked at his hands he saw signs of it developing there. Not being familiar with the symptoms, William thought to send for an apothecary.

As he stepped from the room he became aware of people standing below stairs, looking up and murmuring. As he descended the stairs the crowd melted away but as they went he caught the word smallpox.

Looking down at his hands he turned them over examining them closely, shocked at the thought of the terrifying disease. As he examined them a young, badly scarred, serving girl appeared before him. 'Sir,' she addressed him, 'I've been sent to care for you. I've had smallpox and they say you can't get it again if you survive it so they've asked me to tend you.'

'Thank you,' he murmured, hardly hearing or understanding in his horror.

He returned to his bed stunned by the thought of being badly scarred...if he lived. A typically 'Handsome Hay', he was horrified at the thought of being ugly.

His young nurse brought food and wine and tended his every need but was shocked a day later when a trickle of blood ran from William's mouth. His skin had started to darken as blood oozed from his veins to spread and form dark patches. Fearing for his life, William requested a writer to the signet to be sent, in order to make his will, but none would come. In desperation, William sent the girl to go with all haste and bring materials so that he could record his own will. Glad to be out of the room the lass gladly obeyed only to return within the hour to find William's body, blackened and dead, upon the bed.

CHAPTER 27

Following Erroll's death, a messenger was sent to Slains from Edinburgh. He bore condolences on William's death from Parliament and wishes for Elizabeth and the child's good health. He also carried the news that, although Parliament had decided that Elizabeth was to be William's guardian along with Alexander Hay of Delgatie, his God Father, the Erroll lands would be held by the Crown until the child reached the age of twenty-one years. In many ways, Elizabeth was relieved. Although her husband had made his surviving cousins' stewards of the lands in Erroll, they had to be overseen and she felt overwhelmed at being widowed, with a young, difficult child to care for, and Slains Castle and its estates to run, without the added burden of Erroll lands.

Two years after the death of William Hay, 5th Earl of Erroll, whilst the king was still only twelve years old, the Queen Mother, with the help of Arran, overthrew Albany's regency and King James V was invested with full royal authority. Her attempts to guide him, however, were thwarted the following year when Douglas returned from England and took control of the king and government.

Determined to be free of Douglas, Margaret gained an annulment of her marriage to him and married Henry Stewart. Douglas was furious and had Henry arrested on the grounds that the marriage had not been approved.

George Gordon, 4th Earl of Huntly, and George Hay, grandson of William Hay, 3rd Earl of Erroll sat on the Privy Council who agreed that the king was mature enough to govern and in doing so would create more stability for the country than having power struggles amongst his would-be guardians.

King James had endured the rivalries between his mother, Douglas and Albany for long enough. On receiving this advice from his Privy Council, although he was only sixteen years old, in 1527 he proclaimed his majority and began, as King of Scotland, to rule in his own right. He had Douglas, Earl of Angus, and his family removed from power and declared a traitor and had his new step-father created Lord Methven.

James was concerned about the spread of Protestantism into Scotland following his uncle, King Henry VIII's break with Rome and, although he wanted to reform the Catholic Church in Scotland, this was a step too far.

'Our clergy are abusing their power,' he told his council, 'all over Scotland clerics grow fat and rich. They take mistresses and have bastards which church monies are used to support and educate. They accept bribes for favours and neglect those in need.'

Members of the Privy Council struggled to keep a neutral expression knowing as they did of James' own mistresses and that he already had three illegitimate children; But none the less, they agreed with him that change was needed. 'Patrick Hamilton is preaching heresy in my land,' continued the king.

'You must rid yourself of him and kill this foul weed at the roots,' they advised. James took them at their word and had Hamilton burned at the stake in St. Andrews.

In gratitude for his advice and support, the king gave George Hay the beautiful Margaret Robertson, grand-daughter of John Stewart, 1st Earl of Athol, to be his wife. Their marriage proved to be fruitful with the births of Elizabeth, Andrew, Margaret, John and Lawrence within five years.

⋘⋙

King James sought to strengthen his alliance with France in the hopes of support, should he need it, against the English who once again presented a threat. News of King Henry's orders for the destruction of churches and monasteries was causing great concerns that a Protestant ruler in Scotland could bring similar actions. The king's council advised a marriage with a daughter of Francis I, king of France and negotiations began for the hand of the frail Madeleine of Valois.

King Francis protested that Madeleine's health was too fragile and James decided to visit France in person to arrange the betrothal. During his stay in France, James went boar hunting with King Francis where he took the opportunity to convince Francis that it would be to the benefit of both nations if the marriage were to be arranged.

The talks were successful and a fabulous ceremony took place to celebrate the marriage at Notre Dame in Paris. Francis arranged for six painters to prepare the decorations and there were days of jousting at the Chateau du Louvre.

At his entry to Paris, James wore a coat of crimson velvet slashed all over with gold, cut out of plain cloth of gold, fringed with gold and all lined with red taffeta.

Within months Scotland was in mourning for the death of the young queen and James, once again, needed to find a bride who would secure Scotland's alliance with France.

The widowed Marie of Guise was a devout Catholic, which James saw as a major attribute, and barely eighteen months after his first marriage, Scotland saw her king once again wed to a French woman. True to form, James wasted no time in fathering children and two sons were born to him and Marie within two years.

Once again, Scotland was thrust into mourning as each of the young princes died. Their sister Mary proved to be of stouter stuff and thrived in the royal nursery.

James continued to prove his potency by fathering six more illegitimate children and acknowledging them with titles and honours.

James, Earl of Moray was a stout young child and before long was displaying the dominant characteristics which would bring troubles to Scotland as he grew.

The next meeting of the Privy Council was dominated by religion.

'King Henry presses me to follow him in breaking with Rome,' complained the king. 'He must know that this is impossible. The Pope is God's chosen leader for the Church. No man can place himself before him.'

Erroll and Huntly were amongst those who fervently agreed with the king but there were many amongst the nobility who, along with the English Queen Mother, would follow the English king in breaking away.

'Most people are in agreement with you, Sire,' offered Erroll. 'In spite of the all too obvious shortcomings of many of the clergy, they cling to the old faith which they know, and are loyal to you.'

❧

Over the next few years William Hay, 5th Earl of Erroll's health began to deteriorate. He frequently coughed and was lethargic, causing Elizabeth, his mother, to fret about him and give him whatever he asked rather than distress him. As a result, he was proving to be a strong-willed and headstrong boy. Alexander was of a mind to send the boy to Huntly who would tolerate no such conduct and thrash the boy soundly should he transgress but Elizabeth worried about his health and refused to let him go.

Lady Helen Stuart was the king's choice of wife for William. Her father had been murdered some years earlier when she was ten years old and James was determined to secure a good marriage for her.

William found his bride unattractive and boring but was obliged to obey the king. Never the less, William decided to use the situation to his advantage and petitioned King James to grant a special license for serving him heir to his father as 6th Earl, Constable of Scotland and Sheriff of Aberdeen notwithstanding his minority.

King James considered William's request. He had heard stories of William's behaviour but put it down to frustration at not being able to handle his own affairs. James himself had taken on the full role as king at sixteen and would not, therefore, deny William for his youth and granted his request.

At Edinburgh, the Lyon-King-at-Arms and the other heralds met. William Carara, the messenger, had been brought before them, for his many oppressive actions upon the people and especially upon the poor tenants and workmen of the Abbey of Coupar and the surrounding district. The Lord Lyon had heard of Crarar's behaviour on many occasions and the man was bold enough to brag of it.

Lord Lyon and the Heralds ordered Crarar's arms to be taken from him and his person to be delivered to the Lord High Constable to be punished at the Queen's pleasure as an example to others. It was unfortunate for Crarar that it was to be Erroll's pleasure too. After a very brief trial, Erroll sentenced the prisoner to be dragged on a hurdle to the place of execution and then hanged.

⁕

Erroll's wedding, which was held in Holyrood, was a lavish one of great ceremony, with no expense spared and nobles from many parts of Scotland in attendance.

The first months of their marriage were spent at Slains where William treated his bride with contempt and verbal abuse. His coupling with her owed less to love than to lust. Helen found William's attentions quite repulsive. He pawed at her and forced himself upon her declaring that he would have his rights as a man. She found it easier not to struggle but to let him assuage his lust and be done with as soon as possible.

Distressed and frightened, Helen determined to write to her brother for help. She was in her chamber seated at her writing desk when William stumbled through the door. It was clear that he had been drinking and was at his worst. Helen recoiled as he approached; making a grab for her, staggering forward and only stopping his fall by leaning on her desk. Papers were scattered and fluttered to the floor. William took one which remained on the desk and waved it in front of her face. 'What's this, is my pretty bride writing pretty poetry?' he mocked.

Through the haze of wine, he scanned the words meaning to read it in belittling fashion. As he took in the words she had written his expression changed from mockery to anger. His cheeks flushed and his bloodshot eyes bulged.

'You would send these lies to your brother?' he demanded. 'How dare you!' and with this, he struck her with the back of his hand. His ring caught her on the cheek leaving a bruise with the impression of his family crest and a trickle of blood.

305

Stirred by the sight of blood he began to tear at her clothes.

'Miss use you do I?' he roared. 'Well, I'll use you well now.' Ripping her clothes from her shoulders he stripped her naked and threw her onto her bed. In spite of her struggles he satisfied himself smothering her screams with his bruising mouth. When he had finished he rolled off her leaving her barely conscious and stumbled from the room laughing.

Helen's ladies ran to her as soon as he left. They were shocked to see her bruised and bloodied body and made haste to bring water and cloths to sooth and bath her.

Within a short time, it was clear to Helen that she was with child. Even then William taunted her that she must enjoy his lovemaking or she could not have become pregnant. The next spring she gave birth to a baby girl whom she called Jean.

'A girl,' sneered William, 'my mistresses give me boys and my wife bears a girl!'

'And God help her with a father like you!' she thought but dare not utter the words for fear he would strike her. Instead, she bowed her head and bore the insult praying for the day she would become a widow.

Her brother Matthew visited to congratulate her and William on the birth of their daughter. William was determined not to leave Matthew and Helen alone together but Matthew was so shocked by her weakness and detecting a scar on her cheek he asked William to give him some time to speak with her alone – a request William could not refuse.

As soon as William left the room a tear trickled down Helen's cheek. She had not the strength to sob. Matthew scooped her into his arms and soothed her with gentle words, assuring her she would soon recover her strength and be well again. As her body shook with her grief he held her away from him.

'What ails ye lass?' he asked looking at her and knowing that the trouble went deeper than exhaustion. His finger went to her cheek and he looked more closely at the mark. Although the cut had healed he could make out three impressions in what appeared to be a shield. His expression changed from one of compassion for his sister to one of fury as he realised the implication. Laying her gently back on her bed he strode from the room to seek out the Earl of Erroll.

As Matthew turned through the doorway, William appeared. He knew in an instant that Matthew knew the truth.

'The lying bitch!' he exclaimed. 'I never touched her. You cannot believe her lies!'

'Your words confirm my thoughts,' growled Matthew. 'Helen told me nothing but the scar you left spoke for her and against you! You left your mark on her for all to see; you bastard!' Matthew took William by the throat and would have done for him there and then had not William's guards arrived.

Thrusting William from him, Matthew wiped the hand that had held William's throat. 'Use your whores but do not ever lay hands on my sister again. If I find you have been in the same room as her I will see you hanged,' he promised.

Knowing that Matthew would be as good as his word, William turned; brushing away the hand of his guard who tried to support him, and stumbling unsteadily down the stairs.

༄ঌ৵

In spite of his weakness, William railed against the restrictions placed on him and took every opportunity to dominate those around him.

'You live off my money!' he barked at his mother; his hands making fists as he leant towards her threateningly. 'How is a man of my status to dress as he should when you use up so much of my money? I am my father's heir and the Erroll money and lands are mine!'

'The king has decided on the lands. I have no say in that, but I will not allow you to throw away the fortune that your ancestors worked so hard to earn. The money which I spend is my own, my tocher, given by my father in my marriage contract.'

William turned on his heel and, throwing the door open so hard that it slammed against the wall, he flounced from the chamber, his long blue robes swinging behind him as he swept down the stairs.

∼✶✶∼

The market at Peterugie was busy with farmers buying and selling produce and traders who arrived on ships from foreign parts offering spices, fabrics and luxury goods. Dogs snarled at each other over scraps and entertainers sang and played to earn their supper. A farmer drove a flock of sheep through the street to sell and a boy sold pies from a tray hung about his neck. William may not yet hold the lands of his fathers but he was Constable of Scotland and had the rights of his office. The Earl of Erroll had the rights of the market and a fee was payable from the stall holders rents and those of visiting traders.

Erroll also had the right to try felons. Markets always attracted pick-pockets and thieves hoping to benefit from the crush of people and buyers being distracted by purchasing goods. Those arrested were held until they could be tried by the market court and William arrived just in time to sit in judgement.

In the foul mood that he had the felons were given a harsher deal than they might otherwise have expected. William's father saw the benefit of making those who broke the law pay for their offences by working long, hard hours in recompense, but the new earl wanted revenge for his perceived grievances and took out his anger on the petty criminals.

Pickpockets were put in the pillory with their ears nailed to the wood and a boy of ten who had stolen a loaf from a stall was sentenced to hang. The market officers were shocked and tried, discreetly, to suggest lighter punishments but William would not listen to them. He calmly stood, his thirst for vengeance assuaged, and as the officers bowed to him he strode from the market court.

When the court had stood down, William turned on the market bailiff. 'I will take the market fees now,' he declared.

'My lord, I cannot hand them to you now. They must be counted and sent to Slains to your mother.' William was furious and demanded the money immediately. In the face of his lord the man feared to disobey and handed a heavy purse to him. William hefted the purse in his hand before putting it on his belt, disappointed that there was not more in it. Struggling with a fit of coughing, William mounted his horse and turned for home.

On his arrival at Slains Castle, he found the king's messenger closeted with his mother. Having no respect for her and a great sense of his own importance William did not hesitate to enter. He was pale and exhausted by his day's ventures but was determined to take control of the situation. The messenger stood and bowed to him as William sat in a throne-like chair upholstered in red damask and trimmed with gold braid.

'What have we here?' he asked arrogantly, 'Are you entertaining men, mother?' His mother blushed but was furious at the suggestion. Before she could respond, the king's messenger interrupted. 'King James bids me advise your mother that he has chosen a husband for her.' He personally hoped the new husband would keep this young man under control but knew better than to express his thoughts.

William began yet another bout of coughing and took out a handkerchief to stifle the coughs. When he removed it the messenger noticed blood on the cloth but made no mention.

When he could finally speak, William asked, 'So, my mother is to marry. Does this mean that she will be spending his money instead of mine? Who is my mother's new husband to be?'

'Ninian Ross 3rd Lord Ross of Halkhead,' came the reply. 'He is much favoured by the king since his father died at Flodden with the old king.'

'Then you will be moving from Slains, mother.'

'I will indeed,' she replied with relief that she would soon be spared her son's behaviour.

William was delighted that he would finally be free of his mother's criticism but concerned that he would no longer be able to pressurise her into giving him money. He knew that the money was kept in the wall safe in his mother's antichamber but she kept the key on her chatelaine. He was determined to lay hands on the key before she left to marry Ross and to this end, he formulated a plan.

At supper, William played the fine host displaying all of the behaviours expected of a man of his station. As master of Slains, he sat at the centre of the table with his mother beside him and their guest on his other side. He made polite conversation asking after the king's health and many political matters.

When the meal was concluded he retired, leaving his mother to entertain their guest. Whilst they talked, William watched from the shadows, waiting for his mother to retire. When finally she went to her room he waited a while to allow her to retire and fall asleep. When he was sure she would be sleeping, he silently lifted the door catch and slipped through into her chamber.

Stealthily moving across the room, William found the peg where she kept her chatelaine. Holding the bunch in his hand so that they did not make a sound, he lifted the keys off the peg and slipped through into the anti-chamber. As soon as he was clear he hurried his steps to the wall safe. Opening the door he lifted a brass-bound casket from the safe and hurried out. It would be stupid to try to travel by night so William returned the keys before retiring. He hid the casket under his bed until it was light enough for him to leave Slains.

Seagulls screamed and chickens ran about the yard as William emerged at dawn demanding that his horse be saddled and his guards make ready to ride with him to Edinburgh. The journey was long and they were forced to stop several times due to William's coughing. He tried to disguise his frailty blaming his horse's saddle or lameness for the interruptions which none of the guards was fool enough to question.

When finally they arrived in Edinburgh, the travellers went directly to the castle where William demanded an audience with the king.

'The king is not here,' he was told. 'The king is at Stirling Castle for the month.'

Furious to be thwarted in his quest to have the money from the lands of Erroll given into his control, William took himself into the town to find entertainment. He had not gone far from the castle gates when he realised the folly of wandering into the town unguarded. The smell of the rubbish in the streets and the pigs rooting through piles of discarded foodstuffs made him recoil.

Finding the nearest tavern, he sat down near a crackling fire and ordered wine. Heads turned to see the fine gentleman who had arrived alone and could afford more than ale. William did not notice the hush which greeted his arrival and soon a low hum of conversation replaced the silence. He had emptied his glass many times before the landlord came to ask for payment. Carelessly pulling out a handful of coins, he threw them onto the table and rose to leave.

No sooner had he passed through the door than a shadowy figure followed. As he turned into an alleyway to relieve his full bladder a woman approached him. Her matted hair was carelessly flung over her shoulder, tied in a scarlet ribbon which matched her lips and painted cheeks. Silently she put her arm around him and turned him about. 'That's a fine sword you have in your hand,' she said with her head tilted to one side, 'Fancy a bit of swordplay?' Flattered he laughed which brought on his cough again. Wiping his arm across his mouth he put his mouth over hers and kissed her so roughly that she almost lost her footing. He pressed himself against her and scrabbled with her skirts. As he did she was aware that what she could feel was not just his tarse rising in admiration for her finer points, but a purse of substantial proportions.

William was only half-aware of what he was doing as he took her until his exertion caused his cough to resume so badly that he could not continue and fell away from the whore gasping for breath. The pimp, who had followed him from the tavern, was waiting in the shadows and seeing William unable to defend himself or give chase he put his arm against his throat pinning him to the wall and grabbed the purse wrenching it from his belt. As the thief made off down the lane, William lurched forward aiming to give chase but struggled to breathe and fell unconscious in the lane.

At first light, a street boy saw what he first thought was a bundle of fine clothes. Hoping to make some money he leapt on them to lay claim before anybody else appeared. He jumped back when he found the owner was still wearing them and was disgusted when he found that the wearer was dead; a stream of dried blood on his face.

Fearing the risk of being accused of murder, the lad ran away and it was an hour later that William's body was found and reported to the castle. The description suggested a person of quality and the guard were sent to recover the body and bring it to the Castle chapel where William's guards identified his remains.

Lady Helen felt a twinge of guilt that she had longed to become a widow and grieved for her daughter who had lost her father, but in her heart, she rejoiced that she would no longer have to suffer William's abuse and her daughter would grow up loved and cared for.

The death of the Queen Mother removed the king's allegiance to England and when King Henry invited him to meet at York, James declined. Henry was furious at the slight and prepared to invade Scotland.

It was one of the many duties of the Constable to gather men to fight when the king demanded but Jean was not only an infant but a girl and parliament did not think it seemly for a woman to try to order the barons to supply men to fight.

Although she could inherit the titles and lands of her father, parliament discussed options for a male family member to, not only be her guardian but also take on the responsibilities. They concluded that her father's cousin, George Hay, was a suitable person and as he was next in line he was the obvious choice. The barony had been in the possession of the crown for over nineteen years during William Hay's minority and as he had died before reaching twenty-one years of age he had never taken control of them.

Having made their decision, the crown transferred into George's hands the lands and baronies of Erroll, Capeth, Inchiref and Fossoquhy in Perthshire; Cowie in Kincardine and Slains in Aberdeenshire, making him 7th Earl of Erroll. George agreed to pay 4,000 Merks to Helen as Dowager Countess of Erroll and that he would marry one of his sons to Jean at the king's pleasure.

Shortly after the agreement was signed, King Henry invaded Scotland. Initially, events favoured the Scots when Huntly defeated the English army of Robert Bowes at the Battle of Haddon Rig, but the Battle of Solway Firth, three months later, due to the Scottish leaders vying for control, dashed Scottish hopes. It was a humiliating defeat as they had considerably greater numbers than the English and although King James was not present at the battle, on hearing of it, he fell into a great depression and withdrew to Falkland Palace in a state of collapse.

'The king has taken to his bed,' Huntly was told, 'he has struggled to bring the barons to work together for the good of Scotland and now the English have the upper hand because of their feuding amongst themselves. He is in despair and will not rise.'

The queen was distressed by James' despair. 'Your Majesty, the queen's labour has begun,' his yeoman of the wardrobe, John Tennent of Listonschiels, told him. 'I'm sure she will be delivered of a fine son this day. But nothing would rouse James from his bed.

When news came that Mary had produced a girl, James became delirious, lamenting about his standard being captured he slipped into unconsciousness never to awake. The six day old Mary was now the Queen of Scotland.

❧

Two factions immediately began to form amongst the Scottish nobles. Some wished to maintain the Catholic faith and others to embrace Protestantism and both wished to gain control of the new queen.

Some preferred to continue the Auld Alliance with France whilst peace with England appealed to others, but Moray had been made Regent and he, a Protestant, wasted no time in making Scotland a Protestant country.

❧

The marriage of the new baby queen was of paramount importance as the future of Scotland depended on it and she was soon betrothed to the young Prince Edward of England, much to the dismay of the Scottish Catholics and those who frowned upon an Anglo-Scottish alliance. Henry's insistence that Scotland break from the Auld Alliance was the final straw and the Scottish Parliament broke the engagement. King Henry was furious, and with the words,

...Put all to fyre and swoorde, burne Edinborough towne, so rased and defaced when you have sacked and gotten what ye can of it, as there may remayn forever a perpetual memory of the vengeaunce of God lightened upon them for their faulse-hode and disloyailtye.

Do what ye can out of hande...to beate down and overthrowe the castle, sack Holyrood house, and as many townes and

315

villages about Edinborough as ye may conveniently, sack Lythe and burn and subvert it and all the rest, putting man, woman and child to fyre and sworde without exception, where any resistance shallbe made agaynst you...

...passe over to Fyfelande and extende like extremityes and destructions in all towns and villages.

he sent the Earl of Hertford north to try to force the Scots into complying.

At Slains Castle, George Hay met with George Gordon to draw up a contract of marriage between Erroll's daughter, Margaret, and Huntly's son John. 'It's good of you to come and bear witness for the contract,' he said to his kinsmen, Peter Hay of Megginch and Alexander Hay of Delgatie. 'Hays and Gordons have married numerous times but in these troubled days, it is good to be sure of each other's support. Alexander Ogilvy and George Gordon of Schewess will bear witness for Huntly', George continued.

The ongoing friendship between the two noble families gave each security and encouraged the alliance of other powerful families to their camp.

The plans of Erroll and Huntly were to be changed dramatically in the coming years when Alexander Ogilvy paid a return visit to the Gordons. 'I am greatly troubled by the behaviour of my son, James,' he confided in George Gordon. 'I am of a mind to make your son, John, my heir in his place.'

George was surprised to hear this news. 'I knew he was a trouble to you but are you sure you wish to disinherit him?'

'I have made up my mind. John is an honest man. I would trust him to manage my property and people fairly and wisely. I would speak to him now if you would summon him.'

George was proud to hear that his son was held in such regard and pleased to see the lands and title endowed on him. He sent for John to attend them immediately and within moments he entered making a low bow to Alexander.

When he had explained his intention, Alexander added that John would be required to take the name of Ogilvy if he accepted the proposition which he did most willingly.

Ogilvy's disinherited son did not take his loss lightly and cursed his father vowing to challenge the arrangement when he died.

'You might have trouble with James Ogilvy,' George Gordon warned his son. 'He's a bad lot which is why Alexander has disowned him.'

'Alexander's decision is quite clear. What can James do about it in law?'

'He will not necessarily use the law, but if he does he will find people to back him. There are always people who will swear whatever you ask if the price is high enough…or the threats dangerous enough.'

'So what do you suggest?'

'Well, if his wife, Elizabeth, outlives him, you should marry her and strengthen your claim. In the contract Alexander and Elizabeth have their life rent on the estates. If you marry her she still has the estates.'

'But I'm contracted to marry Erroll's daughter, Margaret.'

'We must speak to George Hay and see if we can buy you out of the contract.'

'This will mean that instead of a young and beautiful wife, I must marry a woman of over sixty years.'

'It need only be a marriage in name. There are plenty of women you can take to be your mistress if you so wish.'

'Well, I'll not wish to bed an old woman!'

Erroll understood the position which John Gordon was in and had no wish to see him threatened by James Ogilvy but asked that they wait until the case arose before scrapping the contract between John and Margaret unless Erroll found a suitable husband for Margaret in the meantime. Huntly gratefully agreed to the conditions.

⊷⊶

The death of Queen Mary's grandfather, Henry VIII of England, in 1547 left his son, the staunchly protestant Edward VI as King of England. Edward continued his father's attacks on Scotland and the Scots suffered a terrible defeat at the Battle of Pinkie Clough, George Gordon, Earl of Huntly being taken prisoner by the English and taken with them into England.

'This is a black Saturday,' Erroll observed at the Privy Council meeting. 'Our people suffer greatly at the hands of the English. Does the English king really believe we can be convinced to give a Scottish queen to them as a bride by force?"

'Aye, tis a rough wooing indeed' the council members agreed. 'Better our Queen be taken to a place of safety until she is older.'

James Hamilton, 2nd Earl of Arran, as next in line to the throne of Scotland, should Mary not survive, was appointed regent. He was of the Protestant faith which was of great concern to many of the Scottish nobility who wished Scotland to remain a Catholic country. In order to prevent him influencing the young Mary, Erroll and many other Scottish nobles, signed an agreement to support taking the regency from Arran by suggesting that his father's divorce, and, therefore his second marriage, were invalid, making Arran illegitimate. Catholic Mary of Guise would be favoured by this.

As soon as the Queen Mother had control of her daughter she sent Mary to France, to be brought up as part of the French royal family.

In due course, Queen Mary was married to the frail Dauphin, Francis.

᭞᭞

1552

When George Hay had been called to a meeting of the Privy Council, he left his wife, Margaret, in labour with their next child. She was safely delivered of a son and in George's absence named him after his father.

George was a man of his word and on his return from Edinburgh he invited Jean Hay, daughter of William Hay 6th Earl of Erroll, to be Godmother to the new baby. He also honoured his promise by betrothing his eldest son, Andrew, to her. Although Andrew was seventeen and Jean thirty-two, he had no objection to the match. He knew that he would eventually succeed to the title Earl of Erroll and that it was only as a result of his father's agreement that this was so. He also found Jean more attractive than many younger women of his status whom he would otherwise be expected to marry. On his marriage, he was to be given a charter of the lands of Slains and Erroll.

A year later Jean gave birth to a fine healthy daughter whom they named Helen in memory of Jean's mother.

CHAPTER 28

The reign of King Edward VI of England was destined to be a short one. His death after just six years as king was followed by Lady Jane Grey, daughter-in-law of the protestant Duke of Northumberland. Her brief reign was replaced by that of Henry VIII's daughter, Mary Tudor – a staunch Catholic.

The year after their marriage, Francis succeeded his father as king, making Mary, Queen of France as well as Scotland.

When Mary I of England died and Elizabeth became queen, many Roman Catholics considered Mary of Scotland to also be queen of England, as they believed Henry VIII's marriage to Anne Boleyn to be illegal. As a result, when Francis died the next year, Mary decided to return to Scotland.

John Knox was becoming a thorn in the side of the Queen Mother by organising the Protestant nobles into the Lords of the Congregation. Information reached Erroll that she had outlawed Knox and his followers. Knox reacted by preaching a sermon in Perth which roused his listeners to riot. The parish church had been spoilt and two monasteries nearby had been attacked, stripped of any trace of idolatry and vessels and vestments stolen. The Protestant army had stripped St Andrew's Cathedral and burned Scone Abbey before turning their attention to the churches of Edinburgh.

Mary of Guise had fled to Dunbar for safety and the protesters had proclaimed their government at the market cross in Edinburgh.

George Hay was informed with all haste and sent a messenger to offer her his house at Erroll for her comfort, should she wish it. Mary declined and set about negotiations with the rebels and agreed to suspend the laws against heresy but being ill, she withdrew herself to Edinburgh Castle. Within a short time the Queen Mother was dead.

❧❧

1560

George Hay's daughter Beatrix was only hours old when he left Slains Castle to set out on his journey to greet the returning Queen with the rest of the Privy Council. She landed at Leith to a welcome from the Catholic supporters and rode to the Palace of Holyrood which her father had had lavishly decorated for his wife.

Following the advice of James Stewart, her half- brother, she took a moderate line, allowing the reformed Presbyterian Church some ground but the Protestant reformers, including John Knox, were appalled that she was hearing Mass in her own chapel. At the same time, she found no great favour with the Catholics, as they doubted her commitment to their cause.

Stories of her leniency towards the Protestants reached the ears of the Pope. Concerned about her zeal for the Catholic faith he decided to send the fanatical Jesuit priest, Father Edmund Hay, rector of the Jesuit College in Paris and brother of Peter Hay of Megginch, to Scotland, to ascertain Mary's commitment. Lord Erroll was keen to meet with Edmund as he had not seen him for some years. He invited him to dine with him at Holyrood on his arrival at Edinburgh and was taking the opportunity to ask about matters in Europe when a messenger arrived asking for an audience with him. Entry was granted and a travel-stained figure stood before the Earl. Recognising the man as one of his grooms from Slains Castle, George was alarmed and stepped down to meet the man. As he feared, there was dreadful news.

Margaret had not recovered from the birth of their daughter and had developed childbed fever which had claimed her life. Seeing that George had received bad news, Father Edmund moved to his side. 'Come, we will pray together,' he directed leading George to the palace's chapel.

George returned to Slains Castle as soon as he was able. As he and his guards entered the courtyard he was struck by the normality. Chickens scratched the ground in search of grubs; women sang and laughed together; the sound of hammer on metal in the smithy and the smell of bread baking. It seemed wrong that his wife could be dead when everything else went on as usual.

As people realised he had arrived, they fell silent in respect for his loss and George slipped from his horse to enter the castle.

Margaret's body had been laid out in preparation for her funeral and as he knelt beside her to pray, their children, who had gathered at the castle, slipped into the room and knelt beside him.

Andrew, George's eldest son, had been delighted at the birth of his own first son, Alexander, but had left his home in Erroll to return to Slains when his mother died. His own wife had suffered several miscarriages since their daughter had been born and he had been concerned for her safe delivery during the confinement but she had been safely delivered of a fine strong son and was recovering well.

He spent hours sitting with his father, following Margaret's funeral, talking about their families and Andrew's own childhood. He reminisced about the Christmas that his father had given him his first suit of armour, emblazoned with the Hay arms, and how he stumbled about trying to walk in it. He was delighted to find that his father's memories of events seemed fine as they chatted about Andrew's first attempts at riding and sword fighting.

It was not until he asked his father about more recent events that he became concerned. George clearly struggled to remember the names of people he knew well and events which had happened within the last few weeks. Andrew worried that, if this became known at Court, his father might lose people's confidence. These were troubled times and the populous of Scotland needed to be sure of the Privy Council's competence.

꒰ঌ ঌ꒱

On his return journey to Edinburgh, George stayed for a week at Erroll. It was good to spend some time with family and friends and to visit a number of his tenants. Andrew travelled with him and each enjoyed having company for the journey.

When they arrived at Erroll, Andrew's wife, Jean, greeted them warmly asking how their journey had been and enquiring sadly about Andrew's younger siblings. He took her arm as they talked and led her inside, concerned for her so soon after the birth of their son.

'The child and I are fine,' she assured him, turning to her father-by-law and giving him a sad smile.

After they had dined, Andrew sent for wine and they spent the evening chatting about family members.

As the evening drew on, servants brought tapers to light candles and stoked the fire to warm the room but George begged to be excused early, claiming that the journey had made him tired, and retired to his chamber.

'How did you find my father?' Andrew asked Jean.

'Well, I thought; perhaps a little tired.'

'Did you notice he struggled to recall Helen's name?'

'What of it? He has a lot on his mind. Lots of people stumble over names.'

'But she is his grandchild. And I have notice he forgets other things and gets confused.'

'I'm sure he's fine. I'll pay careful attention whilst he is here and see if I notice anything.'

'Thank you, my love. Perhaps I'm worrying needlessly.'

The next morning, George spoke to his son about his estates. 'I must confide in you, Andrew, my years draw on and I am finding it troublesome of late to deal with matters of the estates whilst also attending the Queen and her Privy Council. The demands are great and I find I am absent all too often when the needs of my lands require my attention. I am of a mind to pass more of my properties into your name. They will, of course, be yours eventually, but I feel it would be in the best interests of all if I were to do this now.'

Andrew was relieved that his father chose to transfer the properties to him and wondered if the problems he had witnessed in George were due to stress but chose not to speak of it at this time.

❧

On her return from France, Queen Mary had found conflict between various factions had begun again. James Hepburn, Earl of Bothwell had an open quarrel with the Earl of Arran and the Hamiltons, which upset here greatly, and although the Earl of Arran was later declared mad, Bothwell was imprisoned in Edinburgh Castle without trial only to escape later that year and establish himself in Hermitage Castle.

The Queen was becoming a close friend of Bothwell and later that year permitted his marriage to Lady Jean Gordon, daughter of the Earl of Huntly and attending the wedding herself. During the festivities, Mary approached George Hay. 'I was sad to hear of your loss, Lord Erroll. It is wretched for a man to be without a wife.'

George bowed low before replying, 'You are too kind, your majesty.'

'I am of a mind to redress the situation, Erroll. Lady Helen Bruce would be a suitable wife for you and I would see the wedding take place as soon as it can be arranged. I have need of your services and would not have you delay.'

'Thank you, Your Highness,' replied George, somewhat bemused as he had not yet thought of taking another wife.

When a rider arrived at Edinburgh demanding an audience with the Queen, Mary sent a servant to find the cause of the fuss. 'The fellow says he has news of my Lord Bothwell,' the girl reported, 'He had apparently been injured and is like to die.'

Mary leapt to her feet. 'Bring him in!' she ordered.

The poor fellow was exhausted but able to relate that Bothwell had been injured at Hermitage Castle and was asking for her in his delirium. The Queen ordered that the man be fed and given a bag of coins for his trouble and sent for her maidservant to ready her clothing for travel. The poor girl tried to protest that it was only a few weeks since Mary had given birth to her son but her protests were swept aside. Mary would ride to Hermitage Castle to discuss 'matters of state'.

CHAPTER 29

At Slains there were great celebrations. George's wife, Helen, was to give birth in a month's time and preparations for her confinement were underway. George was making plans for a brief visit to Erroll to see his first grandchild. The messenger had reported that the boy was healthy and the image of his father. As George gave instructions to staff about what he would need preparing for the journey, Helen suddenly moaned and bent forward. 'What ails you, Helen?' he asked as he rushed to put a supporting arm around her waist. 'Is it something you ate?' At over sixty years of age, George was proud to be about to become a father once again. He knew the risks of childbirth but this child should not arrive for a month yet. Surely it could not be coming so early. He was horrified when it became clear that the child was about to be born and Helen's ladies ushered him out of the room.

Pacing the hall, he stopped to empty a glass of whisky and refill his glass before resuming his agitated bustling about. In less than an hour, he was summoned to Helen's bedside and pressed down onto a chair by Helen's maid before being handed a bundle of shawl's with a tiny child inside. Helen had given birth to a daughter.

The servant's had already sent for a priest, knowing that the chances for a child born so early were slim. As soon as he arrived, the priest hurriedly prepared to baptise the child asking George to name her. They had already decided that if the child were a girl they would call her Eupheme and without more ado, the priest proceeded to baptise the child. George was shocked to see how tiny the child was and how weak it's mewling. He looked up at the maid who shook her head before dashing a tear from her eye and turning to rush from the room.

He sat and nursed the tiny bundle as Helen slept, exhausted and shocked by the early arrival of the child. As he parted the shawl to peep at his new daughter, a tiny hand appeared from between the folds. The little fist opened and closed before feebly relaxing back onto the wrap. He was surprised at himself as he felt a tear trace its way down his cheek. He, who could go fearlessly into battle, was brought down by such a tiny infant.

The next day, Helen tried to feed her daughter but the infant had no strength in her to suckle and whimpered from hunger. A young maid suggested using a cloth as a wick for the little one to draw milk from a dish and trailed one end in the milk whilst offering the other to the baby's lips. The little one rooted feebly to find food but would not take the cloth into her mouth. Gradually her efforts stilled and she slept again, leaving her mother distraught and desperate to find a way to feed her in the faint hope of building her strength.

As she slept the infant's breath was hesitant and broken until finally, it ceased. Helen snatched her up shaking her and begging her to breath until the noise of her cries brought George back to the room. He held Helen in his arms with the baby between them until Helen began to sob in acceptance that the child was gone. He held her into the night, both of them looking at the child and crying together until they had no more tears. When Helen's maid silently approached them, George gently lifted Eupheme into her outstretched arms and wrapped his own around his wife.

Little Elizabeth could not understand the loss of her tiny sister and fretted for her asking where she had gone until her nanny gently lifted her into her arms. 'God sent Eupheme to us for a short while but now she has gone back to him,' she assured the child. As they left, George heard Elizabeth's chatter, questioning about her tiny sister and complaining, 'But I wanted her to play with me.'

∽ ∾

There seemed to be nothing George could do to distract Helen from her misery. He felt that they must leave Slains Castle for a while to allow her to start to get over their loss. Alexander Hay was thinking of making some changes at Delgatie Castle and welcomed them to come and discuss his plans.

The fiery-headed Alexander welcomed George and Helen with the young Elizabeth and suggested her nurse-maid take her to play with his own children, whilst he entertained her parents. Leading his guests into the great hall he sent for wine to refresh them. He commiserated with them on the loss of Eupheme but move rapidly on to ask for news of Queen Mary. George told him all that he knew but news of events in England was slow to reach Scotland.

After they had dined, Alexander told them of his plans for the castle.

'There is much unrest in these parts as followers of the Protestant faith seek to convert everybody to their ways. I will never give up my adherence to the true faith of Rome and would protect my family and castle from the attacks of the reformers. We have been troubled in the past by attacks from power-seeking lords, and by those who would destroy all who support the Queen, but the recent developments in the use of artillery have me doubting how long we could withstand an attack. Trebuchets can cause much damage but cannon will take down the walls faster than we can repair.'

George looked at the plans which Alexander had had prepared. 'You plan to build the walls between eight and sixteen feet thick and a turnpike stair within the wall. This part looks wrong,' he suggested, pointing to the stair as shown on the plan, 'the stair looks to be far too wide.'

'It will be five feet wide. Big enough to take furniture up and allow people to pass on the stair. It grows narrower as it ascends but sweeps up to the Great Hall. Do you not think it will be fine?'

'It will be grand indeed but if soldiers gain entry they will have easy access up such a stair.'

'They will not gain entry. That is the reason for the thickness of the walls – to keep them out.'

George nodded his head thoughtfully. He looked at the other features of the design and thought it well planned. Alexander told him of proposals for painting the beams in the ceilings which Helen was most interested in and made note of the idea to use at Slains on their return.

The men continued to talk of the new building throughout George and Helen's stay. The cost would be enormous but Alexander was confident that the estates were doing well. The manpower shortage which had followed the devastating losses at Flodden was gradually recovering and stone masons from Europe could be employed where necessary.

The next morning George asked Alexander if he had ever thought of strengthening Delgatie as the new canon would devastate the walls as they were. Alexander was puzzled as they had looked at the plans together the previous night. He presumed that the confusion was a result of George and Helen's tragic loss, so, without reminding George of the fact that they had discussed the matter, Alexander brought the plan to his desk and unrolled it.

'I see you plan to build the walls between eight and sixteen feet thick.' Alexander furrowed his deep brow but resisted reminding George that they had discussed this.

❦

George Gordon's concerns about his son John's inheritance from Alexander Ogilvy proved to be right. John received the Queen's agreement to his marriage with Alexander's widow but it was not a comfortable arrangement. His new bride expected their marriage to be a full one and not just a marriage of convenience and threatened to announce that it had not been consummated. Her attitude towards John was scornful and bitter and in no way encouraged him to wish to bed her. He for his part was spiteful, regretting giving up his young bride for this woman who could have been his grandmother.

James Ogilvy appointed lawyers to act for him against him but when John was summoned to the Court in Edinburgh, the two met and a fight ensued in which Ogilvy was injured so badly that John was imprisoned. Managing to escape, he fled to one of his castles.

Early in 1562, the Queen decided to visit the north of Scotland. When she arrived at Aberdeen, she was met by the Countess of Huntly.

'Your Majesty,' she began, bowing deeply, 'My son is wrongly charged. He was attacked by Ogilvy in the street and sought only to defend himself. He had no intention of injuring him but Ogilvy was drunk and stumbled. It was an accident which caused his injury. I beg you to intervene and clear my son's name.'

Mary barely looked at her before announcing that there was nothing she could do for John unless he surrendered himself at Stirling Castle.

The countess assured the Queen that he would do so and retired to take the news to her son.

John agreed to go to Stirling but discovered that Sir James Stewart's uncle was to be his keeper there. 'I would not be safe in his hands,' John told his mother. 'It is likely that I would not come from the Castle alive. James Stewart is a Protestant and hates me for not converting to the Protestant faith. He would see me dead if he could.'

When the queen heard that John would not surrender himself she flew into a rage stamping her foot and declaring that the countess of Huntly took her for a fool and had deceived her. Her ladies in waiting sat near the windows concentrating on their needlework and keeping their heads down to avoid being drawn into her rage.

❧❦

Erroll and Huntly had long been close friends, as had their fathers before them, but when George Gordon and his son went against the crown, George Hay, in faith to the Queen, could not support him.

Moray was determined to get rid of Huntly and persuaded Mary that if she crushed Huntly, Queen Elizabeth of England would look favourably on her claim to be the next heir to the throne of England.

When George Gordon invited Mary to Strathbogie she was in no mood to be Huntly's guest and suspected a trick but sent the Earl of Argyle and the English Ambassador, Randolph as her representatives.

When they returned, Randolph reported to Mary that Strathbogie was very finely appointed and suggested that Huntly had more than any subject should have. The seeds of Mary's jealousy were sown. Frustrated at Huntly's failure to hand over his son she set off towards Inverness.

When Mary and her troops arrived at Inverness Castle, Alexander Gordon, Captain of the castle, refused to hand the royal castle over. Shocked by this turn of events, some of Gordon's followers changed allegiance and went to support the queen, enabling her troops to easily take the castle. Alexander Gordon and five others of the garrison were summarily executed.

Satisfied that Inverness Castle was safely returned to the crown, Mary set out to return to Aberdeen and was met by a tumultuous reception from the people and declared that she would stay in the city for forty days or until peace was restored in the county.

When Mary heard that Huntly had a royal canon at Strathbogie, which had been given to him by Arran, she demanded its immediate return and sent Captain Hay to the castle to try to capture Huntly. When Captain Hay, the royal messenger arrived at Strathbogie he was treated with respect.

When George Gordon heard that the Queen demanded the return of her canon, he replied, not only the cannon, which was her own but also his body and goods were at her disposal. He considered it strange that he should be treated in this way because it was not him but his son who had offended the Queen.

'I would risk my life to capture Finlander Castle and Auchindoun for my Queen if she only commands me to do so,' he told Hay. 'I desire that this be reported to Her Majesty from her most humble and obedient subject.'

Hay took the words of Huntly back to the Queen at Aberdeen. He was shown into a grand hall and discovered Mary in conversation with Lord James Stewart. The Queen asked what news he had from Strathbogie and Huntly's message was faithfully reported to her. James Stewart sneered and bent to whisper to Mary who tilted her head to listen before dismissing Hay.

Huntly sent his messenger after Hay to take the keys of both castles to the queen. As the rider arrived he was met by James Stewart who questioned him about his request to speak with Mary and denied him entry, taking the keys himself and placing them safely in his room where they would remain.

Huntly and his son were ordered to appear before the Queen and Council at Aberdeen but George Gordon feared placing himself in the hands of his enemies and declined. Encouraged by James Stewart, Mary sent troops to attack Strathbogie but Huntly's guards had raised the alarm and the earl escaped over a low wall at the back of the castle. It was just two days later that John Gordon attacked Stewart's forces as they attempted to take Finlander Castle. The Gordons were declared rebels and the surrender of their castles was demanded.

For his own protection, Huntly mustered five hundred men and marched them towards Aberdeen to the Hill of Fare in Midmar. Here he positioned his troops near Corriechie Burn and met the Earls of Moray and Atholl with a force of two thousand men. Moray, Atholl and Morton surrounded his camp. Moray's men were ordered to attack but many of them would not fight against Huntly, as they knew him to be a good man and faithful to the Queen; throwing down their spears they left the battle.

Gordon's men, thinking they would pursue the fleeing soldiers, threw away their spears and drew their swords in readiness but Moray's second line stood firm with pikes extended. Huntly was horrified to see one hundred and twenty of his men killed and many, including he himself, were taken prisoner.

George Gordon was mounted on a horse in readiness to be taken back to Aberdeen but before he had even left the battlefield he suddenly and silently died. Shocked at this sudden and unexpected development, Mary gave orders that his body be embalmed and taken to Edinburgh for trial. His son, John, was executed. Huntly's cousin, John, Earl of Sutherland, fled to Flanders.

Following the battle, Queen Mary went to Delgatie Castle and stayed for three days as the guest of Alexander Hay. On her arrival she found George Hay and his son, Andrew, to be there also. 'Erroll, it is good to see you. I hear you are to be congratulated on the birth of a daughter.'

'Thank you, your Majesty. My wife and I have indeed been blessed with a healthy child.'

'And what name have you given her?'

'My wife wishes to call her Isabel.'

For a moment, Mary hesitated. She had expected George to call his daughter after her but on reflection, she decided not to question his choice and merely nodded in acceptance.

Andrew drew his father to one side. 'Would it not have been wise to call the child after our Queen?' he asked.

George seemed puzzled but covered his confusion by turning the conversation to his son's own child. 'How is young Alexander progressing? He must be walking now.'

Andrew's response was hesitant. 'He is fit physically. He gets to his feet unaided and can totter across the room but there is something amiss and I cannot decide if the child is willful or perverse but he does not respond when spoken to. He makes sounds but is not speaking as his sister did at this age.'

'It will come. All bairns are different and some speak sooner than others. And when they do you will wish them not to!' he laughed.

⌘

It was only when Queen Elizabeth still refused to meet Mary that she realised that Moray had tricked her into defeating his personal enemy, Huntly, and furthering the Protestant cause. She was furious with Moray and withdrawing her trust in him and the Protestant Lords she turned back to the Catholic faith.

Erroll was dismayed to learn that, at the next sitting of Parliament, his erstwhile friend, Huntly, Sutherland and eleven other earls and barons of the name Gordon were forfeited.

❧

1564

News had arrived from Erroll that Andrew and his wife, Jean, had been blessed with a son, whom they had called Francis, and, although Andrew had been delighted at the birth of their first son, Francis was rapidly becoming his favourite. He seemed more alert and responsive even at such a tender age than his elder brother and turned to look at every sound. Suddenly, Jean gasped. 'What ails you?' Andrew enquired, rushing to her side.

'It has just occurred to me why Alexander seems strange.'

'Strange? In what way?'

'Have you not noticed that he lies silently much of the time? He does not cry as most babies do.'

'Surely you don't want the child to be distressed?'

'Of course not. But babies normally cry and he very rarely does; nor does he react when I enter the room. He does not turn his head or look up. When you spoke to me in the nursery, Francis turned to you. Come with me.'

She led Andrew to where Alexander was sitting, playing with a toy horse. 'I want to try something,' she told him. As they entered, Alexander continued to play, ignoring their arrival. He had his back to the door and Jean signalled Andrew and Alexander's governess to stand still as she walked over to the child. Jean clapped her hands behind Alexander's head. He continued playing quite uninterested.

Andrew strode forward. 'He's just ignoring you. I'll teach him to treat his parents with respect!'

Jean snatched at his arm. 'Look,' she said, pointing at Alexander. He has still not reacted. 'I don't think he is ignoring us; I don't think he can hear us.'

'Are you sure? Let me try.' Andrew picked up a metal box and dropped it on the stone floor with a clatter. Alexander continued as if nothing had happened. Andrew stepped in front of the child who startled as his father came into view and grinned up at him. Andrew looked at Jean.

'It seems you are right. He responds well enough when he sees me but not to sound. I will ask the Royal Physician if anything can be done.'

Andrew sent his squire to make ready for him to leave for Edinburgh that afternoon. Taking his leave of his wife he promised to do everything possible for their son.

On his arrival at Court, Andrew made his way straight to the quarters of the Royal Physician, Bourgoing, and explained his son's problem to him.

'Of course, I would have to see the child,' Bourgoing explained, but there is little that can be done to cure deafness. Some have tried pouring acid into the ears but it causes great distress and I have not heard of any success result from it. Others push probes into the ear to try to open them. I could attempt this if you wish.'

Andrew acknowledged that he would appreciate any help and sought permission from the Queen, for Bourgoing to accompany him to Slains.

The queen was sympathetic and readily agreed, wishing the child well and Bourgoing every success.

On their arrival at Erroll, the accompanying entourage was instructed to obtain refreshment and be available when required.

Andrew sent one of Jean's ladies to the nursery to fetch the boy down and invited Bourgoing to take a seat.

'What will you do?' Andrew enquired, his restless hands in his lap betraying his anxiety.

'Ah, here is the child now,' Bourgoing observed. You will see how I first assess him and then I will tell you what I propose to do.'

Little Alexander walked hand in hand with his nurse-maid. His eyes roamed around the room taking in the features which he was rarely permitted to see. As he turned he startled as he saw the visitor and made a bow as he had been taught, first to his father and then to their guest. Bourgoing bowed his head in response with a gentle smile and held his hands out to the boy. Alexander looked to his father, who nodded permission and the child went towards the stranger.

Bourgoing said nothing but watched as Alexander studied the fabric of his fine robes and tentatively stretched out a small hand to touch the shiny fabric.

'Do you like my robe?' Bourgoing asked. Alexander continued to finger the pattern wordlessly. Speaking louder the question was repeated. Alexander looked up at him with a quizzical expression and murmured a sound.

Andrew was becoming angry at what he perceived to be his son's rudeness and rebuked him sharply. He was shocked when Alexander completely ignored him and would have struck the boy for his insolence had not Bourgoing raised his hand to stop him. Turning the boy around, the physician pushed him away towards his nurse and almost immediately called, 'Alexander!'

There was no response from the child and with a knowing nod, he indicated to the nursemaid to take the child away. She looked to Andrew who nodded his ascent and waited until they had left before asking Bourgoing for his opinion.

'The boy hears absolutely nothing,' he declared.

'How can you be so sure? He was only here a moment or two.'

'I shall demonstrate,' the physician told him. 'Turn away from me and remain looking at the far wall.'

Andrew was puzzled but complied.

'Andrew!'

Andrew spun around, 'What?' he asked still confused at the man's behaviour.

'You see? I called your name and you could not help yourself; you turned to me.'

'So what does that prove?'

'Everybody responds to the sound of their name. It is natural. People can ignore other words which may not be addressed to them or they may not be interested in, but everybody responds to their name. The child was next to me and I called his name but he did not react. It was as if I had not spoken. The only explanation is that he did not hear. If you want further proof I suggest you make sudden noises behind him when he does not know you are there and such like but you will find I am right.'

'This is true, I have done so. Then what can be done?'

'Nothing.'

'Nothing? Are you sure?'

'I am certain. We could torture him with acid in his ears and other such things as fools have tried but it will be to no avail and would be cruel. The boy cannot hear and will never hear. He will also never speak as nobody can learn to speak without hearing. We learn to speak by copying sounds. Those who cannot hear sounds cannot copy them.'

'Why has this happened?' Andrew demanded. 'Jean was careful throughout her pregnancy and the birth was straightforward.'

'Are you and Jean closely related?'

'Why, yes. We are cousins.'

'There are those who say that it is not good to marry too closely. This is why the church forbids marriage between those who are related in the first and second degree.'

'But we had a dispensation from the Queen!'

'That is as maybe, but the Queen is not God and he is our judge in all things. The fact remains that we see problems like this all too often in couples who are closely related.'

'Nonsense! I have heard it said, but surely it has been disproved. There are many who require a dispensation to marry and have children who are fit and well. Our other son hears perfectly. I will not believe this.'

Bourgoing shrugged. 'Have it as you will, but I must warn you that any future child you have may be similarly afflicted.'

Jean had arrived just in time to hear his last words. Her shock was clear. 'What does he mean?' she demanded of Andrew.

Andrew was horrified. His son was destined to become the next Earl of Erroll; Lord High Constable of Scotland; Sheriff of Aberdeen. How could he carry out his duties with no hearing and no speech? He took his wife's hand and sat her next to him. With the help of the physician, he tried to explain the situation.

'Then you will wish to have our marriage annulled!' she exclaimed.

'Peace, woman; I will do no such thing. There is no proof that what he supposes is correct. We have two healthy children and will have more. You are my wife and so you shall remain.'

That evening, when they had recovered a little from the initial shock, Bourgoing sat with Andrew and Jean and explained what the future would hold. What behaviour they might expect from Alexander and how they could help him to learn social skills if nothing else. Their only consolation was that their other son, Francis, could hear perfectly.

Somewhat reassured, Jean relaxed a little and, remembering her duties to their guest, she offered him wine before they retired.

Sleep was a long time in coming to both of them that night as they talked about the evening's revelations. When Andrew finally began to snore, a tear trickled down Jean's cheek, rapidly followed by another until she was sobbing her grief into her pillow.

CHAPTER 30

Queen Mary knew that it was important that she marry and produce an heir. Sitting with her ladies she mused on the prospect of marrying Don Carlos of Spain but realised that Elizabeth of England would be furious with her if she married him as he was a Catholic.

She drew the thread through her tapestry and looked up as the door opened. A footman introduced the visitor as Lord Darnley before retreating, leaving behind a handsome young man who entered and approached her bearing a message. He bowed deeply before kneeling before her. Bidding him rise she heard his message before inviting him to join the company for a while. Inviting him to take a seat on a stool beside, her she questioned him about his journey to Edinburgh and his interests. Finding that they shared a passion for hunting, Mary invited Darnley to join her the following day when she was to travel to Stirling for a hunting weekend. Darnley, believing himself to be almost the queen's equal being her first cousin, readily agreed and begged to be excused in order that he might prepare for the journey.

Darnley was a highly educated, sophisticated and charismatic young man and over the next few weeks, Darnley was often at Mary's side, flattering her with his admiring comments and sharing her interests, but keeping his visits short enough to entice her to desire more of his company. Taking himself off to Stirling Castle for a while, Darnley planned to make Mary wait a while before she could share his company once again. What he had not planned for was contracting measles from a servant in the castle. What began as a disaster for him, developed into a triumph when, as soon as Mary heard of his illness, she set out for Stirling to nurse him back to health herself.

Mary was becoming infatuated with Darnley, enjoying his flirtations and admiring his youth-full figure and good looks. She decided that her quest for a husband was over. She would marry Henry Stewart, Duke of Albany, Lord Darnley.

When it was announced on 28th July 1564, the eve of their wedding, that Scotland would henceforth be ruled jointly by the King and Queen of Scots it was too much for the Scottish nobles to swallow. The twenty- two-year-old bride wore her widow's black gown and was entirely outshone by her 19-year-old groom's bejewelled outfit. Although the Catholics of Scotland accepted her marriage, the Protestants, including Moray, were incensed, but in spite of their protests on Sunday 29th July 1565 Mary and Darnley were married in the Chapel-Royal of the Palace of Holyrood. As Mary celebrated the Catholic Mass, Darnley turned and strode out of the chapel.

It was not long before Mary saw Darnley for the deceiver that he was. His intrigues with her Protestant opponents were a constant worry to her and raised voices were often to be heard in her chambers. 'I am carrying your child and yet you prefer to go out drinking with your cronies! You come back well after dawn and never come to my bed.'

'Why would I come to your bed?' he threw back at her, 'You have the child you wanted in your belly and I have no desire to bed a pregnant whore.'

'You dare speak to me in that way? You said you loved me.'

'I loved 'the queen',' he replied pointedly.

Mary was devastated. She had been told he had been cavorting with women and he always smelt of drink. He returned so late that he never left his bed until midday and avoided her whenever he could. Even at table Darnley flirted with other ladies, ignoring Mary and causing mutterings amongst the courtiers. Darnley considered himself to be Mary's superior and asserted his authority even in their bed.

But Mary was not the feeble female he took her for. Gathering Erroll and other advisors together, she explained her plans. The legend on the coinage was to be changed to read, Mary and Henry, by the grace of God, Queen and King of Scotland, where previously Henry's name had appeared before her own. He was also to be denied the right to bear the royal arms.

Darnley was furious and plotted to take his revenge. His father, Mathew Stuart, Earl of Lennox and William Maitland who felt slighted when Mary appointed her musician, David Rizzio as her secretary, conspired with him. James Stuart, Earl of Moray was also drawn into the plot.

Maitland was a close adherent to James Stewart, Earl of Moray and as a dedicated supporter of the Queen, he hated to see the way Darnley was treating her and abusing his position. He watched as Darnley flirted with other women, including Maitland's own wife, and how he favoured his drunken cronies over the Queen. Although anxious to remove Darnley, Maitland was not fool enough to believe that he could assassinate him without dying for his work. In an effort to support the Queen, Maitland saw a strong Privy Council as the way forward in the hope that they could persuade her to take their advice. He appointed Alexander Hay of Delgatie as his Deputy Clerk of the Privy Council and it was Alexander who in due course drew up the bond in which it was agreed to get rid of Darnley.

Unaware of Maitland's plans, Darnley had ideas of his own. If Moray and the exiled Lords in England would agree to grant Darnley the 'crown matrimonial' in the next Parliament, and in so doing make him lawfully King of Scots, then Darnley would switch sides, recall and pardon the exiles, and restore their estates. Finally, he would re-establish the religious status quo as it had existed at the time of Mary's return from France.

The success of the plot depended upon there being a scapegoat, whom they could blame for tricking Darnley and being responsible for the recent swing towards Catholicism. David Rizzio seemed the perfect victim; the handsome and well-groomed personal secretary to the Queen, and the man, who Maitland had suggested to Darnley, was sleeping with his wife. Rizzio had, at one time, been Darnley's lover. He felt betrayed and was ready to take his revenge on both Mary and Rizzio.

The Four Marys, Seton, Beaton, Fleming and Livingston, ladies in waiting to the queen, gave her comfort and support, sitting with her, playing cards and sewing to help her pass the time. They had all been with Mary since they were young girls having travelled with her to France and had taken a vow of chastity after Francis died promising not to marry until the queen re-married. When the Queen had married Darnley, they were free to marry and Mary Fleming had sought permission to wed Sir William Maitland, the Queen's illegitimate half-brother and Secretary of State. The Queen was delighted to give the match her blessing.

Mary Seton's family had been close to the royal family for generations; her mother was Lady-in-waiting to the queen's mother and Darnley was her cousin.

As secretary and a great friend to the queen, John Hay of Talla was Mary's Master of Requests; He was also in debt to

Darnley as the result of a number of card games and had been recruited by Maitland to assist in Darnley's undoing.

Darnley and a group of friends were regulars at the local taverns. When the taverns closed they frequented one of the many brothels to be found around the streets of Edinburgh and it was there that they spent most nights. Darnley was well known there and his knock was answered by a gaudily dresses girl of about twelve years of age. Her face was painted with bright red lips and rouged cheeks and her dress revealed more than she would have liked. Sweeping her into his arm, Darnley staggered into the main room and collapsed onto a sofa pulling the girl onto his lap.

An older woman entered who was clearly the madam of the house and Darnley called to her, 'This one new is she? I like 'new' ones.' His comment was met by laughter from his friends.

'I kept her pure and sweet, just for you,' the woman assured him. Darnley kissed the girl's neck roughly. When she squirmed and tried to get away the woman reminded her to be 'nice' to the gentleman and she reluctantly stayed on his lap.

'If she doesn't know how to be nice to you, you could get Mary to teach her. She seems to know how to be nice to Rizzio,' quipped Hay.

Darnley was on his feet in a second. 'Rizzio! You're right, she is always with him.'

'I bet he's in her skirts right now,' suggested another of the men.

Darnley, although he had no desire to be close to Mary, hated to think that he was being cuckolded and resented Mary's affection for Rizzio.

He was not going to miss his fun tonight but he would deal with Rizzio tomorrow. Grabbing the girl by the wrist he took out his anger on her as the others cheered him on.

When Darnley woke the next day his head throbbed. Struggling to clear his mind he threw back a glass of wine that his groom brought to him and thought back to the previous night.

'Send for Hay and the others,' he demanded. As Darnley's friends lived as part of the court, it did not take long to gather them in his room.

In a short time, they had decided that Rizzio must not just be 'punished' but dispatched. Darnley knew how much this would hurt Mary and spitefully wanted to cause her as much pain as possible.

It was 8 pm on the night of Saturday 9th March 1566. David Rizzio frequently joined the Marys in the evening for cards and to sing to them and had been invited to stay for supper. As he and the four Mary's sat in the Queen's supper chamber enjoying the meal with a group of friends, Lord Darnley and a large group of conspirators passed through the Palace of Holyrood. Rizzio had just left the table and was reaching for his lute when the door burst open.

Darnley entered first, to restrain his heavily pregnant wife. Lord Ruthven who was amongst them was suffering from a fever and close to death. He wore a suit of armour under his cloak and entered the room with the words, 'It would please Your Majesty to let yonder man Davie come forth of your presence,'

Mary, realising the danger that Rizzio was in said, 'Leave our presence under pain of treason.'

Ruthven told Darnley to seize his wife and fighting broke out amongst them. Rizzio hid behind the queen's dress whilst her other friends struggled to protect Rizzio and get Ruthven out of the room. At that moment the other plotters entered the room and tried to stab Rizzio. Mary saw the knives and thought they would turn on her next. She was six months pregnant and feared Darnley planned to be rid of both her and the child in order to take the throne.

When Hay pulled out a gun and held it against her belly she stopped struggling. David Rizzio was dragged screaming from the room and stabbed repeatedly before being thrown down the stairs.

The four Mary's rushed to their mistress as she sobbed hysterically. 'David!' she called repeatedly as they hushed and tried to comfort her. Mary Seton rushed off to get an herbal draught to sooth her and before long she was sleeping.

As Rizzio's life was ending, 150 miles away another life was beginning. Andrew Hay and Jean had a new son, Thomas. As her lady handed the child to its mother she looked carefully to see for signs that something might be wrong with it; checking fingers and toes and looking into his eyes. The baby did not take kindly to being handled so and expressed his annoyance loudly.

'Well, he makes enough noise,' she laughed, convinced that all was well, and handed him back to be wrapped in bindings.

The maid smiled reassuringly and rocked as she walked.

Over the next days, the queen discussed with her confidants, what she should do now. She was still married to Darnley and was too proud to prove her critics right. They decided that the best course of action was to turn Darnley against the plotters. They gathered ideas for ways they could discredit them in his eyes and encourage him to realise the danger he

347

would be in if he was implicated in an attack so close to the queen. Their plan succeeded; in the days that followed, Mary skilfully managed to persuade her husband that the plotters were using him for their own ends. and a week later, after a public reconciliation, Mary and Darnley left Holyrood under cover of darkness and made their way to Dunbar Castle but in spite of this, she would never forgive Darnley's treachery.

The Marys had feared that the queen would miscarry after the terrifying murder of Rizzio and in fear of childbirth she had written her will when she retired from the court for her confinement she sent for a sacred relic to be brought to her room.

As she laboured to deliver the child, the head of St Margaret, which as Father Edmund Hay, brother of Peter Hay of Megginch, described, *'Her skull is enclosed in the head of the bust whereupon there is a crown of silver gilt, enriched with several pearls and precious stones'*, watched over her.

On 19th June she gave birth to a healthy boy in a tiny apartment in Edinburgh Castle.

Mary insisted that a message be sent to Darnley immediately to tell him of the birth of his son in order that he could prepare for the prince's christening but the reply which she received was that Darnley would not be attending the child's christening. 'It is as I feared,' she confided in Mary Seaton, 'my husband will deny his son if he can. I must ensure he acknowledges him as his own or my prince may be denied his birthright.'

Darnley had accused Mary many time of having an affair with Rizzio and she was determined to secure her son's right to the throne in due course. She sent for Darnley as soon as she was washed and recovered from the birth to make his acknowledge that the child was his.

'My lord,' she said, 'God has given you and me a son, begotten by none but you. I am desirous that all here, both ladies and others bear witness: for he is so much your own son that I fear it will be the worse for him hereafter.'

The people of Scotland were delighted with the birth of a male heir to the throne and the baby's baptism at Stirling Castle was celebrated with three days of festivities.

In England, Queen Elizabeth was not about to celebrate. 'Alack,' she cried, 'The Queen of Scots is lighter of a bonny son, and I am but of barren stock.'

CHAPTER 31

Six shadowy figures entered Craigmillar Castle. Their black cloaks showed that they were men of distinction but their behaviour was that of villains. They went through into a back room and closed the door behind them. Maitland and Moray had called them together to broach the question of the removal of Darnley and were about to take Huntly, Argyll and Bothwell into their confidence.

With them sat William Powrie, George Dalgliesh, John Hay of Talla, and John Hepburn of Bolton – servants and followers of Bothwell and committed supporters of the Queen. It had been decided between Maitland and Moray that it was worth the risk of including their enemy, Bothwell in order that they could later lay the blame at his feet but Bothwell, in his turn, had brought his supporters as witnesses.

Moray had little to say during the meeting, leaving the talking to Maitland but Bothwell took to the plan with alacrity. His ambition to marry the queen would be served well by the removal of her husband. Maitland hoped for a union between England and Scotland; whilst the Catholic Darnley remained this would be nigh on impossible.

As they sat around the table, Hay took out a bond which had been prepared on the orders of Maitland and drawn up by his kinsman Alexander Hay of Delgatie. By the end of the meeting, every man there had signed and Darnley's fate was sealed.

Darnley had recently been unwell with a fever. He had a rash on his face and swellings in his neck and groin causing Mary to send him away to Glasgow for fear of the baby or herself being infected but promising to visit him there.

On his arrival, his father told visitors that his son had smallpox in the hope of deterring requests for an audience but servants talk and it was not long before it was known that he had, the great pox - syphilis.

Mary arrived soon after and spent some time closeted with her husband. During the evening, she sent for ink and paper that she might write a letter and, having sealed it, dispatched it to Bothwell in Edinburgh. Each day she sent letters suggesting they were of matters of state before insisting that she must leave and deal with matters of great import.

After a short stay in Glasgow, Darnley returned to Edinburgh and lodged in rooms at the Old Provost House at Kirk o' Field.

Silent figures crept into the basement of the house by night carrying sacks of gunpowder which they packed into the cellar.

⊰⊱

'What was that?' Darnley asked his servant, Taylor, sitting up straight in his bed. A scraping noise below had startled him.

'I heard no sound,' insisted Taylor.

'Listen.'

Darnley two sat in silence; Taylor standing beside him. It was some moments before they heard a voice.

Darnley slipped out of bed and stepped silently to the window, taking care not to cast a shadow. Standing to one side of the window, he peered out just as a figure passed so close to the house as to disappear from sight.

'There's somebody there,' he reported in a hoarse whisper. 'I am not safe here. We have to get out!'

Taylor put his hand on the door to go and look for a means of escape, but Darnley stopped him.

'No! They'll hear us. The window is our only hope.'

Throwing open the casement, Darnley looked down.

'It's too far to jump.'

Taylor looked around the room.

'Here, we can use this chair. I'll take the cord from the bed curtains and lower you to the ground.'

As he spoke he pulled the cord out and put it under the seat of the chair, fastening it around the legs and around a bed post before pushing the chair through the window. Darnley sat on the window sill and swung his legs through before lowering himself onto the chair. His man braced the rope around himself and, using the bed post to help to take the weight, he lowered the chair to the ground.

Just as Darnley stood up from the chair, the door opened. Seeing the glint of a knife in the intruder's hand, the servant leapt through the open window, landing with a thud and a curse on the ground below.

In the garden below, other figures now appeared, alerted by the noise. Darnley, still weak from his illness, had little energy to run and Taylor had turned his ankle in his bid to escape. Two of Douglas' henchmen had seen them running across the lawn and gave chase, throwing themselves upon the escapees.

'Pity me, kinsmen, for the love of Him who had pity on all the world!' Darnley cried.

Snatching the rope from the chair, the plotter pulled it tightly around Darnley's neck until he lay still before passing it to his fellow to dispatch the servant likewise. It took just moments to finish their victims.

'Help me to get the bodies back into the house to be....' A tremendous explosion stole his words and the two fled, but in the struggle, Archibald Douglas' slipper was pulled from his foot. He scrabbled around in the dark trying to find it but to no avail and was pulled away by a dark figure to hurriedly leave the scene.

Mary's servant, Bastien Paget, had wed that day so the queen's visit to Darnley had been short. Before long she left to return to the Palace of Holyrood, arriving too late for the masque which had entertained them that evening but in time for the bride bedding.

The Queen retired late but Bothwell stayed up playing cards. She had not been asleep long when an explosion tore through the house at Kirk o' Field, rocking Edinburgh and lighting up the sky.

Rescuers rushed to the house and buckets of water were passed from hand to hand to put out the fire but no sign could be found of Darnley or his companion. It was only as the sun rose that two bodies were found in a neighbouring garden. Suspicion immediately fell on Bothwell and comments whispered behind hands suggested Mary was involved but never more than a whisper was spoken.

The Queen began to spend a great deal of time in the evenings with Bothwell causing more than a few raised eyebrows and looks of disapproval from Mary Seton. When the

Queen ignored the reproving looks from her companion, Seton spoke to her on the matter warning that people had begun to suspect that they were not merely playing cards. 'The gentleman has something of a reputation with the ladies' she warned.

'Just the gossip of idle people who have nothing better to do than criticise' the Queen protested. 'You yourself have seen James enter with papers to discuss with me and act on our decisions when he leaves.' Seaton could only agree but fretted that the Queen was heading for more trouble.

⁂

Bothwell was the prime suspect in Darnley's murder and Darnley's father, the Earl of Lennox, along with other family members, were incensed when they saw Bothwell wearing Darnley's gold armour and realised that the Queen was giving her dead husband's possessions to the man they were convinced was his murderer.

They petitioned for his trial until the Privy Council finally agreed.

⁂

George Hay had been away from Slains for some time and knew that Margaret would be concerned. Deciding to write and tell her that he was well, he set out to apprise her of events in Edinburgh.

'My Dearest Margaret,
   I trust that this finds you in good health and that all at Slains is well.

354

I am sure you will have heard of the death of Darnley and will be worried for my safety. I can assure you that I keep in the best of health and shall return to you at Slains as soon as I might.

The events since Darnley's murder have been complex, to say the least. The popular belief has been that Lord Bothwell was implicated in the murder and Lennox, Darnley's father, demanded that Bothwell be put on trial.

Her Majesty, the queen, was persuaded to this and requested Lennox to attend for the prosecution. I know that she was distressed by this as she kept to her rooms pacing back and forth before sitting dejectedly in her chair beside the fire. I tried to assure her that it was important that the people see justice to be done but she would not be comforted. I fear for her health both in body and mind.

I myself was called to sit amongst the judges at the Tolbooth and I tell you, my good wife, I feared for my life.

Bothwell had over four thousand followers in the city, many of them armed and it was for this reason that Lennox feared to come forth. He travelled as far as Stirling before sending his apologies to the queen that he could not attend as his health suffered. (I fear it would have suffered so much the worse had he entered Edinburgh!)

My Lord Bothwell arrived confidently and in great splendour for his trial.

Her Majesty, Queen Elizabeth of England tried to send John Selby, her messenger, with a letter urging a postponement of the trial but Bothwell's henchmen would not let him pass, nor would they let his letter be delivered and offered him violence! Just then, Bothwell emerged on horseback with Maitland at his side and took the letter to take to our queen.

When they returned, Selby asked if the queen had looked at the letter but was told that she was sleeping and had not been disturbed. And yet, I myself saw her that very moment at the window!

And so, my Lord Bothwell continued to the Toll Booth.

Besides myself, the jury consisted of Andrew Leslie, George Sinclair, Gilbert Kennedy, Lord John Hamilton, (you will remember him from Andrew's wedding), second son of Chatelherault, James, Lord Ros, Lord Sempill, Lord Herries, Laurence, Lord Oliphant, John Forbes, John Gordon of Lochinvar, Lord Boyd, James Cockburn of Langton, John Somerville, Mowbray of Barnbougle and Lord Ogilvy of Boyne.

Bothwell was charged with being art and part of the odious, treasonable and abominable slaughter of the King on 9 February last.(I fear they were mistaken in the date which, I believe should have been 10th.)

In any case, no evidence was brought against my Lord Bothwell so that when we, the jury, retired after seven hours, to discuss the case we had no choice but to declare him innocent. And I must tell you, my dear, I was glad to do so for fear of the mob had it been otherwise.

As he left the Tolbooth, Bothwell was triumphant. He defiantly fixed a note to the door, on which was a challenge, wherein he offered to fight in single contest against any gentleman undefamed that durst charge him with the murder. He then sent for the town crier and paid him to go around Edinburgh and proclaim the verdict.

Given the number of his men around the town, no answer came to his challenge safe in the form of a note which was stuck to the Mercat Cross, stating, 'There is none that professes Christ and His Evangel that can with upright conscience part Bothwell and his wife, albeit she prove him an abominable adulterer and worse, as he has murdered the husband of her he intends to marry, whose promise he had long before the murder.'

I fear that Bothwell now believes that none can harm him.

The mob has now dispersed and I hope to be able to return to you soon.

My love as ever

George.

⟡⟡

Parliament was closing and George Hay was planning to set out as soon as possible to return to Slains. He had found the two preceding weeks particularly exhausting and longed to rest within the walls of his own castle, but that afternoon he received an invitation to dine with a group of lords at Ainsley's Tavern near the Palace of Holyrood and felt obliged to attend.

When he arrived at the tavern, he was shown into a room at the back of the building. Around it sat eight other earls, eight bishops, and seven Lords of Parliament.

Supper was superlative with copious amounts of wine being provided and consumed. George held back and drank slowly, anticipating an early start the following day in order to make best use of the daylight for his journey home.

When the meal was concluded and the gentlemen's glasses were re-filled with port, Bothwell produced a document. Standing to address the gathering, he explained briefly that he wished them all to sign it to confirm his innocence and defend him from accusations regarding his involvement in Darnley's murder. Many of them having sat as judges in the case, they could hardly refuse he reminded them. There was some muttering and a number of hushed conversations began, only to be quelled by Bothwell continuing his address.

The queen could not remain unmarried, he reminded them. It would be better for her to marry a true Scot than a foreigner. Should the queen choose him, they would recommend him as an appropriate husband for her, and pledge to assist in defending such a marriage.

One earl leapt to his feet, only to be pulled by his doublet back to his seat, stumbling as he did so. There was outrage and raise voices as many objected to the man, whom they knew must have been involved in Darnley's murder in some way, offering himself as the next husband for the queen! But Bothwell had positioned his supporters carefully between those whom he knew would protest. They were primed to remind any who objected that they all wanted to be rid of Darnley and whoever had risked all to oblige them should not suffer as a result.

'Are you telling me you found a guilty man innocent?' a hushed voice whispered to Erroll.

During the deliberations, one or two managed to slip away. Argyll refused to sign and showed signs of causing trouble so Bothwell changed tac.

'I present this bond to you only for your consideration. I do not ask you to sign tonight. Please. Gentlemen, enjoy your evening.' And with that, he withdrew.

The following day, George Hay was about to set out on his journey home when the sound of hooves made him look up. Peering through the window, he saw Bothwell with twenty armed men on horses. Some of the men broke away and disappeared to the back of the building. George realised, there was no escape.

A rap on the door followed in seconds and before he could move towards it, the door opened. Bothwell stepped in apologising for the interruption. Two armed men stood behind him, their hands poised over the hilts of their swords.

It was the work of a few moments for Bothwell to tell George that the queen wished her nobles to sign the bond he had shown them the previous night and he had brought it with him for George to sign as he knew he was about to leave and would not wish to disappoint the queen.

Knowing he had no choice if he wished to escape with his life, George signed the bond. The moment his signature was sanded dry, Bothwell whisked it away and turned on his heel. Signalling to his men to follow, he set off to repeat the event with each of the nobles and clergy whom he had entertained the previous evening. Erroll was by now so confused and exhausted that he postponed his journey and took to his bed.

In her naivety, Mary believed that would be the end of the matter.

After Prince James' christening, Mary had left him with the Earl of Mar and instructed the Earl not to give him over to anybody he did not trust to keep him safe even in the face of violence. Now she felt the safest place for him was Edinburgh castle and rode to Stirling to collect him. With her rode thirty men including Secretary Maitland and Sir James Melville of Raith.

When the party arrived at the castle, Mar came out to meet them. Bowing deeply to the Queen, he addressed her formally. 'Your Royal Highness, you gave me orders that I should, in no circumstances, release the prince into the hands of any I thought might present a danger to His Majesty. At this time I feel that to hand him over to your keeping would place him in such danger as you asked me to protect him from. This being the case I shall not release the prince into your care.'

The Queen was outraged but in no position to wrestle her son from Mar's care, she agreed to his offer to let her see the boy.

On Wednesday 24 April, Mary set out for Edinburgh. The sound of hooves approaching at a gallop caused Mary's guards to attempt to draw their swords. When Bothwell appeared with about eight hundred men and took hold of Mary's horse by the bridle. His men took the Earl of Huntly' Lethington and Melville captive as Bothwell took Mary to one side. There was a heated but whispered discussion between them before Bothwell openly said, 'If Your Majesty would permit me, I will escort you to my castle at Dunbar, for safety'. She agreed to accompany him and indicated to her guards to comply.

They arrived at Dunbar at midnight. As soon as they arrived, Bothwell swung down from his horse and stood beside the Queen swearing that he would wed her. Lifting his hands up to assist her he held her waist and lowered her to the ground. As soon as her feet touched the earth, he put his arm about her, and, in spite of her protests, took her inside the castle and up to his chamber.

Unsure as to whether this was horseplay by the Queen and the gentleman, the guards were unsure how to react. They were Bothwell's own household and guards but nevertheless bound to protect the Queen. As she did not call to them to rescue her, they stood and watched as Bothwell took her away.

Once in his chamber, Mary giggled. They had planned to make it look as though Bothwell had imprisoned her and she took great enjoyment in pretending to be his prisoner as he made love to her. 'There, now you will have to marry me,' Bothwell whispered in her ear as he lay back on the pillows. Mary giggled in response and kissed him passionately.

The first day after their arrival at Dunbar, Melville was freed and rode with all haste to Edinburgh to raise help to free the Queen.

When he returned to Dunbar with a force of citizens armed with farm implements, he was told that the Queen was playing golf with Bothwell. There was much murmuring amongst the crowd who had left their homes and farms, on the word of Melville, to rescue the Queen.

On 12 May the Queen created Bothwell Duke of Orkney and Marquis of Fife. - James Cockburn, Patrick Hay of Whitelaw, and Patrick Hepburn of Beanston were knighted at his investiture. Soon after, Erroll received a summons to attend the wedding of the Queen and Bothwell.

Having no choice but to attend, he prepared a letter to his wife, inviting her to come to Edinburgh and join him. Elizabeth was delighted. News of events had reached Slains Castle from time to time by way of travelling hawkers and musicians, tempting her imagination and thirst for more information and not least her concerns for George.

She arrived in Edinburgh on 14th May to a warm welcome from George. Her maids immediately went with her luggage to George's chamber in Holyrood to unpack and prepare her gown for the wedding. George and Margaret spent the evening in his chamber where he tried to explain the complicated events of recent months but struggling to remember what had happened.

'My duty is to protect the Queen' he explained, 'and I will do so to the last drop of my blood; but it is difficult to know if she wants to wed Bothwell or is being forced. If he is forcing her, what hold does he have that she does not resist? I know she always likes a strong man to lean on but if he really killed Dudley as people say, how can she marry her husband's murderer?'

'I thought Bothwell was married to Huntly's daughter,' Margaret mused.

'He was but the marriage has been annulled on the grounds of consanguinity…even though they had a dispensation from the Pope.'

'The man certainly knows how to get what he wants!'

'If he did rape the Queen, as they would have us believe, why doesn't she have him arrested? They went out playing golf the next day. It doesn't sound as if she was too unhappy about it.'

'Isn't Bothwell a Protestant?'

'Yes, and that's causing concern to all parties. There are rumours that Mary now follows the Protestant faith.'

The next day George and Margaret dressed in preparation for the wedding. The procession to the Great Hall in Holyrood was as colourful as could be expected for any royal wedding but the excitement which might normally be expected was replaced by concerned faces and a tense atmosphere. The wedding was according to Protestant rites and George noticed that the Queen looked depressed. Not what he would expect of a willing bride.

Scotland was once again divided; some were in favour of Mary and Bothwell and others against. The Lords opposed to them gathered an army and Mary set out with Bothwell to gather forces to face them, leaving Sir Patrick Hay of Whitelaw in command of Dunbar. Moving from place to place they were disappointed to find few men would follow them. Finally, on 15th June 1567, they met the army of the confederate Lords led by Kirkcaldy of Grange at Carberry Hill.

Mary expected Huntly to appear with men from the Catholic northern Lords, but on such a hot day, when the rebels were sober and her men were drinking wine, she decided not to wait fearing that her men would be in no fit state to fight if they were allowed to consume much more.

The rebels were coming out of the sun and her men were facing into it. The rebels were being supplied with food by the local people but many of her force were deserting through hunger and lack of commitment to her cause.

Robert Birrell, a burgess of Edinburgh, wrote in his diary that night,

'The 15 day being sonneday, the armies came within view. The one stood upone Carberry Hills, with 4 regiments of shouldiours, and six field-pieces of brasse: the uther armey stoode over against it, messingers going betwixt them all day till near night; dureing which parley the Duke fled secretly to Dunbar, and the Queine came and randred herself prisoner to ye Lordis, quho convoyed her to Edinburghe to the Provost's Lodgeing for yat night; Sr. Symeon Prestone of Craigmillar being Provost for ye time.'

'It is almost evening' Mary pointed out to Bothwell. 'We cannot succeed if it comes to a battle. I will negotiate for your freedom.'

'Don't be a fool, Mary. They will never let us go free' he returned. Mary saw they had no option and sent a messenger to the rebels.

None of the opposing Lords wished harm to the Queen and readily agreed to her surrender on her terms; that they let Bothwell leave the field freely and return her to Holyrood to remain as Queen.

Bothwell kissed Mary passionately before mounting his horse and riding away with John Hay of Talla, Hepburn and Cullen.

Mary watched as they rode into the distance, raising her hand to wave she realised that Bothwell was not going to look back and sadly she lowered her hand and turned away.

Bothwell and his followers made their escape to Aberdeen where they boarded a boat. It was only when they reached the coast Norway that they were arrested for not having the correct papers.

Taken to Denmark, King Frederik was about to release them when news came to him that Bothwell was wanted for the murder of Darnley.

'I cannot release you,' he told Bothwell, 'but nor do I wish to send you back to Scotland.'

Over the next weeks, news of events in Scotland from traders came to the king's ears which led him to understand that Mary would never be accepted as queen again. Losing interest in Bothwell he sent him to Dragsholm Castle where he was chained up in a stinking cell. There was a barred window high in the wall allowing rain, wind and snow to penetrate the filthy cell but doing little to freshen the putrid air.

As days turned into weeks and then months, Bothwell could be heard muttering to himself. The mutters gradually turned to ravings as he beat his head against the floor, unable to rise and denied company he gradually descended into madness.

CHAPTER 32

In Scotland, two days after Bothwell had left the field at Carberry Hill, Mary was taken prisoner and held at Lochleven Castle, home of the Dowager Countess Douglas of Lochleven.

Moray, the Queen's half-brother, was returning from France to become Regent of the Queen's son, Prince James.

A boatman rowed Mary out to the island on Lochleven where the Douglas Castle stood. She sat in her room on the third floor and looked out onto the loch. She startled as the key turned in the lock and the door to her chamber opened. The guard stood back and Lord Erroll stepped past him. Dropping to his knee he took Mary's hand and placed it to his lips. 'Your Highness,' he said, 'I trust you are well and being cared for.'

Mary was delighted to see one of the few men she could trust. 'I am as well as might be, Lord Erroll. But you risk much in visiting me here.'

'Ha! I feel as if I might be in my own castle of Slains,' he observed. The castle was, indeed, very much like that of Slains, being laid out in exactly the same way and very much surrounded by water. The day was hot, yet within the stone walls the air was chilly and Mary shivered. 'I have been summoned to attend the coronation of your son, James, as King of Scotland.'

'And will you go?'

'How can I attend in my role of Constable of Scotland at the coronation of a king when his mother, the Queen, still lives?' he asked. 'It is my duty to protect you, not to see you usurped. It would be wrong and I shall not do it.'

'You have always been a faithful servant Erroll. There have been few who have been true to me as you have. You have always given me true council and stood by your Catholic faith.'

'You honour me.'

'It is kind of you to visit me Erroll but you must go. There is great danger for you here.'

Lowering his voice George promised, 'I shall go but I will gather your supporters and rescue you from here. I will send you a messenger when all is ready.'

Mary smiled her thanks but doubted that he would succeed.

Bowing, George Hay left and she heard the key turn once more in the lock.

Barely an hour after the visit, Mary was gripped by a sharp pain and groaning she sank onto the chair. As the pain subsided she called out to the guard for one of her ladies to be admitted to her room. It was not long before she realised what was happening and when her maid arrived she was helped onto her bed.

The pains continued into the night until, in the early hours of the next morning, she miscarried twins.

Mary was left weak and miserable. Born to be a queen, her life had been one trouble after another. Those who should have served her had taken advantage of her; those she had loved had abused her love. Her only living child was taken from her and would be used by her enemies to take her throne from her. What, she asked herself, did she have left to live for?

It was some time before Erroll was able to fulfil his promise but when Mary was told once again that she had visitors she looked up hopefully expecting to see him.

The figures who entered her room struck terror in her heart. Not the longed for Lord Erroll but Lord Ruthven and Lord Lindsay entered. Her maid was pushed from the room and the door slammed behind her. Unlike Lord Erroll they did not bow to her but thrust a document in her face. Their ultimatum, abdicate or die. They were deadly serious and Ruthven stepping behind her chair put his arm around her forehead and pulled back her head. She felt a chill of steel against her throat as his blade pressed into her tender skin.

'You will sign,' he growled as Lindsay handed her a quill. He drew an inkwell from his cloak and unscrewed the top. Mary dipped the quill into the ink and, with tears in her eyes, she signed her name.

No sooner was the document signed than the men left her room and made their way directly to Stirling to arrange for the coronation of the one-year-old James as James VI of Scotland.

William Douglas had been absent from the castle when Ruthven and Lindsay had forced her to sign her abdication. On his return, he was horrified to hear of their actions and feared for his own future. Sending immediately for his scribe, he had a legal paper drawn up, which stated that he was not present when the Queen signed her 'demission' of the crown and did not know of it, and that he offered to convey her to Stirling Castle for her son's coronation which was the following day, which offer she refused. Taking the paper to Mary's chamber, he begged her to sign it in the hope that he would be vindicated of complicity. Bowing her head sadly, in the realisation that, like so many of her nobles, he was more concerned for his own neck than hers, she signed.

William was terrified that others might gain access to the queen as Ruthven and Lindsay had done, either to threaten her or even to free her. Either way, he himself would be held responsible. His solution was to appoint his wife, Lady Agnes Leslie, as the Queen's chief female companion. She was to remain as such for the duration of her ten and a half months of imprisonment, accompanying her throughout the day and often sleeping in her bedchamber.

Erroll was angry and frustrated when the news was brought to him, but, determined to free his queen, he continued, with a few close friends, to plan her escape.

In spite of Agnes' personal supervision, on 2 May 1568, a message was smuggled to Mary's room telling her to be ready with her maid at midnight. When the appointed hour came, a hooded figure opened the door of Mary's room and threw back his hood. Mary's heart leapt and she smiled broadly at the familiar face of Sir William Douglas' brother, George. A finger was raised to his lips to warn her to keep silent and a wave beckoned her to follow. Stealthily they made their way down the winding stone steps and out into the chilling night air. The short distance round the castle wall and down to the water was covered in moments.

Climbing into the boat, Mary shivered with fear and cold. Her rescuer removed his cloak and wrapped it around her as the boatman dipped the oars into the water and pulled them away to freedom and the safety of Dumbarton Castle.

When Sir William learned of her escape, he was so fearful that he took out his dagger, and, pulling open his tunic, he attempted to stab himself with his own dagger.

CHAPTER 33

Curious to see the building progress at Delgatie Castle, Helen asked George if they could journey north and visit Alexander for a week or two before he was recalled to the Royal Court. George always enjoyed visiting Delgatie and readily agreed. On their arrival, it was clear that work was well under way.

'Greetings, Alexander. I see you are making some changes here.' Alexander was puzzled that George should seem surprised but without comment, he led them into the new building and showed them around. George was amazed by the size of the stairs and spoke as though he knew nothing of the plans. During the course of their stay, Alexander became increasingly concerned that George's memory was failing. He was reluctant to point this out to Helen and tried to compensate for the lapses in the hope that it was a result of stress and nothing more. He showed George the new cannon he had purchased and explained that in the present times of unrest, both religious and social, it was prudent to be prepared for an attack. Many of his older guns were unreliable and overheated very quickly. The newer ones were less prone to blowing up and could be fired more frequently.

On their return to Slains, Isabel's nanny brought her down to greet them. George dismounted and helped Helen down. The horses were taken by the groom and George turned towards the steps as his daughter was brought to the door. George turned to Helen in surprise. 'We have guests,' he said in surprise.

Looking around, Helen wondered who he was referring to. Following his eyes, she saw Isabel waving down and looked towards George smiling in the belief that he was joking. 'Didn't you say you were going to discuss getting some new cannon like Alexander's,' she prompted. 'I'll go and see the children whilst you find the armourer and talk about your ideas.'

'Was I? Oh, yes, an excellent idea,' agreed George who was beginning to find strategies to disguise his failing memory. 'We are so exposed to attacks from sea, here at Slains, that more cannon are essential.'

As time went on, Helen noticed more and more that George was frequently forgetting where he had put things; what he was going to do, and even people whom he had known for years. Her concerns grew for his well-being when she found him wandering around the castle declaring that they must make ready to go to Slains. When she found him she led him gently into their chambers and sat him comfortably in front of the fire with a glass of mulled wine. 'I have a longing to visit Andrew at Erroll,' she told her husband as she took a seat opposite him.

'Andrew? Oh, yes,' he blustered, 'Andrew. Must see Andrew again. Good man; one of the best.'

Helen spoke to her maid and told her to make ready for a visit to their estates in Perthshire. The woman nodded and left to tell the other servants to prepare.

The entourage was quite informal but Helen requested additional men to join them for her husband's safety.

When they arrived at Erroll, Andrew was in his study with Andrew Tulidef who was signing a bond of man-rent. George Hay of Newraw, who had been one of the witnesses for them, came out to beg their patience and explained that a carriage had lost a wheel and delayed Tulidef's arrival. George was clearly bewildered as to who these people were and looked pleadingly at Helen to explain. 'Newraw, how are you?' she asked approaching one of the visitors and giving George a clue as to the man's identity.

'Newraw, good to see you,' Erroll said shaking him by the hand.

'We will take a little refreshment whilst Lord Hay is engaged in business,' Helen said, taking George by the arm and leading him to the window seat. 'I always love the view here, don't you, George?'

The scene was familiar of old and George finally felt comfortable. 'When I was a young boy we would come to visit my Uncle William here. Where is he? Will he join us for supper?'

'Your Uncle died alongside your father at that dreadful battle at Flodden,' Helen reminded him.

'Dead! No! A wonderful man. Such a clever man; especially in divinity. He knew the New Testament as well as if he had written it himself. He would always choose his words with care and never speak to hurt or humble a man no matter how lowly.' A tear came to his eye as he remembered and he brushed it away unashamedly.

Andrew came to join them apologising for having been engaged on their arrival. 'Father, it is good to see you. Mother, are you well?'

'I am quite well,' Helen replied, 'but your father and I wished to talk with you.'

'Let us talk over dinner,' he suggested and led them to his table where a servant waited with an ewer of water to wash their hands. The meal was accompanied by conversation about the estates and developments in farming. Concerns about the religious reformers were expressed and what the future might hold with the Queen a captive in England. When George expressed concern on hearing this, Andrew was shocked, knowing that his father had been instrumental in her escape from Lochleven. As they took a final glass of wine, Helen reminded George that he had said he was tired and would retire early.

'Did I?' he questioned. Andrew knew that he had not and looked quizzically at his mother.

'I will join you very soon,' Helen promised and George, reluctant to let them see that he had no recollection of such statement, took his leave of them.

'Is father losing his mind?' Andrew asked his mother.

'He is well advanced in years and I fear he struggles sometimes to remember things. Sometimes he seems fine and then he will say something odd. He asked for his uncle earlier and was most distressed when I told him he had died at Flodden. He can reckon and discuss estate matters quite soundly and then say something entirely out of keeping with events. I just don't understand it. I have even found him wandering in the barbican not knowing where he was.'

'This is most worrying. Perhaps if you both stay here rather than returning to Slains, I can support Father and represent him when he needs to attend to his duties.'

'That may serve well, Andrew. Thank you. Your father is into his seventh decade and he finds his duties exhausting now. I must send a messenger to Slains to make arrangements for Isabel.'

He lifted his glass to empty it and Helen noticed that his hand shook. He quickly put the glass down and rose from the table declaring they would retire and, taking her hand and placing it on his arm, he lead her as far as her chamber before placing a kiss on her cheek and taking his leave.

A week later the alarm was raised. Erroll had not been seen since early evening when he had retired to rest before they ate. As Andrew and his wife Jean, along with Helen had taken their places at table, they had become aware of George's absence. Helen sent a maid to their room to rouse him believing that he had slept longer than intended but was horrified when the girl returned to report that he was not there.

'Don't worry,' Andrew reassured her. He will be enjoying the gardens or looking at the new portraits in the gallery. Staff were sent searching indoors and out but none returned with news until a lad ran in, forgetting to bow and rushed up to Andrew crying, 'My lord, The Earl has gone riding!'

'Oh, no!' exclaimed Helen. 'He will have no idea where he is and will get lost.'

'I don't think so,' reassured Andrew. 'I have noticed that, although he forgets things almost immediately these days, his memory of long ago remains good. He will know these grounds as well as any man.'

Helen had to agree that his words were true and took courage from them.

Andrew called for his horse to be readied and forty men to accompany him. He sent for his riding cape and promised to return with his father. Ten-year-old Francis had heard the shouts and begged to be allowed to ride with them. 'Well enough,' his father decided, 'an extra pair of eyes could be useful.'

Francis was thrilled. He did not often get a chance to take part in a search and he loved his grandfather dearly. The party set off with Andrew dividing the men into small groups and giving each group a route to take.

Whilst the men were away, Jean took Helen to sit in her solar and sent for wine. 'Francis is a credit to you,' she told Jean. 'How do his brothers do?'

Jean looked away and when she turned back, Helen saw the glitter of tears in her eyes. 'I fear that Thomas has the same affliction as his brother. It is too early to be sure, but he displays the same behaviours.'

'Oh, my dear! I am so sorry. To have one child so accursed is dreadful but two is unbearable.'

'His nursemaid sometimes thinks he responds to a sound but I fear it is wishful thinking. Alex can never carry out his duties should he become Earl of Erroll. Andrew is to meet with Parliament to seek an act to have him set aside. It is terrible to see my sons so.'

'But at least you may take comfort in the children's love.'

'Indeed I do; and yet.....'

'What is it?'

'Alexander sometimes seems to hate me.' Jean broke down and sobbed.

'I'm sure you are wrong, Jean. Why would he hate you?'

'I'm sure I do not know but he pushes me away and screams the most terrible screaming. It goes right through me.'

As if on cue, a dreadful sound reached their ears. Jean rushed from the room and flew up the stairs to the nursery. Helen followed as quickly as her older legs would permit. When she arrived in the doorway, it was to witness Alexander thrashing around and uttering a dreadful noise somewhere between a scream and a gurgle. His eyes were wild and his nurse was being pummelled by his fists. Jean tried to intervene but drew back gasping. Helen saw three lines of blood down her face where the boy's fingernails had scored her. Now the boy was rolling on the floor screaming and grasping to grab anybody who came within his reach.

'Stand back,' Helen advised. 'He will exhaust himself soon.' Leading a distraught Jean from the room, she asked, 'Does this happen often?'

'Every day,' she replied. 'And it is getting worse. He throws things and bites people. He's like an animal.'

'Then Andrew is right to speak to parliament. I am so sorry Jean but I fear he will never take his place in Scotland.'

Sounds in the courtyard brought their attention back to the Earl's absence. Francis was first to enter with the news. 'I found him!' he exclaimed, 'Grandfather had fallen from his horse. I saw the riderless horse and found Grandfather lying nearby.'

Helen gasped. 'Is he hurt?' she asked rushing past Francis into the yard. Andrew had sent for a carriage to bring his father back as he was too weak to re-mount.

'I'm fine,' George told her brushing away hands which would support him out of the carriage. As he stepped out he stumbled and, were it not for a stable lad who instinctively reached out and caught him, he would have fallen to the ground. The lad apologised when he realised he had laid hands on the Earl but Andrew re-assured him that he had done well.

Helen took George's arm in courtly fashion whilst discreetly supporting him and maintaining his dignity. She led him inside and ordered brandy to be brought to revive him. George sat slumped in the chair in sharp contrast to Helen's upright posture. When he struggled to raise the glass to his lips she sprang to her feet and took it from him. 'I think, when you are ready, I should like to rest a while. Will you accompany me?'

George readily agreed and before long they were in their chamber.

Helen helped George to disrobe and don his nightgown before helping him to mount the steps to the bed. The maid had turned down the covers in readiness and Helen lifted his feet onto the bed before covering him with the counterpane. He slept almost immediately and she sat beside the bed with her hand on his arm.

After a while, her eyes gradually closed in the peace of the room and she slept for some hours before Andrew silently opened the door. He stepped into the room and looked at the motionless figure on the bed. Putting his hands on Helen's shoulders he gently squeezed to rouse her.

'I'm afraid father has passed away,' he told her. Her eyes darted to her husband's body and she gasped as she saw that Andrew's words were true.

Catholicism was now illegal and Donald Campbell, who had been the Abbot of Coupar Angus, had not been to George's liking. The Abbot had had five illegitimate sons and numerous daughters, much to George's disgust. Now the Earl of Atholl, who had been given the lands of the abbey, had nominated the protestant Leonard Lesley to be Commendator of the abbey.

In the circumstances, Andrew and Helen agreed that to bury the Earl at the abbey would have been contrary to his wishes. They were also reluctant to make further gifts to the abbey since Campbell was gifting much of the Abbey's wealth to members of his family. It was finally agreed that George Hay would be buried at Erroll and Andrew's brother, Thomas who was parson of Turriff, would take the service.

George had been widely respected amongst his peers and many would have gladly attended his funeral but Helen knew he would wish a Catholic service and the risk was too great. A private, family service was arranged and it was only after it had been accomplished that news of the earl's death was sent abroad.

Andrew accompanied Helen back to Slains Castle. Jean remained at Erroll for a while as she had recently discovered that she was carrying another child and Andrew though it too dangerous for her to travel. He had written to parliament explaining about his eldest son's affliction and requesting that his titles pass to his second son, Francis, when the time came. He had also set a guard of two burly men to watch over Alexander who was becoming increasingly violent.

Andrew spent his first weeks at Slains getting to know his new tenants and renew his acquaintance with the castle people. Being apart from his wife, Andrew found the services of one of the serving girls most acceptable. A small, pert young lass whose parents were both in the Earl's service; she hoped to be elevated to lady's maid by finding favour with the Earl but also found herself with child and before the year was out, Andrew was father to a base born daughter, Agnes. Recognising his duty, he saw to the welfare of the child and ordered that she be brought up with his own children.

Andrew rode out hunting with his falconer and Master of Hounds and used the excursions to call at Clochtow, Whinnyfold and Ward of Cruden to meet his people and see how they lived their lives. He was sympathetic to the plight of the fishermen whose hard lives at sea were made more difficult when the catch was poor. Their women folk walked many miles around his lands selling the fish that their men had caught and then returned home to care for their families in the tiny, two roomed But-n-Ben cottages that they called home.

It was whilst he was visiting a young family who lived within his feu that a rider on a fine but exhausted mount arrived with news from Erroll. Andrew's wife had succumbed to the dangers of childbirth and left a baby daughter, motherless.

Andrew was horrified and returned to Slains Castle immediately. Lady Helen already knew of the tragedy as the rider had called at the castle seeking his master before being re-directed. She had anticipated that he would wish to travel to Erroll as soon as possible and had given orders to the servants to make ready for his departure.

It was too late that day to set off but at first light the next morning he mounted his horse and turned it towards the gates. A small entourage of twelve men travelled with him bearing his pennant and providing a guard.

'How sad,' Helen mused, 'to have given up her right to the title of Erroll when she was young, and now, as she finally became Countess of Erroll, she is taken by the Lord'.

Andrew had his wife laid to rest near her uncle, George, and according to the Catholic rites, before collecting his new daughter and her wet nurse to return to Slains Castle.

By the time they arrived back it was dusk. Candles had been lit within the castle and torches burnt outside to permit work to continue for a while longer. Helen came out when she heard the horses arriving and stood at the top of the wooden stairway looking down sadly at the tiny child who was waking and beginning to demand food. She reached down and took the child into her arms whilst the wet nurse entered and removed her cloak. Helen took her to the nursery and gave orders for refreshments to be brought to her as soon as the child had been fed.

Andrew was weary and begged to be excused before retiring.

By virtue of his role as Constable of Scotland, Andrew was obliged to spend a great deal of time at the Royal Court. He took great pleasure in his duties and found the bustle and intrigues of Court fascinating but tiring.

Although little over forty years of age he was beginning to feel the rigours of age. His muscles ached when he awoke in the mornings and he was becoming clumsy. A goblet would slip from his grasp during dinner or a document flutter to the ground as he fumbled with the rest trying to regain his grip. He began to walk with short shuffling steps and the tremor in his hands, which he had noticed some time ago, was becoming more pronounced. He did his best to conceal his physical problems knowing that his enemies would take advantage of any weaknesses; there were enemies around every corner.

Sleeping at Holyrood seemed also to be a problem. He would awake with nightmares and shout aloud, to the alarm of his groom. Word began to spread around the Court that the Earl of Erroll was becoming feeble. Whispering behind their hands as he passed, courtiers would snigger and gesture behind his back and yet, disturbing as this might be, it faded into insignificance compared to the pains which he sometimes suffered. He was becoming increasingly aware of his hand trembling when he was at rest and would hold it with his other hand to still it. 'I am being poisoned!' he told friends. 'These reformers wish me dead for my Catholic faith.' There was some truth in this, it could not be denied, but he was not as great a threat as some to the Protestants.

❦

The arrival at Slains Castle of Peter Hay of Megginch's son, Patrick, was most welcome. Andrew was always interested in the welfare of his tenants at Erroll and enjoyed catching up with news of friends and family. It took his mind off his ills and youthful company was always welcome. Had he known the true purpose of Patrick's visit, he would not have been so pleased.

⋙⋘

On the first of August 1576, at 2 am, in the depths of the darkness, at Slains Castle, a light thud announced that a ladder had made contact with the castle wall. Shadowy figures rose up the ladder and slipped silently into the castle courtyard. The rush of the waves coming against the shore and the sound of muffled voices within the bakehouse were the only sounds in the castle yard. Not a dog barked because the scent of the figures was familiar to them.

Lord Erroll's brothers might have been thought to be sneaking back from a late engagement with ladies of easy virtue, entering as they did, were it not for the fact that they were accompanied by Peter Hay of Megginch and twelve men at arms.

Andrew's brother, Lawrence, gave a hoot like an owl. A grating sound witnessed the drawing of the lock on the castle door by Patrick and as it shifted, the figures slid through the opening. The figures clearly knew their way around the castle and whilst Andrew, Earl of Erroll, and his servants slept, they spread out around the castle. The men at arms rushed to the chambers of Andrew's servants and at a given signal, burst into the rooms, snatching weapons from the bedsides of the sleeping men and locking them in their rooms; helpless to defend their master.

Being a light sleeper, Andrew was disturbed by the sound of the catch on his door being lifted. He reached for his sword before the man was upon him and picking up a chair he flung it with all of his might at the figure. He passed through the door and stumbled down the stairs to the main hall, where he slammed the door closed and pushed a chest against it. Heavy blows told him that the men would not be deterred. He wondered why no guards had been roused by the noise and looked around for a means to escape.

The weight of three men against the door forced the chest to move and in moments they were clambering past the obstacle to strike at Andrew with his sword. Although heavily outnumbered Andrew gave a good account of himself. He dodged behind his table grabbing silver plates to hurl as he held off his attackers. A downward blow caught his attacker on the arm slicing into flesh and drawing a curse from him. Andrew whirled round as he sensed a man behind him, but not fast enough. His brothers were younger and fitter than he was and it did not take them long to send the sword spinning from his hand and to hold him fast. Although there was only the first faint light of dawn creeping through the shutters, Andrew could see that the men were armed with swords, daggers and pistols.

'Don't be stupid and you won't get hurt,' said a familiar voice. 'Now, get up!' it ordered. Andrew was forced to his feet and peered into the darkness as he was bundled through the door and down the stairs. His eyes were gradually becoming accustomed to the dark but he was unable to control his clumsy decent as hands pushed and pulled at him until they had descended four flights of stairs. He knew that he was now in the cellar and a grating sound told him that the cover was being removed from the dungeon.

'What are you doing?' he begged and was rewarded with a blow to the ribs. 'You were told not to speak,' he was reminded.

'We agreed not to hurt the clumsy old bastard,' Lawrence's voice said. 'He's no good to us dead; the Earldom would only go to John. I'll go down first or the fool will fall and break his neck. You go back and see that the bairns are brought here.'

Lawrence turned and stepped onto the ladder to descend into the deeper darkness. Andrew was turned around and felt hands grab his ankles guiding his feet down onto the rungs of the ladder. A strong pair of hands pushed him down until his head was below the floor. When he felt his feet reach solid earth, he was pushed to the ground and more bodies descended the ladder. There was a crack as a flint was struck and a light burst into life. A branch of candles was lit and the darkness retreated. Andrew's arms were grabbed from behind and he felt a rope being bound around his wrists.

Looking around he saw that his captors were his brothers, Lawrence, George and Alexander accompanied by armed men. One he recognised as Harry Herst, Lawrence's man at arms, but the others he did not know.

'What on earth are you doing?' he blustered. 'Where are my children?'

'You'll find out soon enough,' came the reply. 'Leave him there. Did the others get the weapons from the guards and lock them in?'

'Aye,' said one of the armed men. 'All secure.'

Scuffling sounds and muffled cries witnessed to the arrival of Andrew's sons as they were forced to join their father. Unable to hear and now not even able to see their father's reassuring gestures, Alexander and Thomas were terrified. Francis tried to reassure them by taking their hands and holding them tightly but fear gripped them none the less.

The captors had made their way back up the ladder, taking the candles with them and leaving Andrew tied uncomfortably and in complete darkness. Although the boys were not bound, there was no possibility of escape from the pit. Francis tried his best to untie the knots which held his father's bonds but to no avail. The rope was tarred and would not give to his small fingers.

By the next day, Andrew was cold, stiff and hungry. It was midday before he heard voices above and the sound of the grid being removed. A figure lowered the ladder and descended into the dungeon followed by two more. Andrew's brothers stood before him and taunted him.

'Look at you, you sick old fool. You can barely walk, you shake and you're losing you mind. Call yourself an Earl? I should be Earl and Constable of Scotland not a feeble bastard like you,' Declared Lawrence. 'Scotland needs strong men to rule. If you don't do as we ask you will, 'disappear'. A nasty fall onto the rocks below your beloved castle; an accident with a knife; thrown from your horse; anything can be arranged. You could die right here and your body would be found at the foot of the cliffs and your children with you.'

And so it went on, day after day. Andrew's brothers would threaten and menace him into agreeing to do what they asked. He was roughly handled and left tied in the dungeon with little to eat and drink and shivering in the cold with his children frightened and helpless. Francis' attempt to grab Lawrence as he descended the ladder was rewarded with a kick which sent him sprawling across the dirt floor. As a result of his efforts, his hands and legs were tied to prevent further attempts.

On 16th August, his captors returned with a support of five soldiers. A bundle of papers and a pen were thrust in front of Andrew. 'Sign!' he was ordered.

'What are they? There is not enough light to see.'

'No matter. I've waited long enough. Just sign.'

The blanks they presented Andrew with were designed to pass his property to his brothers and their accomplices. The first blank document was in favour of George, giving him the life-rent of all the Kirktown of Slains for life for a small yearly payment to the College of Aberdeen.

Another blank was to Lawrence, at his pleasure, of the life-rent of the two parklands of Claschbanye, and land in the Barony of Erroll, for all the days of his life.

A third was to Alexander of £40 yearly with the provision that he should travel with William Hay, parson of Turriff to make him give up the parsonage of Turriff and give it to Alexander for life, and, should William not be happy with this, to give up £40 to have been taken from Inchmichel.

Another blank document to Lawrence, George and Alexander and their accomplices was for jewels, gold, silver, charters, evidence, clothing, furnishings and other goods.

Exhausted and weakened both physically and mentally, and in fear for his sons' welfare, Andrew scrawled his signature on each of the documents. As they were snatched from him he cursed his captors, only to receive a kicking for his trouble.

Once the documents had been removed from his presence, one of the guards cut the ropes around his wrists and left him rubbing them to restore the feeling before beginning to struggle up the ladder.

Peter Hay of Megginch immediately sent his sons to Erroll in search of Andrew's principal servant, Neil Neilson. Their hope to find him at there was dashed when they were told that he had gone into the town of Perth on behalf of his master. Their luck changed when, stopping to wet their throats at an inn, they heard a familiar voice. Peering around a doorway, Patrick saw their quarry. He darted back to his brother to tell him excitedly of his discovery and the two men slipped out of the inn to await their victim's departure.

It was not long before Neil stepped into the street, a little the worse for his refreshment, and, putting a hand against the wall of the inn to steady himself, set off to return to Erroll. He had gone but five paces when a hand came out from an alleyway to grab his tunic and drag him into the shadow. A glint of steel flashed as a knife was drawn and a spurt of blood bore witness that his throat had been slit.

When he was finally free of the dungeon, Andrew went through the castle releasing the castle guards. Each of them apologised to their master for not being able to defend and protect him but Andrew made it clear that he did not hold them responsible. He did, however, order them to ride to Edinburgh and take a report of the events to the king. Andrew was furious to have been held captive by his brothers but was determined to deal with them correctly and not risk his status, reputation or, indeed, his life by acting rashly. He set out the incident in a clear and rational way, telling the king that the documents had been signed under duress and that he now revoked and annulled every one of them.

When his letter had been dispatched, Andrew prepared to set out for Turriff in order to warn William of the events and the document relating to him. Whilst in the area Andrew planned to stay at Delgatie Castle. He was most impressed on his arrival to see the developments. The tower had been completed and final extension with the battlement walk above the string course was about to be started. He could not help thinking that, with such defences at Slains, his enemies would have had greater difficulty in gaining access, and was determined to rectify the matter on his return. He stayed at Delgatie for some days, enjoying the new apartments and discussing religion.

When Andrew discovered that his brothers were attempting to claim the rents and rights granted to them in the documents which he had been forced to sign, he wrote to King James reminding him of the incident and his repudiation of the documents.

Besotted with Esmé Stewart, Sieur d'Aubigny, first cousin of James's father Lord Darnley, the king had neglected to respond to Andrew's initial letter but was determined not to let such corruption thrive in his kingdom. He wrote now to all provosts and magistrates that Andrew Hay, as High Constable, had right to try and imprison trespassers, invaders, shedders of blood, within 4 miles of the king, re-affirming that powers and rights were his. Nothing had changed and Andrew's powers were re-affirmed.

To further assure Andrew of his support and confidence, James invited him to marry Agnes Sinclair, daughter of the Earl of Caithness.

Knowing that he had only one son who could possible take on the responsibilities of Constable of Scotland on his demise, and being all too aware of the frailty of life, Andrew knew that he must marry again. The king's proposal seemed sound and a marriage agreement was drawn up between George Sinclair, Agnes' father, and Andrew Hay. Due to the honour done to her through the marriage, Andrew was called upon to give little of his estate in the contract but received a significant tocher from Sinclair.

Agnes had never been an easy daughter to control showing none of the deference a father would expect of an obedient daughter. She was strong willed and outspoken; but this was hardly surprising for a member of such a disagreeable family, her brother, John, having burned a cathedral in pursuit of men from the Clan Murray who had taken refuge in the steeple. Alexander Gordon, 12th Earl of Sutherland divorced his obnoxious Sinclair wife, Agnes' sister, and her father George Sinclair invaded and ravished the lands of the Clan Sutherland leaving a trail of widows and orphans in his wake.

It did not take Agnes long to realise that she had been married to a husband who was not in the best of health and to decide to take advantage of the fact. Knowing that two of

Andrew's sons were deaf and could not speak, she planned to put about a rumour that Andrew was not caring for his sons whilst at the same time convincing the boys that their father planned to overlook them. Should she succeed in bearing a son, she would work to secure the earldom for him.

Within a few months, Agnes was able to tell Andrew that she was carrying his child. Although he was becoming increasingly angry at her deriding comments, malicious comments to and about his children, and flirting with every man who entered the castle, he was, none the less, delighted that he was to be a father again.

When she succeeded in bearing a son, Agnes demanded that he be called George in honour of her father. Andrew was happy enough to comply as it was his father's name also and he was weary of the troubles and arguments with his wife. At times he would believe that Agnes was plotting to kill him and was very wary of stoking her wrath knowing the reputation that her family had.

What Andrew had not anticipated was his wife's venom in plotting with her nephews, and Peter Hay of Megginch and his sons, whom Andrew had still not forgiven for holding him and his castle captive.

Fully aware of his wife's potential for deposing his sons, Andrew decided to make a further attempt to have his eldest son's hearing investigated. He requested a private audience with King James and with all due respect, explained his dilemma.

'It is a sorry situation indeed,' sympathised the king, crossing the room and stroking Andrew's arm. We cannot have a Constable of Scotland who has such an impediment. It would be an impossible situation but I am concerned about the stories of your son's violence, Andrew. Is there truth in this?'

'Your Majesty, my son suffers the frustrations of his affliction. He cannot communicate through speech and often struggles to make himself understood. Those of us who know him well can usually understand what he is trying to tell us but sometimes the hindrances are such that he is overcome with emotion.'

'That is, I suppose, understandable. I have heard that there is some progress in this area amongst French physicians. It may be that they can offer some help.'

'I would do anything to help my son, and spare no expense, Your Majesty.'

'That may be so but I cannot spare you to travel to France. In these times of unrest, you are needed here in Scotland. However, there is a surgeon in Dundee, William Duncan, whom I will command to accompany Alexander to France to seek medical assistance. He will also be more able to understand the interventions that they suggest. If you are agreeable, I will arrange this immediately.'

'I am most grateful, Sire.'

Whilst Alexander Hay was in France with the surgeon, Agnes gave birth to their second child. She was now determined that her sons would benefit from her distasteful marriage to this frail old man, as she saw him.

❦

It was becoming increasingly difficult for Andrew to run his estates and he was reliant on his family and managers to care for the management of them. Although he continued to take command of the collection of revenues, his supporters kept records for him as his hands now shook uncontrollably.

Agnes sneered to herself as her husband struggled to cope with stairs and with many day to day tasks. Knowing that he planned to ride to Delgatie she declined to accompany him, blaming a headache and keeping to her chamber as he left. As she watched from the window of her bower, she laughed as he was helped to mount his horse, struggling to lift his leg. His groom and ostlers helped him with great respect, knowing him to be a fair and honest master whom they had all come to love, but Agnes saw him as no more than a route to power and wealth.

As soon as Andrew had made his plans known, Agnes had summoned her brothers, her father's illegitimate sons, Patrick and John, to attend her. William Sinclair's brother, John, had strangled him to death before being taken prisoner by their father and Agnes believed that by supporting her nephews she would hold them in her power. A scratching at the door indicated their arrival and Agnes bade them enter.

Dismissing her maids she indicated that they should be seated. The young men looked about them at the fine hangings and portraits which adorned the walls and the beautiful curtains of her bed and windows. They were the finest they had ever seen and their eyes glittered with greed.

'I see you are impressed,' Agnes smirked. 'My husband is a powerful and wealthy man but also a man who is feeble in both body and mind. On his death, all of this will go to his sons. Two of them are idiots and the third is not yet of age. I have two sons to provide for and I will see that you all benefit if you help me.'

'Indeed, those fools will be easy to deal with. We can remove them while your husband is away.'

'Idiots! Do you not see? It needs to be done carefully. If you kill them you will be captured. Their father may be weak in body and mind but he is still the High Constable of Scotland and can have you put to death. No. It must be done in such a way that we get his lands and property 'legally'.'

'And how do you propose we do it, aunt?' asked John

'We will get him to sign everything over to us. Land, property, everything.'

'Will he do that?'

'My God, Patrick, you are no sharper than a lump of dough! We will draw up documents for him to sign, and when he dies we will produce the papers giving everything to us. John, you are a fine scribe, you will draw up the necessary papers but leave the names of the recipients and the properties blank. We will fill those in when Andrew has signed them. Fold them in such a way that there are spaces for us to do so. I will give you the parchment you need and tell you what to write.'

True to her word, Agnes produced a number of parchments and ink. John had been well schooled and was able to produce the documents with ease. Contracts, bonds and obligations, indentures and appointments, investments, charters, precepts, instruments of sasine, confirmations and ratifications thereof, procuratories and instruments of resignation and all other such properties of the Earl of Erroll, along with his lands lordship and barony of Erroll, and even Slains itself, were to pass to Agnes and her family. The contents would destroy the Earldom of Erroll. John Sinclair wrote for many days, recording whatever Agnes told him to and smiled to himself gleefully in anticipation of his own share of the bounty of their fraud.

At length, the parchments were filled and Agnes, finding no more within the castle, provided John with paper to complete the documents.

When the last one was drawn up, Agnes secreted them away in the chest in her bower, locking it securely and hiding the key about her person.

'I have written as you asked but fear that as soon as he realises what we have done he will denounce us for this,' said John.

'Fear not. He will have no idea what is in these documents and we will keep them until he dies. It will not be long now,' She assured him.

Over the following months, she presented Andrew with the blank documents for him to sign whilst he was putting his signature to other documents. Hurriedly interrupting, she would slip the papers before him suggesting they were household matters which he had no need to read through but required his signature. Having gained his signature upon them she would prevail upon John Cunnisoun, his steward and others present to witness his signature. Although they were surprised to be asked to do so, on household documents, none saw fit to question the Countess' actions.

At the least suggestion of his questioning the number of documents which suddenly needed his endorsement, she led him to believe that he was imagining that he had signed them previously and these were the same ones. Not wishing to draw attention to his forgetfulness before witnesses, Andrew questioned no further.

When each bore Andrew's signature, Agnes took them to her room and waited until he had gone to bid farewell to his visitors. Now she went into his room and, melting a little wax in the candle which stood on his desk, she dripped it onto the documents and pressed his seal into the soft wax. Returning to her room she secreted them away in her chest again until such time as she would be able to use them.

The next stage of her plan was to set Andrew's sons against him. Knowing them to be obedient and respectful to their father, she gradually gave them to believe that their father believed that none of them was capable of becoming

Earl of Erroll. She drew attention to every kind gesture he made towards her sons and feigned distress at his least reprimand of Alexander, Francis of Thomas. Slowly her seeds of uncertainty took root and Francis began to believe her. He indicated as much to his brothers and they too watched as their father played with his youngest children and pampered them. Their fears grew, and in spite of their erstwhile respect for their father, they began to question his orders. Andrew could not account for this unexpected and unwarranted change in their behaviour and his anger at their disobedience only fuelled their belief in Agnes' claims.

It was not many months before Agnes devised a method of ridding herself of her husband; even before death should claim him. Telling Andrew that she was planning to visit Erroll, she set out to meet Peter Hay of Megginch and presented him with two of the documents which she had tricked Andrew into signing. Peter was surprised to see Andrew's signature and seal on documents which gave away the inheritance of his children to Agnes' children. Agnes feigned fear and distress that Andrew should treat the children of his first marriage in this way, and, claiming that Andrew was also being unfaithful to her, she suggested to Peter that he must inform the king. She explained to Peter that Andrew was not of sound mind and that his abuse of her and his children was as a result of this and must be revealed to the king immediately. Telling him of his lack of tutelage of his children she cited their disobedience as a result of this and furnished Peter with some of the documents which she had tricked Andrew into signing to show to the king. Peter needed no encouragement to do anything which was to the detriment of his kinsman. He was envious of Andrew's rank and wealth and was delighted to have the opportunity to see him undone.

When Peter's letter arrived at Holyrood, the king was with his lover, Alexander Hay of Easter Kennet. James had prevailed upon Maitland of Lethington, clerk to the privy council, to nominate Alexander as Clerk of the King's register, on a salary of 150 merks, in reward for his favours.

James was furious when he discovered the contents of the letter. 'That Erroll should betray his sons so is outrageous,' he fumed. 'I shall write to him instantly on these matters and demand his explanation.'

Peter Hay's words had been damming, claiming that Andrew's sons were being so badly brought up that they did not obey or respect their father; that he despised his eldest son, Alexander, and was doing nothing to help him overcome his deafness; that he gave away the monies that should, in due course, come to his sons and that he was disrespectful of the king himself.

James immediately set about challenging Andrew Hay and suspended his rights, demanding that he should hand over his estates and responsibilities to his sons without delay and set about freeing his wife of the bonds of marriage – a development which Agnes had not foreseen.

Andrew's health was, in fact, declining rapidly. He saw people and objects which were not there and sensed touches which had not happened. He would feel a hand on his shoulder and whirl around only to find himself alone. His hand shook more obviously now and he could no longer still it by use of the other hand. Whilst walking he would sometimes suddenly halt and could not advance for some moments.

When the King's letter arrived at Slains, Andrew read the contents with horror. In his weakness, his legs would no longer support him and, were it not for the swift action of his steward, John, he would have fallen.

'Fetch me my pen. I must reply to the King immediately,' he ordered.

'My Lord, if I may assist you, I should be honoured to do so,' offered John, knowing that Andrew struggled to write of late. John had served Andrew and his father for decades and was in his confidence. His offer was gladly received and Andrew set about responding to the King. His distress became anger as he realised now why his sons had become disrespectful of late and how they had been poisoned against him by his wife and his enemies.

Reminding the King of how, five years ago, the very Peter Hay who had made these allegations, had held him prisoner in his own castle and become his enemy, Andrew denied neglecting the children of his first marriage and offered to subject himself to the judgement of any true men who were not his enemies. In answer to the King's request that he hand over his lands immediately to his sons he, bearing in mind his heir's handicap, cited his youth as justification for not doing so but, reassured James that he would find a wife for Alexander, of his son's liking, that he may produce heirs of his own.

Much to his own regret, Andrew explained that his contract to marry Agnes had been made between himself and her father who had since died. His heir was yet young to deal with such an issue and therefore he was at a loss as to what might be done.

'Lord Erroll gets above himself!' declared the King on the receipt of Andrew's letter. 'Does he deny his signature on these documents? Summon my Council. Does he refuse to obey me? I will have Erroll's compliance and obedience or have his titles from him!'

In spite of Erroll's protests of his obedience to the King, James wrote again to him demanding to know if Andrew would abide by his findings and the decision of the King's Council.

Regardless of his failing health Andrew stood fast to his conscience. Replying that the findings were much to the detriment of himself and his estate he asked to have the keeping and guidance of his children returned to him as they were still minors. Almost overcome by his emotion he told the King of his love for his children and that their minds had been poisoned against him by Peter Hay and other of his enemies, reminding James of the terrible way that Peter and the other conspirators had treated him and murdered his servant in Perth. He concluded by requesting an audience with James and before a committee of honest men so that he might tell him face to face the truth of his case.

King James was not accustomed to being challenged. Erroll's reply was not the grovelling obedience he had come to expect and infuriated him still further. Alexander Hay of Easter Kennet feigned shock at Andrew's response and stroked James' arm seductively before taking him into his arms and hugging him with soothing noises.

'My poor James. I should never treat you so,' he assured the King. 'I don't know what my kinsman is thinking to write to you in such hurtful way. If I were in his position I should cherish my King and obey him in all things.'

'You speak truly, Alexander. Perhaps I should do just that. I should give you the property of Lord Erroll. Fetch a parchment now and I shall do so right away.'

Thrilled beyond his wildest dreams, Alexander bowed deeply and summoned a servant to fetch what was required.

'Sit,' ordered James, and dictated to Alexander what he would have him put. Declaring that it was through the Earl's failures to look after his children properly and neglect of his duties and debts, the King gave all of Andrew's goods to his Counsellor, Alexander Hay of Easter Kennett. On a second document, he had Alexander record his resolution concerning the Earl himself. Andrew was to be put to the horn. His daughter, Helen was to keep her tocher but resign her lands to her brother, Francis on condition that he ensure her the money for her tocher. The King himself would choose her husband rather than her father.

Andrew's eldest son was to be taken to the Castle of Edinburgh to be assessed as to his capability to become Earl in due course and to be questioned about his father's treatment of him. Should Alexander be able to indicate that he was willing to sign over his right to become Earl to his brother, Francis, all of Alexander's needs were to be met and also those of his younger brother, Thomas.

Andrew was to give up his castle or be accused of treason. His marriage to Agnes was to be ended and any with a claim against the estates were to submit their claim to Francis and he to deal with it.

Andrew was at Sandend when the letter from the King arrived at Slains. Blissfully unaware of his wife's duplicity and sure that his health was failing fast, he thought it was time to write his will.

Before leaving Slains he had given some thought to finding a wife for his second son, Francis, who alone of his sons had escaped the curse of deafness. Margaret Stuart, daughter of the Regent Moray, was an excellent match in regard to station and royal lineage. She was young but seemed in good health and the prospects of her bearing sons seemed excellent. The match was arranged and the marriage took place, much to Agnes' annoyance.

Now that Francis marriage was contracted, Andrew felt that all of the sons of his first marriage were provided for.

It remained for him to make provision for his present wife and sons. Eighteen thousand merks was to be taken from his estate to be divided between Agnes and her children. A princely sum but not the fortune she had dreamt of.

When Agnes discovered that her plans had failed she was furious. In spite of her 'perfect' plan, now she would lose her husband and any rights to his estate; her son would not become the next Earl of Erroll and Andrew, having been put to the horn, was an outlaw. All of his goods had been given to the King's molly and Helen would get a good marriage. It could not have been worse!

When Andrew returned to Slains Castle he was devastated to receive the King's judgement. He could not conceive of why James who, until recently, had held him in good favour and whom he had always served well, should now believe such lies about him. In his weakened state the shock shook him badly. John, his steward, helped him to mount the steps. Reaching his chamber he prepared the Earl for bed and sent for a draught of poppy juice to sooth him. Andrew's shoulder length hair was now completely white and his erstwhile strong features were aged and wrinkled. At almost sixty years of age, Andrew's appearance added a decade to his days.

'What my enemies have failed to do to me in battle, my wife has done with a pen,' he lamented.

⁂

Perth was bustling with people who had come to the town's market. Farmers brought their livestock and crops to sell and merchants offered every conceivable commodity. Fine wines from France and beautiful fabrics from all over Europe and Asia were to be found alongside ribbons and pies.

A number of servants from Erroll had been sent to buy goods and were enjoying a day away from their regular duties. A cart had been brought to take the goods home and it was not unlikely that one or two of them might be in need of it to return them home after partaking of the local ales.

The noise of the market was echoing around the square where the Mercat Cross indicated the town's right to host the event. Taking care that light fingers did not relieve them of their purses, they spread out amongst the stalls to seek the goods they needed. Calum, assistant to the ostler, had been given the task of finding a new bridle and was wandering around looking for a seller of leather goods. Laughter coming from near the Mercat Cross drew him towards it. A group of travelling players were entertaining the crowd and Calum paused to watch. A young juggler threw balls in the air and caught them deftly before asking members of the crowd to offer him their knives to juggle. Hands reached out towards him with all manner of blades. He took his time, making a show of examining each one whilst trying to find three of similar size to use. A hand reached over the heads of the crowd to offer a fine blade, etched with scrolls and flowers.

As the juggler put out his hand to take the fine offering, the owner suddenly dropped to the ground. The crowd parted as he fell amongst them. There was a scream as an old woman yelled, 'Plague, he has the pestilence!' Others took up the cry and in seconds the square was ringing with screams and shouts as people tried to get as far as possible from the victim. Traders packed away their goods, careless of how they were stored; trays were upset by figures pushing past. Street urchins and thieves took the opportunity to help themselves to unforeseen treasures and crammed pies into their mouths as they rescued them from the fallen trays.

The staff from Erroll raced back to their cart and threw themselves up onto the boards. The reins were slapped on the horse's back and they set off at a gallop.

The alarm was raised as soon as they arrived and all gates were secured to prevent access to any who may have been in contact with the victim. Erroll was far enough away from the town to be isolated from the townspeople so it was hoped that staying within the walls would be sufficient to keep them free from infection.

A messenger was sent immediately to Slains with news of the outbreak in order to alert them before any pedlars who might be carrying the disease arrived there.

Arriving at Slains Castle only hours after Andrew's return, the messenger rode in and was greeted by the yard boys who took his horse to be cared for while he requested an audience with the Earl. Always aware of the importance of being informed about matters on his master's estates, John woke the Earl and helped him to leave his bed and slip on a gown. Andrew granted an audience immediately. The man, dusty and exhausted, bowed to the Earl as he entered.

'I bring grave news,' he began. 'There is another outbreak of the pestilence in Perth. I hear it has spread to Edinburgh also so I came to warn you of the danger of going to Court. The King retires to Stirling for safety.'

Andrew smiled wryly at the suggestion that he might ever go to court again. 'We must close the gates to all. John, go now and ensure that we have sufficient supplies. You did well to bring the news so quickly.' He told the man. 'I will see that you are rewarded for your pains.' With that, he drew a handful of coins from his purse and pressed them into the fellow's hand. 'You must go to the kitchen and refresh yourself. Stay the night before you return to Erroll.'

Expressing his thanks, the man took his leave and made his way to the kitchen. The day was well on and the meal had finished but cook found some choice cuts of meat for him and a mug of ale was produced. When he had refreshed himself, he was shown to the hall and found a place near the fire to sleep for the night.

It was past midnight when a turnspit heard groans. Rubbing his bleary eyes he pushed himself up on his elbow and looked around to see who was making them. An unfamiliar figure lying near the fire was curled up, moaning and rocking in pain. The lad clambered to his feet and crept across to bid him be silent lest he wake everybody up. As he leant over the figure, by the light of the fire he saw the man's neck was swollen and black. He leapt back with a gasp. In spite of his lack of years, he knew only too well the signs of the pestilence. Without a second thought, he yelled, 'Plague!'

There was a scuffling as everybody in the hall rushed to get away. Only the prone figure of the sufferer remained. Andrew's steward was roused by the noise below and was making his way down the stairs to find the cause when he was met by a guard. 'Keep the Earl in his room,' he advised. 'The pestilence is in the castle!'

Turning on the stairs he returned to Andrew's room and woke him.

Andrew was shocked and afraid. The pestilence had no respect for age or station. His man assisted him in dressing and the Earl began to give orders immediately for the welfare of his people.

'Bring the Countess to my chamber he ordered. We must plan together.' Nobody was to enter or leave the confines of the castle boundaries. Fresh food would be fish caught off the coast. All food was to be rationed until it was safe to leave and get supplies.

The following day, Agnes, neglecting her duty to oversee the servants in this time of crisis, went to complain to her

402

husband about his son, Alexander's, disobedience and behaviour towards her. 'You have only yourself to blame he grumbled. If you were more understanding towards him…..'

'Understanding? He's little more than an animal!' she declared. William Duncan had returned from France with Alexander a week ago, only to explain that there was nothing to be done to make him hear. The surgeons there had poked and prodded, causing Alexander great pain and frustration but to no avail.

'I will not have my son spoken of thus!' protested Andrew. He cannot hear. That is no fault of his.' In his rage, the veins in his neck bulged drawing Agnes' attention to them. It was then that she screamed.

'What now!' Andrew groaned.

'You have it! You have the pestilence!' Agnes told him fleeing from the room to save herself.

Andrew was a good master and his people would lay down their lives for him. Nothing was too much to ask of them and none, save his wife, hesitated to volunteer to nurse him. It was decided that those who had already been in contact with the master should be the ones to care for him as there was every possibility that they too had contracted the dreaded disease.

Within two days Andrew's suffering was over and his body was laid out for burial. Before the week was out, fifty-two of the castle people also succumbed to the disease. Only one of those who contracted it survived. The turnspit.

The King's decree was not actioned in full. Andrew was dead and could not be put out of the Castle. His goods would pass to Francis as James still insisted on Alexander and Thomas being taken to Edinburgh Castle to be assessed, and Alexander Hay of Easter Kennett would not receive the spoils of Agnes' plot. Agnes' son would not become Earl of

Erroll; nor would she be the wife of an outlaw and would be free to marry the unsuspecting Alexander Gordon of Strathdon, brother of the Earl of Huntly. Having dared to challenge his brother's intimacy with the king, he would pay the price through his marriage.

Andrew's body could not be taken far for burial for fear of spreading the disease. The minister at Collieston church agreed to bury the Earl but insisted on a quiet ceremony to avoid the spread of the disease.

The downy shadow on his upper lip betrayed the new earl's youth but in spite of his lack of years, Francis Hay was an intelligent and perceptive young man. Soon after his brother, Alexander, had been judged to be incapable of taking on the responsibilities of Constable of Scotland, Francis matriculated as Earl of Erroll. It did not take him long to discover Agnes' role in his father's fall from grace. He wasted no time in informing of the king of his findings and in due course Agnes was brought before the king and his council to explain her actions.

Andrew's erstwhile wife made such protestations of her innocence, and that she had never seen the incriminating documents before, that she might otherwise have been believed, but the evidence brought against her was so strong that the king ordered her to produce any outstanding documents bearing Andrew's signature that she might still hold and summoned the other conspirators to appear before him.

All who held documents, giving them rights appertaining to the Earl's land, which had been created between the dates of Andrew's birth and death, were to be produced to be authenticated.

The statute being signed it could be hoped that Francis could now hope for a period of peace to become accustomed to his new role and setting straight all matters pertaining to his estates.

It was no to be so.

Determined not to accept the role of obedient wife, Margaret made herself as disagreeable as possible. Now the chatelaine of Slains Castle she flounced around giving orders to servants in the knowledge that Francis would be furious with her decisions. Finding a girl churning milk into butter she ordered her to leave it and fetch her some wine. Knowing she would be punished and the butter would spoil, the girl hesitated and was rewarded with a furious outburst and threat of being sent away if she did not obey immediately.

'I want the bed linens changed every day,' she ordered the housekeeper, 'and these wall hangings are horrific. Take them down and put them on the floor. I would rather walk on them than look at them.' Not wanting to disobey but fearful of her master's wrath and the damage which might be done to the valuable tapestries, the woman bowed and left the room but sought out her master to have her orders confirmed or denied. Francis was horrified. 'Touch nothing,' he commanded. I will speak with Lady Erroll. And with that, he strode off to find her.

Margaret was sitting at her dressing table with her maid brushing out her hair. A tangle caught in the brush and Margaret turned in a passion to strike the girl.

'Leave us,' ordered Francis. He expected his servants to attend to his every need and demand but always treated them fairly and with respect. 'I will not have my people treated in this way,' he declared. 'They work hard and without them, you would live a much less comfortable life.'

'Ha! You call this comfortable?'

Francis was not accustomed to being spoken to in such a manner and glared at her. 'You will be silent, madam, and do as I bid you!'

'Make me!' she challenged. In two strides, Francis was across the room and swinging her from her feet he put her face down across his knee and, lifting her dress he spanked her soundly.

Rather than being subdued by such treatment, Margaret was aroused by it. 'You like it rough sir?' she questioned before raking her hands through his hair and pressing her mouth against his.

Francis raised both hands and pushed her from him wiping his mouth with the back of his hand.

'You will remain in your room until I say you may leave,' he ordered and strode from the room to find a guard who would ensure that she did his bidding. She flounced across the room and threw herself onto her bed but it was only after she heard the key turn in the lock that she permitted herself to weep. She hated the isolation of Slains; the weather and the sea crashing around them; the deep haar which blocked everything from sight; the distance from the excitement of court. She found Francis physically attractive but he was too serious and she was too young. She did not want to be a brood mare to bear children year after year; if she were honest she was terrified of childbirth. All that she knew of it was the pain women suffered and that many of them died.

When Francis finally permitted Margaret to leave her room, as Countess of Erroll, she demanded to be taken to the Royal Court. Francis was wary of taking her, new as he was to such things and knowing her propensity for causing trouble. Finally, he decided he must present her to the King but warned her to behave in a manner becoming to a countess.

Initially, her introduction to Court life went well but at the King's ball that autumn a new figure came into Margaret's life. The sixty-eight-year-old William Forbes was a charming and handsome man. In spite of his years, many of the ladies found him charismatic and were entertained by his tales of valour and chivalry. Always dressed in the very finest materials, tailored in the height of fashion, his silver locks gave him a distinguished and rather a roguish look. As he approached Margaret Hay he swept her the deepest of bows, taking her hand and planting a lingering kiss in the palm whilst raising his eyes to give her the most wolfish look she had ever seen. She almost expected his nose to grow long and sprout whiskers! Holding her hand high it was the work of a moment for him to slide his arm seductively around her waist, waiting for the musicians to strike up, his fingers exploring her waist.

As he returned her to her seat at the end of the dance he sat next to her, so close that she could feel his breath on her bosom, and asked her to tell him about herself. The request was a mere gesture as he really wished to tell her about himself and proceeded to do so as soon as she paused for breath.

His first position at Court was as Gentleman of the Bedchamber he explained which cause Margaret to giggle. 'And were you successful in the bedchamber?' she asked coquettishly.

'I must have been, he gloated. I am now father to eighteen children!'

Margaret laughed unrestrainedly drawing the attention of those around her. Francis heard her voice and, turning to see who she was with, he stormed across the room. Taking her arm he bowed to Forbes. 'You will excuse us, Sir. My wife is tired.'

'No, I'm not. I'm just beginning to enjoy myself,' she began but before she could do further damage to both of their reputations, Francis had removed her from the room and, with a bruising grip on her arm, he escorted her to their chamber. His words to her were plain and powerful. Never again would she find herself at court whilst she remained his wife.

'And you will not entertain people without me present!' he ordered.

Pouting and furious she dared to answer him back, swearing that she had no wish to remain his wife and would return to Slains the next day to pack her clothes and return to her aunt's house.

The following morning King James sent for Francis. He was sure that tales of his wife's behaviour had reached the king's ears and he prepared his words of apology as he made his way to the King's privy chamber.

'Erroll, be seated,' bade the King as Francis made his bow. 'I have news for you. I have heard this morning from Edinburgh Castle. Your brothers have been examined by my physician and they have both been declared insane. I'm sure that you understand that this means they are unable to care for themselves and so it is my decision that they shall stay under the guards at the Castle for the rest of their lives.' Francis was shocked. He wanted to protest that if people took the time and made sufficient effort to communicate with his brothers they were of sound mind and yet he knew that it was true, they could never live a normal life and care for themselves. At least they would be safe at the Castle and he had met their guard. A kinder and more understanding man could not be found in the kingdom. He thanked James for his kindness and care of his brothers and sadly left to deal with his wife.

By the time he reached their chamber, Margaret had gone. Her maid had packed her clothes in her kists and the two had taken a carriage to fulfil her threat.

It was two weeks before Francis heard from his wife again. A letter was delivered to him with her seal. He took it to his desk and sat down to read. Breaking the seal angrily he read:

> *The gear within Slains, as following which my lady desires;*
> *item of feather beds 30,*
> *item of bolsters 24*
> *item of pewter plates 8*
> *item of trenchers 28*
> *item of spits 4*
> *item of racks 2*
> *item of pots of brass and iron 15*
> *item of pans 8*
> *item of barrels within the place 38*
> *of this 33 barrels for ale*
> *item of ten quart stoppers 4,*
> *with one chopping board,*
> *item of chandeliers 11,*
> *of these two of wood,*
> *item two mortar with their pestols.'*

The furnishing of Logie which my lady desires as after follows which extends scantily to the half:

In Logie according to the inventory 21 pair curtaining hereof, my lady desires ten pair, one of the purple velvet beds and hall furnishing thereof, curtains, pillows, matt tasselled sheets of Holland cloth with one pair of bed sheets and two pair of head sheets, six pillows, six cushions of Holland cloth, one pair of curtains of blue and white wool, two pair of green plaiding curtains

Item one pair of curtains of green serge

curtaining for curtaining for beds and curtaining lining to go around it.

Item one pair of curtains of red murtkey,
one pair of curtains of bewsey

Item one pair of droggatt curtains green and red

Item One pair of curtains red and white

Item one for curtaining and one boutgane of black growgrame

Item seven aress works with one sewn covering eriss silk

Item of feather beds 12

Of bolsters 12

Item three white embroidered bolsters

Item of Scots coverings 16 - there of five red and yellow lined

Item of bed plaids seven

Item of filled cushions and one fillit 36

Item of linen covers 27

Item of blankets 32

Item five pair of linen cloth head sheets

Item of linen sheets 25 pair

Item of rind sheets 6 pair

Item one long green cloth for one high bed

Item three little green bed clothes for chambers

Item of linen serviettes four score and ten

Item two linen cupboard cloths

Item of linen hand towels 10

Item of linen board-cloth (tablecloths) 8

Francis sat back in his chair and put his head in his hands. His body began to shake until he threw back his head and roared with laughter. Tears ran down his cheeks and he realised it was the first time in years that he had really laughed.

'For a lass of fifteen summers she knows what she wants!' he chuckled.

Once his humour had tempered, he sat down to pen his reply.

'To my lady's greed and unreasonable desires, it is answered. That seeing the hall furnishing found in the House of Logie and the remainder of the furnishings left here in Slains is all over little to furnish one of the places, My Lord can spare no part thereof.'

When news arrived at Slains that Margaret was carrying Francis' child his emotions were mixed. He had no reason to doubt that the child was his in spite of her flirtatious behaviour. The child would be his successor but he had no great desire to see his wife return to Slains. He wrote formally to Margaret requesting her to return in spite of his misgivings and yet was furious when she replied that she had no intention of ever returning either to him or to his castle on the cliff's edge. Instead, she offered to spend her confinement at his house at Erroll. Francis saw this as a good solution, planning to keep the child when it was delivered and permit his troublesome wife to return to her aunt's house. On receipt of his agreement, Margaret's ladies began to pack her goods into kists is readiness for the journey. Suddenly Margaret felt a rush of something warm on her leg. Looking down she saw blood on her feet. She shrieked bringing her ladies rushing to her side. Sobbing and shouting for help, they helped her to her bed and tried to stop the bleeding. It was soon clear that she had lost the baby and the fight was now for her life. A messenger was sent to Slains Castle to inform Francis but before they had reached him it was too late.

Saddened by the loss of his child, Francis was none the less relieved. Had the child survived it would have been brought up away from its mother. Having lost his own at six years old, he knew the pain of not having a mother to turn to.

Francis was nineteen years old and looked back over his life so far. His mother was his father's cousin and had born two sons who were unable to hear or speak, brothers to

Francis and his younger sister, Helen. His grandfather had been heavily involved in the intrigues surrounding Queen Mary. He himself had been imprisoned with his father and brothers by his uncles. He still could not go near the dungeon without memories of their ordeal pressing in on him. Agnes, his father's second wife had plotted against Andrew and had almost destroyed the House of Erroll.

It was only after his father's death that Francis was able to demonstrate the truth to the King and clear his father's name and have the titles, properties and estates restored to himself in full.

His ailing father had died of plague and Alexander and Thomas, his brothers had been taken away from him and declared insane.

Now his wife and child had died.

Francis clung to his belief in the Catholic Church for support, taking solace in the scriptures and relishing the glorious music.

CHAPTER 34

1587 was to bring Francis some sport.

Having been forced to leave Slains as a result of her outrageous behaviour towards his father, Agnes Sinclair has taken up residence at Inchestuthill where she planned to live quietly until her deceit was forgotten. What she had not expected was that Colin Campbell, whose wife had recently died, had decided to take another wife. As he had something of a reputation for unruly behaviour, there were none who knew him who would offer their daughters to him. Collin decided to remedy the situation by taking a hundred men with him to Inchestuthill at night and, under cover of darkness, they set fire to the gates. The moment the alarm was raised, Agnes lifted her skirts and ran as fast as she could for the door. She knew only too well how fast a house could burn and was determined to flee in order to save her own life without thought for others.

As soon as she appeared, Colin and his men violently took her and held her captive, twelve miles from Inchestuthill, with the intention of using her according to his filthy appetites and lust. Had she not been rescued by the Earl of Atholl and his servants he would have done so.

Francis had not had such good entertainment in many years. He made up his mind to visit the Earl of Atholl and hear the tale from his own lips and sent straight away for pen and ink in order to write and ask for a convenient date.

Atholl was delighted to host Erroll at his home and introduced him to his only unmarried daughter, Mary. Mary Stewart could not have been less like Francis' first wife, Margaret. She was demure and faultlessly obedient. Her beauty overwhelmed Francis so that he felt compelled to ask for her hand before he left for fear she be betrothed to another before he returned. 'Of course we would need the King's permission,' he reminded her father but I do not foresee a problem. Being greatly burdened by debt, Atholl was delighted to gain such a match for his daughter and Francis was content to accept a minimal tocher.

Both Francis and the Earl of Atholl being staunch Roman Catholics, they wished the marriage ceremony to be a Catholic Mass and decided that it would be best if the ceremony were held at Slains Castle. Francis referred to his first wife's recent death as justification for a quiet, private ceremony with a few close friends as witnesses.

During the course of the ceremony, a curate approached the priest and beckoned him to one side. After a moment's whispered conversation the priest returned and, with a serious countenance he continued the wedding. As soon as the proceedings were concluded he addressed the gathering to announce that news had arrived that Queen Mary had been executed by Elizabeth of England. The assembly was shocked. Mary had sought support from her cousin, Elizabeth, and although Elizabeth had held her prisoner for years rather than supporting her cause, none had expected this outcome. The news had a sobering effect on the marriage celebrations and was yet another blow for Scottish Catholics.

The King's reaction surprised his people. He denounced it as a 'preposterous and strange procedure,' and yet took no action, knowing that his mother's death laid clear his way to succeed to the throne of England on Elizabeth's death, should he uphold his apparent adherence to the Presbyterian faith.

Frustrated by his inability to openly worship as a Catholic, James decided to deal with at least one of the biggest issues in Scotland; that of the continuing rivalry between the Scottish nobles. He invited his nobles to a celebration at Holyrood for his twenty-first birthday. None could refuse as to do so would be seen as rebellious and provoke the King's displeasure. During the celebrations, James held up his hand for silence and spoke to the gathering in earnest, urging them to set aside their differences and forswear their feuds by drinking three solemn pledges to eternal friendship. They were powerless to refuse and all complied but their gesture was meaningless. When James then announced that they would process in pairs to take their places at the banquet table which had been prepared at the Mercat Cross, they were incredulous at his naivety. Fireworks were launched and cannon fired to celebrate the occasion and free wine was provided for the onlookers who looked on in amusement.

Francis Stewart Hepburn, 5th Earl of Bothwell, a charming and intelligent villain, had long been a favourite of the King who found him, not only witty but also physically attractive. The Earl was also fierce and lawless, renowned for feuds and loose living, and fantasised that the crown of Scotland might one day be his. James repeatedly forgave his transgressions in the vain hope that trouble would dissolve like the mist on the hills. Bothwell knew that the King's threats were hollow and continued to court trouble in both religion and with the aristocracy. However, Bothwell's veneer of French culture covered his capricious nature and James was beset by rumours that Bothwell was involved with the Black Arts and it was not long before he was accused of plotting against the King.

Captured and imprisoned in Edinburgh Castle, it did nothing to quell the rumours when he managed to escape.

Such was Bothwell's audacity that he gathered men and outlaws and attacked the Palace of Holyrood, smashing doors with hammers and setting them on fire, causing the king to retreat to a tower for safety. It was only when the Common Bell summoned the people of Edinburgh to Holyrood in the king's defence, that Bothwell fled. The king pursued Bothwell down to the borders without success and the earl was to have the last laugh as James was thrown from his horse into the icy waters of the Tyne.

※

Unlike Francis' first wife, Mary was gentle and timid and he was enthralled with her, going out of his way to find ways to delight her. Mary, although not many years older than Margaret had been, had respect for the Castle people and treated them kindly. She knew how to run a castle and would visit each family most days, to see if all was well with them. Her weekly rides to the outlying cottages were appreciated by even the humblest tenants. When she saw suffering she was sympathetic and would take with her a basket of bread and pies for those in the greatest need. Her regular visits were unannounced and when she came to a tiny cottage near Ellen one day she was distressed to hear a child sobbing.

'What ails you child?' she asked the girl. A streaky face looked up and the little one quickly bobbed a curtsey and wiped her face with her ragged skirt, making the streaks even worse. Unable to drag out a word, she pointed in the direction of the stream where a man was bending towards the water and pushing something down with a stick.

'Hoy there!' she called. The man turned and, seeing who the visitor was, pulled his forelock and approached.

'What are you doing which is causing the child such distress?' she asked.

'Cat had kittens,' he said. 'We can't feed no more mouths so I'm drownin' em.'

The child began to wail again. 'Could you not keep one?' Mary enquired.

'Don't need one. Bairn will get over it.'

Mary looked sadly at the child. 'Why don't I take the kittens and keep them at the Castle? I could tell you how they are when I come to visit and when you are a little older, perhaps we will find you a job and you can stay at the Castle. You are obviously a caring person so I'm sure we can find a job for you. How would that suit?' she asked looking at the father.

'One less mouth to feed I suppose,' he grumbled. And so it was agreed. The bundle of kittens, dripping with water, was rescued and put into the basket for the return journey.

Francis was in the courtyard when they returned. As he helped Mary from her horse, she reached up to her guard and took the basket from him. 'What on earth...' he began.

Mary explained and looked up at him with such pleading eyes that he laughed. 'You are such a softie,' he laughed taking her in his arms. Speaking over her shoulder he told a stable lad to find milk for the kittens and put them in the stables where they could learn to catch mice and rats to earn their keep. Mary put her hand into the basket and pulled out a tiny grey and white kitten.

'May I keep this one as a pet?' she begged. 'I'll call him Bruce after Robert Bruce who gave this castle to your ancestor.' How could he deny her? At last, his life was turning around.

When he was called to Edinburgh to attend the king, Francis left Slains with a light heart. The summer had been kind and crops had been good. Francis had decided to spend a night in his mansion at Erroll to break his journey south.

Darkness had fallen by the time he arrived and the flicker of candles could be seen through the windows. Dropping from his horse, he strode up the steps to the door which his steward held open in readiness. He was helped off with his cloak and handed over his hat, the feather in which reflected his own exhaustion.

'How do I find you, Donald?' he enquired.

'In the rudest of health, my Lord Erroll,' came the reply accompanied by a bow.

'And my estates in Erroll?'

'All is well sir. There was some flooding of the river in the spring but the land has benefited. There were forty cows swept downstream but all were found well enough.'

'That is good to hear. And what of Megginch? Is he giving you any trouble?'

'Not at all, Sir. His eldest son is recently married and has his own affairs to tend to. The younger boys are being educated away from home; the youngest in France. I do not expect any more trouble from them.'

'That is good to hear. I shall retire now Donald; it has been a long journey.'

The following day began with the early arrival of a herald from Edinburgh bearing the news that the Armada, which Philip of Spain had sent to attack England, had been defeated. It was a shock and a huge disappointment for Francis. Had they been successful, England would have been returned to the Catholic faith and Queen Elizabeth might have been replaced with King James. Following so soon after Queen Mary's execution it was a dreadful blow to Francis and all Scottish Catholics.

Francis rode around his estate before setting off for Slains. Arriving at the old Motte, he saw that it had fallen into disrepair and would need much work to restore it. On returning to the mansion he gave orders that demolition begin on the old building immediately.

On arrival at Edinburgh, he rode directly to Holyrood house and settled into his chamber before presenting himself to the King.

When he was granted entry into James' privy chamber, Francis took off his hat and swept a deep bow, coming to rest on one knee. He was surprised to see Lord Huntly in the King's chamber. He had heard that Huntly had the King's ear but did not expect him to be present at a private meeting.

'You may arise, Erroll. Come and sit here by me.' Francis obeyed. 'I wanted to be the one to tell you,' continued James, 'Your father's wife is to marry.' Nothing could have prepared Francis for this news. After her behaviour towards his father and later her kidnapping – which rumour had it was not entirely repugnant to her – he did not expect any self-respecting nobleman to offer for her. He was tempted to ask who her next victim was but curbed his tongue and was glad he had done so when Huntly enlightened him. 'My half-brother will wed her.' Alexander Gordon was the Earl's illegitimate brother and a thorn in his side. 'They deserve each other,' he smirked.

'And how fares your new wife?' James enquired, 'Will there be a young Hay before long?'

'I pray so, Your Highness.' But in truth Francis was dreading Mary giving birth to the child she had so recently told him she was carrying. In order not to distress her he had feigned delight, but knowing that so many women did not survive childbirth, and Margaret's death being still fresh in his mind, he feared she might not survive the ordeal.

'I too will be taking a wife before long,' announce James to the surprise of both Francis and George. The King's preference for men was widely known but of course, the succession was a necessity and much as Francis and other members of the Privy Council had urged him to do so, they had expected their pleas to be met with resistance.

'I am to marry Anne of Denmark. The marriage ceremony will be by proxy and will be before the month is out,' he continued without enthusiasm.

'Take my hand Erroll; I would have you re-assure me.'

Francis could not refuse the king's demand but when James kept hold of the outstretched, gloved hand stroking it and edging towards his bed-chamber, Francis slipped his hand out of the glove, withdrew the other and handed it to James. 'I would have you accept these as a gift, Your Majesty, as you clearly find them to your liking.' James took a step closer and would have swept Francis into his arms and embraced him, had not his groom knocked at that moment.

Thwarted, the king commanded the man to enter. Clearly flustered and distressed, the groom conveyed a message that a rider had arrived from Slains Castle with news that the Countess of Erroll was taken ill and Frances required to return home as a matter of urgency.

The king nodded his consent and Francis hurried from the chamber with a mixture of relief and concern. Dashing to the stables he found that orders had been given for his horse to be made ready and was waiting for him. His guards were mounted and ready to leave. The party rode at full gallop, changing horses at Stirling and Dundee to make the most possible speed.

Francis spurred his horse on as they approached Slains Castle, racing down the lane and through the outer gate without stopping. As he entered the bailey he swung down from his horse and rushed up the wooden steps into the tower.

Mary lay on her bed looking no more than a child herself. Her face was pale as she reached out her hand towards him. She looked so tiny he could not bear to see her so. Her maids fussed around her not knowing what to do.

'Leave us!' ordered Francis. He sat beside her on the bed.

'I fear I have lost our child,' she whispered. He saw a tear trickle down her cheek before she turned her head away. Gently placing his hand under her chin, he marvelled at the softness of her skin as he turned her face towards him.

'Do not distress yourself. There will be others.'

His kindness was her undoing and she gave vent to her grief. Francis slipped his hand beneath her and gently lifted her towards him to hold her in his arms. He gently rocked her for some time and when he felt her body had relaxed, he gently lowered her onto her pillow. As he leant forward to place a kiss on her cheek he paused. Horror overwhelmed him as he realised she was no longer breathing. Roaring his denial he crushed her to his chest. A guard opened the door but realising the cause of his master's cry he gently closed it again. As others approached he held out his arms to forestall them with a shake of his head. The castle was plunged into mourning.

❧

On 2/8 November 1588, George Gordon was appointed Captain of the Guard and yet in spite of this and of having signed the Presbyterian confession of faith, he continued to plot for the Spanish invasion of Scotland and worked closely with the many Catholics residing in the north.

Many of his duties were at Holyrood and it was here that his treasonable correspondence was discovered. King James shook his head sadly and ordered Huntly's captaincy of the guard to be taken from him and that he was to be imprisoned in Edinburgh Castle. The next day he sent for him. He was finding the Catholic Lords useful to hinder the dictatorship of the Kirk and was, himself, discreetly seeking the aid of the Spanish king to help him to secure the English throne. When Huntly stood before him, his head high and his countenance confident, the guards were dismissed and James questioned Huntly about his actions.

George would not deny his faith and James did not wish to punish his favourite. He was convinced that Huntly's plan was to put him on the throne of England, so permitted him to dismiss the correspondence with a few well-chosen words before turning the conversation to less political matters.

Within the hour all charges were dismissed and the King commanded Huntly to stay and dine with him. Within days, his duties were restored to him. It was only due to Chancellor Maitland's protests that Huntly's duties were once again removed from him and he was sent back to his estates in the north.

Huntly was not a man to be crossed as the severed limbs of his enemies, which adorned the walls of Strathbogie Castle, demonstrated. He had had two cooks from an enemy clan roasted alive as an example to all and was capable of fearsome deeds to any whom he disliked.

Confident of his safety, just five months later, Huntly raised a rebellion in the north and was joined by Bothwell who hoped to destroy Maitland. The rebels were soon overpowered and forced to surrender, by the king's forces, at the Brig 0'Dee. Taken to Borthwick Castle, Huntly was imprisoned for a short time, only to be freed once again on the king's orders. As soon as he was set free, Huntly made his way to Slains Castle. Francis welcomed him expressing his disbelief that Huntly could, apparently, do as he liked with the King's blessing. George sat back in his chair and grinned at Francis. 'Well you see,' he explained, 'I could pay the penalty for my actions with one end of my body or the other and I chose not to lose my head!' Francis' look of shock made George roar with laughter. ''Tis a great price to pay admittedly but my milliner is happy.' The earls rocked with laughter until they ached and called for more wine.

৵৶

Whilst at Holyrood, Erroll and Huntly spent a great deal of time in each other's company.

'I cannot live with my conscience,' Huntly confided. 'I was prevailed upon to sign the Presbyterian confession of faith but in my heart, I cannot deny the Catholic Church.

'It is the true faith, Gordon. We must support each other in our belief as we do in our lives.'

'Would you pledge your support to me as I would to you?'

'I should not hesitate to do so.'

When Francis returned to Slains Castle he immediately contacted a Writer to the Signet to arrange an appointment in Aberdeen when both he and Huntly could be present. A contract between the earls was drawn up committing each earl to defend the other against all save the King and to behave like brothers in their defence of each other. Each man saw the bond as a strengthening against the controversies which surrounded them and against their enemies. It was a matter of honour that each of them adhered to their pledge but also a guarantee to each, that the other would come to their aid should the need arise.

Once the document had been signed, Erroll and Huntly returned with all haste to Slains Castle. Francis had received a message that Spanish Ships had been seen travelling north and he knew that his long awaited gift from King Philip had arrived.

When they arrived at Slains, the ships could not be seen. The sea was rough and worsening and the haar was thick. Seagulls screamed overhead as they were pulled about by the strength of the gathering wind. It was all the earls could do to keep their feet as their words were snatched away by the gusts. Bending low into the wind and pushing their way towards the entrance, Erroll knew that to try to reach the ships would be impossible until the storm abated. He and Huntly sat before the fire and drafted a letter to be taken back to Spain, expressing their regret that the Armada had failed.

'We should suggest that Spain uses Scotland for a base to attack England,' Huntly suggested. 'If they land soldiers here we can have them marching to England in no time and some can remain here to help us to restore the faith.'

By the following dawn, the mist had lifted and the sea was much calmer. Francis was awakened with the news that the Spanish ships were anchored offshore and were lowering a boat. His groom helped him to dress and he rushed down to see five swarthy men pulling a small boat up on the south bay. His men had gone down to meet them and there was much arm-waving going on as they tried to understand the Spaniards. He joined them on the beach and ordered his men to fetch ropes. A simple A-frame stood at the top of the cliff and within moments a rope as thick as a child's wrist was attached and thrown down. Erroll's men launched two of their own boats and rowed hard towards the ships.

It took several hours before they finished unloading the cannon which King Philip had sent from the ships and into the boats to bring them ashore and then hauled them up to the castle. Finally, six small but powerful cannon and a large number of cannon balls stood in the bailey to be admired by Erroll and Huntly. The castle people stopped their work and approached in awe at such fine weapons.

Eventually, Huntly put his arm around Francis' shoulders and the two went inside. 'It was not a complete success,' Erroll told Huntly. 'There was another ship the Santa Caterina. She was thrown onto the rocks in the bay and her hull was holed. She sank before dawn with all hands. Had she survived we would have had three more cannons.'

'No good dwelling on what might have been. These are excellent weapons; powerful, manoeuvrable and complete with ammunition. Philip has been generous.'

Before the ships left, Huntly spoke with the captain of the flagship and handed him a package of documents. They made their farewells and watched as the ships turned about and set sail for home. Within the week they were intercepted by England's forces and the package of letters was in Elizabeth's hands.

King James had just returned from a hunt when he was presented with a letter from Elizabeth demanding he capture the traitors and imprison them. He mused for a while on the question of whether it was treason or not given that it was not their own king whom the earls were plotting against, but decided not to risk his chance of succeeding to the English throne by saying as much and instead, imprisoned Huntly.

That evening James dined with Huntly in his apartments.

1590

Remembering the problems surrounding his elder brother and his own succession to the Earldom, Francis recognised the importance of producing heirs and at twenty-six years old and engaged as he was in potentially dangerous situations, the need grew urgent. Loath as he was to replace his beloved Mary, he knew that he must take another wife. His cousin's wife, Christian Douglas had a sister, Elizabeth who was of age to be married and, if he could not marry for love, as he felt he would never do again, he could at least marry a beautiful wife. The Douglas sisters were known as the Pearls of Lochleven and thought to be the most beautiful young ladies of the Scottish aristocracy. Elizabeth was also very intelligent and feted at court for her sonnets. Her grand-father had had the family title of Earl of Morton and associ-ated lands restored to him some four years earlier and her father was anxious to restore the family's status and fortune. He questioned Francis about his past attempts to restore Catholicism to Scotland but Erroll refused to agree to give up his plans. Considering the king's favour towards Huntly and Erroll and his failure to punish them, Douglas decided that marriage of his daughter to Francis was a shrewd decision.

When Francis approached the King for permission to marry her, James pouted and was reluctant to agree, having hoped that Francis would become his intimate. He made a final attempt to tempt Francis to his side, which the Earl avoided with clever words and flattery. Finally, resigned to the fact that Francis would never be persuaded, James gave his permission.

So soon after his previous wife's death, nobody ques-tioned the lack of ceremony for his wedding but at least in part, his motivation was his desire for a Catholic ceremony.

1591

The following year brought Francis the son he had hoped for. In spite of his fears, Elizabeth was a healthy and sensible woman and gave birth to their child at Slains Castle to the great delight of Francis and all of the castle people.

Remembering his brothers' affliction, Francis repeatedly made noises around the child watching for his reaction until Elizabeth became so tired of his behaviour that she begged him to desist. He smiled down as her and placed a kiss on her forehead, his long, black hair sweeping across her face and his moustache tickling her. 'We shall call him William,' Francis declared. 'And I detect he shares his mother's beauty.'

Francis was so taken with his wife's beauty that he sent to Edinburgh for the finest artist to paint portraits of himself and Elizabeth, as soon as she was recovered from the birth.

Not all was such a pleasure to Francis as the Provosts and Baileys of Edinburgh, concerned that a rebel such as the Earl of Erroll, who had been, in recent times, accused of treason and declared a rebel, should continue to hold his title of High Constable of Scotland and have the right to prosecute and sentence criminals. They appealed to the king to remove his rights and transfer them to themselves.

Anxious to maintain order in his realm and unwilling to challenge the rebel Earls, James wrote back to the Provosts confirming Francis' rights and ordering the Provosts and Baileys to support the Earl of Erroll in his duties and not to encroach on his rights in any way. The authorities were furious at this response and determined to challenge Erroll's actions whenever they could be seen to be controversial in any way.

❧❧

It was little over a year later when Francis Hay welcomed the Earls of Huntly and Angus to Slains Castle. They ate together with Elizabeth in the tower house before Francis begged his wife to excuse the gentlemen as they had matters of importance to discuss. Elizabeth was already expecting their second child and was happy to leave them whilst she said goodnight to William and retired herself.

The earls discussed at length what actions they should take to return Scotland to the true faith. 30,000 Spaniards were to be landed from the Netherlands, 5,000 of whom were to establish Catholic control of Scotland whilst the rest marched south to England. Each of the earls knew the possible consequences of their actions and each was prepared to risk all, even their lives, for their faith. Finally, they decided to send a man of their own to the King of Spain to beg for aid, in the belief that, with some assistance, they could get King James into their hands, convert Scotland to Catholicism and avenge the death of Mary Queen of Scots.

Huntly's relationship with the king was still benefiting him and now he was commissioned to capture James Stewart, the Earl of Moray, and bring him to trial. Believing himself invulnerable, and knowing from his own experience, how loath the king was to actually take action against troublemakers, Huntly, instead of taking Moray prisoner, slashed him a fatal blow across the face with his sword. As Moray sank to the ground, mortally wounded, he told Huntly, 'Ye hae spoilt a better face than yer ain.'

Knowing Huntly to be well favoured, his enemies, aware that they would get no satisfaction from the king, took action themselves and ravaged Huntly's lands.

The rebel lords were charged with treason but once again freed by the king with orders for all Catholics to renounce their faith or leave the kingdom. The demand was met with unrest amongst the highlanders, who wanted to lose neither their chiefs nor their faith, and a refused to comply. James was furious and attainted all the lords who were involved.

Meeting at Strathbogie, the Catholic Lords decided to commit the task of conveying the request for help from Spain to their friend George Kerr. Letters of authority and other blank letters were prepared signed with their names. Seals were made in paper so that they could be copied in wax when they arrived in Spain and then used to seal the documents.

George Kerr was sent for and questioned in order to ascertain his allegiance and willingness to undertake such a dangerous mission. His instructions were, on his arrival in Spain, to write in the letters the message which they had given him verbally. They particularly instructed Kerr to say that they would send their sons to Spain or Flanders, as hostages, if Phillip of Spain wished.

Had Elizabeth been present she would undoubtedly have raged at the suggestion that her tiny son might be sent away. As their meeting finished a dark figure slipped from behind a curtain and melted away into the depths of the castle.

Kerr made his way to the south west of Scotland and took a boat to the Isle of Cumbrae. Here he spent some time seeking the captain who was to transport him to Spain. Having found him, the two approached the ship. Lurking in the shadows, a figure slid stealthily towards them. As Kerr set foot on board, Andrew Knox, minister in Paisley, leapt forward and snatched at his tunic. The guard lurched towards him and grabbed Kerr by the arm, bending it up behind his back and thrusting him against a wall before landing a jaw-cracking blow to his face. As Kerr doubled in pain his other arm was grabbed and pulled behind him. A small chest containing the letters fell to the ground.

Rope was bound tightly around his wrists and around his neck preventing him from making his escape. Lashing out with his foot, Kerr struggled to free himself but the chill of steel at his throat halted him and in seconds he was bound fast. A second figure had taken the captain and a gasp betrayed the knife which slid between his ribs before his body was consigned to the water.

Kerr was half dragged and half carried away to the authorities. A brief search revealed the papers he carried. The purpose of blank documents with signatures was a mystery to his captors but they were suspicious enough to thrust Kerr into a cell until he could be passed on to the king's guards. The letters which had been found on his person were sent to the Queen of England. Robert Bowes, her diplomat, examined the suspicious papers. All that could be seen were signatures. He had some experience of espionage and believed that they had been written in white vitriol – invisible ink. On closer examination, he realised that this was not the case and, not wishing to appear a fool, gave orders for Kerr to be examined.

When Kerr was hauled from his stinking cell and dragged along a corridor, he knew what was come. The mingled smell of blood, vinegar and excrement made his body recoil. The air left his lungs as he was thrown onto a bench where his wrists and ankles were strapped down. The sound of metal on metal turned his head to see a long poker being drawn from a stand and thrust into the fire. Within moments the end glowed red and then white. The hulk of a being who stood over him plunged the poker into a bucket of water to demonstrate how hot it was. The hiss as it cooled made him strain against his bonds.

Again it was thrust into the fire and while it heated the thug offered mercy if Kerr should talk.

The poker hovered above his face yet Kerr shook his head. He smelt his own flesh burning as the unbelievable pain ripped through him. As the instrument was removed he became aware of a warm wet sensation on his britches. Again the poker was heated. This time it came across his chest. Darkness overcame him but its mercy was to be short as the bitter smell of vinegar brought him back to suffer again. When still he did not talk, his tormentor went to the foot of the bench to which he was fastened and a groaning indicated the turning of a wheel. Within moments Kerr felt his joints strain in exquisite pain. Laughing at his moans the thug walked off to leave him to suffer. Each half hour he returned to turn the wheel again.

Finally, Kerr could take no more. He could barely utter the words, 'I'll tell you.'

It was only then that he revealed that the letters were to be filled in by William Crighton, a Jesuit who had worked and studied with Edmund Hay, son of Peter Hay of Megginch, to initiate a Spanish invasion. He would complete the pages with Spain's demands, to which the Catholic earls would have conceded.

Elizabeth, alarmed at the thought of Spain and Scotland uniting against England, sent men and money to King James, with orders for him to persecute rigorously all those who were concerned or suspected.

The three earls and their fellow rebels retired to Caithness where they would be protected by Scotland's natural features, but Angus was intercepted, imprisoned in Edinburgh Castle and sentenced to death.

When his prison door opened, Angus was on his knees praying. He fully expected to be led out to the scaffold and was surprised to be hushed by the guard. A Catholic supporter, the man was willing to risk all to help Angus to escape. He followed silently, stopping when the guard touched his arm and moving against the damp, slimy wall to prevent give-away shadows. Footsteps approached and the guard indicated to Angus to keep still. As the footsteps grew closer he felt a tug on his sleeve which drew him deeper into the shadows. Closer and closer the figure came until, holding his breath, Angus felt the man pass within inches of where he stood, before passing on.

The guard whispered to him to remove his shoes. If they could hear footsteps so could others. With his shoes in his hand, he followed his rescuer. When he finally found himself outside the castle walls he walked purposefully away for some distance before breaking into a run and making good his escape.

Undeterred by Angus' arrest, Huntly and Erroll, decided, as they dared not send their signatures so soon after the other affair, to send an English priest, John Cecil to Spain, with an account of the situation in Scotland, and to petition Philip for support.

Gathered together at Strathbogie, they composed the account between them.

The King is 26 years old and has been married four years. He has no children, nor is it expected he will have any. He is a man of small spirit, quite given up to his pleasures and the chase. He depends upon the Queen of England, more from fear than otherwise, as he is very timid and hates war. He gives no attention to the Government, is of no religion or fixed purpose, and allows himself to be swayed by those around him. Two or three times he has been captured by the competing factions; and he follows either of them without difficulty whilst they hold him. He does not seek to free himself, and has therefore lost prestige with his subjects, and the object of each contending faction is to capture him, and rule in his name. He does not seem to resent this.

The Queen is sister of the king of Denmark. She is more sensible and discreet than the King, and sees his littleness and poor government. It is understood that she would be glad for him to be in the hands of the Catholics, whom she secretly favours. She has told several Catholic ladies, and particularly the mother of Lord Seton, that she is really a Catholic, and prays by the rosary.

Dividing Scotland into two parts, namely, north of Edinburgh and south of it, the principal Catholics in the northern portion are the said earls of Huntly, Angus, and Erroll, as well as the earls of Athol, Sutherland, and Caithness, and a great number of barons and knights. Indeed, in this part there are few heretics, except the low people and officials in the cities. The southern part is richer and more populous, and there is at present no earl really Catholic there, as the two that remain, namely, Morton, and Glencarne, are heretics; and Bothwell who used to be on the Catholic side, although a heretic, is in exile in England, because twice last year he surrounded the King in his palace to take him. The other earls—of Argyll, Cassilis, and Eglington—are boys, and almost powerless. Their religion is unknown, but some of their guardians are well inclined. But what is of most importance is that in this part of the country there are many barons and gentlemen who are good Catholics. They are lords Hume, Seton, Sanquhar, Claude Hamilton, Livingston, Herries, Maxwell, Semple, the abbot of New Abbey, and others. Of gentlemen there are Ladyland, Lethington, Johnstone, Eldersley, the three brothers of lord Seton, and many others of the same sort. In the court and around Edinburgh the most powerful man is the duke of Lennox, a Frenchman, and a relative of the King, a young fellow of 23, very well inclined in religion, as his mother and brothers are Catholics. The King loves him dearly and would like to make him his heir, if he could, but the queen of England does not like it, and favours the house of Hamilton. The power of the Duke centres in the court, and he holds the office of Lord

Admiral, whilst the earl of Mar is captain of Edinburgh Castle. The earl of Mar is a young man of the same age, married to his (Lennox's) sister. Both of them will follow the strongest party, although on their own account they are enemies of the Queen (of England). Those who now have the King in their hands are the men who were exiles in England, and entered Scotland four years ago with the Queen's support, capturing the King in Stirling Castle. These are the earl of Morton—a Douglas— president, lord Glamys, Treasurer ; Maitland, Chancellor, who has now retired from court; Carmichael, Captain of the Guard; and the provost of Glenlouden, all persons of low condition except Morton, who can do but little, as the head of his own house, the Douglases, the earl of Angus, is a Catholic. The rest are powerless, and hated by all but the preachers and the queen of England. The King, it is understood, is anxious to get away from them, although out of fear of the queen of England he dares not say so. There are also the earl of Ross, Sir James Chisholm, the King's Steward, and Colonel Stuart, all of whom are Catholics.

The people generally outside of the cities are inclined to the Catholic faith, and hate the ministers, who disturb the country with their excommunications, backed up by the power of the queen of England, by aid of which they tyrannise even over the King and nobles. They have passed a law by which anyone who does not obey their excommunications within 40 days loses his rank and citizenship. This is enforced by the aid of the dregs of the towns and the English ambassador. The nobles and people are sick of this tyranny, and are yearning for a remedy. They are looking to his Majesty for his support for the restoration of the Catholic faith.

The Demands of the Catholics of Scotland for their deliverance.

First, the opinion of the above-mentioned nobles is, that with 3,000 foot soldiers sent either from Brittany or Spain to the south and west of Scotland, with arms for as many more, and stores for two months after their arrival, besides the funds herein-after mentioned, they would be able at once to take the King, and defend themselves against all the force of England.

The port of debarkation will be in one of the provinces of Carrick, Coyle, or Cunningham, where there are many safe harbours, and all the gentry around are Catholic. The desire of these gentlemen is that with part of the foreign force, and their own men, they should at once go and capture the King, and the two cities of Edinburgh and Glasgow which they think will be very easy. They would then like to reduce the rest of Scotland, and turn out or capture the principal heretics, and fortify the castles, which are all now utterly unprovided. They would then raise men, and make ready to resist the forces of England, which they think will be in Scotland in about two or three months.

The money they will want is 100,000 ducats, which they would wish to be brought by the commander his Majesty sends, or his commissary, so that he could pay for the things necessary from time to time, without distributing any of it to the lords, as has been done on other occasions, without any profit at all. The place that the lords have fixed upon as best for the landing is a bay called Lochryan, in the province of Carrick. The mouth is very narrow and can be easily held, and it is very deep inside, well protected from all winds. There is a town on one side called Intermessan, which may be made impregnable. To this place men and stores can be sent from all parts of Scotland by land and sea, and also from the neighbouring Catholic counties of England. Ireland is less than a day's sail distant.

To this port also may be sent ships, etc., from Spain or elsewhere, by two routes, one by St. George's Channel, and the other round Ireland, which is quite safe and only two days longer. From Nantes to the port in question ships usually go in five or six days.

The lords think it will be unnecessary to send cavalry, at least at first, as they have plenty there of their own to cope with the English in Scotland.

They think that amongst the 3,000 or 4,000 men his Majesty might send Colonel Stanley, with his regiment of 1,000 English and Irishmen, now in his service in Flanders. They might go without attracting attention to Brittany, and there join the Spanish force; and then proceed to Scotland under the general appointed by his Majesty. The footing his Majesty now has in Brittany will greatly serve to conceal the Scottish enterprise, and it will also serve as a refuge or point d'appui in case of need.

Finally, these gentlemen are sure that, with his Majesty's help, they will capture the King at once, and will deal with him as his Majesty orders. They will convert to the faith the whole of Scotland, and keep the queen of England so busy that she cannot molest his Majesty, either in Flanders, France, or the Indies.

They think it would be very advantageous that the earl of Westmoreland and Baron Dacre, with other English gentlemen in his Majesty's service in Flanders, who are natives of the north of England, should be sent to the east of Scotland, when the Spanish contingent has landed in the west. They should not go with Colonel Stanley, to avoid suspicion. If the Scots soldiers in Flanders are also sent to the east coast they should land at Lord Seton's port, near Leith.

If his Majesty needs more information he is requested to send back to Scotland with the person who brings this some Spaniard of experience to treat with the gentlemen, and see the places in question. But this must be done with all secrecy and speed, as the present state of affairs will bear no delay. If his Majesty cannot send the aid requested the greater part of the gentlemen named are determined to leave the kingdom, as they cannot maintain themselves against the devices and strength of the queen of England, who fears her ruin more *from Scotland than any other part of the world, and is determined to undo her opponents there.[1]*

James himself had been aware of their plans but, in the mistaken belief that the plan was to put him on the throne of England, he had held his hand, whilst at the same time negotiating with Elizabeth to become her heir. Being thwarted by the Catholic clansmen of the north, he was unable to capture them and soon gave up the chase.

Elizabeth sent her ambassador, Sir Robert Bowes, to James to press him to do his utmost to capture the earls but James confided to him that, 'if he should again pursue them and toot them with the horn he should little prevail.'

It was expected that the Scottish Parliament would pass an act of forfeiture against the conspirator's lands but it was not to be and yet again they were forgiven for their Conspiracy of the Spanish Blanks, on condition that they submitted to the Kirk. James called for the text of the submission to be brought to him and sat for some hours modifying the text until it resembled something he thought they might deign to sign. Finally, the earls were ordered to appear before the king on 5th February.

Furious at the King's failure to act against the Catholic Earls, the Synod of Fife immediately excommunicated the conspirators, who condescendingly consented to stand trial in their heartland, Perth. The Kirk was very suspicious of this and, on 17 November 1593 they convened a Committee of Security, demanding that James postpone the trial until they were ready to prosecute. Alternatively, they would assemble in force at Perth to pursue the defendants, 'to the uttermost'. Fearing civil war, James was finally spurred into action. The Estates declared a compromise which banned the Catholic religion and required the Earls to conform by 1st February 1594. They rejected the Blanks as evidence and so the charges of treason could not stand. Erroll and Huntly laughed when they heard at the demands and decided to ignore them; nor did they obey orders to leave Scotland.

It was not until October that King James finally managed to intercept them. He examined them himself and allowed them to convince him that the letters referred to their support for the Jesuits. Although sceptical, he realised that they offset the power of the reformed church. Accepting their explanation, he once again set them free.

The Judicial Court, on 11th April 1594, recorded that Masters David MacGill of Cranstoun-Riddel and John Skene of Curriehill, advocates to the king, produced the summons of treason raised on the king's orders, against William Douglas, Earl of Angus, George Gordon, Earl of Huntly, Francis Hay, Earl of Erroll and Sir Patrick Gordon of Auchindoun, knight, whereby they were summoned to have appeared before the king and his justice on 18 May last, to have answered to the crimes and points of treason and lese-majesty contained in the summons. The advocates produced eight blanks in paper, two signed by the Earl of Angus only, the other two by the Earl of Huntly only, the other two signed by the Earl of Erroll only, and the other two by the three earls and laird of Auchindoun. They also produced the seals of the earls imprinted in paper which had been given to George Kerr.

There were numerous signed statements of Master George Kerr with a letter written and signed by him, they said, of his own free will, by which the whole treasonable trafficking against the religion, the king, his estate and realm was confessed. The treasonable reason for which they were sent was to be filled in by the council of Spain and Master William Crichton, Jesuit, regarding the sending to Scotland of men of war, and of 30,000 Spaniards to come to Scotland

and land in the west, where 5,000 would have remained in Scotland to assist the earls in altering the religion of the country.

The council found that the accused were guilty of treason and summoned them to appear before the king. Those charged with delivering the summonses were ordered to do so at their dwelling places, or by public proclamation at the market crosses of our burghs of Edinburgh, Haddington, Lanark, Aberdeen, Perth, Banff etc., and other necessary places where they are or live, on notice of sixty days, in such a way that a summons of this kind could reasonably reach their ears, that they should compear before the king or his justice on 20 May next in parliament to answer to justice regarding their treasonable crimes.

John Blindseil, Bute Pursuivant, summoned Sir Patrick Gordon of Auchindoun, knight, at his dwelling places of Auchindoun and Gartly. After knocking six times at the gate, he affixed a copy of the letters translated into English on each one of the gates. Alexander Hay in Aberdeen, George Grieve, stabler in Edinburgh, and Henry Bell, servant to Laurence Peacock, doctor in the grammar school of Edinburgh were his witnesses.

The summons was delivered in the same way to George, Earl of Huntly at Strathbogie

Francis, earl of Erroll was personally apprehended and a copy given to him

John Blindseil also delivered a copy of the summons to the market cross of Banff, the head burgh of the shire where Sir Patrick Gordon, George, Earl of Huntly and Francis, Earl of Erroll dwelt, and openly proclaimed the Earls traitors and affixed a copy of the letters translated into English on market cross.

Robert Fraser, Unicorn Pursuivant, delivered the summons to William, Earl of Angus at his dwelling place of Douglas and to the market cross at Lanark and Haddington.

When those charged with issuing the summonses reported that they had done so, the court of parliament then declared that William, sometime Earl of Angus, George, sometime Earl of Huntly, Francis, sometime Earl of Erroll and Sir Patrick Gordon, sometime of Auchindoun, knight, each one of them, having committed and incurred the special crime of treason and lese-majesty, all their goods moveable and unmoveable, as well lands as offices and other things whatsoever belonging to them, to be confiscated to the king and to remain perpetually with his highness in property in time coming, and their persons to underlie the pains of treason and utter punishment appointed by the laws of the realm.

Francis prepared to set off for Strathbogie, shaken by the summons but sure of the support of Huntly, whose favour with the king seemed to endure whatever he did. Before leaving Slains he stopped at Clochtow, the nearest farm on his estate at Slains and just to the north of the castle. His approach was seen and Morag, the farmer's wife came out still holding her distaff. Dropping a curtsey, she explained that Roddy, her husband, was out tending to a sheep and offered to send for him.

'Do so,' Francis ordered, 'I must speak with him before I leave.'

Morag called to her youngest son, who was chopping wood, to run and fetch his father. She invited Francis to enter their home and fetched him a glass of wine.

'How fares your bonnie wifie?' she enquired.

'It is of Elizabeth that I would speak,' he replied.

At that moment Roddy entered. Snatching his cap from his head he bowed low to his lord and master. 'I trust all is well, my lord.'

Francis explained that all was far from well, he himself being charged with treason and his lands and property forfeit. Although he did not anticipate the threats being carried out, there was always a risk that some fortune seeker might decide to endear himself to the king and Francis' powerful enemies by capturing him or his family.

'Elizabeth is to be confined soon with our third child and my son, William and daughter, Ann, are yet infants. If I should be forced to leave Scotland, Elizabeth could not possibly make the journey safely. I could not take two infants with me as I will be forced to travel in Europe. If this should come to pass I want you to take them into your home and care for them. I will see you well rewarded for this kindness.'

'Sir, our home is larger than most in these parts but it is still just a humble farm house. It is not fit to house a countess and her children.'

'It is the safest place for them. The king's men would not seek them in a farmhouse and will expect them to be miles away at the home of a lord. Besides, in her present condition, Elizabeth cannot travel far.'

'I would be honoured, sir. You and your good lady have shown us many kindnesses and I will do all in my power to help.'

Satisfied that Elizabeth would be safe and knowing that none of his people would give her whereabouts away, Francis continued on his way to Strathbogie.

'Take heart,' George Gordon told him. 'They have called us to appear before them. They have not arrested us. Your summons was handed to you; they could have taken you then but they didn't.'

'You are right, but our property is to be taken. We will lose everything.'

'Francis, you know the king loves me and will never go through with it. Now I have a plan.' Huntly outlined his proposal to Francis for their next course of action.

Whilst they were talking an urgent knock came on the door of Huntly's chamber. News had been brought to the castle of the arrest of four Papal agents for espionage in Aberdeen. Furious that the town councillors had imprisoned the agents, Huntly and Erroll sent armed men to threaten the king's officers with death should they not be released immediately. Knowing Huntly's reputation for barbaric punishments of those who disobeyed, the council decided to free the agents but inform the king immediately. A burly, bald-headed burgess waddled to the room in which the agents were held and unlocked the door. Red with anger and unable to bring himself to tell them they were free to go he waved his arm to indicate that they should leave. At the same instant, a messenger set off for Edinburgh with the news.

For King James, this was a step too far even for his favourite. With orders to the Earl of Argyll to capture the rebels, James prepared to travel with his forces to confront them in person.

In just two years, Huntly and Erroll had gone from being favoured advisors to the king to Catholic rebels. Although they laughed at the king's weak willed attempts to make them comply, they were furious with the Kirk and those who were determined to make them deny their faith.

Erroll and Huntly knew that Strathbogie was under observation and met at Slains Castle to discuss their plans. Both had the support of their own people and in addition bonds of Manrent in which other powerful barons pledged their support. Between them, they were confident of raising over a thousand men to fight their cause.

'We will face much larger numbers from Argyll's army,' observed Francis, 'but we have God on our side and no matter how many they present, we will be victorious!' George Gordon shook him by the hand.

'We also have a number of artillery pieces which they will lack,' he laughed referring to the canon which King Philip had sent.

On the 3rd October 1594, the Catholic Earls of Huntly and Erroll, with 800 horsemen and 1,200 infantry, stood in the face of about 7,000 untrained highlanders, led by the Protestant Earl of Argyll, fighting on foot and armed largely with pikes and farm implements.

A harpist along with the pipes and drums led the men forward into the narrow space. It was a battle that none would forget.

The armies met at a place called Belrinnes in the district of Glenlivet which was in Huntly's territory. His men were posted on the south side of a mountain, so steep that footmen could barely keep their hold.

Argyll was trapped with his pikemen hemmed in behind the baggage train. His archers and musket men were quickly routed by Erroll and Huntly's cavalry before Argyll's officers could bring the pike-men into position. As Argyll continued to try to get his men up the hill, Erroll's artillery and Huntly's vanguard forced them back yet again.

By midday, both armies withdrew to re-gather their forces before plunging back to challenge each other again. Argyll deployed his archers and muskets whilst he got his pikemen into formation but the thunder of hooves made him spin round to see Erroll and Sir Patrick Gordon of Auchindoun with 300 horse, charging down the hill, and his men taking to their heels.

John Grant, an ally of Argyle, had been bribed by Huntly and as the artillery fire blazed, Grant led his men away from the battle. Argyle's infantrymen were defenceless in the face of the gunfire and lances. Some were mown down by guns, then to be attacked by Erroll and Huntly's mounted men as they charged forward. Erroll threw himself courageously into the fray, striking to left and to right as he led his men forward. Argyll watched as 2000 of his men fled. Courageously, the remaining highlanders regrouped.

The steep mountain was proving a problem for Erroll's horsemen and they were forced to turn their horses and advance at an angle to the enemy. This resulted in their flank being exposed and their horses suffered considerable damage from a flight of arrows. Seeing this, Huntly attacked Argyle's centre, making straight for his standard, and better ground, where their horses could operate with efficiency. The Highlanders, who were without lances, and so unable to fight back, were driven down the other side of the hill and fled in panic.

Maclean of Duart grabbed Erroll's standard and held it up triumphantly to the cheers of his men. Surrounded by his followers, Erroll had taken an arrow through his arm and disappeared from the sight of the highlanders and the cry went up that he was killed.

Glad to escape the fighting, a youth of no more than 13 summers grabbed the reigns of a horse, whose rider had been killed, and leapt into the saddle. Kicking hard with his heels he turned it in the direction of Slains and rode for all he was worth back to the castle to take the news of Erroll's death.

Huntly, seeing Erroll's plight moved on Argyll with 700 horse. Hundreds of the highlanders were killed and the manoeuvre drew Erroll's attackers away from him, allowing him to reform his troops and come back into the attack. Spurring his horse forward he felt a thud against his leg and suddenly his horse wheeled to the right as he lost the strength in his left leg. Looking down he saw blood coursing down his thigh. It was some moments before the pain hit him and yet still he fought on striking to left and right, cutting down Robert Fraser, the king's herald, and bellowing directions to his men. And then; oblivion. Loss of blood and pain had claimed his consciousness and Erroll hung in the saddle. His horse, aware that its rider was no longer directing it, slowed and stopped. One of his horsemen grabbed the bridle and led his horse away from the battle to safety where Francis was eased out of his stirrups and lowered to the ground. Whilst he was mercifully oblivious, the arrow was snapped and pulled from his arm and the bullet removed from his leg. Blood continued to leak in copious amounts from both wounds as they were bound.

The chief of Maclean stood fast against the assault of the horsemen but was at last forced off the field by his own soldiers, and Argyle himself was taken from the battlefield, weeping with anger.

As Erroll regained consciousness he found Huntly grinning down at him. 'Looks like our losses are few,' he informed Erroll. 'No more than seventy I would say. Argyll has lost over four hundred. He did well for a lad of eighteen,' he acknowledged.

The highlanders dispersed into the hills and Huntly would have pursued them but Argyll's wife was Erroll's sister by law and he asked Huntly to spare him for her sake.

'Elizabeth would not have her sister a widow and I would not have Elizabeth distressed,' he told him. He was also aware that if they followed the highlanders into the hills they could be attacked by men who were far more at home in the wilds than they were themselves. He was sure that having beaten the king's army, they would now be hunted down. As he was helped to a cart to return home Erroll told his herald, 'If Huntly loses Strathbogie, my Slains will be sore hurt.'

His words were prophetic.

King James was furious that Huntly and Erroll had dared to stand against him. His Herald, his beloved Robert Fraser, had not only been killed in the battle but his body had been found pierced by three spears, symbolic of the three Catholic earls. All of his life, James had been subjected to the power seeking nobles of the land. He had overlooked Huntly, Erroll and Angus outrageous behaviour and allowed them to follow their own faith, largely unhindered, but now they had tried his patience too much. On October 29th He appointed his cousin the Duke of Lennox as his Lieutenant in the North and gave orders to destroy Erroll's and Huntly's castles.

Lennox's sister was Huntly's wife and not wishing to see her hurt, he sent for Fergus Campbell, his herald. 'Ride now to Strathbogie and bid Huntly to leave Scotland before I arrive as I have orders to destroy his castle. Do not linger but when you have told him, go on to Slains Castle and tell Erroll the same for I must be about the king's business within the day.' Barely pausing to bow his acknowledgement, Fergus spun about and ran to the stables where he mounted and galloped north.

Lennox gathered twenty men and had barrels of gunpowder loaded onto waggons. Two cannons were brought out on their carriages and horses harnessed to them. He would travel more slowly than Fergus and hoped he would have time to give them his message.

Fergus arrived at Huntly's castle, travel-stained and exhausted. Delivering his message he warned Gordon that Lennox was no more than two days behind him and to make his escape whilst he could. Gordon ordered many of his treasures to be packed and removed to the homes of his tenants, with promises of rewards for their safe keeping, before instructing his groom to pack his finest robes and a selection of necessary items into his travelling kists to be taken with him to the coast. 'Lord Erroll still suffers from his wounds and will never make it to Banff. We shall have to sail from Peterugie. Tell him I will meet him there.'

Turning to his wife, George took her in his arms. I cannot take you with me. My journey will be filled with danger. Your brother will see that you are not hurt.' She nodded her agreement with a tear in her eye. 'Come back to me as soon as you might,' she begged.

As soon as he had refreshed himself, Fergus continued to warn Erroll.

Having no real desire to destroy his sister's home and in the sure belief that James would soon, yet again, forgive Huntly, Lennox carried out the king's orders but inflicted only limited damage to Strathbogie. Even so, the sounds of the explosion echoed through the countryside and reached Fergus' ears as he raced on to warn Erroll.

Fergus reached Slains Castle well after dark. Hammering on the gates with the handle of his dirk, he was rewarded with a cry to hold his hand and identify himself. 'Open the gates you idiot. I come to warn your master of danger.'

'Well, we are safe in here with the gates locked,' came the drawled reply. 'Seems you might be the one in danger, out there. We don't open the gates after dark.'

The noise of Fergus' hammering had alerted Francis and before the herald could tell the gatekeeper what he would do to him if he didn't open the gate immediately, the earl had appeared holding a lantern and was pulling the bar away to admit the messenger.

'What news do you bring?' he demanded.

'My lord Lennox bids me warn you that he has orders to destroy your castles, Sir. He is setting out as soon as he can make ready and says you should make haste to leave before he gets here. He brings gunpowder and cannon. He has already reached Strathbogie and it is no more.'

Francis swung around to the crowd of people who had been drawn by the shouting. His first thought was for his family and he sent a maid to rouse Elizabeth and get her dressed. Another was sent to fetch his children. Three guards were told secretly to accompany his wife and children to Clochtow, where they were expected, and remain with them whatever happened. His personal guard he sent to fetch the small kist from the safe in his room.

Whilst he waited for his family to be made ready, he called for two of his guards to ride to Delgatie and warn his cousin of the approaching danger.

When Elizabeth appeared he held her close and spoke softly to her. 'I must leave for a while. The king is understandably angry and is sending his men here. I have arranged for you to stay at Clochtow until I return.'

'But I want to come with you!' Elizabeth declared. 'I am your wife and will face whatever befalls you by your side.'

'Elizabeth, you cannot. You will be confined within days. You cannot travel. You will be safe enough at Clochtow and I will be safe aboard ship before the night is out. The children need you and I cannot travel quickly with you all by my side. You serve me best by remaining here where I can be sure of your safety.'

Elizabeth knew he was right and, not wishing to frighten the children who had been brought down by the maid, she put her arms around them and explained that they were going to have an adventure. William was rubbing his eyes and asking why they had to get up in the middle of the night and Ann was whimpering. The thought of an adventure appealed to William and he was soon wide awake and jumping around.

The guards had prepared a cart in which Elizabeth and the children were soon safely bundled and it bumped and jolted its way up the narrow lane to the farmhouse.

Relieved that his family were safe, Francis turned to the castle people who were rushing around gathering their few possessions.

At that moment the man he had sent to Delgatie returned. Francis rushed over to see why he was back so soon. 'Sir, as I rode for Delgatie I crossed paths with Ewan coming from that castle with the same message for you. Lennox has already reached Delgatie. The west wall is destroyed but due to the strength with which the new structures were built, they withstood the attack. There was only one casualty; the maid Rohaise was killed trying to rescue a dog that was in an upstairs room'

Francis turned back to his people.

'I must leave you and travel overseas but I shall return. You have been faithful to me and served me well and I shall look to see you all return here soon. For now, I must ask you to seek your own safety. My tenants will care for you if you work for them in return. I pray that God will keep you in his care and bless you.'

Francis' guards were urging him to mount his horse and leave and people were moving away to prepare to leave their homes. Still suffering from the wounds he had received, Francis was helped up into his saddle, stifling a moan as the wound in his leg protested. As they reached the brow of the hill he turned in the saddle to look back at his beloved Slains. There had been no time to remove furniture, curtains, treasures or paintings but he had his life and his family were safe. Vowing that he would return, Francis spurred his horse on.

By the time Francis arrived at Peterugie, Huntly had secured their passage on a ship sailing for France. There was little to take on board and they were soon under sail. The sun began to rise and as they sailed towards it, they heard an explosion. Looking west, Francis saw a cloud of dust rising from Slains. Flashes lit the air as cannon were fired bringing down more of his beloved castle. Slabs of the granite walls tumbled and slid down towards the sea. Unable to watch he turned away. George Gordon stood beside him and in unison they said: 'We shall return.'

[1]'Simancas: July 1593', in *Calendar of State Papers, Spain (Simancas), Volume 4, 1587-1603*, ed. Martin A S Hume (London, 1899), pp. 603-606. *British History Online*http:// www.british-history.ac.uk/cal-state-papers/simancas/vol4/ pp603-606

Information about the murder of King James I from Scotland Magazine.

About The Author

Pamela Rotheroe-Hay of Megginch was born in 1955 and the importance of being a, "Hay" was impressed upon her by her father. She retired after 36 years as a teacher and moved to Scotland – the home of her ancestors. When she first moved north, she lived in the house behind the ruins of Old Slains Castle and was inspired by its history and location to delve into the lives of the Hays who lived there. Pamela has always had a great love of history and in more recent years, historical and genealogical research. As the organising secretary for Clan Hay, she is fortunate in having contact with a number of very knowledgeable historians including the present Earl of Erroll, Chief of Clan Hay.

Her research provided the historical foundation for The Hays of Slains, but the novel seeks to paint a picture of the lives of the inhabitants of the castle and the adventures they might have had.